Balumakazi: Native

Balumakazi: Native

Maidem Kayem

To order additional copies of this book, contact:
Xlibris
1-888-795-4274
www.Xlibris.com
Orders@Xlibris.com
771132

Contents

DESCENDED FROM EGYPT

T HE HIGH PRIEST coughed, cleared his throat, drank some
more palm wine, and began the story.

'*Baluma* means "the people find rest". The Baluma are descended
from the house of a great king called Amen. The sacred writings refer
to him as the founder of our religious beliefs.'

The high priest stopped to let silence take its place.

'When we were in Egypt,' he continued, 'there were thinkers,
doctors, and warlords. The thinkers were the teachers who studied
many things and proposed methods of livelihood improvement for the
people. The doctors sought to discover the cure of any ailment, physical
and spiritual, and the warlords developed defence strategy to protect the
empire. The great King Amen was a thinker.

'We worshipped several gods at that time, with the sun god, Ra,
being the greatest of all the gods. Amen had ascended the throne just
around the time when he had completed his edification in the priestly
order of Ra. Once enthroned, he began studying the concept of divinity
in depth, a concept that had always intrigued him as a child. The results
of his study led him to purport that the sun could not be a deity in itself
but rather that some force had created the sun. Therefore, if the sun was
the greatest of all creation, it followed that the force that had brought
the sun into existence was superior to everything else.

'Thus, Amen further purported that the force that had created the
sun had also created everything underneath the sun, and hence, worship
and adulation should only be made to that one force. He proceeded
to abolish the practice of polytheism and institute monotheism, the
practice of worship to the one and only supreme deity, which he named
Si, a decision which made him several powerful enemies.

'Nevertheless, King Amen was determined to see monotheism prevail. He ordered the destruction of all temples dedicated to the lesser gods and erected new temples for the worship of the one and only supreme Si. All priesthood orders were merged into one for the worship of Si, "the force that created the sun and everything underneath the sun".

'This new system did not go down well with the priests. What would become of their families? It was a complete disaster. During the harvest season, besides the royal tax that was, of course, mandatory for all citizens, additional sacrifices were required of the farmers and herdsmen. In total, thirty-six separate offerings were made to each of the priesthood castes. Everyone understood that this was a necessary procedure to have the priests pray for blessings for future harvests and fertility for the herds. This was a superb arrangement for the high priests who could take a lion's share of the offerings for themselves and their families, and the rest of the priestly caste could share the rest. No one, at least not on the priests' end, complained because it benefitted everyone. The farmers and herdsmen formed the bulk of the 'tax-paying' population, and so even in a year of drought, there was plenty for the priests.

'As with everything, some people always tried to default on sacrifices. This could not be tolerated by the priests, first, because people might just discover that blessings could happen at a lower cost in sacrifices and, second, because the survival of the priestly castes depended on holding a psychological whiplash over the people. The priests therefore used spies to identify defaulters and arranged for very bad things to happen to them. For example, if a sacrifice could not be forcefully taken, arrangements would be made in secret to raid the culprit at night. Farms would be destroyed and cattle stolen. Complaints were handled with explanations centred on divine justice. The priestly orders of Geb, god of the earth, and Nout, god of the sky, were notorious for these underhand tactics.

Besides the harvest, there were other opportunities for reaping off the people. Desperate couples wanting sons – as is the case, for even today, in certain cultures, a son was a prime asset – would usually be gently persuaded to sacrifice a small fortune for this great need. The priests had a nice little trick to handle this. When the birthing time came, the priest would have the lady in question brought to the temple. Once the baby was born, if it turned out to be a girl, the priest would quietly have the baby girl exchanged for a baby boy who had been stolen from another woman. It didn't end there!

'Nine days after the birth of a child, a priest was called in for a "dedication or naming" ceremony. During this ceremony, the priest would dedicate the child to one of the gods, usually the god his order was dedicated to, and then lift the child up towards the sun, make incantations, and announce to the audience what destiny was beheld for the child. A poor sacrifice meant a poor destiny. No one wanted that.

'The idea of "one god" was therefore a source of great distress to these priests. What indeed would become of them? For the people, Amen's praise song would hint that he himself must be the one god, for his heart was kind and his decisions wise. "He sees the suffering of the people and heeds to their cries," they said, but the lingering sound of their music would soon be quietened and replaced with wails. Amen would not live to see the next moon.

'A cup was lined with a powdery substance, a drink was poured and drunk, and then some more was poured and drunk, and the king slept and never woke. The next two successors who dared to continue with monotheism suffered the same fate. The third successor, King Shenu, was wiser. He abandoned the monotheist school of thought and allowed the people to go back to worshipping several gods, and the priests re-established their livelihoods.

'However, not all the people in the empire were unconvinced about Amen's purporting. The return to polytheism and the destruction of monuments built in Amen's honour, coupled with his mysterious death, raised questions that the new establishment refused to address. In the years that followed, discontentment grew amongst the people, particularly because under the monotheist system of worship, with the merging of all the priestly castes, the farmers and herdsmen could afford the "offerings" required for blessings. The reintroduction of polytheism meant returning to the hardship of thirty-six offerings, which they could only afford by starving most of the time.

'The root of the discontentment was in the tribe of Amen and his close family circle. They believed the king had been murdered because it was unusual for a young king to die in his sleep, and nobody believed in death by natural causes. The king's life was not for any mortal to take. Doing so would annoy the ancestors and evoke a curse on the land and its people, and already, three kings had died prematurely.

'Over the years, fear and superstition continued to increase in the king's family and tribe. A group of noble men of the king's tribe got together one evening and decided that the best way to avoid an irrevocable curse was to escape the empire. But escaping the empire to avoid the curse was just nearly as hazardous as staying in the empire and bearing the curse. The king's tribe was principally made up of hunters and farmers. They had no soldiers nor warlords, so fighting their way out was not an option they could consider. The nobles decided it would be best to leave peacefully but finding a good reason to leave would take a long time to plot.

'Their opportunity came a few harvests later when drought hit the western part of the empire, where they lived. Many a herdsman lost several herds of cattle, and crops kept on drying up in the soil. The farmers and herdsmen had to move eastwards of the empire, where the climate was still good to feed animals or borrow land to plant crops. Even the hunters had to move eastwards because the animals in the nearby bushes and forests had migrated eastwards for water.

'The nobles in Amen's tribe seized the opportunity. They wrote to the king, informing him of their desire to ask some of their hunters and farmers to move southwards in search of humidity. With the east becoming increasingly over-occupied and difficult to govern, the king replied, approving the move.

'The exodus began, first in small batches of a few dozens, and then increased to a few hundreds. The farmers and hunters packed up their families and whatever else they could carry and moved slowly. No suspicion was raised because the move had been approved by the king.

'A few months later, over four thousand people had moved southwards, and they kept on moving. It was not until the next harvest season, when the climate got better in the western part of the empire, that questions were raised about the farmers and hunters who had migrated southwards and did not seem to be returning to their homes, by which time about nine million families had moved.

'The king's informants got suspicious as whispers about the preparation for a rebellion in the north and east began to spread. The peoples in the east were grumbling about the excessive tax their prince had imposed on them the previous year for the land they had lent to the farmers from the west. They were also dissatisfied with their prince, whom they claimed was not a true "son of the soil" because he was born by a womb from the west. Even though his father was from the east, his mother was from the west, and in their culture, a person was considered to be of the tribe of the woman who gave birth to him. Open threats had been made by nobles from the prince's own family to get rid of him.

'The northern peoples were complaining about the neglect of their region – deteriorating buildings, city walls, and roads, coupled with increased crime and insecurity. The previous year, the prince of the north had not remitted taxes to the royal treasury on the grounds that he was unable to collect the usual quota and preferred to wait to collect the full amount before remitting. In truth, the king had lost control of the prince of the north and of the region entirely.

'Just to be sure, the king's informants travelled westward to make enquiries. It did not take them long to confirm their suspicions. On an ordinary day in the west, the market squares were so crammed, it took pushing and shoving to get from one shop to another. The temples were noisy and jammed with people bringing animals and crops for sacrifice and screaming to get audience with a priest. The town squares began to fill up during the late hours of the afternoon. Men would sit there, drinking and cracking jokes, a favourite spot after a hard labour day, and the temples wouldn't be emptied until late into the night. Children screamed and played in the streets the whole day long until sunset. The western part of the empire was usually referred to as the heartbeat of the empire, but this time, the market squares, the temples, the town squares, and even the streets were almost deserted. The king was informed!

'The fleeing people had settled south-westwards from the empire on the first stretch of plain land they could find because the women and children were too tired to continue. They had arrived there after a long and tedious walk through a forest bordering the empire. Fortunately, the forest had been dried up by the hot season, and there were no wild animals in sight that a handful of hunters could not kill, these served as dinner occasionally.

'It was only a few weeks before the wet season set in. Here, on this new land, during the wet season, there was more rain and less sunshine, so the crops did not grow as well, but at least the people were hopeful. It was empty land, but slowly, they began to build, starting with shelters and then more permanent homes. The men built the huts, and the women decorated them with drawings and paintings. This new-found land, whose natives had apparently deserted it, became their home. They discovered streams running fresh water and fruit trees the children loved to climb into and play. Life on a different land was not the same as it was back in the empire, but at least they were comfortable. The hunters quickly established a defence order and the farmers a market. There were few priests amongst them but enough to organise and establish a small priestly order. The nobles appointed a ruler from amongst themselves, and a kingdom was born.

'They were not a homogenous people because even though they shared a common ancestry, there were different vernaculars, about twenty-three, coming from the different histories and interactions with people of other clans. Nevertheless, they were all too happy to have escaped the empire unscathed, and that gave them a sense of oneness – for a while, at least – until they all heard a sound they were almost forgetting.

'At first, the sound was unrecognisable, the elders and nobles dismissed it as the noises from the forest that separated them from the empire and calmed the people down. But the sound became louder and more recognisable by the day until it became unmistakable – *fanusi*, the warrior's drum. That was what they called the drums that the warriors of the empire beat to announce their approach to the enemy. The warning was simple. Surrender or die!

'Panic engulfed the newborn kingdom. The women, especially those with young children, were frantic. Surrender was not an option because everybody knew what surrendering meant. They had seen it before with people who had lost wars against the empire – men cut in half in front of their families, women defiled, children maimed, the tribes condemned to perpetual submission and indignity.

'Kimotomba, the newly appointed ruler of the fleeing peoples, summoned the nobles for a meeting. They decided to take their chances and flee farther southwards. It was difficult to estimate at what distance the warriors were from them, so they couldn't waste any time. They had to be off before dawn, or that dawn would be their last.

'The word was sent round, and the families packed whatever they could and set off in groups of about five hundred families each. As they moved, the women and children were kept in the middle, the men on the edges, and the hunters, now turned warriors, brought up the rear. By the time it was the next dawn, they had travelled quite a distance, but they could still hear the drums. Fear kept the fatigue and pain away, so they kept on walking, only stopping to rest from time to time. By the next dusk, even the fear of getting captured was not terrifying enough to persuade them to continue another mile. The people virtually fell to the ground, exhausted. After a few hours' rest and some food, the retreat continued. A few days and nights later, the drums were almost inaudible.

'The people, now relaxed, could better organise their flight. The warriors decided that since it was cooler during the nights and sunnier during the days, the people could walk at night and rest during the day, in the shades of the trees, to give the women the chance to cook properly. The food that the women had wrapped, which they had been feeding on for the last few days, was getting rotten, and fresh food needed to be cooked. Besides, it was easier to find wood to make a fire to cook during the day.

'One early morning, as the people stopped to rest, cook, and wash, deafening screams came from the direction of a nearby stream. The warriors of the empire had, in fact, not ceased the chase but simply ceased to beat the drums to follow the people silently behind, and the first legion had caught up with them. The hunters and farmers and, in fact, any male who was strong enough to hold a spear ran to the defence. Women and children ran for cover in the chaos. The people had been taken completely by surprise. Luckily, the first legion was not large enough, and the hunters quickly overpowered them. Still, the small battle lasted quite a few hours and resulted in more than a few hundred deaths.

'That evening, Kimotomba summoned the nobles. He suggested they bury the dead in a mass grave in the nearby bushes and cover the grave with grass and leaves to conceal it from the next legions chasing them. The families could then take the heads of their loved ones for remembrance since the heads would be easier to carry. Second, the retreat would be continued the next evening to give the people a day to mourn and preserve the heads for the journey with herbs and proper wrapping. The nobles agreed with the second suggestion. They all agreed that the people needed a day to mourn and pack up again. The first suggestion, however, triggered an argument because the people would not want their loved ones buried with the warriors from the empire. Their spirits would not rest if they were laid beside an enemy. Furthermore, Kimotomba had not sounded as convinced about this escape as they had hoped. He had not touched on the one point that the elders wanted to discuss the most – what should be done to prepare for surprise attacks and what strategy should be used in battle.

'The small but very significant issue under the circumstances was that Kimotomba was not a warrior himself and had no insight on defence strategy. He was just as confused as every one of the nobles and even more shaken by that morning's attack. Furthermore, unbeknownst to anybody, he was getting exhausted from the journey and the pressure of leadership and had been contemplating abdication.

'The nobles, realising his confusion, began to discuss amongst themselves a suitable defence strategy. Some suggested that the hunters be allowed to decide for themselves, others reconsidered the option of surrender while others suggested offering sacrifices to Si for protection and safe escape. This last argument was quickly put to rest because it was difficult enough finding food to feed the people, let alone animals for sacrifice. A decision could not be reached that night.

'In the early hours of the morning, the nobles met again. This time, they arrived at a decision. It was no use worrying about how the hunters should be trained to protect the people because their small number could not face the might of the other army in any case. The nobles began to discuss a way forward.

'All agreed that they should take a different course but differed in what direction they should go. One of them proposed that they change the course of the journey and travel westwards. Some preferred to go eastwards instead. Others simply preferred to continue further southwards but with a slightly different angle. By the time the sun was overhead, they had still not agreed on a single course. By sunset, each decided to take their people in the direction they wanted. And so the newborn kingdom split. Some went west, some farther south and others east.

'The group that travelled eastwards did not have too many hunters, so their priests guided them, telling them when to stop and where to stop and in what direction they could continue. The people travelled for a long time. As they journeyed on, they would stop from time to time for a few weeks to let the pregnant women give birth or rest when they were too heavy to walk. There were some who died along the way. The dead person's head would be cut off and kept in remembrance of them. Not everyone continued on with the group. Whenever they got to a fertile place with good climate, some families would prefer to settle there, and so the group became smaller and smaller as the journey continued.

'Finally, they got to a place just beside a rainforest. They decided to settle there and use the forest as a safe haven if ever they should be attacked. This new place, they called Lumani, the place of rest.

'And that is how we came to be called Baluma.'

The high priest had come to the end of his story. He sipped the last of his palm wine, stood up with the help of a long bamboo stick, and stretched his aching muscles.

Until then, the children and young people had been listening to him in silence, taking in every word. He was always a great storyteller, and when he found enough energy to sit by the fireside in the evenings, the children and young people always gathered around to listen to his fascinating stories of the history of the kingdom and their people. They always marvelled at his wisdom and knowledge of everything.

It was said that his mother died giving birth to him, that he had been raised by a crocodile in the forest, and that that was where he got all his wisdom from. His nickname was Mfile Nzuzu, 'the old crocodile'. Nobody knew his real name.

'Everybody of my age is in bed, so I better be gone like a good old man.'

With that, Mfile turned around and strode slowly into his shrine, leaving the children still staring as he walked away.

BOOK I

*From the Scourge of Slavery to
the Claws of Colonialism*

CHAPTER 1

And so they chose to live, but so what if they had died?
We choose to live, giving up dignity and honour and
pride, and then we live. And then what? What is life
without honour?
Honour is the only thing worth living for, and it is the
only thing worth dying for.
I would rather die like a king than live like a slave!

Maidem Kayem

LUMANI WAS A beautiful place with an exotic landscape.
There were nine main hills, and each hilltop was shaped like
a horn, with the tip of the horn looking upwards. From a distance, it
seemed as if eight of the horns were humped in the direction of the
ninth horn, which was at the top of the largest hill. There were nine
clans that lived around the nine hills, with the king belonging to the
clan that lived around the largest hill. The three pillars of the tribe were
the king, the patriarch, and the high priest. The king was commonly
referred to as the supreme leader of the tribe and supreme commander
of the army. The patriarch was the father of the tribe, the owner of the
land, and the protector of posterity. The high priest was the voice that
mediated for the people through the ancestors to God.

The structure of governance had been thus established because of
an old adage they had, that 'to whom wealth is given, power cannot be
given'. The king, by virtue of his position of kingship, was esteemed to
have boundless political power, so the patriarch inherited the land and
all its wealth. The king's duty was to protect the tribe and the patriarch's
to provide for the people. The patriarch typically guided the people on

where to farm to get a good harvest and settled land disputes between families.

The priestly order was particularly well structured with nine levels of authority and a high priest or priestess at the head of it. The authority of a priest was determined by his spiritual maturity and ability to 'make things happen', and only the priests knew what that meant. There was never any argument about succession or authority in the priestly order because each priest knew exactly who amongst them could make what happen. The priests of the neighbouring kingdoms always expressed great respect for the Baluma priestly caste.

Each of the nine clans of the Baluma was headed by a prince. In the king's court, they belonged to a council called the Nine or, as they called it, Ngui. Then there was another council called the Eighty-One, consisting of noble men and women and other people of the nine clans who were revered for varying achievements. This council was exclusive so that each clan would have equal representation. This council, they called Wemtii.

The Baluma also had a very well-structured judiciary system enforced by the king and the two councils. There were four main kinds of punishment depending on the crime committed, and punishment was meted out with caution. A person could be made to pay a fine, exiled, killed, or condemned to slavery. People were made to pay fines when they had committed an act of disobedience, exiled when they had committed an offense against the ancestors, or, in the case of rape or incest, taken to the outskirts of the kingdom and killed. In the case of theft, they were condemned to slavery. A person condemned to slavery was marked for life, and their family would be ostracised for generations.

The punishment of slavery was enforced in cases where a person had stolen land from a widow and her children or harvested from a farm that was not theirs and left the owners to starve. Depending on the magnitude of the theft, the person could be condemned for several years or for life. Once condemned, the person would be assigned to either the king's palace or to another household. All their property would be seized and given to the person from whom they had stolen.

A condemned man's wife could either follow him to his place of work or could return to her family. The slave was required to work for their master, and their master, in turn, had a duty to take care of the slave as he did everybody in his household. If the master was kind and the slave showed good behaviour, the master could set them free before the end of their time of service and reward them with property and land to grow crops and restart a good life. The king, the nobles, and other rich men owned several slaves.

* * *

Baluma was not a warlike tribe. They were traders, farmers, and brokers. Because they rarely ever expressed aggression, they enjoyed affable exchanges with the neighbouring tribes. Whenever there were festivals in Lumani, the people always invited the neighbouring tribes. The king of Baluma visited and was visited by the neighbouring kings on several occasions. There was an established trade-by-barter system between Baluma and their neighbours to the west, the north, and the south.

With those on the western border, they exchanged food crops for cloth and jewellery. The people of the west were considered very vain and flirtatious. The Baluma women did not like their men going west to trade. They always complained that whenever their men stayed there for too long, they returned a little offbeat, shaving their beards more carefully and more frequently and paying more attention to themselves and the quality of food their wives cooked. Even more annoying, the men would sit around in the evenings, talking about how good trading in the west was, and that made their wives wonder whether 'trading' was not a euphemism.

To the north of the kingdom, there were tribes of herdsmen. The Baluma exchanged their food crops and medicines for cows and other animals that the northerners brought. The Baluma learnt from their northern neighbours how to tend cows and sheep, a practice that they had long forgotten about and was uncommon in Lumani until peaceful relations with the north had been re-established.

It wasn't legend but a historical fact. One sunny afternoon, a man rode into Lumani on a horse dressed in several pieces of cloth and his head wrapped all over so that one could barely see his eyes. His hands held a rope that led to the horse's mouth (a weird thing for a Baluma). He said something through the cloth in a strange language. The man sitting behind him on the same horse translated in a tired voice that they wanted to see the king. This second man was not so wrapped up, even though he had a similar cloth wrapped around his head. His face and neck had a skin colour that was recognisable to the Baluma. The first man who had spoken in the strange language had skin on his hands and around his eyes that was not quite so usual. It looked like the skin of the people the travellers said lived across the great waters. Even though his eyes were of normal colour, the skin looked as if he had been severely burnt by fire.

The men on horseback rode to the king's palace and, after a while, came out, got back onto their horse, and rode off out of Lumani.

The next time the men reappeared, they had two other horses with them, each carrying two men dressed as with the first ones. The one in front was wrapped up, the skin around his eyes and hands looking burnt, holding a rope that led to the horse's mouth, and the other man behind looking very tired but with a skin colour that seemed more normal and acted as the translator for the one in front. This time, the king received them along with the high priest and the patriarch. A small crowd gathered around the palace to get firsthand information.

The men had come with a message from a person they said had been sent by God. They said the Baluma were not living righteous lives because they ate pork and drank palm wine. These messengers had been sent to warn the Baluma to change their ways and accept this new way of worship where they would not be allowed to offend God by eating pork and drinking palm wine. That was the same message the king had been given by the first man a few days back. The king had asked the man to give him time to speak with his high priest and patriarch and to return in a few days for an answer.

The high priest ran out of patience, explaining that the Baluma also believed in one god but that they believed that God had put the land

and everything on it at the disposal of the people. Palm wine was tapped from trees that God had grown for them; how could it be a bad thing? And pigs, which lived in the bush, had also been put there, along with the other animals, by God at the people's disposal, so how could that be a bad thing either? After arguing over palm wine and pork for a while, the messengers came up with a proposition. They had cows for sale if the Baluma could get rid of the pigs, at which point the king asked them whether they were traders or messengers, and a very fiery brawl ensued.

The men were sent off with the understanding that if they returned, they would be taken to the outskirts of the kingdom, their heads severed and put on sticks as a warning to anybody who would attempt to threaten the peace of Lumani again. The men left but, just as the king had anticipated, came back with swords, and a barbarous war began. The Baluma army was not as skilled as the enemy, but they had the advantage of the rainforest to the east of their kingdom, where the women and children could run to for safety whenever they were attacked. The forest was always their refuge.

The Baluma warriors knew all the nooks and crannies of their kingdom, so hiding and trapping the invaders was not arduous. Battle after battle, they kept on pushing the enemy outwards. At the end of a few weeks, they had pushed them completely out and reseized the kingdom. With the war being now at the borders, the women and children could return to the kingdom.

The invaders had called for and received reinforcement. As the war waged on, the Baluma army realized that the northern tribes had been conquered by these enemies and had submitted to their strange way of worship. The kings of some of the northern kingdoms sometimes sent messengers to the Baluma king, offering a peace treaty in exchange for submission to their new-found way of worship, but the Baluma were adamant about their own way of worship. The king rejected the offers, and the war continued.

The war lasted about twelve years before the last legions of the invader gave up, by which time dozens of Baluma princes and hundreds of warriors had been killed. The invaders, seeing themselves defeated, made a final peace offer, which came as a surprise to the Baluma because they had not realized they were winning the war. The offer was for unconditional peace and to establish trade between their kingdoms and the Baluma.

That was how the trade between the Baluma and the northern peoples re-began. As time went by, the relations evolved from skeptical to affectionate and finally to somewhat friendly. Some Baluma men even took wives from the north. But the Baluma were still too reticent to let their women go north.

* * *

The Baluma also had good doctors who were known to cure all sorts of ailments, so the neighbours always came to Lumani to get cured when their own doctors could not help them. This was common of the peoples to the southern borders, who were typically a fishing people. Their own land was bordered southwards and westwards by great seas. They had lots of fish and other seafood; these, they exchanged with the Baluma for medicines. They fetched the fish from the seas and then salted and dried the fish to preserve for the journey.

The Baluma nicknamed the southern people 'the fish men' and often teased the traders who came. The southern peoples, in turn, nicknamed Baluma 'the elephant people'. Before setting off on a journey to trade with Baluma, the southerners would joke that they were going to see the elephants. This nickname was given because the Baluma prevented the southerners from hunting elephants in the forest beside Lumani, and during festivals, the elephants always came to feast with the Baluma as if they were the tenth clan of Lumani. The Baluma forest guards would sound their trumpets to a special tune, which seemed to beckon the elephants. When the elephants would stroll out of the forest, the people would fetch water and fresh vegetables. The animals would sit there, drinking and eating and playing with the children the whole day long. At sunset, the bull elephant would sound his trunk, and the school would walk slowly back into the forest.

The southern peoples said the Baluma liked to 'play with food'. 'Those animals should be in the pot, not in the forest,' they would say.

However, the reason for protecting the elephants was much deeper than the southerners understood. There was a fable in Baluma that had been told to every generation. Every parent told their children the story as if they had been there themselves.

The Baluma previously hunted every animal in the forest without discrimination. The elephants were rarely seen around the forest. It was as if they had migrated farther or come closer, depending on the weather. Whenever the hunters saw an elephant, it was an opportunity to kill the rare animal. Elephants were precious because they had lots of meat and fat. A medium-sized one could feed a whole clan for weeks. The women loved to dry the meat and preserve to feed their families slowly until another elephant could be found.

There was, however, one particularity about the elephant: it was a very vindictive animal. For every elephant killed, the people were sure to suffer. Noticing one of theirs was gone, the school would return a few weeks later and raid the clans, destroying houses and farms, eating crops and overturning everything in their way. Then the elephants, when their anger was pacified, would go back into the forest, only to be seen a few months later after another hunt and feast of elephant meat. To protect the people, the king created a forest task force. Young men from the clans closest to the forest were trained and put systematically on guard. Whenever they saw the elephants approaching, they would sound trumpets to alert the people to take cover. This was how the Baluma lived in the era when they still used to hunt elephants.

During that era, the legend went that whenever the land was plagued by an illness for which the doctors did not have a cure, the doctors would go into the forest and camp there to search for a cure until one was found. This was because they believed that the forest had a leaf to cure every illness. On one such occasion, a group of doctors went out to camp in the forest to find the cure of a strange rash that had recently plagued the land. Amongst them was a young doctor who had given birth a few weeks before and, because she was still nursing, had to take her baby along. In the middle of their second night in the forest, a strange catlike animal attacked. The young doctor rapidly strapped her baby to her back and ran for her life, along with the rest, but in the midst of the commotion, the baby slipped from her back. It was only when they had got back to the clan that she felt her back for her baby and discerned what must have happened. She cried and cried for days because the other doctors wouldn't let her go back to fetch her baby. The king sent a few hunters into the forest later on, but they couldn't find the baby.

A few days later, the forest guards noticed an enormous elephant at the edge of the forest. They blew the trumpets to alert the people to run for cover, and they seized their spears. This was unusual because the elephants always attacked as a school and only when one of theirs had been hunted. It had been several months since the last elephant had been killed and the school had disseminated their wrath. So what could this lone one possibly want? The forest guards stood there, wondering whether to attack and how. The elephant stood there for a while and then began to walk slowly with her trunk curled up, directly towards the forest guards, who held spears at it, feigning courage.

As it got closer, the forest guards noticed it was a female and that there was a baby elephant walking shyly behind her. They understood that her trunk curled up was not a sign of aggression but didn't know what to do. She stopped in front of the guards, unfolded her trunk, and put down a bundle of dust and leaves. The guards were raising their spears at her when they noticed a smaller but stouter male elephant walking towards them less peacefully. When he arrived, he stood beside the female, and the baby moved backwards. The female bent down and pushed the bundle forward. The guards picked the bundle up; it was the young doctor's baby. He was alive and well despite the dust and had a strange green pulp in his mouth and on his fingers, which he was sucking on. The forest guards, realising what had happened, dropped their spears and brought water to offer to the elephants to express gratitude. The three elephants, seeming to understand the gesture, began to drink.

In the meanwhile, the guards informed the king, who gave immediate orders. The doctor was informed and a feast thrown to celebrate. The stouter elephant, the male, stood up and blew his trunk, and a few moments later, seven other elephants had joined the feast. The elephants were given cabbages and other vegetables to eat and allowed to stay for as long as they wanted. The king decreed on that day that the Baluma shall no longer hunt elephants and will protect the elephant schools from the hunters of other lands.

The legend continued that ever since that day, the elephants, as if to return the people's goodwill, never came to destroy farms or clans. Instead, they would come to the edge of the forest, blow their trunks, and wait to be invited in. The forest guards would inform the people, and instead of running for cover as they did before, the people would come out with water and food for the elephants.

* * *

The southern traders or 'fish men', as the Baluma called them, usually came to Baluma during the wet season after the harvest. However, on one occasion, they surprisingly came to Lumani in the peak of the dry season. Even more surprising was that they had not come for medicines as they usually did. This time, they had come to exchange fish for slaves. The slave owners were not sure whether trading condemned men was moral, so they referred the matter to their king. Strange as this exchange was, the Baluma king authorised the exchange, and the trade began. The fish men would come to Lumani at whatever period of the year they chose to trade fish for slaves. The only thing the king bothered to emphasise was for the slave owners to indicate to the buyers the number of years each slave had been condemned to avoid punishing a slave for longer than the law allowed.

A few years later, when some slaves who were expected back had not returned, it caused anxiety, and the Baluma king wrote to the kings of the southern kingdoms to enquire about the slaves who should be freed and sent his emissaries with the letter. When the emissaries had still not returned after a few months, the king sent two nobles to the south. The same thing happened. The journey to the south and back did not take more than two or three weeks, but it had been already four months since the nobles had left. The king decreed that no more slaves should be sold to the fish men and called the Ngui and Wemtii councils for a meeting.

The councils made a note of the number of slaves sold by using sticks to represent each slave; the height of the stick indicated the number of years the slave had been condemned to. All the nobles and rich men who had sold slaves to the southerners came forward and put down their sticks. Three hundred and seventy-one slaves had been sold, of which one hundred and eight were due back in the kingdom but had not returned, and sixty had been condemned to life so were never expected back. The nobles agreed that the situation was worrying and decided that once the fish men returned, they would find out what was going on.

It didn't take long for the fish men to return. The warriors captured them and took them before the king. They confessed that they did not buy the slaves for themselves but rather to resell. There was a trade that had been established at the coast. White men had come from across the great seas on very large boats and had made an agreement with the southern kings. They would give slaves to the white men in exchange for liquor and other things the men brought. It really wasn't a mutual agreement. The kings had had no choice because those who refused to agree had suffered harrowing consequences. Their kingdoms had been burnt down and the people captured and put on the great boats. The fish men said that the white men had strong medicine. They had weapons that had never been seen before, and even the strongest warriors could not defeat them. Every slave who had been taken to the coast had been put on the boats. They had returned to Lumani because there were no slaves left in the coast; even the emissaries and noble men from Lumani had been put on the boats. The white men had promised to return the slaves in a few years, but everybody knew that wouldn't happen.

The king nodded. The fish men were taken away and dragged to the outskirts of the kingdom. Their heads were severed and stuck up on sticks that were planted in the ground as a warning to the enemy.

The fish men never returned, but the southern warriors did. They came during the wet season as the fish men usually did, although this time, the Baluma were not expecting them. They stayed in the bushes for a few nights and observed the people at close range, and then they entered the kingdom one night and captured people, especially small families living in isolated areas where there were not many men to fight. It was only in the morning that the people noticed the disappearances. The next night, the same thing happened. The councils held again, the nobles decided that the forest guards and warriors should be put around the clans at night, and when an intruder was caught, a trumpet would be blown to wake the whole clan to fight.

It happened exactly as they had planned it. The following night, the southern warriors were overpowered and killed despite the fact that their weaponry was superior. The guards continued to guard the clans for about a year and, every now and then, caught intruders. Sometimes they could not kill all the intruders but killed at least enough to send the remaining ones running for their lives.

The people were just getting used to the situation when it got worse. One day, just as the sun was setting, the southern warriors attacked again. This time, they had come in greater numbers, and they were better armed than before. The southern warriors attacked the first clan just when the people were on their way back from the farms, carrying large baskets of crops.

The children were running around their parents, playing and laughing merrily. A little boy tugged his mother's loincloth a little too much. The cloth loosened and fell to the ground. The boy froze. His mother dropped her basket to pick up her loin to cover herself. She wrapped it back up with such great care, and he knew what that meant. He was just a little over four years of age, but he had had enough experience to know what that 'careful finishing off of something she had been doing before he interrupted' meant. He looked at his mother and felt dead already. He spun and ran in whatever direction could take him away.

She ran after him. He was like a house fly you think you caught, only to open your hands and find that you missed. The adults around laughed and pretended to try to catch him but always let him slip away. They knew as he did that there was no refuge for the kind of trouble he was in. When one of the adults tried to catch him, he took a turn right and ran towards the bushes. He was running so fast, his mother couldn't catch up. She gave up the chase and stopped, but he was still running from the fear. She shouted to him that she would be waiting for him when he got home, so unless he intended to be someone else's son, he had better come back and take his punishment immediately.

She turned around back to the group. They were yelling so many things to her that she could not distinguish clearly enough. All she could hear was 'Kubi! Back!'

Kubi was her son's name. She was about to presume they were asking him to be obedient to his mother when the terrified looks on their faces made her spine stiff. She turned around, and it happened in a flash: Kubi running away from her, the southern warriors charging towards them, aiming their weapons, a warrior pointing a weapon at Kubi, and then Kubi cut in two. Parts of his little body flew into the air.

Her heart didn't have time to stop. She screamed and ran towards what had been her son but didn't get there. The warriors aimed at her, and in a matter of moments, she and her son would meet in the land of their ancestors.

The warriors charged towards the terrified crowd like a stampede of buffalos. Baskets, crops, and human parts flew around the air. The warriors rampaged through the clan, killing whoever they could not capture. They seemed to know every possible hideout in the small clan. Even the babies and children hidden behind rocks and under grass heaps were found and killed if they were too small to sell. Some men and women tried to fight back, but their efforts were futile. They were easily overcome by the southern warriors' superior weaponry. The warriors chained the people they captured and moved to the next clan, leaving some warriors behind to warden the people they had just caught. Amongst them was Nubami, Kubi's father.

It had been six years since he had brought home a beautiful western woman as a second wife. Nubami had gone to the west that season to trade for cloth to resell in Lumani when he met his second wife and was so taken that he paid her dowry almost immediately with the cloth he had bought. So instead of bringing home cloth, he had brought home a wife. His first wife was unable to bear children, and she had accepted his family's decision that he get a second wife to bear him children, but she had not thought the woman would be that beautiful. When his first wife returned from the stream, she had broken a calabash on the poor woman. In the first year, there was a lot of rivalry between the two wives, especially when the second conceived, but once the baby was born, the little one's joyful cries filled the house with cheer and peace, and the two wives reconciled.

As Nubami sat on the ground, staring, he was in a trance. He had seen his two wives and son explode and all his friends cut up. His mind persuaded him that this was all a hallucination.

In the second clan, the warriors caught the people less unaware because night had already fallen, and the forest guards were in position. However, because of their superior weaponry, the warriors quickly eliminated the forest guards and attacked but not before the guards had alerted the people. In the bushes surrounding this second clan, a handful of boys were checking the traps they had set for bush rats when they heard the screaming. Some of the boys ran back to the clan but didn't live to understand what was going on. Two others stayed, Mwami and Bula. Mwami recognised the sounds and thought of running to the nobles in the clan at the next hill to alert them so that they could send their warriors out. He turned to Bula to tell him the plan, but Bula was no longer by his side. Mwami could see Bula running off in the distance and realized too late that the rumours about his friend had been true.

Bula was the son of Tanu, one of the prominent nobles of the Wemtii. Well known for his generosity and foresight, Tanu was a light-skinned man of average height with drooping jaws and a pointed mouth that protruded so obviously that with his slanted eyes, it gave him the cunning look of an old fox. It was said that if Tanu asked you a question that seemed simple enough to answer either in the affirmative or negative, you would be foolish to speak without asking yourself what either answer would imply. Tanu was influential in the Wemtii. He had eight wives and thirty-one children and was preparing dowry for the ninth. He had one of the biggest compounds in the clan, several slaves, and several plots of land. Everybody held him in high regard. Tanu had always felt strongly about slave owners treating their slaves in a humane manner and had even adopted in secret some of the children of his slaves to avoid them being ostracised from the community. Tanu was one of the first nobles who had gone to the king to express the people's concerns about the slaves who had not returned and anchored the first few meetings they had on the subject, expressing disappointment about those who didn't see a problem with the slaves not returning.

It was during the meeting that was held prior to the capturing of the fish men, some had observed a somewhat reticence on Tanu's part to put his own sticks forward but dismissed it as tiredness since the meeting had taken the whole day. The nobles were therefore bemused to observe an obvious shift in Tanu's stance towards the trade of slaves shortly after the fish men had been killed and began to watch Tanu more closely after that. It was Tanu's peculiar carriage in the subsequent meetings about placing forest guards that raised eyebrows. Tanu was silent for the whole meeting and kept his eyes down but for a few comments he made in passing from time to time about slaves being slaves and that people should be free to sell them. The elders had taken keener interest in Tanu since then but observed nothing much until a few months later when he offered to go southwards to negotiate with the southern kings on behalf of the Baluma. In spite of the peculiar behaviour, the king and nobles decided to give him the benefit of the doubt.

Tanu travelled down with his son Bula. When Bula returned later without his father, the rumours began to spread that Tanu had joined the southern slave traders and was making a great deal of wealth from the trade. Nobody ever confirmed the rumours, but almost everyone believed them.

Mwami had not believed the rumours until he saw Bula running away that night. Mwami had been living with his auntie and her husband in the clan that had been attacked, but he did not go back to fetch them. He knew it would be of no use. He ran for the clan at the next hill.

By the time Mwami got to the hill, he had been running for a lifetime. He was given fresh water to drink to catch his breath and then invited to tell his story. He told them all he knew and affirmed the story about Bula and Tanu. Needless to say, the people had already deduced that even before he came to the part.

This second battle was much bloodier than the first, and left very few alive. Even amongst those captured, most were injured too severely to survive the journey to the coast. The injured ones were abandoned there to die, and the warriors chained the healthy survivors and returned to the first clan to return southwards with those they had captured.

The king and councils met the next morning, and a decision quickly arrived. The families would move into the forest, and the warriors would hold the fort. The generations that had fled into the forest before, during the era when the herdsmen attacked, had all passed, but the Baluma were always conscious of their age-long culture of seeking refuge in the arms of Mother Forest whenever war spread beyond the periphery of the kingdom.

The Baluma packed and began to move. It took quite a few weeks, but it was well organised, and since the dry season was approaching, the people felt happier in the cool shades of the forest trees. The warriors stayed behind to protect the kingdom.

The southern warriors took their time in returning, but they did. Meanwhile, in the forest, the high priest prophesied that this war, unlike the previous one, would last generations. New warriors were trained cyclically in the forest and sent out to guard the land. Sometimes they vanquished, and sometimes they were vanquished and captured. Every now and then, the southern warriors would get as far as the edge of the forest and capture a few families. The Baluma moved farther into the forest under the guidance of their priests until they were no longer within the reach of the southern warriors. The Baluma warriors continued to defend generation after generation. Kings died, kings were crowned, and the Baluma continued to fight. Trade continued with the northern peoples and sometimes the western peoples.

The Baluma counted the generations by the number of kings who were crowned during that era. They counted thirteen, including the king who had led them into the forest. Of the thirteen kings, seven had died in battle, four had been captured, and two had died in old age. The fourteenth king to ascend the thrown would live to lead the people home.

Through the generations, the Baluma told their children beautiful stories about the kingdom that was once theirs, about the festivals and the crops they used to plant, and the children told their own children in turn. From generation to generation, only warriors who lived mostly on the land to protect it could come home and tell stories about Lumani with greater detail. The people had resigned themselves to the situation and were losing hope of ever returning to Lumani when suddenly, the high priest had begun to talk about the 'calming of the waters'. It renewed the people's hope about returning to Lumani, and with guidance from the high priest, the people began to pray for 'the great return'.

In Lumani, the attacks became less and less frequent, but the people still remained in the forest for fear of surprise attacks. The high priest began to speak of visitors approaching. These ones, he said, were not coming for slaves but had words in their mouths that he could not understand. They were travelling from place to place, speaking the strange words, and were on their way to Lumani.

The warriors were on guard one afternoon when they saw some white men approaching them, dressed in white robes and holding books. Walking alongside the white men were natives of other tribes carrying bags. The warriors did not notice any weapons, so they deduced that these must be the same men the high priest had spoken of. The men approached them with respect and asked to see their leader. It was during one of the times the king was on a supervisory visit to Lumani. Two kings ago, it had been decided that though the king was supreme commander, he should not be allowed to lead the warriors to battle any longer. The people had grown wary of losing kings in battle. From then onwards, the king would stay with the people in the forest and only go back to the land to supervise when the high priest could 'see' that there was no danger. The king therefore appointed an *afomi* (second-in-command) from amongst the warriors to lead the warriors in Lumani permanently while he stayed with the people in the forest. Once the king got clearance from the high priest, he would take a few weeks off to check on the warriors. It was therefore during one of such supervisory visits that the white men in white robes paid a visit.

Hundreds of years of war had spelled the warriors' scepticism. They tied the men up in spite of their peaceful demeanour and seemed a little surprised when they offered no resistance. Instead of leading the men to the king, the warriors preferred to lead them to the *afomi*. This person, Wandi, was known for his generosity with blows from his machete and bullets from his gun. He had been a warrior long enough to see his father and seven of his brothers killed in wars against the slave takers. Wandi was never in any mood to show mercy to invaders; he carried an anger in his heart that even death could not quench.

Still tied up, the white men were dragged to Wandi. One of the white men said something, and another one (a native of the south who spoke the Baluma language) translated.

'Peace be with you and all around here.'

Wandi murmured something about peace or blood, and the warriors around roared with a laughter that filled the air. Then, the men still tied up told them the purpose of their visit, to bring them a message of salvation. They spoke about a supreme deity and his boundless mercy and compassion for all who came to him. They said that this god had a son who had promised good things for all who believed in him.

All the while the men talked, Wandi looked at them in utter bewilderment. The high priest had cautioned that the visitors spoke a language he did not understand, but Wandi had never imagined their words would be this far from reason. Wandi was still glazed in his thoughts, wondering what to do with them when they were done talking, when something the men said caught his attention: 'forgiveness for all who had wronged you'. He struck his machete on the ground, and there was immediate silence.

He glared at them and asked them to explain what they meant by the word *forgiveness*. He wasn't sure what exactly they meant, but he was sure he did not like the idea. The men explained, using examples Wandi was familiar with, like seeing his brothers killed. Just to be sure he understood them correctly, Wandi asked the men specifically whether they were asking him to forgive the southerners and white men who had killed his father and brothers. The men replied that this was what the 'son of God' was expecting of him. Wandi rolled his eyes and did not say a word after that. When the men were done talking, Wandi gave orders for them to be untied and their books returned to them. The men preached to the warriors around and then made their way out of the kingdom, promising to be back in a few weeks.

Wandi informed the king personally about the guests and the strange words they had spoken. They both laughed and made jokes of the white men, their strange robes, their word, and their books. To his amazement, Wandi found himself feigning amusement. He could not figure out why he had lost his appetite since afternoon. He had just been informed that his second wife had given birth, and he would be returning home in three days for the naming ceremony of his eleventh child. He should have been a happy man, but he couldn't eat or drink anything. He found difficulty finding sleep that night. He kept on tossing and turning until almost daybreak.

Suddenly, Wandi was in the middle of a battlefield somewhere on the outskirts of Lumani. He was striking a man to the ground with his machete when he felt something sharp hit his left shoulder. As the man he had stricken fell to the ground, he looked at his shoulder and realized that he had been hit by a bullet. He grabbed his shoulder to stop the blood from spouting. Looking sideways, he saw his elder brother (Vumanga) falling to the ground. Everybody was fighting everybody. There was so much confusion and blood everywhere.

Wandi got to Vumanga and started to drag him out to safety. His brother's chest and belly were open, and he could see the intestines. He knew his brother wouldn't survive, but at least he had to drag him to the cave and let him die there so that he could be given a decent hero's burial later on. As he dragged his brother, he saw the white man in a white robe following him, telling him to forgive the people who had shot his brother. He looked down at his brother's chest and saw Vumanga gasping for breath and then giving up the ghost with a smile.

As Vumanga drew in his last breath, he touched his arm and said slowly, 'Forgive them, Wandi...'

Wandi opened his eyes and was thankful he had been dreaming. He knew that his brother would never say such an absurd thing. He got off his mat, rolled it up, and went out to take a bath.

The naming ceremony of his baby (a girl he had always wanted to replace his mother) had gone excellently well, and he returned to Lumani with his spirit buoyant and had long forgotten the white men and their strange teachings. He did admit that the white men and their words of forgiveness had a strange effect on him. Every time he had tried to submit to the principle, he experienced a feeling of relief, a feeling that took the weapon out of his hand but completely contradicting his role of *afomi* and thus causing him great discomfort. He had concluded that was the kind of effect nonsense talk would have on anybody who wasn't a coward.

Those white men, he told himself, had never seen a war; if they had, they would not be saying something so foolhardy. Besides, as the high priest had told them at the naming, no man who came in God's name could bring war. Theirs (Si, the god the Baluma worshipped) was a god of peace who only urged his people to defend when needed but never to attack.

So how could the same people who had come with war and bloodshed to take people who had never committed a crime as slaves claim to also come in the name of Si? Wandi questioned.

While he did admit the ones who had come for slaves had different faces from the ones who came to preach, still, they had the same skin colour and talked with the same accent and in the same language; Wandi refused to be convinced there was a difference.

Life continued as usual for a long time after that, with Wandi in charge of Lumani and the people in the forest. The southern slave takers had not reappeared in almost three years, and Wandi and his warriors were beginning to wonder what that might mean. They were tempted to suspect that the southern slave takers had changed strategy when the white men in white robes returned.

The white men still had their books and translators with them as they had before. They approached respectfully as before and asked to see the leader. This time, Wandi had more patience for them. The strange talk was becoming entertaining. He placed both palms behind his head and stretched backwards to rest on the trunk of the tree on which he had been resting before the *interruption* as the men began their sermon.

He was more preoccupied with the strange withdrawal of the southern slave takers. When he was a child, his great grandfather had told him stories about the war against the northern invaders. They said that towards the end of the war, the invaders attacked less and less until the attacks ceased completely. Then they had received a letter from the northern kings asking for a peace treaty. Wandi sat there, wondering whether this was the same thing happening for a second time. He had been a warrior since he could stretch his left hand over his head and touch his right ear without bending his head. He had grown up in war. Though he had spent his life until then hoping that he would live to see the end of the war and get a glimpse of peace before he died, the thought of peace somewhat scared and excited him; he was not sure what peace meant. He was a child who had been born during a time of war. He did not know what peace meant. He smiled at the thought that the girl he had always wanted might indeed see a time of peace in her life.

The white man was saying something about a prince of peace when Wandi decided that he could bother to let his guests have his attention. Wandi thought he had no difficulty understanding what the white man meant by *prince of peace* ('That is, a prince who makes peace,' he rushed to conclude).

He wanted to go back to the subject of forgiveness. He asked the white man what he thought of the slave takers, whether they too deserved forgiveness, and, for a reason he could not explain to himself later on, expected the white man to agree with him that they didn't. The white man smiled and began to talk slowly as if he had read Wandi's mind. He talked about two goats for sacrifice, one to be offered to God and the other carrying the sins of the people away; the one that carried the sins of the people away was called the 'scapegoat'. The first goat was sacrificed to God for forgiveness and the scapegoat pushed over a cliff to take the sins of the people back to the evil one. Not forgiving meant holding onto the scapegoat. All the sins of the past would remain. The only way to get rid of that sin was to push that scapegoat over the cliff and walk home free. This did not mean, though, that the offender would not be judged by the same God for his sins against one. By the time the white man had come to the end of his sermon, Wandi was even more confused than he been before.

While he was still trying to wrap his head around the concept of forgiveness and a goat carrying sins, he noticed that some of his men had been listening with more keenness this time than they had the last time. It made Wandi console himself that he was not the only one in the situation and feel relieved.

* * *

A few months later, the decision was finally made to let the people return to Lumani. When King Tozingana made the announcement to the people, there was silence for a few moments, and then after that, as if they had digested what he had said, the people let out a sound of joy that had not been heard for centuries.

The Baluma returned shyly to the land, settling in the areas bordering the forest for a while before spreading outwards. There was still a lot of leeriness because even though it had been three whole years since the last attack, the horror stories told by the warriors who survived were chilling enough to make even a strong man convulse. The 'great return', as the people called it, was properly organised with a particular number of warriors assigned to each group resettling. Occasionally, people cried wolf, so the warriors and other trained guards had a tough time getting the people resettled with little commotion. Once the people returned, the white men in white robes asked for permission to settle. The king cut up a piece of land on the outskirts of the kingdom around where the attackers used to come from. This was to shield the Baluma so that if the attackers returned, they would find the white men and their southern servants first, and that would alert the warriors.

There were four white men in total and seven helpers who doubled as interpreters. The white men and their helpers settled neatly. They built huts and sheds that they used as homes and as preaching grounds, and before long, the crowds began to grow. Most of the people came out of curiosity in the beginning but gradually took interest and began to ask more and more questions to the point where the white men were forced to make a question-and-answer session part of the daily program. The greater part of those interested were the young people, and they eagerly got involved with what they called 'the work of the church'.

Once the initiation rituals began to gain popularity amongst the Baluma, there was increasing disconcertion in the priestly order. The high priest (Pa Ngunep) was particularly disturbed that the people who were converting to this new way of worship were the young men and women – the future of the Baluma. He chose to do nothing about it just yet.

When the young people were ready to be integrated as members of this new religion (which later became understood as Christianity), the white men began to teach them about the initiation ritual to the religion, which they called 'baptism'. This was a ritual in which the person in question would be made to bow his head, and the white man would say some words, pour some water over the person's head, call that person by a new name, and welcome the person as a new member of the religion. The person being initiated needed to abandon the teachings of the high priest (which, according to the new religion, were false teachings), the god of their ancestors, Si (who, according to the new religion, was a false god), and the name he or she had been given by his family (which was contrary to the law of the new religion). Wandi did not have the patience to attend the preaching and the rituals himself, but he listened carefully as his wives discussed the issue whenever they came home from these sessions.

Wandi's second and third wife had grown interested in the preaching but were too afraid to ask him for permission to attend. They were not sure how he would react. They tried to persuade his first (his favourite), but she was not interested. Wandi had not given his approval but hadn't directly disapproved either. When his wives served the evening meal, he would enquire about the religious session of that day and feign a disinterested look.

* * *

At the turn of the century, hope began to return to Lumani. But by some evil twist of destiny, another problem came along, even more terrifying than the slave takers.

A group of white men, armed with guns and other unfamiliar weapons, came into Lumani and asked to see King Tozingana. Even though the white men were armed, because they did not show any aggression, they were led through. They met with King Tozingana and offered a truce. To protect the Baluma from other white invaders, they could establish Baluma as their protectorate. They informed the king that the southern kings had already done so, and their territories were now protected. They would build schools and roads in the kingdom, and in return, Baluma would show solidarity with them by abiding to the laws that they proposed to keep order and ensure what they called an 'improvement' of livelihood. The king and his counsel turned the subject over and over and finally came to the conclusion that if these people were offering protection, then perhaps there were more dangerous invaders on the way. Besides, word had come from the south that the trade of slaves was over and that the southern kings who had accepted this same kind of truce were doing well, and their kingdoms were prospering. King Tozingana decided to accept the truce.

Wandi was skeptical about the decision. He liked to believe that his army could defeat any other. After all, he had led the Baluma army for fourteen years, so what sort of protection could these *new* white men have to offer that his army couldn't? There was something about this truce that he felt uneasy about, but the councils persuaded him that that was the trauma the *bad* white men of the past had caused him. They convinced him that this was the new method all the other kingdoms had adopted, and they were doing well. Wandi accepted reluctantly, but something inside told him they were being naive.

Wandi left the meeting with his heart unrested, so he went to see Abimi. Abimi was more than just a brother in arms. They had grown up together in the forest, trained together as warriors, passed their manhood test, and been admitted into the army on the same day. Both men had fought battles together against the southern slave takers and had risen in rank almost together. Both men knew that Wandi was only the superior because Abimi had sustained an injury in one of the wars that had almost paralysed his right arm, which was the stronger arm. Over time, Wandi had trained Abimi to use his left arm, and Abimi had excelled but was still a little slower. So when the time came to choose the next *afomi*, Wandi was the natural choice.

When Wandi entered Abimi's compound, Abimi had no difficulty figuring out who had come because the children always got excited when Wandi came and ran out to greet him. They led him to Abimi's house, telling stories and asking questions all at once. It was interesting to see the other side of a warrior known for mercilessness on the battlefield. The children were never afraid of him, the women always loved having him around, and all young men wanted to be him someday. Even during the era before 'the great return', Wandi never had to worry about his family back in the forest. They would never starve because the other families would take care whenever they were in need. His reputation of mercilessness was only in the perspective of his enemies; to his people, he was a shield, true to his name Wandinendi (shortened as Wandi), which, in Baluma, meant *safe haven*.

Wandi entered Abimi's home, and as they always did, they served palm wine and drank the first two horns in silence. Wandi rubbed his eyes to begin the conversation. When he was done telling Abimi of the decision that had been taken and of his reticence, he explained the depth of his suspicion.

'Abimi, we must never forget that these people are the same ones who tormented us for fourteen kings. You and I were both born in the forest, and how many of our children have been born to us here on our land? We only just returned from the forest, and already, these same people who kept us away from our land for so many years are now willing to protect us? For free? And from who else?'

Abimi thought about it for a while and then tried 'Wandi, perhaps these ones who are willing to protect us are different from the ones who took us. Remember that while the southerners were trying to sell their people and ours, we were trying to protect our people and theirs. Remember even traitors amongst us, like the infamous Tanu. A person would say that all of us are the same, but we both know there is a difference. So why can't we see a difference in these white people? Besides, there are the people of the church here whom several of our people have joined, and they have been peaceful, at least so far. I admit that I neither agree with this new way of thinking and their strange rituals nor understand how Si could choose to be a shepherd, but I can see that these white men in white robes are different from the ones who sent southerners here to take people. These other ones who have come with weapons have shown us no aggression so far, so why should we not welcome them? Besides, if they ever show aggression, we will show them exactly whose land this is.'

Wandi was still not convinced. He thought about it in silence and then shook his head and said, 'Abimi, I understand. But I maintain that there is something about these people, all of them, the white men in white robes and the new protectors, that I do not like. Let us see what time will have to say.'

* * *

The new protectors returned to Lumani with servants (natives from neighbouring kingdoms), horses, and vehicles. The king gave them large plots of land around every hill and in every clan. The white men built temporary shelters, and before long, more joined them. They were all armed, and soon, there was a small army of white men in every one of the clans in Lumani.

By this time, Wandi was getting really suspicious because he had been watching the men closely. If ever this army, instead of protecting the people, turned on them, they would be completely trapped and easily subdued. These 'protectors' had superior ammunition and were living in the heart of the kingdom; it would be a perfect attack. Besides, the people had grown so used to seeing white men amongst them that they had stopped watching their movements or being suspicious. Some women were even rumoured to be meeting the white men in private.

Wandi decided to discuss the matter in private with King Tozingana. He chose a rainy afternoon to go to the palace. Rainy afternoons were good for such secret meetings because the sound of their voices would be swallowed up by the sound of the rain and thunder. He was ushered into Tozingana's presence with little protocol.

As soon as he started speaking, Tozingana interrupted to say he had been having the same suspicions himself but had been wondering whether it was not too late since he had already signed the treaty. The two men looked at each other speechlessly for a few moments, and they both knew that the time was right to send for the high priest.

The first words the high priest spoke when he looked up from the calabash confirmed their suspicions and desolation. 'We have been strangled.'

They both looked at Pa Ngunep (the high priest) in dismay, hoping he would revive their despairing hopes as he usually did, but this time was different. Pa Ngunep's eyes met theirs, and he crushed every iota of hope they had with his words:

'A cobra has skin like dust. It mingles its way into the sand unnoticed and lies beneath patiently. The children play and chant songs that the cobra enjoys, and once he gets thirsty, he rears his head and bites whom he chooses. You only feel the sting of a cobra. Nobody ever knows where a cobra hides or sees him rearing his head.'

Pa Ngunep's message was clear. It was too late.

Wandi refused to be defeated so easily, cobra or no cobra. The next morning, he woke Abimi and the other commanders and informed them of his meeting with King Tozingana and Pa Ngunep's words. He was relieved to find that all agreed with him and were ready to fight, except for a few who wondered aloud if there was anything they could do about what was to befall them. The Baluma warriors got together at sunset.

Another thing Wandi was noted for (besides his mercilessness with the enemy) was his charisma. He was a natural commander, an attribute that had earned him the respect and loyalty of all his soldiers. Wandi reminded his men of all that had happened to their people, from the wars with the north through the southern slave traders to their return to Lumani. He hinted suspicion of the so called 'good white men' (the religious men) and opinionated that he did not trust them not to be in league with the 'cobra'. Abimi agreed, much to Wandi's surprise. None of those present, not even Wandi himself, realized that those words were of prophesy.

The warriors planned on a strategy of attacking the cobra's shelters and gave themselves about a week to prepare and observe the enemy, but the cobra did not wait that long to strike. The next morning, they went round all the homes, dragged out every young person (men and women), and made them march to the shelters they had built. The largest cobra stood on a stool in the front so that everybody could see him. He had a bulging stomach and a long beard, while the others circled the people, holding guns at them. They used an interpreter, someone from the south who had learnt their language. The people were divided in three groups. The first would fell trees in the forest, chop them up into logs of wood, and bring back, the second would cut grass, and the third group would dig wells around. Nobody objected. The people were shocked beyond words.

They worked the whole day non-stop without food and were only allowed to return home in the evening. Wandi and his commanders had not been there because they had gone to the forest before sunrise to prepare themselves, sharpen their weapons, and revise their assault strategy. They returned in the evening to the horrid news. Abimi insisted on patience and training and preparing the warriors properly before attacking the cobra. Wandi knew it would be a bad idea to attack the next morning, given that they were not yet prepared, but his emotion would not listen to reason.

Ill-prepared and driven by sheer emotion without logic, Wandi and his men charged at the white men when they came round the next morning to get people for forced labour. The cobras shot in disarray. It was difficult to know who set the houses on fire, but in a matter of minutes, roofs were up in flames, with people fleeing in all directions. The warriors cornered and killed several cobras before they could get any reinforcement. Wandi charged towards a cobra standing a few feet away. The cobra saw Wandi approaching and aimed his gun, but Wandi seemed faster than the bullet. In two strides and a blow, he seized the gun from him. The young cobra dropped dead more from fear than from the blow, and Wandi continued on.

A few hours later, Wandi and his men were overpowered and tied up. Standing at six-foot-four and over three hundred pounds, it took six strong cobras to pin him down. Wandi and his warriors were left to sit under sun the whole day. The women and children were made to pull away the corpses, and the rest of the men (who were able to work) were lined up and sent to fell trees in the forest for wood to be used in the construction work. Abimi sat beside Wandi in silence. Not a word was exchanged between the two men for the duration of captivity.

For seven days, the captured men were not given food, only water to drink occasionally. They were woken and beaten just after sunrise and then tied up and made to sit under the sun for the whole day in a place that had no trees, so there was no shade, which had been specially pointed out by the large cobra with the big belly. At sundown, they were dragged back to the prison, and a rope was tied around their legs and then strapped to a heavy piece of timber perched against a wall so that they were hanging upside down for the night. They were always given a whipping before the guards retired.

During those seven days, Wandi had time and pain enough to reflect on the past. Every time he closed his eyes, he seemed to see his brother Vumanga saying, 'Forgive them, Wandi.' Wandi resorted to keep his eyes open. The men were bleeding all over. The room smelt like rot because some of the men's wounds were rotting.

Wandi turned to his right and saw a large heap, and some substance seemed to be dropping on the heap. He managed to shake his blood-streamed head to see better. He noticed a large shiny stone. As he concentrated harder, he realized it was held up by a large armband. Wandi's bloodshot eyes widened as he took it in.

King Tozingana had been captured along with them. Unbeknownst to them, the king had later joined them in the squeamish that had led to this dilemma. Wandi moved his eyes from the armband downwards to the head of Tozingana and then upwards to a horror he had not experienced since the wars with the southern slave takers: the feet of Tozingana hanging from the rope that had strapped them and blood dripping from them unto what Wandi now realized was a lifeless body. Observing the feet carefully, he could see that the feet were too neatly separated from the body as they hung from the log of timber strapped to the rafters of the roof. Wandi, even through bloodshot eyes and a blood-streamed face, could deduce that a machete had been used. But still, he refused to close his eyes. He turned his head to the other side and right into the eyes of Abimi. He knew from the look on Abimi's face that Abimi had seen and understood the same horror, but both men said nothing even then.

The next day, the men were made to carry the body of the man who had once been their king. They were led by a guard to a place where a pit had been dug. The young men who had dug the pit were still standing there with shovels and hoes. Abimi stared at one of them in particular. Wandi noticed Abimi staring and followed his eyes to the young man. The two men moved their eyes to look at each other. Wandi knew that Abimi had something to tell him about the young man.

The body of Tozingana was dumped into the pit, and the young men began to put the earth back into the pit. Wandi and his men were made to watch. By sunset, they were flogged again and then allowed to go home.

* * *

When Abimi got home, there was a preacher waiting for him in his compound. Fr. Thomas Gooding had come on invitation of Abimi's first wife to offer his condolence for what had happened and to tell him about the 'good news'. Abimi was not in any mood to receive him, so the Father Thomas apologised and promised to return the next day when Abimi was rested. Abimi went straight to bed. In all the wars he had fought, he had never seen this kind of inhumanity. In Baluma, it was dishonourable to treat even an enemy in that manner. He was determined to wake up the next morning from this horror.

Wandi put his head on his pillow, closed his eyes, saw Vumanga again, and opened his eyes. At daybreak, with eyes still opened, he got up, went out for a fresh bath, and asked for breakfast, which his youngest wife brought to him. He ate in silence. For the first time since he had married her, she felt afraid being beside him, so she excused herself and left. He didn't answer or even notice she had left. He finished his meal, took his gun and machete, and walked slowly into the forest, where the other warriors were already waiting for him.

'To the death!' Wandi roared.

'*To the death!*' the warriors roared back.

The forest carried the echoes of their voices. The trees came alive. The birds of the forest squawked and flew from tree to tree. The sun rose in approval. Even bush rats and moles came out of their holes.

'I am Wandinendi, eighth son of Morewa, fourth son of Shesweh. You all know who my father was. You all know who my brothers were and the kind of blood that runs in our veins. So you know that I would rather die like a king than live like a slave. If anybody here disagrees, leave now, and I will hold you no grudge.'

He struck his machete into the ground.

* * *

When Abimi returned home that evening, his first wife told him excitedly that Father Thomas had been waiting the whole day. He sat down. Father Thomas rushed over apologies for the recent events, which he called 'unfortunate', opened his book, and began to read. Needless to point out, Abimi didn't hear a word of what was being read. Father Thomas went on to talk about the essence of marriage and the divinity of such a covenant, which he insisted could only be between *one* man and *one* woman. He went on to preach against polygamy as a transgression of God's law of love and family.

Abimi stood up and looked down at Father Thomas. 'I have four wives. Assuming your religion accepts my marriage to the first, what do I do about the other three?'

Father Thomas got up clumsily. 'Send them back to their families. Most unfortunately, because they have sinned against God by entering into unholy unions with you, they will not be allowed to remarry nor to receive Holy Communion according to the law of God.'

'And my children?' Abimi glared.

'Send them with their mothers. They are the product of a sinful relationship.'

Abimi dragged Father Thomas by the arm all the way to the entrance of his compound. 'If I should ever catch you or one of yours around this compound again, your soldier brothers will not be able to rescue you in time.' And he threw him out.

Abimi turned around to go back into his house when he spotted his first wife hiding behind a banana tree. She jolted and ran back into her house.

He should have known she was behind all this. Abimi shook his head.

* * *

The rumours spread about King Tozingana's death. Some said he had been killed while fighting, while others said he had died of brief illness, and yet some said he had fled the kingdom. Nobody but the cobras who captured him and Wandi's warriors had the real version. Wandi and Abimi informed the Ngui and Wemtii of the real version, and they all chose not to tell to preserve the dignity of the king. The kingmakers sent word out, which concurred with the rumour that Tozingana had died in the skirmish, and since no one ever saw a king buried, it was easy to get away with such a story. Still, there were rites that had to be performed with certain ornaments Tozingana had been buried with to determine who the next in line would be.

Abimi spoke to Wandi for the first time since they had been captured. 'Brother, do you remember the young man I was staring at on that day?'

Wandi nodded.

'He is the son of Mbunti, the palm wine tapper. He joined that religion a few months ago and has been doing a lot of what they call church work or whatever they call it.' Abimi rolled his eyes.

'Then he can lead us to the grave of King Tozingana?' Wandi enquired.

'Of course or by the god of my ancestors he will die by the one arm I have left,' Abimi swore.

Abimi was at Mbunti's front door before cockcrow the next morning. He banged on the door of the little house so hard that he almost broke it down.

Mbunti came out, trembling, wrapped in only a light loincloth. 'What could be the trouble, my brother?' he asked.

'Don't call me brother while your son betrays the land that will receive his bones. Bring him here, that church worker-traitor son of yours!' Abimi roared.

Mbunti did not have to send for the young man. He had already heard the banging and the roar and had come out to meet the two men. Abimi spat on him and dragged him out by the throat, leaving Mbunti's wife screaming in agony, 'Please, please don't kill him! He is the only son I have got!'

Mbunti crept away to put on a decent loincloth and rushed to Father Thomas.

When they were some distance away from the palm wine tapper's house, Abimi let go of the young man's throat and asked him in a hushed voice, 'Now what is your name?'

'Wilfred,' the young man answered and then dared to continue. 'Forget about who I was in the past. I am now a renewed man in the name of my Lord and Saviour Jes – '

Abimi's left hand landed to silence him. 'You should never have forgotten who you were, Nyomi.'

The young man looked at Abimi, puzzled, but Abimi didn't give him the time to ask how he knew his real name.

'Now take me to where our king was buried.'

They got there soon enough and began digging. Some elders and Wandi had followed a few yards away and arrived soon after. Once they dug to the decaying body, the stench that filled the air was so revolting, Nyomi (now Wilfred) started to run. Wandi caught him and threw him back to Abimi.

'Get down in there, young traitor,' Abimi scolded.

The boy threw up on his way down. He pulled out what the elders instructed: the ring, the armband, the earring, the anklet, and the decaying head. An elder wrapped the accessories up, and they started to go away. Wandi and Abimi followed. Nyomi was left there to cover up the pit alone. The sun was already rising.

Nyomi had just finished when the prison guards met him at the pit, and he had no hesitation explaining what happened, but the cobras had more important things to do than to spend time wondering why these savages needed a dead man's head and accessories. They let Nyomi go home. Father Thomas was waiting for him there.

'Wilfred, my son, God has spared you. Now tell us what they did to you.'

When Wilfred was done recanting all that had happened, Father Thomas promised Mbunti that he would take the matter to the authorities (and by that, he meant the new cobra government). Mbunti asked Father Thomas to take caution not to reveal their names for fear of retribution from the people. However, by the time Father Thomas got to the cobras, he had forgotten his vow of secrecy.

A group of armed cobras were dispatched to Abimi's compound to arrest him one early morning. Abimi was out in the forest camping and training. Three of his wives were out in the farms. Only one who had only recently given birth was there with the rest of the children. When they arrived, she explained that Abimi was not home. The cobras rampaged the compound, destroying everything, burning the buildings, and taking Abimi's three eldest sons along with them. Somebody ran into the forest to inform Abimi.

Wandi wouldn't let Abimi go back. He had Abimi tied up to prevent him. At sundown, Wandi dispatched a few warriors. One set off to Mbunti's house, another to Father Thomas's house, and another to the prison where he knew the boys (Abimi's sons) would be kept.

The warriors carried out a clean job. By the next morning, there were a few dead bodies, including one identified as Father Thomas's, and Abimi's family was safely in a neighbouring clan.

Pa Ngunep carried out the funeral rites, and the ancestors pointed out the new king: Ottuwa, third son of Tozingana.

CHAPTER 2

*After the pride and arrogance but before the vengeance
and mercilessness, all I can see is a man who, just like every
other, wants to live and love.*

Maidem Kayem

WHEN OTTUWA TOLD his family that he wanted to
marry Lemi, the daughter of Gemo, his whole family
objected. Even his great-granduncle, Kolezi, who was usually too tipsy
(from liquor) to speak at such a gathering, steered his large blurry
eyes open.

Lemi was from the Tebo tribe on the other side of the eighth hill,
which bordered the kingdom to the south. During the era of the slave
takers, when the Baluma had moved to the edge of the forest bordering
Lumani on the east, their warriors sought to protect Lumani and the
neighbouring kingdoms (including the small Tebo kingdom).

Amidst the disappearances, the Tebo warriors were discovered to
be making secret deals with the southern peoples to kidnap the Baluma
people. It was then that the Baluma warriors had moved their people
farther inwards into the forest but were careful not to let the Tebo
warriors know the hiding place. The Baluma had never confronted the
Tebo on this issue because it could have caused a war between the two
tribes and division at a time when neither could afford it.

However, the name Tebo became synonymous to treachery amongst
the Baluma. No reason except 'we already have a wife for him' or 'we
already have a husband for her' was ever given to the Tebo. Every
marriage between the two tribes was vehemently rejected by the Baluma.
The real reason for the antipathy remained a tribal secret.

Ottuwa, in insisting to marry from Tebo, was therefore met with a very angry reaction from his family, especially after they had told him the truth about the grudge. However, Ottuwa was not convinced about the argument and didn't see why he should hold onto a grudge that old. When Ottuwa continued insisting adamantly despite his family's opposition, Kolezi asked for silence and began to speak. Even though Kolezi was a well-known drunk, he was always invited to family meetings because from time to time, he would say something that could resolve a complex issue in a very simple manner. Nobody was ever sure when or whether to take him seriously, but in moments like these, somewhere between tipsy and hallucinating, he would speak words of wisdom.

Kolezi looked Ottuwa in the eye and asked, 'Have you understood why we don't want you to marry Lemi?'

Ottuwa replied that he had.

Kolezi asked a second question. 'Do you still insist on marrying her?'

Ottuwa replied that he did, and Kolezi concluded, 'You therefore agree that we need to protect ourselves from your wife?'

Ottuwa wasn't sure exactly what his uncle Kolezi meant by 'protect ourselves' but said that he agreed as long as they would let him marry Lemi.

Kolezi curled his lips up in a cunning smile, which Ottuwa could not understand. When Ottuwa left the meeting, Kolezi and Ottuwa's mother (Dami) went to see the high priest.

In Baluma, children were important to every marriage because they confirmed the ancestors' approval of the union. Not having children meant that the ancestors were displeased with the union. When Lemi couldn't conceive, she became an object of ridicule. Ottuwa's mother, Dami, was curiously very understanding of her barrenness, so the insults came mostly from Lemi's own family, and that made her even more miserable.

Kolezi then persuaded Ottuwa to marry again, someone from a good clan to appease the ancestors and bring everything back to order. Ottuwa married again. He chose Aruma, who was from one of the nine Baluma clans, and this time, the family approved.

The large cobra puffed and pulled again at his pipe, contemplating how to teach these savages a lesson they would remember. He contemplated the killings and pondered how meticulously the attacks had been carried out. It even crossed his mind that perhaps the attackers had been helped by some of the native recruits who worked with them. After thinking about it for a while, he dismissed the idea because the recruits had proven themselves to be even more enthusiastic about the new government structure than even the cobras. They were good and faithful servants just as they had been taught in church.

Father Thomas was a keen advocate of the principle of submission and had been brought there on special recommendation from prominent members of the church and the archbishop. Until his death, Father Thomas had done an excellent job of grooming obedient church workers. No matter how much the cobra administration taxed them, the church workers paid willingly and even reported defaulters. They also cleaned the church and church premises and the homes of the clergy and the cobras every day for meagre returns, which they never complained about. At harvest time, they brought their harvests to Father Thomas for blessings and offered him the best produce, which he shared generously with the cobra administration. Father Thomas was loved and adored by the church workers. He had instructed them to cooperate with the cobra administration that he said had been sent to make their lives better for the service of God. It was these church workers who had been the first to report the incident immediately after they had arrived work that morning. Father Thomas's dead body, lying in front of his house and covered in blood with a deep throat wound, was first discovered by one of the mass servants who fetched water for the cleaning of his house every morning.

The large cobra called in three others, barked out orders, and went to have some breakfast. The three cobras assembled groups of young men and dispatched them to every clan of the nine hills. Once the men arrived at a clan, they would go straight to the house of the cobra in charge and transmit the message they had been given. The cobra would get together another set of young men who would go around breaking houses and seizing women and children randomly and then tie them up and drag them to the main clan where the large cobra resided. There, they were prisoned in cages made of cane and straw built next to the administrative building. At sundown, the women and children were shoved into a metallic container about six feet high and eight feet in length and breadth. There was no space for some of them to stand so the women carried as many children as they could to contain the number. The men locked the container and whistled as they walked away. No men were taken because the orders were to capture only women and children on that day.

The next day, another rounding up was done, randomly as usual, but this time only men. They were tied up and prisoned in the same cages as the women and children had the day before. From the cages, the men could hear the moans of the women and children in the metal container. They had not been let out since the doors had been shut the night before. Some of the men could recognise the voices of their sisters and wives or daughters calling out from the metallic container.

The young men were given the ultimatum to cooperate or be put with their families in the container. Some young men conceded and were led away, while others who refused were led into the same container holding the women and children. The young men who refused to cooperate were squeezed into the metallic container since there was not enough space, and one could hear bones breaking on the inside as the doors were squeezed shut.

* * *

Word got to Wandi in the forest about the imprisonments and the young men who had been set free. Nobody knew what had actually happened or what the young men had been told, but being a good commander, Wandi figured it out. He and Abimi arranged to go and see Ottuwa that evening. In the meantime, the warriors were getting agitated and worried about the people who had been taken. Some of them had been told that their wives and children were amongst those taken. They wanted to react quickly and free their families. Wandi calmed them down by reminding them of the first battle they had undertaken without much thought and the end result of that. The men went back to training. Nobody stopped to rest. The anger kept them training non-stop until sundown when they sneaked back into the clans.

When Wandi and Abimi got to Ottuwa's compound, he had already been waiting for an hour. He had something interesting to tell them besides the imprisonments. He had been escorted to the residence of the large cobra a few hours back. Contrary to what he had expected, he wasn't imprisoned. Instead, the large cobra offered him some liquor and engaged a discussion about the administration of Lumani. He talked about the plans he had ahead – buildings, bridges, roads, and so on. All the cobra wanted (or so he said) was to be allowed to develop the land with no resistance from the people. This is the reason he had sent for Ottuwa. He wanted Ottuwa to talk to his people and persuade them to be cooperative, and in turn, there would be no more punishments or retaliation from his administration.

Wandi and Abimi asked spontaneously and simultaneously, 'And what did you say to him?'

Ottuwa hesitated. 'Well, I said I will think about it,' he said with his eyes glued to the floor. He could feel Wandi and Abimi staring at him, so he sighed and surrendered. 'Well, OK, well, well, I told him what I thought he wanted to hear.'

'Which was?' Wandi and Abimi said again simultaneously and obviously less patiently.

'That he could be assured of the full cooperation of my people.'

Wandi thought about it for a while. 'That was the right thing to say, but it bothers me that you didn't sound like a king.'

Ottuwa lifted his eyes to Wandi and knew it would be useless to try to explain himself. So he simply said, 'Help me.'

Abimi could not believe his ears. His *king* was asking for help.

The three men went on to discuss the retaliation of the cobras, the people who had been taken, the ones still imprisoned, and their worry about the young men who had been sent home. None of them had recanted what happened at the administrative residence, and they had refused to answer any questions. All three men agreed that if the young men were unwilling to say anything, it could only mean that they had conceded to cooperate, also that if they were not willing to reveal why or where the others were being held, it could only mean that the others had either been killed or were being tortured for not cooperating.

Wandi decided to get a group of spies to watch those young men closely and also to plant spies in the cobra administration to keep a step ahead of the cobras. Abimi suggested that women would make the better spies, especially on the cobra administration, because the cobras needed women to cook and clean their residences. Wandi hesitated because he felt that that might compromise the women's security. Both men settled on recruiting young men instead. They could pose as cleaners and errand boys for the cobras. Besides, the native women wouldn't know how to cook the kind of food the cobras ate.

'Probably sand,' Abimi joked.

The attack strategy of the warriors had to be revised because both Wandi and Abimi knew that soon, the cobras (through their native spies) would discover that the forest was being used as a training camp. Wandi and Abimi would discuss that later.

Wandi told Ottuwa to take charge of recruiting the spies and to keep on telling the cobras *whatever* they wanted to hear. He fixed his eyes on Ottuwa long enough for the king to understand the undertone. *Ottuwa needs to start acting and sounding like a king if he wants to be respected as one.*

As Wandi and Abimi walked back home, they talked about Ottuwa's strange reaction to the cobra. Surely, the king could as least pretend to have courage in front of the cobra for the sake of his personage. The two men remembered how on that sunny afternoon, the high priest had sighed when he raised the ring to announce the name of Ottuwa as successor to Tozingana and said something about a king unlike any others but a man with the strength of a woman. The witnesses to the ritual had expressed their surprise because Ottuwa, as far as they were concerned, was the least likely to be chosen to succeed his father. This, for two reasons.

First, of all Tozingana's children, he (Ottuwa) was known as a good orator but wasn't known for any kind of strength that they could understand. He was docile and always willing to make peace instead of fighting as any young man with a natural Baluma-male instinct should. Second, he didn't seem to ever show off any kind of pride or arrogance in being a man as was expected of every typical Baluma male, especially one who would be king someday.

The priest had explained that from what he could see, the ancestors had pointed to a different kind of strength that Baluma had never witnessed before. This kind of strength, although different, would be right for the times. The witnesses had objected vehemently, but the high priest had reminded them that the ancestors had spoken, and their will could not be tempered with. If anyone else should been enthroned instead of the one they had chosen, such a person would meet a death that would be difficult to understand or explain. And so Ottuwa had been enthroned.

Walking back home that evening, Wandi and Abimi wondered what the 'strength of a woman' could mean and pondered how a 'woman's strength' could prove to be useful in these circumstances.

At the next sunrise, Wandi and Abimi met with the other warriors in the forest and began to re-strategise. It was decided that they would henceforth not confront the cobras in head-on attacks but organise sporadic attacks in strategic places that were important for the cobras: their homes and offices from where they administered their government. As many had observed, several of the cobras were beginning to settle in Lumani with their wives and children. That was good because the warriors could retaliate effectively in the measure that whatever the cobras did to their families, they could do same to their families to inflict the same kind of pain.

Days and weeks went by, and Wandi still had no information on what had happened to the captured people. He was getting worried. Ottuwa had assured him that he had set up a team of spies and sent them out, but the response was too slow for Wandi. When he went back home one evening, he decided to call Uwa (his matriarch, the first wife), whom he knew was always observant of everything. He usually called her a shadow because she seemed to know about everybody and everything going on but never offered him information unless he asked.

Uwa listened to Wandi as if she had been expecting him to bring this up sooner than later, and as he spoke, her expression assured him she could be of help.

'They took the women and children and locked them up in a metal prison. Then they caught the boys the next day, asked them whether or not they were prepared to cooperate with the cobras. Some agreed. Others didn't. The ones who refused were locked up with the rest in the metal prison, and then the ones who agreed were told to feed information periodically on what is going on amongst us.'

'Uwa, whoever told you this must be one of the boys who agreed to cooperate,' Wandi shared.

'Yes, he is Nsika, the grandson of Mama Sawa. I went to see Mama Sawa when Nsika was taken to console her. As we sat there talking, Nsika came home but wouldn't talk to us. A few days later, Mama Sawa called for me, so I went, and there was Nsika in tears. He told us everything. He said that amongst them who had agreed to cooperate, no one was sure who to trust anymore. The white men had told them that they would be caught and locked up with the rest in the metal prison if ever they told anybody about the agreement. If they cooperated, they and their families would be preserved from punishment or forced labour.'

Wandi said intently, 'Why did Nsika decide to tell you and Mama Sawa?'

'Well, from what he said and the way he said it, my thinking is that the guilt was killing him. Mama Sawa is the only family he has left. And since we have taken care of them, ever since the tragedy, Mama Sawa feels indebted, which is why I think she called me.'

'Do you think he might have spoken to anyone else?' Wandi enquired.

'Well, from the fright in his eyes and the hush in his voice, I don't think so. He was shaking so much, he had to repeat for us almost every statement he made because he couldn't get his words out right a first time.'

Wandi didn't have to ask Uwa not to tell anybody else about what she had just told him before he let her go back to her house. They both knew she wouldn't.

* * *

Wandi worried for how long the cobras intended to keep the people in the metal prison. A warrior's instinct told him the people would not be back ever. He decided to go and see Ottuwa again to ask what was going on with the espionage task force. Abimi was not sure he would be able to control his temper if Ottuwa sounded remotely like he had the first time, so he opted not to accompany Wandi. Abimi wasn't wrong. Wandi came back, totally out of temper.

Ottuwa had not set up the task force because he was worried about what the cobras might do if they found out. He said he would rather wait for 'the right time'. Wandi chose not to argue, realising that if he wanted the job done he would have to do it himself. He went home and asked Uwa to bring Nsika to him.

Nsika trembled as he stood waiting in front of Wandi's house. He had never met Wandi alone. The few times he had, he was accompanying his grandma to say hello and to thank Wandi for one or another thing he had done for them. Nsika loved Uwa because she was warm and motherly (he had never known or felt a mother's love). Uwa personified motherhood for him. He was never sure what to think of Wandi, who was stern and had an overpowering personality, and so had never had the courage to offer any word other than 'Thank you, Papa'.

Nsika's mother had given birth just shortly after his father had died. His father's family had blamed his mother for killing their son and had sent her back to her mother's place. Mama Sawa, a widow herself, struggled to feed from the little garden around her house. When her daughter had died not long after from grief and the baby survived, she had run to Uwa in tears. Wandi had never given his opinion on what happened between the families of Nsika's father and mother, nor had he ever discussed the subject, but he had taken on the role of providing for and protecting Mama Sawa and the baby as the Baluma culture required of a father.

Wandi came out of his house and asked one of his children to bring two stools. He invited Nsika to sit with him and began by asking Nsika to repeat what had happened at the cobras' residence. Nsika asked politely if they could go into the house to have the conversation. He was too afraid to speak outside in case any of the other spies saw him there and told on him.

Wandi calmed him down. 'If the spies are as vigilant as I think they are, they already saw you standing in front of my house. They are already watching us. If we go in, they will suspect something, whereas if we stay outside, they would think you are just here on a courtesy visit, so calm down and act normal. I am your father, and you have come to see me.'

The word *father* coming from Wandi was all Nsika needed to calm down. He started talking in a voice that was low enough for a passerby not to clearly distinguish the words but high enough for Wandi to hear.

When he was through, Wandi asked him, 'Can you cook?'

Nsika said yes, surprised at the turn of the conversation.

Then Wandi said, 'Go and call for your grandmother.'

When Nsika returned with Mama Sawa, Wandi told her to go to the house of the large cobra and ask for Nsika to be employed to work in the kitchen as a sweep or cook under the pretext that they had nothing to eat and could benefit of the little payments he would get from there. Nsika would then watch them carefully and report back to Uwa.

Wandi's warmth melted Nsika's fear of him, so for the first time, Nsika offered, 'I can speak the cobra's language.'

All three adults (Mama Sawa, Uwa, and Wandi) turned to the boy in surprise.

Encouraged, he continued, 'Father Thomas used to teach us whenever he read from his book. His boys know the language very well, and they used to teach us after service every Sunday, so I can understand and speak quite a little.'

'How did you learn so fast?' asked Wandi.

Nsika dropped his eyes to the ground, not sure how to explain. Mama Sawa, understanding Nsika, explained that she had been amazed herself at how fast Nsika learnt languages. He was already fluent in the languages of the northern and southern peoples from whom they bought meat and fish occasionally.

Wandi took in every word. He was silent for a moment and then smiled at Nsika. 'Smart boy. So you listen carefully to what they say and report on every word you hear.'

Nsika was elated to be of use to Wandi. He beamed.

Wandi sent word to Ottuwa to use the same strategy to recruit spies. There were many young people around who had begun to understand the white man's language through the tutoring of the new religion, and they could use that to their advantage. This time, Ottuwa prove useful.

The next morning, Ottuwa called a meeting of young people. He started shyly and doubtfully as he always did until some cobras and overzealous church workers joined the crowd. Noticing them, he changed his tone of voice to sound commanding and ordered for his people to show full cooperation to the white men (whom he described as 'good people') to live peacefully. He spoke as if the large cobra was sitting right next to him. He sounded convincing and convinced about what he was saying. This surprised and enraged most of the true natives since they knew how much King Tozingana had opposed the cobras and their treatment of the people and naturally expected his successor to walk in the same footsteps. Meanwhile, the bewildered look on the people's faces gave Ottuwa an idea of how he could go about this cobra administration. That moment was the turning point in Ottuwa's destiny and perhaps in the destiny of Baluma.

Later that day, Ottuwa summoned a few young people who had been recommended by the Ngui and gave them instructions on how to report back without blowing their cover.

* * *

Wandi and his commanders agreed it was time to start the attacks. They mapped out the areas in which the cobra administration had built residences, the church premises, and the residences of the clergy and cobras. Wandi was taking no chances. If he had ever doubted his instincts, his discussion with Uwa that night had dissolved all doubt. The new church was involved with the cobra administration. Some of the warriors whose wives were already going to the new church recanted that their wives had told them that the new priest in church had been preaching to them about obeying the cobras and their new government, the same way Father Thomas had preached.

The first place marked for attack were the prisons in which the people were being kept. It had been nine weeks since they had been taken with no news about when they were going to be released. Nsika's first task was to locate the metal prison. He swept around the large cobra's compound but didn't find it. The next morning, under the pretext of going to fetch water, he searched around the bushes surrounding the cobra's residence. Somewhere behind a eucalyptus tree, he saw what looked like a heap of grass. As he approached it, he noticed there was a metal container beneath the grass but couldn't hear any sounds coming from inside.

The warriors chose a dark night to creep into the bushes around the cobra's residence. It did not take them too long to find the container following Nsika's directions. They easily found the entrance and broke it open. The decaying bodies fell out. The men had to stop their noses to the smell. It was a horrible sight. The bodies were unrecognisable. The warriors tied cloth to their noses and tried to pull the bodies out but couldn't continue after a while of struggling because there were too many. Wandi estimated at least two hundred and fifty heads. He clenched his teeth, apprehending that the people had simply been locked in the container and left there. His heart sank as he came to understand the depth of it: to starve or suffocate to death, whichever came first. He ordered his men to leave the bodies there. The cobra administration would have to use to church workers to bury the bodies because the stench would sooner than later get to the large cobra's house.

The nearest cobra's residence was barely a mile away. They poured oil on the grass around and torched it, spread the oil to three more residences, and then ran home. The fire soon got to the homes, and as the warriors got farther away, they could hear the cobras running out screaming. Some of the screams seemed to be coming from children, but they felt no remorse.

The cobra administration could not figure out what had caused the fires, so there was no punishment meted out this time. Besides, no cobras had died. They had all been able to run out before the fire consumed the houses. Groups of young men and women were rounded up and made to rebuild the cobra residences to replace the burnt ones.

Meanwhile, training continued in the forest. Wandi and Abimi decided it was time to intensify attacks. With the information being fed to them by Nsika and other spies in the cobras' entourage, they would know when to strike. The next best moment was during the church celebrations the following weekend, which almost all the cobras and native converts would be attending.

Wandi and Abimi went over the specifics for the last time as they walked back home from the forest together. Wandi was explaining something when Abimi flipped his eyes in sign language to tell him to hush up. Wandi stopped, and they continued in silence for a few feet when Abimi suddenly looked left, and Wandi's eyes followed.

A white woman was on her way home with a baby on her shoulders. The woman obviously had a lot of difficulty carrying the sleeping baby, and on closer look, she seemed to be in tears. She also had one eye that was red and swollen. The two men watched her carefully, head to toe, as she passed by. They could see she was in pain, but none of them offered to help. The horror of their people in the metallic container two weeks ago, coupled with their own personal suffering, had numbed their feelings.

The woman fell to the ground a few paces off and lay there for a while, crying, before getting herself and her baby back up to continue walking. Wandi and Abimi watched until she disappeared from sight before they carried on with their discussion.

The church celebrations started quite early. The cobras, the church workers, and other new converts made a considerable crowd. The church workers at the cobras' residences had been given the day off to attend the service and rest. There would be a procession round the main clan led by the priest holding a huge cross and then back to the church for a service. Nsika had managed to capture the words *Christ the King*. Wandi had his men in place at a safe distance, watching the cobra's residences to indicate when everybody had left for the church. The season was good for the plan because the Hamattan had just set in. Wildfires were common in Lumani during this period. The Baluma knew their land and how to prevent wildfires from ravishing their clans but had not shared this secret with the cobras.

As soon as the homes were emptied, the warriors went into action. With some oil and fire, they set alight the grass just around the houses nearest to the grass fields, and in a matter of minutes, the houses had caught fire. The wind did the rest, spreading fire from one residence to another. Wandi and Abimi watched from behind some bushes. As the fire raged on, with nobody seeming to be running out of the houses, most warriors concluded that there were no people in the houses, and that, they felt, was rather unfortunate as hate and vengeance had taken precedence over their strife for riddance of the invaders.

Suddenly, a white woman ran out of a house, carrying a child and screaming. The warriors let her get as far away from the house as possible and then rushed towards them as if to rescue them but, once they got close enough, caught them, tied them up, and carried them into their forest hideout.

Wandi and Abimi were at the place in a short time. They both recognised the woman; she was the one they had seen the day before. Her child, clutched to her chest and crying as well, could have been about two or three years of age. They needed to use a translator to communicate with the woman. Luckily, some of the warriors had learnt the cobra's language considerably well enough to translate, but the woman was too hysteric to say anything reasonable. Wandi could not talk to her in that state, so he had the men make the woman and child inhale an herb that sent them straight to sleep.

The church was still in procession when some parishioners noticed smoke coming from the residences. The native church workers were sent to the residences to find out what was going on, but by the time they got there, the houses were almost in ashes. They could hardly save anything. The word was sent to the parishioners at the procession, and someone whispered to the priest leading the procession. Father Robert interrupted the procession to make the announcement to stop the ceremony and asked the faithful to return in about an hour to continue with the service. The church workers rushed to fetch water from the stream to help to put out the fire, while the cobras, their wives, and children stood around moaning about the property they had lost in the fire.

One young cobra rushed to a particular house, which was already in ashes, and screamed, 'Christy! Christy!' and then 'Maria! Maria... Oh lord, oh lord, no, no.' He tried to get into the blazing house, but the other cobras stopped him.

The large cobra walked around the premises of the burnt houses as if looking for a clue to a puzzle. After scrutinising the houses and seeming not to find the clue, he turned his attention to the grass around. He noted that the fire had carefully selected the grass it had claimed. There was a straight line separating the burnt grass on their end from the untouched grass on the other end. He looked towards the bushes and narrowed his eyes, called one of the native church workers, and spoke to him. The man ran towards the bushes where the fire had come from, looked around, ran back to the cobra, and said something. The large cobra looked around again before turning back for the houses.

The church workers helped clean up the church after the procession, and the service concluded later on. Father Robert thanked them and, as usual, offered them a meal in his kitchen, while he and the other cobra 'faithful' had a meal in his living room.

* * *

What the large cobra hadn't noticed as he looked around the bushes was Abimi's keen eye between the blades of grass in the distance. Abimi crawled back, drew Wandi's attention to what he had just seen, and asked for the woman to be woken up. When she came around, Abimi asked her what she had been doing in the house when everybody was at church. The woman replied. The translator explained as Wandi and Abimi fixed their eyes on the woman and child.

Her child had been down with a high fever since the morning before. She had gone the during the day to the large cobra's house to ask for some medicine for the child from the stock, but he had refused to give her any on the pretext that there was none left. She knew he was lying because she knew supplies had just come in a few days back and told him so. The large cobra gave her an evil look and asked her what she was prepared to do to save her child. She had tried to hit him, but he had grabbed her, punched her in the face, and thrown her out with her child. When she arrived home crying, the native woman who worked as the maid had given her some herbs to make the child drink. The child was feeling much better in the morning just before the fire started.

When the translator was done, Abimi asked conclusively, 'So who is Christy, and who is Maria?'

The woman looked at Abimi, wide-eyed, expressing a surprise that Abimi was getting tired of recently. Wandi almost laughed at Abimi's expression.

'I am Christy, and my daughter is Maria.'

The translator did not have to translate that because from the gestures she had made, it was clear who was who.

Wandi and Abimi retreated to talk.

'She's a woman. Let her go with a warning. If she says anything, we will come back for her. She has a baby to protect. She will be careful, and from what she says, she is not in good favour with the large cobra,' Wandi advised.

'She is a woman, which is precisely why we cannot take the risk of letting her go with a warning. She *will* talk,' Abimi said impatiently.

Wandi considered it for a moment. 'We can't keep them too long, and we can't keep them here in the forest with us without the warriors getting any... *ideas*,' he dared to finish. 'Besides, it is a matter of time before the other cobras discover where we are. Why don't we let her go and then move from here, which was what we intended to do in any case?'

Abimi grabbed Wandi by the arm. 'We don't have to take them along. We just need to bury them alive or kill them and *then* bury them. She and her daughter should have died in the fire anyway. Have you forgotten the container? Wandi? So soon? What do you think they would have done if it was our woman and child?'

Abimi's words were so true but too raw. Wandi took in a deep breath to fight against himself. His sense of humanity was failing him, so he tried to hold on to his spirituality. 'Abimi, Si does not allow us to hurt people who have done us no wrong. It will bring a curse on our warriors. Si does not allow us to kill in this manner, and this woman and child have not done anything wrong.'

'Oh, does Si approve of the invasion as well, warrior priest?' Abimi scoffed, stepping back.

Wandi never liked it when Abimi got into moods like this. Abimi was a fun-loving man; nothing ever killed his humour. He was always a breath of fresh air for anyone who had the honour of meeting him. Even during the era before the 'great return' when they guarded Lumani and sometimes lost hope of ever regaining peace and returning to the land, Abimi still found the humour to crack the lousiest of jokes. One thing that his humour concealed was his sensitive nature, which only Wandi knew about. There was a fragility to Abimi that he consciously used his humour to conceal. After every fierce battle, Abimi would retreat into a small cave far away and cry all night by himself.

One evening, not long after Wandi's brother, Vumanga, had died, Wandi went to the same little cave to cry on his own. Vumanga represented a lot to him. He was the eldest and a second father to Wandi. He had taught Wandi everything he knew about war – how to anticipate a blow, how to detect the assailant's weapon, how it would be used and the first move the assailant would make, how to kill swiftly and painlessly, how to dock and curve to avoid the assailant's weapon – so that war became an art in Wandi's mind and every battle a dance. Wandi had been anointed *afomi* nine days later, succeeding his brother. He had kept a brave front more for his pride than to give the people faith in him, but back in Lumani, he couldn't hold back any longer. The nine hills reminded him each passing day of his brother and father and mentor. Whenever he could escape, he would creep into Abimi's little cave and bare his heart where he thought nobody would find him.

That evening, while he was crying, he saw a stout figure appear at the edge of the cave and thought he was having an apparition.

The stout figure chuckled. 'Would you like a piece of roast?'

Recognising Abimi's voice, Wandi swallowed and managed, 'Roasted what?'

'Human flesh.'

'Huh?' Wandi puzzled.

'It's just porcupine. We are not cannibals yet.' Abimi laughed. 'But with the way this war is raging, it might not be a bad idea to eat our attackers from time to time.'

Wandi wiped his tears quickly and pretended to laugh.

Abimi squeezed himself into the small space beside Wandi. 'It is OK to cry when nobody is watching, you know.' He paused for a moment and then continued, 'But even better after a piece of roasted porcupine.'

Wandi tried to speak, but his mouth wouldn't let him.

As they ate, feeling Wandi's pain, Abimi continued, 'I too come here to do the same thing once in a long while.'

Wandi almost choked on his meat as he started laughing.

Abimi looked at him in surprise. 'So you think you're the only one who knows where to hide?'

'And how long is a *long while*? Every two days?' Wandi finally managed and laughed so much, tears rolled out of his eyes.

Abimi ignored him and concentrated on his roast. When he was finished chewing the last bone of the porcupine, he said, 'We are warriors, not pieces of dry wood or bones of roasted porcupine, and even before the wood is dried, the tree bleeds, and even before we kill the porcupine, it screams to let its ancestors know, so why not us? What everyone seems to forget is that on the battlefield, we may be vengeful and merciless, but before all that, we are proud men who, just like every other, want to live and love. That is the least we ask, but they won't let us.'

As if he knew what was to follow, Abimi kept quiet. Wandi let out a torrent of tears.

Then Abimi said, 'Whenever you need me, I will be your rainbow' and he always was.

It was perhaps because of this sensitive nature that Abimi was also extremely vindictive. So when he got into moods like this, Wandi knew exactly where it was going to end. Ultimately, because Wandi was the *afomi*, the final decision was his, but he couldn't get himself to take any decision without Abimi's approval. He never had and never could.

He looked at Abimi with pleading eyes. 'Abimi, this looks like it is going to be a long war. We cannot win every battle, and we have to do this one step at a time. Let us let the woman and her child go, and then we move camp as we had decided.'

'OK, we let them go this time, but if that woman or any other cobra should survive an attack they should not have survived...'

Wandi knew that was as much of a warning to the woman as it was to him. The next time, Abimi wouldn't be having this discussion. Whatever cobra got caught would be dead before Wandi could ask.

The men waited until sundown, blindfolded the woman and child, led them to the edge of the forest, and let them go.

The warriors went deeper into the forest and stopped somewhere after a mangrove in the place they called Njuu. That was the place where the Baluma had settled to hide from the slave traders after the Tebo tribe betrayed them. Some of the warriors had grown up in the forest during the era before the 'great return' and knew the area well. Others had either not yet been born or were too young to remember what it was when the tribe had returned to Lumani. Wandi and the elder warriors led the young men there. The warriors cleared the forest and easily built shelters. The only problem they had was the distance from Lumani and therefore from their families.

Wandi knew Njuu would provide safe training grounds. The distance from Lumani was the first reason Wandi had chosen this place. It would take the cobras a long enough time to find. The next reason was that the place was a semi-dry piece of land surrounded by thick mangroves with tall intertwining trees that served as a shield so that if a person was standing on the outside, he would not realize there was life besides crocodiles and other reptiles beyond the mangrove. These trees had served as the boundaries of the kingdom during the era before the 'great return'. Additionally, the shielding mangroves and trees also attracted dangerous insects around that anybody who wasn't used to the area couldn't survive.

Wandi had his men calculate the distance it would take to and from the kingdom, what alternate paths to take, how to cover any tracks left by footprints, and how to camouflage body odours with herbs and perfumes. When they were done, Wandi had redone the calculations himself and cross-checked every detail. Coming from Lumani during the daytime, always before sunrise, it would take them one day and half a morning to cross one way and, when they started off during the nighttime, one day from the kingdom to Njuu. The journey from Njuu was faster, a day if they started off during the early hours of the morning and a night if they set off from Njuu just after sundown. Because of the distance, they could not keep the men in camp too long. They would have to be brought and trained in batches. Wandi decided that for every attack, they would train a different batch that way, they would go into the forest, camp, train, carry out attacks on the cobras, and then go home to be recalled at a later date. With this strategy, they could train even more warriors and hedge the risk that the best might all be caught in a single counter-attack.

* * *

Ottuwa sat there, wondering what the cobra had eaten to make his stomach so large, when he was snapped back to reality.

'These bush fires seem to be particular about where they start and what residences they ravish.' The cobra sipped noisily from his jug of liquor.

Ottuwa said nothing.

'Am I to believe that the bush fires of Lumani know which houses are ours and which mud huts are yours?'

'There are many hypotheses to what happened. One could be that our ancestors are trying to send out a message. Another could be that your people do not protect their houses from bush fires as my people do.'

'Well, that's just two hypotheses,' the cobra cheeked.

'Our people mean you no harm,' Ottuwa tried to explain.

The large cobra waved his hand for silence, and Ottuwa stopped. Nobody did that to a king, but even the cobra of the smallest rank dared anything with the natives and even to him. Ottuwa was becoming used to it.

'You said our houses are not protected?'

'Well, we have been here for a long time, so we know what leaves to plant to stop the bush fires from ravishing our homes. Perhaps you don't have those plants protecting your houses.'

'Instruct your people to plant those herbs around when they start work to rebuild our houses.'

He had Ottuwa led out. But he still wasn't comfortable with the answers he had got. There was something about the fire he knew wasn't started of natural causes or lack of herbs. Ottuwa had sounded consoling, but he was not convinced. He could feel there was a silent hand behind this attack and, on second thought, behind the first.

'Cornell!'

A young cobra marched into the room.

'What news do we have from our young recruits?'

'They went to help Father Robert clean up the church.'

'No, I don't mean the church workers. I mean the ones with whom we had an "agreement".'

'None of them have reported back yet, General, sir. Most are either sick or dead.'

The large cobra expressed surprise but no sympathy. 'OK, come and see me tomorrow after breakfast.'

'Yes, sir.'

* * *

Ottuwa, on the other hand, could sense that the large cobra had not been convinced by his argument. By the crack of dawn, he summoned all the young able men and women of the clan to the palace and requested of them, as he usually did, to help their 'friendly neighbours' to rebuild the houses that had been destroyed by the fire. As the crowd dispersed to get material for work, Ottuwa noticed from the corner of his left eye a young cobra watching him intently. Once the crowd was dispersed, the young cobra marched towards him and informed him that he was summoned to the residence of the large cobra.

This next meeting was even more disturbing. The cobras had marked certain areas of the kingdom on which they preferred to build their new residences, and this would mean resettling the people to other areas of the kingdom. From what the large cobra described, the areas in which they had chosen to resettle were the coolest and choosiest areas of the kingdom, where the breeze was fresh in the mornings because they were covered with shady trees so that the sun did not penetrate too sharply, and in the evenings, it was warm, unlike in other areas of Lumani. These choice areas were typically passed down from one generation to another. The families who occupied those areas had a rich and long history of their land and how it was obtained by their ancestors for posterity. That kind of land was never sold or given away. The land was particularly sacred to those families because their ancestors were buried in the land beside the houses and shrines built in their honour where sacrifices were made occasionally to ask for protection and prosperity. This was the people's real wealth.

Ottuwa could not find the words to explain the sacredness of this land to the cobra, so he offered other areas equally comfortable that the patriarch had not yet allotted in exchange for the land the cobra had marked out for 'occupation'.

The cobra shook his head, saying, 'Talk to your people. They always understand you. We are only asking nicely out of courtesy.'

Ottuwa called the Ngui for a secret meeting that night. That was one cult he could always trust. There were so many rumours of one or another member of the Wemtii being compromised that the Ngui had decided two years ago not to divulge any sensitive information to the Wemtii. All tribal secrets would be held exclusively by the Ngui. Ottuwa let them know about what happened and his fears of what the repercussions would be if the people refused to relocate and the cobras decided to retaliate. He had already counted so many dead or missing, and he didn't want to lose any more. The Ngui agreed to help him persuade the people to relinquish their land in exchange for land elsewhere.

Makafu, the newly anointed high priest, spoke for the first time since his anointing. 'It was not our strength against our adversaries that led us here to this land that we now call our place of rest but the god of our ancestors. I will go into the forest with Wandi tomorrow to strengthen the warriors.'

The Ngui agreed with him.

Makafu was one of the priests who had expressed concern when the new church began to draw attention. He had even attended services under disguise to listen to the message of this new religion. While he found nothing fundamentally wrong with the notion of a god incarnate, he felt insulted that the new religion referred to theirs as a pagan religion. He found it ironical that this new religion should condemn their ancestral adulation as idol worship and yet urge its faithful to bow down in front of a piece of wood shaped in a cross-like form. As if that was not enough, the religion encouraged the men to marry only one wife. This particular point had caused a lot of weeping and gnashing of teeth as several women who were properly married and settled were sent back to their families with their children. The new religion was not just making the people turn their back on their ancestors but also destroying families and the fabric of the entire Baluma society.

Makafu and a couple of other priests had approached Pa Ngunep with their concerns and asked him to authorise them to 'do something' about the spread of the new religion. Pa Ngunep was docile (at least in their perspective), saying that soon, the people would realize what the new religion was doing to them and would come back to their senses. Besides, their own spirituality did not allow them to impose their spiritual beliefs on anyone.

When Makafu was anointed high priest, the priestly order was satisfied with the choice because Makafu was a well-reputed exorcist and a hardliner on traditional beliefs. He was their ideal 'invasion time' high priest.

Wandi was disheartened but understood Ottuwa's plight. Abimi was unimpressed. He would have preferred to put up a fight before ceding the land.

'To what end, Abimi? More dead bodies? There is another way to fight them. That is why I am here.'

Makafu calmed Abimi down and told them about the increasing displeasure in the priestly order about the new religion and how it had affected especially the youth. The people who were converted now saw nothing wrong with the cobra occupation, and so he had advised Ottuwa to make certain they were the ones who were used to rebuild the cobra homes. There was nothing to worry about regarding the snitches who had been planted amongst them because one by one, the priests had identified and *taken care* of them, but he knew that would only serve as a temporary solution because any of the converts could be used any day against the tribe. The priests had decided to watch every new convert to the new religion with a keen eye.

The people moved out peacefully though grudgingly. They were filled with such animosity that even the cobras overseeing the move thought better than to be aggressive. Ottuwa was there himself to make sure no one showed any resistance. As the people passed by him, he kept his eyes down and whispered, 'This will pass.' By the end of a few weeks, all the people in the 'chosen' lands had moved.

On the 'chosen' night, Makafu got his assistants together to prepare the area that had just been occupied. According to Baluma spirituality, the ancestral spirits would be unrested by the new occupation and cause mayhem in the kingdom. The spirits needed to be calmed. They prepared themselves and waited until the time was right for the ritual.

Makafu cut a piece of cloth from the loincloth he was wearing and began the incantations, putting the cloth into the mud from the land, which he had poured into a calabash. He and his priests moved around the 'chosen' areas in a clockwise circle, sprinkling and incanting in low voices until they came back to their starting point.

Makafu pulled the spotless white chicken prepared for the ritual out of its cage, held it by the legs, and then broke its wings and legs.

'You can't walk, and you can't fly, so we will meet you again on this same spot.'

By the time morning came, the chicken was dead. The cobras hardly noticed it as they busied themselves getting the people to work, destroying the homes and grave sites and whatever other structures the people had had there, getting others to fetch timber from the forest and cut them into neat logs for building.

One of the native (church) workers sweeping around saw the chicken and put it in his bag. A few other workers had seen him take the chicken and tried to caution him when the cobras were not watching. They reminded him of the ritual in which a chicken was crippled in that manner and what it signified. He insisted that he was now a 'child of God' and that no harm could come to him. At the end of the day, he took the chicken home and had a bountiful dinner with his family.

He and his family were buried the next Saturday.

* * *

Ottuwa could not stand the humiliation of the displacements, so he had not returned to those areas to watch his people work, even if they were the traitors. He stayed home instead.

Aruma had been watching him carefully and deliberately brought him dinner, knowing he would refuse to eat that evening. She had good news for him that she hoped would cheer him up. When he refused her meal, she tried to start a conversation, intending to introduce the subject she had come for by asking him how he was doing with the cobras. Ottuwa put his head in his palms, and the conversation took the wrong turn. He told her how powerless he felt and how he regretted the day he had been anointed. He had always considered his succession an honour and wanted to serve and defend his people as best he could but had no idea how difficult it would actually be.

'When I was anointed, I hoped to spend the first few years of my reign driving out the cobras, but here, I find myself hoping desperately for one day not to count any bodies of my people. We are dying more now than we did when we were fending off the slave takers. My ancestors must have a short life planned for me. That is the only possible explanation.' He was in tears.

Aruma was so saddened by what he had related that she forgot the real reason she had come in the first place. She excused herself and ran back to her house weeping.

Lemi, who had the same kind of good news, was watching from the window of her house. When she saw Aruma running back in tears, she chose to inform Ottuwa on some other day.

* * *

By the time the work on the new homes for the cobras was done, the cobras realized for the first time that the land that they had chosen was almost surrounded by water, and the few patches of land linking their area to the rest of the dry land were swampy. Getting out of there using the only dry route would take a long time to walk, so they decided to build a bridge over a major stream, separating their area from the rest of the dry land.

Makafu was waiting for that. He marched to the compound of the large cobra and demanded to see him.

The young church worker standing at the door recognised him and said to the young cobra standing beside him, 'Here is the eldest and greatest wizard of the land. Please give him as much respect as you can afford a pagan.'

Both of them laughed.

'Nobody comes looking for the bass. The bass asks for you. You don't ask for him. Hasn't anyone told you that? Or did your apprentices not get word to you in your cave?' the young church worker said mockingly to Makafu.

'You will bring him out here, or this sunset will have a story for you,' Makafu chilled in a low voice.

The young cobra stepped forward, casting a demeaning look at Makafu and holding his long gun, threatening, 'Who is going to have a story, old wizard?'

The young church worker had stopped laughing but still had his mouth opened. He was a native and understood the subtle meaning in Makafu's words. He went to the young cobra's side and persuaded him to let Makafu see the large cobra.

When the large cobra stepped out, he was a little shocked at who his guest had turned out to be. When he was told who wanted to see him, he had been half-distracted reading a letter that had come from home, so he had concluded it would be Father Robert's catechist, a grey old man with much to say. When the young cobra told him who Makafu was, he couldn't believe he had been called out for this, but since he had some time on his hands, he decided he could spare some to listen to the weird man.

'So what have we done against your ancestors?' There was a translator between them who did his job zealously.

Makafu ignored the mockery. He was above small talk. 'You have started work building a bridge over the Akiki River.'

'Oh, is that what you call that small stretch of flowing water? Yes, we have.'

'Stop!'

'Stop what?' The cobra's eyes widened in honest surprise.

'Stop work and use the land with the only path out of the areas you chose. You desecrate the Akiki by building a bridge over it, and we will not let you do that.'

'Who is we?'

'I have said it, and you have heard me clearly, so our ancestors will not say I did not warn you first.' Makafu turned to go.

'Come back here, old man!'

Makafu was caught by two church workers and made to turn around. They pushed his head downwards so that he bowed.

'I could kill you now, but that would be too easy. Nobody will know what happened, and others may try to repeat what you have just done.'

He had Makafu taken out and flogged. Makafu didn't resist or let any sound out all the while. The church workers were elated to have the opportunity to beat up a man who was so revered in the kingdom. It affirmed their authority. It would be a badge of honour in the church community.

When the workers were done with the beating, they dragged Makafu back to the large cobra to show off their good work. A swollen-faced Makafu, with his back covered in blood, was led to the large cobra. Satisfied, the cobra dismissed Makafu but not before saying something the translator interpreted fearfully.

'You will die on the day that the bridge is completed.'

The large cobra didn't have any more time to waste with this old man. He asked the workers to throw him out.

Nsika had been around the house, fetching water, and had watched the whole incident.

* * *

Wandi was getting frustrated at the seeming ineffectiveness of their attacks on the cobras. They couldn't keep on just burning down buildings because the cobras seemed to replace the lost property in no time using forced labour. They needed to do something more effective to hurt the cobras more, but with what and how? He couldn't figure out what they could do to hurt the cobras enough yet with minimum loss to their people. The cobras were few but had superior weaponry and, worse, had no notion about the principles of war according to Si. What worried him most was the converts amongst the Baluma who were now working with the new administration. Wandi tried to hold on to his spirituality, to defend and not to attack, which meant to hurt only those who had hurt him, but he had to admit at that point that even that part of him was stretching thin.

The cobra administration had picked out the poorest, most outcasted people in the kingdom and gave them a sense of self-worth with their new religion, which preached about the greatest becoming the least and the least the greatest, cleaned these people up, and given them special uniforms that they wore to carry out their work. These uniforms were a symbol of the authority of the cobra administration and welded fear, resentment, and hate amongst the natives. These uniformed peasants were more than eager to work with the new administration because they now had authority over people whom they would otherwise have been unable to meet even in a social gathering.

The debate was heated amongst the commanders in the Baluma army. They wanted the cobra's blood, to spill it, to see it, and to smell it. Wandi kept on weighing the long-term impact on the people. They had grown in such a number, it was impossible to move them to the forest as they had during the era of the slave takers. At the same time, he was not sure how or when to retaliate without repercussions on his people. He ground his teeth in agony and frustration.

Abimi was in such pain, he was silent the whole meeting. The warriors continued arguing about possible methods and their possible impact: setting the church ablaze during service, burning the homes of the cobras again, poisoning their food, and so on. Finally, Abimi's eyes flashed, and he broke his silence.

'Where are the weapons coming from? How do they get here? This is our land after all. If we can find the source of the weapons, we can channel them to our warriors and fight the cobra with his own weapons.'

'We will need to learn how to use the weapons first,' Wandi chipped in.

'Nsika can steal one, and we will use that to train until we trace the source of these weapons. Surely, the transporters have a route.'

That was thought-provoking enough. A few hours later, the commanders had come up with a plan that seemed more promising than just burning houses.

Wandi and Abimi left the meeting that evening, both sure of one thing. This time, they were prepared to kill as many cobras as they could, irrespective of the price their people would pay. The last thread binding Wandi to his spirituality was giving way and Abimi's even long before that.

The bridge was in the last stages of completion. The native workers – now turned foremen – supervised the other natives and punished severely anyone who showed signs of even tiredness. As the bridge got to the last stages of completion, it was a marvel to the Baluma and even the foremen. They had never seen anything like it. Children were happy to participate in the building during the day, carrying water, straw, and mud. They even played on the parts that were dry when the foremen weren't watching and ran off as soon as they saw one approaching. They loved especially the view of the stream from the top. The foremen allowed only the white children to play on the dry parts of the bridge because they were the children of the 'bass'.

As the sun dried the last bits of the bridge, the natives were given less and less work to carry out on it. One afternoon, after keen inspection, the large cobra declared the work satisfactory and gave his workers the rest of the day off. The natives, of course, had to stay back to sweep the bridge and the surroundings to make it ready for cobra use the next morning before church service.

He lit his pipe as usual after dinner and sat down on the balcony of his newly built house. He thought about his daughter back home. It had been three years since he last saw her. He recalled how she had cried at seeing him go and how he had almost decided not to take the train that day had it not been for the promise of great fortune on this side of the world to make their lives better. His own father had worked on ships all his life and had died poor. He had joined his father working on the ship when he was a teenager. The work was hard and the pay meagre. They would go out to sea for months and months with little food and under harsh weather. The ships were usually infested with rats of all sorts. His own job had been to set traps for the rats and clean the ship.

Whenever they came back ashore, it was time to catch a glimpse of city life before heading back to sea. The best way to let off the frustration was with booze and women. It was on one of such pastimes that he had met the mother of his daughter. He had gone back to sea a few days later and returned ten months later to have a baby girl put in his arms. Her family had obliged him to 'do the right thing' by marrying her, and so he had. The relationship had grown sour after that because she was a woman with more demands than he could afford. When the opportunity came up a few years later to make a fortune in what they called the Dark Continent, he seized it to make a better future for his daughter.

The job seemed easy at first, but when he had got to Lumani, he realized it was quite an uphill task. The natives were stubborn, and understanding their native language was impossible, at least to him. It did not sound like anything he had heard before, but he was amazed at how easily the natives had got to understand their language. As he sat there, pulling and puffing on his pipe, he imagined his daughter reciting her poems and chasing her pet rabbit around their little garden. He was determined to see her the next summer.

He pulled again at his pipe and puffed. Suddenly, his chest felt as if it was on fire. He tried to cough, but he couldn't get to. It was as if his nose and throat were blocked. He put his pipe down and started for the kitchen to get some water but fell to the ground. The earth seemed to be spinning around him. He could hear the voices of the other cobras in the living room as they laughed and played cards. He screamed as loud as he could but couldn't scream loud enough for them to hear. He finally managed to cough. What came out was a large clog of blood and yellow substance. He stretched his trembling hand to grab a chair but couldn't get to it.

Suddenly, he thought he saw an old man watching him very calmly at the edge of the balcony. He turned his head painfully to take a better look. The old man was holding a short stick, which he was leaning on with both hands, and watching him carefully. He was sure he had seen the old man somewhere, but with all the pain, his memory failed him. He stretched his arm out in a gesture to ask for help, but the old man didn't move. He just stood there, watching him. The cobra was suffocating, and as he drew his last breath, he finally recognised him.

It was morning when the large cobra's body was discovered on his balcony. He had choked on his own blood and vomit. The doctor said he had died of a convulsion after suffering a heart attack.

When Father Robert got the news, he came almost immediately, accompanied by his church workers. They brought oil, cloth, soap, and incense to wash and wrap the body and have a prayer service. The church workers were inconsolable. Their 'good master' had gone to rest.

Each of them told of how much he rewarded those who had worked hard bringing rubber and cocoa for him. The other cobras didn't show as much sympathy, even though they guarded the corpse and assisted at the prayer service. Notably absent were Christy, her husband Kamuel, and their daughter Maria.

As the other cobras went about preparing to have the corpse transported, the church worker who had been there on the day that Makafu had told the large cobra that he would die on the day the bridge was completed went to see his 'master' to remind him of what had happened on that day and what the old man had said. The young cobra laughed at him and told him to stop being ridiculous.

This church worker, now baptised Cornelius, even though dissatisfied with the reaction he had received, obediently went about his duties. He was from the clan that lived around the sixth hill of Lumani. His grandfather had been a servant in the shrine of Pa Ngunep (the late high priest). His father had also served Makafu before converting to this new religion. So Cornelius understood in great depth the impact of spoken words by a high priest, especially coming from one like Makafu. He decided to see another cobra called Cornell (the one after whom he had been named) as soon as he finished work that day.

The two had met for the first time when Cornelius had cleaned Cornell's house after Cornell had arrived in Lumani. Cornelius had done such a good job of cleaning and was also well articulated in the cobra's language that he had greatly impressed Cornell, who then decided to take him as a permanent worker. After a few months of good work, Cornell had recommended him to the large cobra for a 'promotion'. The large cobra had obliged by giving Cornelius the position of chief native guard around his own house. Cornelius admired Cornell so much that he had asked Father Thomas to baptise him Cornell. Father Thomas had persuaded him to take the derivative name Cornelius to avoid confusion, and so he had with pride. Since then, Cornelius had doubled as a house guard and a very effective spy, and Cornell was always willing to receive Cornelius.

Cornelius waited until it was dark enough before setting off for Cornell's residence. He came round the back and tapped the back door three times in their sign language. Cornell excused himself from the small gathering he had invited to his place and went to the kitchen, opened the back door, and stepped out.

'The high priest had told him that he would die on the day the bridge was completed, bass.'

'With what strength would the old man have strangled him?'

'He did not have to do it physically, bass. Those wizards know how to kill you spiritually, but you will die physically.'

'How is that possible?'

'They will perform a ritual, bass, and then speak evil words. I know I saw it before. My father worked with him, remember?'

'OK. I will have him brought in tomorrow for questioning.'

'He will not say anything, bass. We have to kill him.'

'Let us hear what he has to say first.'

'OK, bass. Thank you, bass.'

Cornell went back to the gathering, and Cornelius disappeared into the dark.

* * *

Makafu looked blankly ahead of him as the young workers flung insults at him and made mockery of his dressing and crooked stick. Young cobra Cornell walked into a sudden silence.

'You said that General Merritt would die on the day the bridge was completed. Correct?'

Makafu looked at him blandly. Cornell asked irritably for a native to translate. Still, Makafu said nothing. Cornell tried a few more times. When Makafu didn't react, he decided to have a closer look. He walked towards Makafu, whom he could see was looking at him intently. He stopped a few steps away and stared straight into the old man's eyes. Makafu looked back at him.

There was something in Makafu's eyes that made him uneasy, like a silent whisper to keep his distance. He refused to be deterred. The man looked frail and weak. His clothes were simple pieces of white cloth well wrapped around his waist with a cord to hold them together, a crooked short stick in front of him that he had to hold with both hands to support his bent back, but still, there was an uneasiness he felt about this old man looking him over and over again.

As he drew his eyes back to Makafu, he felt more ill at ease and stepped back. He turned around to leave when Makafu parted his lips.

'Yes, I did, and he did.'

Cornell turned around to see who had spoken. The old man kept his gaze fixed on Cornell, who now stepped farther back. Everybody's eyes were on Makafu, who had spoken without a blemish of a Baluma accent. For about ten minutes, the only sounds around were the birds whistling and the workers in the distance humming.

Shaken, Cornell asked, 'What did you say, old wizard?'

Makafu didn't respond.

'Repeat what you said!' Cornell was raising his voice and drawing his gun just as his assistant, Kamuel, intervened.

'I think a good whipping should discipline the old man.'

Cornell put his gun back reluctantly and stormed out. Makafu now turned his gaze to Kamuel. He opened his mouth to say something and then stopped suddenly. The native guards around, seeing Makafu stop, laughed mockingly, presuming his sudden silence for fear. Only Cornelius and Kamuel didn't laugh.

Kamuel had Makafu taken outside for flogging, but just before Makafu's back was laid bare, Kamuel asked for him to be cut loose.

Kamuel approached Makafu. 'What is it about you that makes Cornell and Cornelius so scared?'

Makafu seemed to be about to respond, opening his mouth again and then stopping suddenly, when the whole place drew dark. Both looked up towards the sky to see the dark clouds that were gathering fast. Lightning struck, and thunder roared almost simultaneously. Hailstones stung, and the pouring began.

'Stay indoors until this clears. The ancestors have something to say, and they don't like to be interrupted,' Makafu managed to say to Kamuel before Kamuel ran off and Makafu stumbled away.

The downpour lasted nine days; the clouds were completely dark for seven. No one could come out of their houses. Even the warriors in the forest were unable to come back. Wandi had the warriors hide in the shelters they had built, but even those began to wear out by the third day with the rain. By the fifth day, they had no shelters left to hide. They had to climb the mangrove trees and make home with the reptiles.

Back in Lumani, there was a flood. People swam from one house to another. Nobody had ever seen anything like this before. The skies just kept on pouring and raining hailstones. There wasn't a minute during those nine days when the rain ceased or even poured lightly. Even at the cobras' residences, water flooded the houses. The bushes were so flooded that the bones of those who had been left to die in the containers were carried by the waters. Other shallow graves dug to bury people who had died either working or beaten to death for opposing the forced labour were washed out, and the bones floated in the running waters. It was as if the ground was cleaning itself out to receive something.

Through it all, Makafu, back in his cave with a handful of priests, kept monitoring and interpreting. There was lightning and thunder nine times a day. Hailstones rained down seven times, and the moon did not come out at night. By the sixth day, it was difficult to distinguish the day from the night. On the seventh day, there was total darkness. The skies only began to clear on the eighth day, even though it was still raining heavily. At the beginning of the ninth day, the sun began to come out, but still, the downpour continued heavily. Towards the evening, the rain stopped suddenly, and then the whole place dried up as though the sun had never stayed out. The tenth day was bright and fresh, but people didn't dare come out. They only peered through their windows and shouted across compounds to find out how their neighbours were doing. Makafu looked through the opening in his cave and smiled. He took his short stick and went to see Ottuwa.

Makafu was not one to dwell on protocol. He simply walked into the palace, sat down on the driest place he could find, and asked the guard to send for Ottuwa. Ottuwa was surprised to see Makafu, even though he was aware of what was happening – the bridge, General Merritt's death, and so on – but he had not thought any of that was worthy of a visit from the high priest. The high priest only showed up at his palace when there was either a meeting of the Ngui or when some other critical issue was at stake. Nevertheless, Makafu was always welcome because even before he was anointed high priest, he had always been a good friend of the family and a distant cousin to Morewa (Wandi's father) and so a distant uncle to both Wandi and Ottuwa.

He went straight to the point. 'Your wife is expecting a baby.'

Ottuwa was at a loss for words. He had thought Makafu had come to talk about the cobras and the recent downpour. 'OK. I hear you, high priest.'

'Yes, you have heard me, but you have not understood. Aruma is expecting a baby, but he will come before his mother is ready.'

'Since you have said so, I will see her after you are gone.' Ottuwa was still puzzled that the high priest should pay a visit to announce a baby.

'Yes, do that.'

'But what about the downpour? This is the middle of the dry season, and we don't have those kinds of rains here.'

'Yes, that was him.'

'Him who?' Ottuwa queried Makafu.

'Aruma's son, the one I have told you she is expecting.'

Makafu looked at Ottuwa, exacerbated.

* * *

Back in his cave, Makafu prepared himself to collapse the bridge. His assistants got the altar ready. When Makafu had washed and cleansed himself, he led the preliminary prayers to start the service. Pouring some water into a calabash, he poured in some sand and began the incantations. The water began to swirl around the calabash, first slowly and then faster and faster until it was almost spilling out. He began to raise his hands, raising his voice at the same time. His assistants did the same.

Their voices were raised louder and louder rhythmically until they became a drumming as the swirling water now took the shape of a whirlwind in the çalabash. The priests dropped their hands, and the water came down, smashing the calabash into little bits.

The prayers were concluded, and the service was over.

* * *

Nsika had no trouble stealing a gun and some bullets from the large cobra's residence as his things were being packed away into boxes. Just to be sure, he stole two, a short one and a long one. He wrapped them up in cloth and hid them stealthily behind the cupboard in the kitchen on which the stove was laid. Nobody ever noticed him going around doing his duties. He never said a word or reacted to anything anybody said. They were not even aware that he understood the language.

Later on, as soon as he finished work, he hid the bag under a pile of dirt and pushed the pile out of the compound to the usual place where he had the dirt burnt. Once the dirt was all burnt, he made his way back home without adding an iota of speed to his step, because he could have been stopped by any cobra or native worker on his way. He acted so naturally that when he got home, Uwa did not think he had been able to get the weapons until he showed her. She hugged him and gave him some dinner.

With the stolen weapons, the warriors were able to begin training on using them. Naturally, the short gun was lighter and easier to use. The long gun, even though it was heavier, was actually more effective. Wandi already had a plan in place to trail the source of the guns. The corpse of the large cobra was to be taken to his home country the next Wednesday.

The spies had to follow stealthily behind in the bushes around to trace the route to the coast. During the era of the slave takers, the route to the coast had been narrow and very dangerous, with kidnappers at every bend and valley, so the warriors stayed away from the route. This route to the coast, from what they had gathered, was different from the one that had been used during the era of the slave takers. It was larger and well cut out. This was the route used by the cobras for transporting cocoa, rubber, and timber in large vehicles to the coast.

The vehicle to transport the large cobra's corpse arrived just as Nsika finished watering the compound. He pulled open the gate as usual to let the vehicle in and then closed the gate. The native workers began to carry boxes into the vehicle. As he listened carefully, Nsika understood that the vehicle was to be driven to the coast and the contents put on the ship early on Saturday morning. When the loading was done, Nsika grabbed a bucket to go and fetch water. There was somebody waiting for him at the stream already, to whom he would transmit the information.

Just as he stepped through the gate, he heard, 'Nsika! Nsika!' It was the voice of Cornelius.

He thought of pretending not to hear but decided against that because if Cornelius started to chase him, he might just end up at the stream with him. Nsika turned around.

'Make sure you clean the house properly when you are done fetching water. There is a new bass coming in on Tuesday.'

That was an added piece of information, and Nsika was relieved he had made the right decision.

He got to the stream just as his counterpart was arriving. As he filled his buckets, the other man pretended to be helping him with the fetching to receive the information. When Nsika returned from the stream, he scrubbed the house extra clean.

Abimi had his men deep in the bushes along the road through which the vehicle rode. They walked for a distance in the bushes, monitoring the truck. As soon as it was out of sight, they got to the road and began following the road to wherever it would lead. It was a straight road with no other criss-crossing roads, so it was easy to follow. They walked for about three days, stopping each time for a short rest. The men fed on bush rats and other small animals they could find. It was easier to walk during the night and in the early hours of the morning when it was cool. On the fourth day, they saw the truck in the distance on its way back. They got their weapons out in preparation: machetes, bows and arrows, and metallic spears.

Wandi and Abimi had both hesitated about this plan because they knew that in the best-case scenario, they would lose at least ten to twelve men. Wandi had even wanted to be the one to lead the ambush, but

Abimi wouldn't let him. Wandi represented too much to the warriors; if he fell now, the war might well be over.

As the vehicle approached the ambush spot, the men held their breath for Abimi's battle cry. Abimi had his attention so fixed on the road, it was as if he was counting the turns the wheels of the car made. He had a long rope in his hand that he had tied to a young stout boar, which he had tamed for good use. The truck wasn't going very fast because a lot of animals usually crossed the road to get from one end of their bush to another. Running over an animal could damage the vehicle, and it was the strongest they had yet.

A few feet from the ambush point, Abimi let loose the boar. The young boar squirmed and rushed on to the road to savour its freedom. The vehicle driver ground his breaks to let the boar by, but instead, the boar, seeing the vehicle, charged aggressively in that direction, causing the driver to slow down almost to a stop.

Abimi drew back his arrow and shot through the windscreen straight into the driver's chest. With that, he let out the battle cry. The vehicle swirled around and ended up on its side. There were three cobras (including the driver) and one native worker in the vehicle. The other two cobras came out with guns as the men continued to rain arrows in their direction.

The bullets were faster than the arrows. Six warriors went down in a matter of seconds. The warriors ran back into the bushes, and the other two white men followed them. Abimi had been praying for that reaction. The warriors quickly climbed the trees, while others distracted the cobras by leading them farther into the bushes. One of the warriors up a tree found a good angle and aimed his arrow, but he missed and hit the cobra on the arm. The cobra yelled in agony and fell to the ground, drawing the attention of his comrade. The warriors took advantage of the brief moment of distraction to send an arrow through his comrade's chest and then closed in on the first one and finished the job with their spears. They rapidly dug a large hole in the ground and threw the bodies in after stripping them of their weapons.

Back on the road, Abimi and a few others had come around the truck to see if there were any others in there. The driver moved, and

Abimi made sure it was his last move. There was only the native worker who was sitting in there, half-conscious. The men dragged him out and bound him. The corpse of the driver was taken to the bush and buried with the other two cobras.

The fallen warriors could not be given proper funeral rites because they could not be transported back to Lumani, so a piece of cloth from each warrior's waist cloth was cut off and preserved for their families. The warriors dug again deeper into the bush and buried theirs in different graves, but they didn't mark the graves to avoid any trail. A bush fire was lit to camouflage the burial sites (of both the cobras and the warriors), and the truck was set ablaze. Some of the warriors began their journey back with their new supply of weapons, while others continued to trace the entire road to the coast. As Abimi walked back with the men, he felt the usual pain after battle but consoled himself that the ambush could have been worse. They had counted only seven dead.

Wandi almost jumped to his feet when he saw Abimi. They inspected the weapons together and realized the new weapons were more sophisticated than the one that Nsika had stolen from the cobra's residence. They woke up the captured native worker to ask him to show them how the weapons worked.

'Nkweni!' one of the young commanders shouted, and everybody around looked at him. 'I know him. We grew up together. Just as I started my training, they said he and his mother had joined the church, but he is not a traitor. He would never betray us.'

'The Nkweni you knew as a boy or the grown-up one?' Wandi asked, raising one eyebrow almost mockingly.

The young commander looked down at his one-time friend, completely shaken. 'Let me talk to him first,' he said, determined.

The others let him talk to the captive while they counted the weapons and grouped each weapon type in different piles.

When the commander had finished with Nkweni, he came back to Wandi and said, 'The cobra's poison is in his veins. He is not speaking like the Nkweni I knew. They have bewitched him in that new religion.

He says the cobras are better people than us because they have clearer skin and longer noses and that their god is superior to Si.'

The others looked at him, stone shocked. Wandi didn't because he wasn't.

'Show us how to use this weapon,' another commander said to Nkweni.

'This one is different from the ones we use. It is the basses who use these ones.'

'What about this other one?'

'I don't know how to use it either.'

'In that case, you are of no use to us, and you know what that means, Nkweni,' said Wandi, moving so close to him that he couldn't breathe properly.

'Please, bass, let me try,' Nkweni said, trembling. He took the first weapon and started trying to figure it out, with the commanders watching closely. He loaded the weapon and tried a few times before he finally shot successfully. Then he tried a second and third time to be sure before teaching the commanders.

He took a second weapon and tried, but this one had a different technique. With the help of one of the commanders, he got to use that one as well. The third weapon was similar to the first in handling. However, on the package from which the gun had been taken was written 'Warning, remove metallic ceiling from barrel and clean before use!' Nkweni had missed that. He loaded the gun as he had the first and aimed.

'Why is the mouth of this one closed?' Abimi asked just as Nkweni pulled the trigger, and *boom!*

The gun exploded in Nkweni's hands, and the shrapnel and hot metallic pieces of the gun flew about. The commanders around covered their faces with their hands spontaneously. Some of them stooped to avoid the metal flying about.

When the smoke cleared, Nkweni was on the ground, gasping for breath. His chest had been struck by several pieces of metal and shrapnel because when the gun had exploded, he had been holding it close to his chest. One of the commanders had been struck in the arm by a small piece of metal, but it was nothing serious.

Wandi went over to have a closer look at Nkweni. He leaned downwards and peered straight into Nkweni's eyes. 'A traitor often meets a peculiar fate.' He put his foot in Nkweni's face, shutting his mouth and nose at the same time.

The young man gasped and struggled and soon stopped moving.

Wandi picked up another gun of the same type. The warriors thought he had gone mad. As he loaded the weapon, the warriors moved back. Only Abimi stayed put. Wandi pulled the metal ceiling off the barrel and cleaned the gun with a piece of cloth and then aimed at a tiny branch holding a fruit on a tree and fired. The fruit came down, and the birds flew off, chirping.

Wandi nodded and ordered, 'Feed the crocodiles.'

CHAPTER 3

*With straight long hair, a pair of strange coloured
eyes that turned blue and green and then black, a straight
pointed nose, and a mouth that could speak a language
I didn't understand, yet somewhere deep within, I knew
there was a semblance.*

Maidem Kayem

DAMI HAD NOT slept properly since Ottuwa had told her
about the Tebo girl he was courting. She had a feeling he would
eventually think of marriage, so she tried to get his father, Tozingana
to dissuade him. Unfortunately, the king ignored it because he was not
convinced Ottuwa was taking that courtship seriously. When Ottuwa
began to talk about marriage, Dami, out of frustration, had gone to
see Kolezi at the bush bar (a thing totally unbecoming of a queen). She
had had no choice because it was impossible to meet him anywhere
else during the day and most of the night. Kolezi wasn't surprised
when Dami told him about Lemi because it had been whispered in
the bar at some point. What surprised Kolezi was Ottuwa's audacity
to contemplate marriage. He had thought this was just one of those
'things', but coming from his mother, even *he* took a mother's instinct
seriously. It was he who had come up with the idea that if, after the
family meeting, Ottuwa still didn't desist, he would take Dami himself
to see Pa Ngunep to get a permanent solution.

'I told you she has given him herbs.'

'Lower your voice, Dami. The witches will hear you and transmit
the message to her.'

Dami lowered her voice, obeying. 'But at least now you understand that I was right. How is it possible that he is still adamant on marrying Lemi? Even after everything we have explained about her people?'

'Pa Ngunep will give us the medicine we need to solve this problem,' Kolezi said as they crossed the last brook to Pa Ngunep's shrine.

They took the rough cleared path leading to the entrance and stopped a few feet off and then both turned their backs to the entrance as required. Kolezi clapped his hands nine times to ask for admission. When they were invited in, they turned around and bent their backs to go into the shrine without looking up. Pa Ngunep lit the incense, invited them to sit, and sat down himself. Dami let Kolezi speak.

'We have some trouble with a stubborn child.' He let Pa Ngunep nod before he continued. 'Ottuwa won't listen and insists on marrying Lemi. Now we know that Lemi is a good woman and that her family is well behaved, but a monkey remains a monkey.' He stopped to let that get home.

Dami couldn't hold back. 'Pa Ngunep, her mother had nine children. Her elder sisters have at least six each, which means Lemi is healthy.'

Kolezi was about to hush her up when Pa Ngunep cut in. 'So why have you come to see me?'

'We came here hoping for a solution to the problem,' Kolezi said before Dami could let out any more.

'There is a cure to every illness, but to find the cure, you need to know what the illness is first,' Pa Ngunep said shortly.

He asked for a piece of a cloth that Ottuwa had used recently but was not yet washed so that it still had his body odour and three strands of Ottuwa's hair. Dami had them ready as she and Kolezi had agreed she should. They knew that that was what the high priest would need for help with *foresight*. The day before, Dami had plucked Ottuwa's hair out cunningly as she hugged him, pretending to have understood and accepted his choice of wife. Then on the evening of the family meeting, as he went off, she had asked him to go ahead, saying she would follow as soon as her cassava was cooked. Once she was sure he was a long way gone, she stealthily sneaked into his room to cut some cloth from a loin he had used that same afternoon.

Pa Ngunep lay down a board and drew an enneagram on it with a piece of chalk, with one angle particularly longer than the rest. He then arranged the board so that the tip of this longest angle was directly opposite him and placed the piece of cloth Dami had given him in the middle space. He broke each strand of hair into three pieces and placed each strand of hair in the spaces between each of the tips of the enneagram, facing the cloth in the middle. He lit three small sticks and, placing them in a triangle around the whole, began his incantations.

Kolezi looked attentively. He was well versed in these rituals, being a retired priest himself, and Dami tried to keep her anxiety down. Finally, Pa Ngunep spoke.

'There are two sons, an elder and a younger. The elder is calm, but the younger is restless. There are two women. Lemi and another one whose face I cannot see at this point. The ancestors point to the younger son as the one they will anoint king, but this elder one is surrounded by confusion and chaos and is in line to succeed as patriarch someday.'

'Why are the ancestors sending us both then?' Kolezi enquired.

'They send whom they please, sometimes to teach us, sometimes to punish us. The elder one is not a bad person, but his mother's family has a different spirituality from ours. Their aura contradicts with ours, which is why there is confusion. He will be on his way soon after Ottuwa marries his mother.'

'You mean the marriage will happen?' Dami said in horror, suppressing a scream.

'Yes. Ottuwa is stubborn. He will marry her. We can delay the child's coming, but we cannot prevent it. We will need to wait until the child is born before we do anything about him.'

* * *

Her mother was a good midwife and had delivered most of her grandchildren herself. Lemi was closest to her mother and, after waiting so long to conceive, decided that she wanted to have the baby with her mother in Tebo. She had to leave soon before she got too heavy to make the journey, so she decided to stop at Ottuwa's chambers on her way back from the market to ask for his permission, but what happened there almost drained the blood out of her.

Dami was scolding Ottuwa. 'We had told you not to marry her, but you wouldn't listen. Now look at the confusion you have caused. We cannot let her child be our patriarch, least of all at this time of invasion. We need unity, not mayhem. I warned you, but the herbs she used were too strong.'

'We have decided to solve the problem as soon as the child is born, so be informed,' Kolezi told Ottuwa.

Ottuwa tried to plead, 'Send Lemi away instead. Let the child grow up in Tebo and never return, but please don't kill him. There is no need to. Remember, he is also our – '

Kolezi interrupted him. 'We wouldn't have come to this point if you had listened to us. The women will soon be at their time, and we cannot let both children meet. The family has already taken its decision, and you have only yourself to blame for it.'

Lemi almost fell on her way back to her house. Aruma, who had just come out to pluck some fruit from a tree, saw her and ordered her maids to help Lemi. They took Lemi back into the house and put her to sleep. Later that evening, Aruma came by to see Lemi, whose maids told her to her greatest surprise that Lemi had left for Tebo a few hours earlier with her Tebo maid whom she had brought along with her when she had married Ottuwa. They had taken nothing with them except a gourd of water for the journey.

* * *

It wasn't two o'clock when lightning began to strike on a busy market day. One bolt caught a treetop and set it ablaze. The fire spread quickly, burning a few stores and causing commotion in the market as traders rushed to put sand into the flames. Deafening thunder followed for the next few minutes, and then the lightning and thunder stopped for a moment to let black clouds gather. The market emptied in a frenzy.

Ottuwa kept on emptying his horn and refilling it as he sat with Makafu in his majesty's chambers, telling one story after another to keep his mind as far away from the delivery room as possible. Makafu simply sat there with his usual bored expression. He had arrived at Ottuwa's palace early that morning to announce that this was going to be the day the child would arrive, but because Aruma was not complaining of any pains and it was sometime before her birthing time, Ottuwa had been doubtful. In the early hours of the afternoon, just as she laid out the dishes for Ottuwa's meal, she felt a sharp pain and went into labour.

The black clouds darkened the skies, and it seemed like a moonless night, even though it was barely three in the afternoon. The downpour of rain and hailstones was ferocious.

Ottuwa couldn't distract himself anymore. 'Will the rain continue for the next nine days like it did the last time?' he asked Makafu.

He sounded so much like a child that Makafu almost laughed. Kings like Ottuwa were the reason he had always insisted to Pa Ngunep that every successor to the throne should be schooled in Baluma spirituality long before he was to succeed, but Pa Ngunep had always dismissed it, saying that the king didn't need to be spiritually knowledgeable himself; he just needed a good high priest. Here was Ottuwa, a brilliant man and proving to be a great politician. His popularity was growing faster than anything Makafu had ever seen, and yet here he was, asking the questions of a little boy because he was ignorant of Baluma spirituality.

'The downpour is just meant to protect him so that our enemies don't hear him cry and know that he has arrived. It will stop as soon as he stops crying.'

Ottuwa heaved a sigh of relief. 'That means he will arrive safely then?'

'He will be here soon with ten toes.' Makafu giggled but stopped quickly, remembering he was a high priest and wasn't supposed to be laughing at his king.

Ottuwa's mind went back to the labour room, and he emptied his horn again.

The middle-aged midwife stood at the doorstep, waiting to get the king's attention. Ottuwa turned around to see the smiling woman. Usually, the baby would be brought to him, but this one was special. He had started suckling hungrily as soon as he was washed and placed on his mother's chest and refused to be interrupted. He yelled so angrily at the midwives whenever they tried to pull him away that they were forced to let him eat and call his father to him instead. When Ottuwa saw the baby, he almost dropped to his knees in awe. The little boy was so handsome and so grossly overweight with a rife appetite. He stopped only once when his father placed his finger on his head before continuing with his meal. The midwives let Ottuwa and Aruma have the moment.

Two years ago, Ottuwa had met Aruma at the 'festival of the pig' (a day on which the Baluma commemorated their victory over the northern invaders). He first saw her with her mother when they brought food to the palace for the festival. She greeted Dami and politely left them as Dami engaged conversation with her mother. Ottuwa knew the family well but had never paid particular attention to Aruma. For him, she was just an ordinary girl like any other. He only took interest in her after that festival when Dami began to talk to him about Aruma. Her father was a noble of the Ngui, a very calm and composed man who had once been an exorcist and worked with Makafu for several years but had given up priesthood to go back to farming because of an almost deadly experience he had had during an exorcism around the time Aruma was born. Ottuwa gradually developed an interest in Aruma and began to visit her family at their home. Even though she was reserved and somewhat shy, she seemed to have a strong opinion on things that mattered to her, such as family and tribe. She had also learnt a little bit about the cobra religion and language enough to teach him a few things. By the time he came to ask her family for her, they both knew they wanted to be married. The bond that formed between them was like a pot of cold water put on a fire that gradually heated up.

On the other hand, with Lemi, it was love at first sight. Ottuwa didn't know much about Lemi and didn't care to know. She was the most beautiful woman he had ever met and wanted to marry her on the day he saw her. It was his family that had delayed the marriage. Ottuwa was determined to fight his family for her, and Lemi was elated to be his first wife. However, once they were married, they were both made to face a reality that neither of them was prepared for. From the disdain

Lemi received from his family (because she was Tebo) and the pressure from her own family for her to conceive to the daily disagreements they had on one or another thing, the marriage took a downward spiral. The distance between them kept on growing. Ottuwa's anointing and crowning only served to widen the already-growing chasm between the two. He became increasing involved with the Ngui and Wemtii councils in trying to protect as many of his people as he possibly could. At first, they didn't see for days, and then those days gradually became weeks, so by the time he was to marry Aruma, the chasm between them was so wide that Lemi didn't feel an iota of jealousy.

As the love Ottuwa had once shared with Lemi waned, what he felt for Aruma strengthened because of their cultural commonness, especially as the pressure from the colonial government increased. Aruma understood Ottuwa in ways that Lemi couldn't.

Sitting there, watching his newborn suckle greedily, he couldn't help but wonder what kind of child Lemi would have had. Two months back, he had been informed by his uncle Kolezi and a few core members of the Ngui that the baby had died a few moments later after birth from swallowing his own tongue. But Ottuwa knew better.

The young baby, satisfied, licked his lips and went to sleep, giving Ottuwa the chance to carry him for the first time. As soon as the baby was put in his arms, he was suddenly filled with a mixture of strength and hope. The baby seemed to take away all his fears and hesitations about the cobra administration. He found himself suddenly willing to put himself in the line of fire to protect his young one.

He closed his eyes to take a breath, but the breath took longer than any he had ever taken. He filled his lungs up to the brim and then opened his eyes and nostrils to empty them. It was a feeling of rebirth and of hope he had never experienced before.

He said to Aruma, 'I will call him Balumakazi', (which in Baluma meant: the breath of Baluma).

* * *

When the new commander did not arrive as expected on Tuesday, Cornell, who was in interim command, decided to give it more time, but by the next Sunday, he was sure there was something wrong. Even though it had rained heavily on Friday, the newly cleared path to the coast was well beaten, so the rain alone could not have obstructed the road. On Monday, he asked Kamuel to take two natives and drive down to the coast to find out. Cornelius requested and was granted permission to go along. Kamuel got a few clothes together and persuaded his daughter, Maria, that he would be back soon and to take care of her mother. Cornelius carried Kamuel's bags into the truck and hopped into the back himself.

They travelled two days before they got to the sight of the burnt car. They almost passed it, but Cornelius's eagle eye made it out before they had gone too far.

He woke Kamuel up. 'Bass, bass, we need to stop and go back a little.'

'Why? What happened?'

'I think I saw something that looked like a burnt vehicle, and the vehicle is big like the one that was sent to fetch the new big bass.'

'OK, let's have a look,' a confused Kamuel offered.

The driver stopped and went back.

'There it is,' Cornelius said as the driver almost went back too far.

The driver stopped and moved the vehicle closer to the wreckage. Kamuel went over the wreckage several times, with Cornelius following and inspecting closely.

'You might be right. This looks like the vehicle, but there are no bodies in here. I wonder what that could mean,' Kamuel contemplated.

'Maybe they ran away when the car caught fire, bass.'

'Let us continue the journey to the coast. We will soon find out what happened.'

Kamuel got back into the car, and the driver ignited the engine. As Kamuel glanced back at the wreckage once more, he noticed that the bonnet of the car was facing the direction of Lumani and that there was a hole in the windscreen as if something had been shot through it.

It was another full day of driving before they got to the coast, which gave Kamuel enough time to think. If the car was turned in the direction of Lumani, one thing was certain: the car was on its way back from the coast. What happened after that was what he couldn't figure out. There were two probabilities. One, on the way back with the new commander, the car caught fire from something like overheating. Two, they were ambushed (which would explain the hole in the windscreen). He dreaded that latter and hoped that once he got to the coast, he would be told something that would eliminate that probability.

'They got off the boat two Fridays ago, sir, and set off by Saturday in the early morn. General Lewis and the boys, sir.'

Kamuel could feel the blood draining out of his spine. 'You mean they arrived here and left?'

'Yes, sir. Why, sir?' the other asked, quite puzzled at Kamuel's drained face.

'He didn't arrive,' Kamuel said, grabbing the edges of the table as his knees shook.

'How do you mean he didn't arrive, sir? There was a vehicle to pick him up. I saw them off myself, sir. And the ammunition was intact. What do you mean, sir?'

Kamuel's head was spinning as the questions rushed at him. He managed to pull out a piece of paper from his breast pocket to write a note: 'General Lewis missing. Send reinforcement and ammunition. Situation ahead uncertain.'

'Get this message faxed back home,' he said, handing the note to the other, who was, by now, even more confused.

'Yes, sir.'

Kamuel had just sat back in the truck when Cornelius took over the questioning,

'So what happened, bass?'

Kamuel was in another world, trying to resolve the mystery. His head was spinning even faster than before.

'Bass, bass, what happened?'

He heard Cornelius's voice in the distance. 'We are going back. Another "bass" will be here soon,' he said, saying the word boss in Cornelius's accent.

'So what happened to the vehicle, bass?' Cornelius asked, not understanding Kamuel's sarcasm in saying the word in a Baluma accent.

'I don't know,' Kamuel answered weakly and pretended to fall asleep.

On the way back, they stopped to take a second look at the wreckage of the burnt vehicle. He scanned the vehicle more meticulously this time but still found no clue as to why the vehicle would have caught fire. To avoid Cornelius's questions, he pretended to sleep most of the way. He had overheard General Merritt talking to the Baluma king (whose name he found out to be Ottuwa) about the bush fires but couldn't make any sense of the king's answer or of what the general had said. His thoughts drew him to the old man whom he had prevented from being killed by Cornell, the same one who had told him something about the clouds and the ancestors. Kamuel tried to make a connection between the burnt car and the old man but couldn't.

He decided to relieve himself by thinking about Christy. She had told him about the inappropriate requests General Merritt was making to her, but he never took her seriously until a few weeks back when Maria took ill and Christy went to ask for medicine for the child. Unfortunately, the general had died before he had had the chance to confront him.

Thinking about Merritt unsettled him as well, so he turned his mind to Maria and how happy she would be to see him back. The next time he was coming to the coast, he had promised her he would bring her along. Kamuel made them stop at a market to buy some fruit that he knew Maria would love.

By the time Kamuel got back to Lumani, he had hardly had three hours of sleep in the three days of travel. Cornelius shook him to tell him they had arrived at his house. Kamuel was thrilled.

Christy couldn't hold Maria back as she jumped out of her chair and bolted for the door, shouting, 'Daddy is back! Daddy is back!'

Kamuel had only just got out of the vehicle when he saw Maria running towards him. He was amazed that she knew the sound of the vehicle that had taken him away from her. When he had bathed and changed, Christy told him of what had happened in the week he was away.

General Merritt was a saint by comparison. What Cornell had done in the week Kamuel was away was abhorrent. They had all woken up to a shattered bridge, and nobody could explain why the bridge had collapsed. Cornell had ordered his men to find out. The workers had been properly supervised and had done so well a job that even General Merritt had been totally satisfied. The fact that the bridge hadn't collapsed on the day after its finishing but almost a week later made it even more difficult to determine what caused the collapse. Cornell's assistants informed him that this could not be the job of an individual or a group of people because of the manner of collapse and the rubble left. The bridge had virtually exploded on its own, and they couldn't figure out what could have caused the explosion because the waters below were calm.

Cornell then decided that somebody needed to be punished for its collapse whether or not that collapse had been the fault of anyone. He ordered his men to seize about a hundred young men randomly and have them summarily executed. Because they were running out of ammunition, there weren't enough bullets to use for the killing, so they knelt the boys down and chopped them up. When the killing was over, Cornell made the families dig a large grave and clean up the place.

As if that wasn't enough, Cornell had made it a habit to abduct women from their homes and have them brought to his. He would send his men out in the evening to bring the women to him. A few days later, he would let them go and have another set brought to him. Those who resisted were taken and never seen after that.

Kamuel threw up.

* * *

Kamuel went to see Cornell later that evening when he felt that he had the strength to face him. He told Cornell of the note he had sent off for more ammunition and reinforcement. He hesitated about the part of the burnt vehicle and then decided to let it out with caution.

'We saw a burnt vehicle by the roadside but don't know what to make of it.'

'Why would you say that?'

'Well, it was difficult to say because it was so burnt and hardly recognisable. There was nobody in it, so it might have been the one we sent, or it might have been from some other cavalry.'

'What did the report at the coast say? Did General Lewis arrive or not?'

'No, they told me he hadn't, and they were beginning to wonder themselves, which is why I left the note to be faxed.'

'Go back to the coast tomorrow and send another note asking for only ammunition. We don't need a new commander. I am taking charge.'

'You?'

'Yes, me. Why? Do you have a problem with that? I was second in command after all. Nobody knows better than me how to administer these people. So take as many boys as you need and go to the coast tomorrow. That's an order.'

'Yes, sir.'

Kamuel was glad he had not told Cornell the whole truth. He noted that Cornell did not seem to be receiving this report for the first time.

When Kamuel got home, he told Christy what had transpired and asked for her to pack a bag. They were both coming along with him. After what he heard Cornell say this evening, he wasn't leaving them behind. Cornell was capable of anything. Merritt had had more dignity and humanity.

* * *

Uwa finished making the soup and served a little in a bowl for Nsika, who was shaking violently. Mama Sawa was in tears because she thought he was going to die. The healer was on his way already. Nsika struggled to eat when Uwa fed him, but every time she took a break to let him digest, he threw up what he had just eaten. So Uwa stopped feeding him to wait for the healer.

The two women left the room when the healer came and sat outside. Mama Sawa couldn't stop crying. She couldn't bear to lose the last person in her family. Uwa consoled her that the boy would be fine, even though she didn't believe it herself.

About half an hour later, the healer came out of the room to the two women outside and told them, 'The boy is sleeping now. I gave him some herbs to put him to deep sleep because he has not slept for the last week. He is really tired but cannot sleep. You need to ask for a priest because there is nothing wrong with his body. The illness is in the head.'

'Are you saying that my Nsika has gone mad? What did I do to anyone?' Mama Sawa was hysteric.

'No, it is nothing spiritual, but the problem is coming from his head. It is only the priests who are taught that kind of healing.'

Uwa calmed her down. 'We will see a priest tomorrow. I know of a good one.' She paid the healer and thanked him.

Nsika's temperature was high and his breathing unstable throughout the whole night. Uwa was not even sure if he was conscious but didn't dare tell Mama Sawa.

At the crack of dawn, Uwa set off to fetch the priest. She explained to him what had happened and the healer's conclusion and didn't need to persuade him to come with her. The priest tied a few herbs together with a little string and put them into his bag.

Nsika was still sleeping by the time they got there. The priest asked Mama Sawa to tell him in detail what had happened with Nsika since he had taken ill.

Mama Sawa explained inconsistently, 'He came back as usual, but this time, he wouldn't eat. Then after some days, he ate, and then he started throwing up. I asked him if he was all right. He said he did not feel like eating. But before that, he had been very shaky about everything. Whenever I called his name, he was afraid, as if I will do something to him, but I have never done anything to him. After some time, I noticed he wasn't sleeping. Just as the healer said, he was tired. I knew, I knew he had a temperature that was not normal. That is when I called his mother.' The last word referred to Uwa.

Uwa couldn't make sense of what Mama Sawa was saying, but apparently, the priest was used to that manner of storytelling.

'Put a pot of water on the fire. When it boils, let me know.'

He took out his bundle of herbs and cut the little string that bound them. He separated the leaves into three different stacks, crushed two stacks into powder, placed them aside, took the third little stack, and put it to Nsika's nose. After a few moments, Nsika began to come around. His breathing became more stable, and his temperature began to drop until he opened his eyes.

Uwa came in to inform that the water was already heated. He asked her to bring the pot to him, and she did so hurriedly, left him with Nsika in the room, and joined Mama Sawa outside to console her (and prevent her from a heart attack meanwhile).

Back in the room, the priest incanted prayers as he poured the powder from one stack of the crushed herbs into the water and placed the pot directly in front of Nsika, who was now sitting upright on his bed as instructed. The fumes filled the little room until the whole place was foggy. Nsika felt stronger and stronger so that by the time the priest began the hypnotism, he could answer clearly.

'Nsika, what do you see?' the priest said.

'I am watching from the kitchen window. They bring them to the house. I have usually seen them tied up like that, but this time, it is different... They do not use the guns because the big bass says there are not enough stones to shoot... I lie in the bush behind a small guava tree... They use the machetes.'

When he was done, the priest concluded, 'Now we are going to lock this story in a cupboard, and whenever you are ready, nature will unlock and tell you again.'

He poured the powder from the next stack of crushed herbs into the water, making incantations the whole while. When it was over, he put Nsika back to sleep. Nsika went to sleep immediately. The priest asked Uwa to make sure Nsika was not woken until he opened his eyes himself.

'What if he never opens his eyes?' asked desperate Mama Sawa, who was still crying.

'He *will* open his eyes whenever he is ready,' he said and then turned to Uwa. 'Just make sure nobody wakes him up.' He glanced at Mama Sawa when he pronounced the word *nobody*.

Nsika only woke the next day by midday. Uwa stayed back the whole while to make certain Mama Sawa did not wake him up.

Wandi had returned from the forest to find that Uwa was not home. The children told him that she had gone to see Mama Sawa because Nsika was ill. He felt anxious, wondering what could have happened, but decided to wait patiently for Uwa.

'Did you ask Natahi what the matter was?' Natahi was the priest who had taken care of Nsika.

'No. I thought I should leave that to you. Priests don't answer such questions from women and definitely not in front of a Mama Sawa.'

'If Nsika needed hypnotism, then the trauma must have been very serious.' Then he remembered a thing he didn't want to forget. 'We are planning to retaliate for the young men who were killed.'

Uwa took in a sharp breath. 'Maybe that is what Nsika saw. He was working at Cornell's place that week. Oh, the poor child.'

Wandi narrowed his eyes, understanding. 'Arrange for him to be transferred to Kamuel's residence. I hear that that one is normal. This Cornell is a beast worse than anything we have ever seen before. Nonetheless, I will see Natahi tomorrow just to make sure Nsika will be all right.' Wandi took Uwa's hand and lowered his voice. 'Uwa, this battle is going to take a very bloody turn. Most of my men were either related to or friends of the young men who were massacred. The raping and torture going on is bolstering their thirst for blood. I am losing control over them by the day. I can no longer swear what they are capable of doing once we attack. If anything should ever happen to me, take your wives and children and run to my mother's family.'

'It won't come to that,' Uwa said in denial.

Wandi sat by Nsika as he slept, pitying him. The boy was too young to have seen what he saw. Wandi cursed himself for letting the boy run errands for him. Perhaps if he had just let the boy stay with his grandmother, this would not have happened, or perhaps he too may have been one of those killed or, even worse, become a faithful church worker and traitor.

Wandi could not decide what the boy would have become, so he decided to let the ancestors handle this case. The boy was so smart and cunning; he had learnt the cobra's language in no time, enough to teach Wandi a little. That was how he had been able to read the writing on the package of weapons that Nkweni missed. It was information from Nsika that had led them to those weapons in the first place. Even after so many months, Nsika had managed to keep undercover, going completely unnoticed. Nsika had been more useful to the warriors than Wandi could ever explain. Natahi had told him not to worry about the boy, that he was *stronger* than he looked.

He wiped the boy's sweating forehead as he woke up.

* * *

The new weapons excited the warriors. Training was much more interesting with these weapons that could kill faster and more efficiently. The commanders spared the bullets and made the warriors train with stones they had shaped like bullets instead. Nonetheless, it was exciting.

As they tested the weapons, they came up with new ideas on how to use them more efficiently. For example, there was a root commonly eaten in Lumani that could be eaten raw, boiled, fried, or dried. These roots had the capacity to absorb water or liquids in good proportions when dried. The warriors got some of the root, ground, and then moulded the paste in the form of bullets and dried. They even used rubber from the trees around. All in all, they were ready for blood no matter how it got spilt. Their anger could be heard in the chants as they trained and in the enthusiasm of their work.

The strategy was different this time. Instead of attacking the clan in which Cornell was residing, the warriors attacked every other clan.

There were more cobras stationed in the clans around than in the one Cornell resided, which was used as an administrative capital for the occupation. In the other clans, the cobras had built schools, homes, and prisons and developed several plantations, and the labour was well organised and effective. The warriors attacked with firearms, killing whatever cobras were in sight, abducting their families from the homes and burning down plantations. The prisons were broken open and all the prisoners freed. There was a fierce confrontation between the natives fighting on the cobra's end and the warriors. Anyone who tried to escape the clans was chased and killed by the warriors. The attack covered four clans and lasted three and a half days. Cornell only got wind of it a week later.

Ottuwa calmed Cornell down, saying, 'I am sure this attack was led by the natives who work in the residences and on the plantations. I have learnt that they are discontented, so the attack didn't surprise me.'

'They said there were fighters, more like soldiers who came into the clans from God-knows-where.'

'No, there has to be a mistake. If there were indeed fighters, it is likely that they came from neighbouring kingdoms, perhaps to settle scores with my people, and that would explain why your people got caught up in the crossfire. But there is no need to worry because this can be easily sorted out. I will instruct my guards to find out what happened, and I will personally bring a report to you.'

Cornelius poured out another drink for King Ottuwa and Cornell and then repositioned himself at the corner at which he had been standing.

'I will need to explain what happened to my soldiers and their families.'

'You are supreme commander. You owe nobody any explanation. If your commanders back in your country think this job is easy, they can come here and do it themselves. Everyone knows the task isn't easy. My people are stubborn and always giving trouble, the reason why the last commander refused to come. I will speak to my people again and make sure they set their eyes out for any assailants. Cornelius here can be of good use in that regard.'

Cornell took in the flattery and believed every word. After the death of Merritt, Ottuwa had manoeuvred his way around Cornell and got into a position of confidence and almost trust with him.

Cornell was the bastard son of a nobleman who had never given him or his mother any recognition. His friends teased and bullied him at school for not having a father, and that stripped him of every iota of self-esteem. As he grew into the senior classes, he bullied smaller boys in an attempt to get rid of the deep hurt he felt. When he was dismissed from school for beating a little boy almost to death, he had, against his mother's wish, gone in search of his father. His father had not received him but sent someone to meet him. This person had got him a well-paying job on the ships and made him sign a paper that forbade him from ever looking for his biological father again. The money was enticing and would guarantee him and his mother a good living for the rest of their lives, so he signed and forgot about his father, at least for a while.

It was on the ships that he had met and commanded Merritt. When his father had died, his stepbrothers had arranged to have him posted to Africa for good, and his life became hell again. In Lumani, he was now assistant to Merritt, a sadist who made it a point of reminding him of the illegitimate manner of his birth and getting him to do the meanest of tasks. In truth, if Merritt hadn't died of other causes, Cornell would probably have hatched a plan for an unexplainable accident, so needless to say, when Merritt died, Cornell was not displeased. He went about establishing his authority by exercising ruthlessness.

Ottuwa had taken interest in the new commander ever since the young man had marched up to him that day to announce that he had been summoned to Merritt's residence. He had noticed the tension between Merritt and Cornell and the nonchalance in Cornell's eyes at the prayer service held for Merritt. Ottuwa had also noticed that Kamuel liked neither Merritt nor Cornell. He therefore took advantage of these cracks in the wall to manoeuvre his way around Cornell, persuading him to make labourers of the church workers and instead making the natives fetch the rubber and cocoa from the forest. Amongst the native workers, Ottuwa had planted his envoys. The workers were to crack the cocoa and coffee fruit, pull out the beans, dry them, and then package them for transportation to the coast. The envoys were charged with drying the cocoa and coffee beans. They made sure to sabotage the work by burning the cocoa and coffee beans so that they would be unusable. The rubber was mixed with poisonous herbs and wrapped up tightly.

To cover up, Ottuwa made them deliver almost twice as much cocoa, coffee, and rubber so that there would be so many loads that a thorough inspection could not be done effectively. The increase in production gladdened Cornell because he had expected to be appointed to take over from Merritt, but instead, his superiors had decided to send in a replacement, completely ignoring him. Cornell needed to prove to his superiors and to himself that he was better than Merritt. He was producing twice as much as Merritt and had managed to tame a once stubborn king. Ottuwa was now a collaborator, getting his people to work without complaining and taking instructions obediently. But for the recent attacks, he was quite exultant about his achievements, and so was Ottuwa.

* * *

Kamuel took his time at the coast. Maria and Christy enjoyed it there. The two natives they had taken along were very helpful since they spoke the local language at the coast. Kamuel deliberately delayed in sending Cornell's message. This role was not what he had bargained for. His orders had been to assist in administering and maintaining peace and order in the kingdom of Lumani and to export the cocoa, coffee, and rubber. The church, he had been told, was there on an evangelic mission to spread Christianity and establish schools and churches. But contrary to that, he remarked that the activities of the church included spying, conspiring, and helping with the brutality of this administration. He contemplated leaving with the next ship that would set sail for home, but his natural problem of indecision was getting the better of him.

Cornelius pointed out to Cornell that Kamuel was taking longer than usual to return and offered to go to the coast himself just in case his car had caught fire. He took care to mention that Kamuel had left for the coast with his wife and child, knowing that that would make Cornell suspicious. Cornell had been wondering himself about Kamuel's delay but couldn't be bothered, seeing as he didn't quite like Kamuel's company. Cornelius was a more useful assistant; the trouble was that Cornelius was a native, so he could not make him command the cobras. Cornell gave Cornelius the green light and made it clear that Cornelius needed to be back with Kamuel and with the next batch of ammunition because they were almost all out and were only holding on by pointing empty guns at the natives.

Exhilarated to be the envoy of Cornell, he got three natives to make the journey with him. Next, he went to Teresa's home, where she lived with her parents. Teresa was a recently baptised girl, about sixteen years old, whom Cornelius had had his eyes on for a long time. He had never got the chance to woo her because she was always around her mother, and his intentions were never pure. A trip to the coast should be luring enough to her family so that they won't ask too many questions about his intentions. Cornelius wasn't wrong; her mother promised to get her ready for the journey the next morning.

So off Cornelius went on his expedition to find Kamuel. He sat in the passenger seat with such gusto, one would have thought he was the commander himself.

When they got to the burnt vehicle, he ordered the driver, 'Stop here and wait in the car for me.'

He went over to the vehicle and inspected it again himself more carefully. He noted that the bonnet was turned in the direction of Lumani but wasn't smart enough to make out what that would mean. He equally noticed that the windscreen had a hole in it. He managed to figure that bit out. The vehicle had been attacked. He had known that the vehicle was supposed to bring back ammunition for the bass. Perhaps that was why the recent attacks in the clans by 'unknown' people had been so effective. Perhaps these people from outside the kingdom had attacked the vehicle and taken the weapons. But what about the people in the vehicle?

He asked two of the natives to scan the bushes around for anything they could find, but they searched in vain. As they continued the journey to the coast, Cornelius speculated on the possibility that Kamuel had noticed what he had and that that would explain his silence thereafter.

They finally arrived at the coast towards evening the next day. Cornelius went straight to work in search of Kamuel. He asked at the port and was directed to where Kamuel was staying. Kamuel wasn't pleased to see Cornelius and made no secret of it. Cornelius humbly gave in.

'I am sorry, bass. We were just worried about you. We thought your vehicle might have burnt or that you were attacked like the other one, so the bass sent me to check.'

Kamuel picked up the last part of his statement (attacked) and gave him a cautious look. Cornelius realized he had said a bit too much and tried to divert the subject by asking after Christy and Maria.

'Did the bass ask you to find out about them as well?' Kamuel asked sarcastically.

'Yes, yes, he is worried about them too,' Cornelius answered, never understanding Kamuel's sarcasm.

'Well, we were just preparing to come back. The cavalry here has offered to provide us with a little ammunition while we wait for the next order. We should start back by tomorrow in the evening.'

Cornelius invited himself for a cup of tea, much to Kamuel's distaste. He talked for almost two hours with Kamuel, answering only in monosyllables, telling about the recent attacks from unknown assailants from other kingdoms and King Ottuwa's ardent cooperation. Cornelius told Kamuel about the fact that the bonnet was turned in the direction of Lumani and the hole he had noticed in the windscreen. He asked Kamuel if he had noticed that.

'No, I hadn't. You're very smart. Make certain you tell the bass first thing when we arrive. I charge you with that task.'

'Thank you, bass. I will make sure to do that. Is there anything I can do for you today or tomorrow before we leave, bass?'

'No, enjoy yourself with Teresa. Here is some money,' Kamuel said and walked out.

Cornelius swamped him with praises. It didn't ring a bell to Cornelius that he hadn't told Kamuel about the company he had brought, yet Kamuel knew, right down to the name of the girl accompanying him.

On the way back, Kamuel and his family were escorted by a small convoy of heavily armed cobras and natives. Maria and Christy had had such a lovely holiday in the coast that they had not wanted to leave. They arrived in Lumani.

'Where is Cornelius?' was Cornell's welcome back for Kamuel.

'Am not sure, sir. I didn't leave Lumani with him, and even though he met me at the coast, he was nowhere to be found when it was time to go, so I thought he had other errands to run for you, sir.'

Cornell cursed under his breath and enquired about the weapons, and Kamuel gave him a detailed inventory. Cornell was not impressed that there were so few weapons.

'There are more coming in a fortnight, sir.'

'OK. Dismissed.'

Kamuel was about to be glad when he heard 'Captain' and turned around.

'I want you to supervise the building of a new bridge.'

Kamuel's jaw dropped. 'What new bridge, sir?' he asked, pretending not to know.

'The one that got destroyed by the natives.'

'Yes, uh, sir.'

Cornelius returned and transmitted all the information he had gathered on his trip about the car and that Kamuel wasn't in a hurry to leave the coast for some reason. Cornell wasn't interested in that second part, even though he knew Cornelius had told him expecting him to take action against Kamuel. He was curious, however, that Kamuel had not noticed what Cornelius had. Kamuel was the most observant man he knew. He decided, just for prudence's sake, to presume that Kamuel *had* noticed but, for one reason or another, withheld that information. The implications of the vehicle being attacked on its way back to Lumani were grave. Who had attacked? Not that he cared, but what had they done of the soldiers and perhaps the new commander? And what had happened to the ammunition in the vehicle?

Cornelius was still talking when Cornell hushed him up. 'About what distance from Lumani was the burnt vehicle?'

'Almost two days' journey, bass.'

'We will go back there tomorrow.'

The next morning, Cornell left Kamuel in charge of administration and took off with Cornelius.

When they arrived at the spot, Cornelius took his bass round zealously to show off how much he had noted. The men scanned the environs again for any clues and moved deeper and deeper but found nothing.

On the way back to their car, Cornell said abruptly, looking down at the ground, '*Stop!*'

'What is the matter, bass?'

'The earth on this area is softer than the others, and the grass is shorter, as if it only just took root. In other words, this area was dug to bury something or someone. Is this area part of Lumani?'

'Yes, bass, but nobody lives here, only witches.'

He made Cornelius clear the small area with a machete and dig. The other men helped, but they couldn't dig deep enough to find anything.

As soon as they got back to Lumani, Cornell began an intensive investigation with Cornelius in charge. First of all, a census needed to be conducted. To get this done effectively, Cornelius dispatched his men in batches to cover each area of the clan. In every household, they needed to take note of the number of people living there and their names and then do a thorough search of the house. The houses of those known to be of the warrior families were searched in greater detail. Somehow, even though the warrior families were known, no one seemed to know who was or was not a warrior in the family, especially since the warriors had, for the last ten or so years, operated under cover. The faces of the warriors were hardly known by anybody now. When the men got to Wandi's residence, they met Uwa, who said her husband was out fetching cocoa and listed everyone in her family. Those who fetched cocoa and coffee were always away working in the forest, so it was normal that Wandi and his four eldest sons should not be home.

It crossed Cornelius mind that the warriors were hiding amongst the people. He didn't believe the warriors whom he had learnt of growing up could have given up that easily. His father had always told him about how great the Baluma warriors were and their victories over the slave takers. What he couldn't figure out was how they could be within the kingdom, living amongst the people, and yet attack from without with such efficiency. Even though Cornelius tried to convince him, Cornell doubted that the attack had come from Lumani. He reckoned that these people were stubborn but not vicious and definitely not warring. In any case, just to be sure, he summoned king Ottuwa.

'The assailants are Baluma!'

'I don't understand, Commander.'

'Our vehicle was attacked in Lumani exactly *one* day from here just on the outskirts. The bodies were buried and the weapons stolen. We saw the bodies ourselves.'

'That cannot be possible, Commander...'

'But it is. We saw the bodies ourselves.'

'It has been more than three weeks since that incident. The bodies must be sand by now. So how could you have seen any bodies?'

Cornell kept quiet, realising that he had been caught in his own trap.

'Why don't you let me talk with the Ngui and bring the culprits to you if there are any in Lumani? We do know that our neighbours have always had a habit of attacking us.'

'I want the culprits here tomorrow,' Cornell ordered.

'Why don't you give me time, Supreme Commander? We need to get the real culprits, or else the real ones will attack again,' Ottuwa said, pampering Cornell's ego.

Needless to say, King Ottuwa had a convincing excuse the next time he reported.

* * *

After weeks of census and Cornelius's men spying on the people day and night, no trace of any warriors could be found. Everybody woke up in the morning and went out to the forest to return in the evenings. Life seemed to go on as usual. But the attacks became more and more frequent and random on schools, churches, residences, and plantations.

Cornell's frustration was indescribable. Even more frustrating was King Ottuwa's insistence that the insurgency was coming from outside the kingdom. They had gone through the forest bordering Lumani on the east in vain. Even more discouraging was that the soldiers got sick each time they returned because of the insects they were exposed to, so much so that Cornell had to resort to using Cornelius's henchmen to get the job done.

To compound his frustration, a rude message came for Cornell from the coast. His superiors were unimpressed with his results. The rising number of deaths amongst the soldiers was making the task of enlisting more for deployment to that part of Africa increasingly difficult. Cornell replied to inform that the soldiers had been sick because of the insects they had been exposed to in the forest and that more frequent supplies of ammunition and medication would be necessary.

A frustrated Cornell invited Ottuwa for a drink that evening.

'How can I get results when am not sure where the enemy is coming from?'

'But you do know where the enemy is coming from – the neighbouring kingdoms. Perhaps you might want to ask the kings there. You have combed my forest and know that if anyone was hiding in there, they would have been caught.'

'The neighbouring kingdoms are subject to command from different cavalries. I can't just walk in there.'

'Perhaps you should send Cornelius to find out,' Ottuwa offered, knowing that if Cornelius went, he would never return.

'No, not just yet,' Cornell said, thinking deeply.

Ottuwa, knowing Cornell, knew he was hatching a plan but couldn't tell what.

* * *

The next time the warriors attacked, Cornell was on alert. It happened during a prayer service that took long because that was the day their 'Lord and Saviour' was crucified (as they believed). They called it Good Friday.

Wandi had his warriors in place. They had done this several times before, so he presumed this would go as usual: set a fire to the church, everybody runs out, destroy the church. He had two of his best commanders leading the attack, so he went home confidently.

The fire was lit, the people ran out, and they began to set fire to the church. The warriors were so engrossed in their task, they did not notice that one or two cobras did not run along with the rest. It was when they had destroyed the building completely that they noticed some cobras around, pointing guns at them. Luckily, they too had guns, so they could fire back. A small battle ensued as the warriors, realising they had been surrounded, tried to break through the ring of cobras around them. Two survived to run back to the forest, with one sustaining a leg wound, but most died in the confrontation. Three who survived were captured.

Cornell came out of hiding to congratulate his men. 'These should be enough to sound the message,' he said jubilantly.

The next day was a dark day for Baluma but one of the brightest for Cornell. He had the whole clan summoned to the main square. The three culprits, which included one of Wandi's commanders, were dragged in. There was a cold wind that blew as the crowd took in the sight. The three men had no clothes on and were streamed in blood and swollen all over, no doubt from lashing, and their eyes could hardly open. They were bound, hands and feet. There was a noose on each one's neck, which led to the one in front of him, and in front of the first one was Cornelius, holding the edge.

'These men set the church on fire and are responsible for all the burnings and killings that have been going on here over the last months. We are going to make an example of them for anyone who intends to follow in their footsteps of defiance,' Cornell announced self-importantly.

Large hooks were pinned through the ribs of the three men, the ropes attached to the hooks strung up over the logs prepared for the purpose. The ropes were then pulled so that the men were suspended in mid-air by the hooks attached to their ribs. The crowd was silent as a graveyard as the horror went home. Cornell looked around, smiling, realising the horror was taking effect. Kamuel stood with his back to the men, stone stiff. Cornelius gave the orders, and spears were driven into the men. When the crowd was dismissed, it took them a few minutes before anyone moved.

Wandi woke up to the news, and the last shred holding him onto his spirituality gave way.

The next morning, Cornelius had a couple of young men rounded up for another 'example'. He had chosen the ablest of young men, but Cornell stopped him and asked him to take those instead who couldn't work, like those who were lame, deaf, blind, or crippled in some way instead because, in his own words, 'We can waste the disabled, but we need the young strong men to fetch the cocoa and coffee from the forest.'

Cornelius obeyed zealously, seizing every young man or woman with a disability in the clan. They were hung by the feet from trees, swords driven into them before a terror-stricken crowd.

The terror began to yield as Cornell soon heard whispers of a resistance from his native spies. Although he was unable to obtain enough information on what the resistance was about or where it was coming from, he did learn of the 'Baluma warriors', a thing he had not heard about in almost twelve years of being there.

Ottuwa persuaded Cornell to let the rest of the captives go. 'They have got your message. It was loud and clear, and I am sure there will be no more traitors amongst my people going forward. Like I had told you, my people are stubborn, but you know a few lessons like these will put them to rest. Why don't you let the rest go? With all the horror they have been through, surely, they wouldn't attempt such treachery ever again. Let them come back to us so we can heal them.'

'Heal them?' Cornell questioned.

'Yes, Commander. They need to be hypnotised so that they do not go mad. That way, they will be of better use to you and me.'

Cornell let them go, not quite understanding what that meant.

On Ottuwa's orders, the rubber, cocoa, and coffee were poisoned extra specially the next time so that even those transporting the raw materials would be affected. If they were lucky, they would come back half dead.

*　*　*

Maria sat making mud huts and cleaning them with water from the stream nearby. Dirtying her hands and dress didn't bother her at all. She loved to wet the earth and mould the mud, designing different shapes of buildings. Whenever her parents let her go outside, she was always up to one or another form of construction. On this occasion, she had not been given permission to play by the stream but had sneaked away from her parent's company as they dozed off during their picnic.

A native girl about Maria's age who was obviously guilty of the same crime also came to play at the stream. Maria, eager to make a friend of her age, went over and asked her what her name was, but the little girl couldn't understand Maria. Not minding the language barrier, Maria pulled her by the hand to show her the mini buildings she was making. The little girl immediately took interest. They quickly made friends and were soon building together, soiling and chasing each other around and laughing their hearts out with childlike innocence.

Unfortunately, their new-found friendship was short-lived as a loud 'Bana!' came from behind them just as they had begun to forget they were both out of bounds.

The two children stopped to see who it was, but Bana already knew who. She thought of running but knew her father would catch her before she had gone two steps, so she gave up and prayed that he would not be angry since she hadn't been away for too long. She was right. He shook his head, lifted her from the ground, and placed her in his arms. His attention now moved to her friend, whom he had only just noticed was actually *white* (it was difficult to make that out before since both were rubbed with mud). Even though she had grown up ever since, he had never forgotten her bright blue eyes and curly brown hair.

The little girl began to smile at him guiltily when 'Maria!' came from not far away, and she ran to her father, who had arrived at the stream around the same time in search of her. The eyes of Bana's father followed the little girl to her father. It was a strange moment for both men as they looked fixedly at each other with their daughters in their arms, each seeming to want to say something to the other but couldn't get himself to do it. It was almost as if they felt that they should know each other as they stood there in a trance.

Wandi came back to himself first and moved a few steps backwards as if to avoid turning his back on Kamuel and then made a sudden about-turn and walked quickly away.

'Oh, Kamuel, you found her!'

Kamuel blinked hard as if he had just experienced an apparition. 'Oh yes, she was playing in the mud as usual, our little piglet.'

He passed the child to Christy, and they started to go back home. Before they descended the hill, Kamuel decided to take a last look at the riverside behind them and around the river in the distance, and there, he saw the man, daughter in hand, watching them walk away.

'Kamuel, come along. It will soon be dark, and this place is dangerous for us at night.' Christy came back and pulled Kamuel away.

He didn't know what to think of this strange fellow. But there was an undeniable familiarity between them. He had noticed that the man had held his daughter in the same protective manner that he held Maria and the way the man had looked at him in the same way he had looked back at him, with neither aggression nor hostility but obvious scepticism. There was, however, something about this man that he couldn't find the words to describe. Maybe it should be *overpowering* or *overly confident*. He knew this man was not the king because he had seen King Ottuwa on several occasions, so who was this man? Kamuel searched his mind for answers but got none.

He began to rethink the cobra mission in Lumani and asked himself what exactly they had been sent here for. Shouldn't they be buying the cocoa and coffee and rubber. They were taking these raw materials forcefully and terrorising the people to get their way. How was that different from the slavery that had just been abolished back home? They had told him these people were pagans. If they were so, why would they have a person they called a high priest? What was it these people believed in?

Kamuel's mind searched for Makafu and found him, remembering the old man and how his loincloth hung weakly from his waist and how lean and frail he looked yet could frighten Cornell, Cornelius, and even Merritt merely with the words that he spoke and the manner in which he had gazed.

When Christy put Maria to bed, she joined Kamuel on the porch outside. She had had the same questions going through her mind about their mission to Lumani, and when they had gone to the coast, she had also thought about getting on to the next ship but thought he would want to continue with his mission.

'We should leave as soon as you have rebuilt the bridge. We'd have thought up a suitable excuse by then. This can't be right.' Christy leaned on him.

* * *

'Do you know the native high priest? The old man whom you flogged some time ago?' Kamuel asked, feigning distraction.

'Yes, bass,' a baffled Cornelius answered.

'Do you know where he lives?'

'Yes, bass.'

'So you can call him here?'

'Yes, bass, but I will need two or three strong men. That old wizard has powers that make him difficult to carry easily.'

'He hasn't done anything wrong, nor have I asked you to 'carry' him here. I want you to simply tell him that I am asking for him.'

'OK, bass.'

Contrary to what he had expected, Cornelius had no trouble getting Makafu to come with him. He didn't go to the shrine because that was forbidden by his new religion but went to see Makafu's assistant at home to relay the message. Makafu came along, and they went off, with Cornelius leading the way, not daring to say a word.

When they got to Kamuel's home, Kamuel, knowing Makafu understood his language, dismissed Cornelius, much to the latter's displeasure, and invited Makafu to tea. The old man wasn't interested.

'Biscuit then?'

'I do not eat such things,' Makafu said, casting his usual bored gaze ahead.

'OK, I'll go straight to the point. I have been charged with rebuilding the bridge over the river. Now as I recall, you had told Merritt that building the bridge over that particular river was not the right thing to do. Would you be kind enough to let me know where it will be OK for me to build a new bridge? I realize there are three rivers.'

Makafu took his time in answering. 'You can build over the Chwa. She has always been calm and welcoming and isn't offended by trespassers.'

'Would you show me the one?'

Makafu rose to his feet. Kamuel followed, and when they got to the place, he pointed with his short crooked stick.

'That one. You can build from there to there.'

'So you're promising me it will be safe.'

'I never make any promises. I simply follow the rules.'

'The rules?' Kamuel repeated.

The old man didn't offer to continue, so Kamuel couldn't query any further.

'Thank you, uh...' Kamuel said, expecting a name but got none.

The work on the bridge began. A week later, when the wood and the sand were ready, Ottuwa was careful to make sure that the wood was not poisoned for the bridge since Makafu had given his approval. Kamuel got the work organised to be completed over the next three weeks. The bridge was relatively short; the current of the water was low, and the river was shallow.

Kamuel selected the people for each task carefully so that each one could do their task without much physical strain. They had two breaks to eat and rest, and at the end of every week of construction, he paid the workers little stipends from the money he and Christy had set aside. The labourers were shocked and skeptical at first, but as he got closer to them over the three weeks of work, they got to appreciate him. He even learnt a few words of greeting in Baluma and taught them a whole lot about building bridges. When the bridge was completed, he made them a barbecue to celebrate. Ottuwa secretly had a cow sent for that occasion, which they roasted.

Cornelius and his master were not invited.

* * *

Now on a path of self-reflection, Kamuel was getting more and more consumed by the feeling of the commonness in humanity: meeting the father of the little native girl and the way he had held her with such protective love (not different from the one he felt for Maria), meeting Makafu for the second time, working with the natives and seeing the way they treated one another (not differently from the society he came from), watching mothers feed babies and the children playing in the mud and grass. He had even got talking to the natives about their religion and was stoned when they told him about their belief in one god and their well-structured priestly order.

All that was tangling his mind and causing him to question more with every breaking of the day, 'What am I representing?'

* * *

When he had finished his tasks for the day, he filled the basins with water and had his usual end-of-workday meal, which Christy always offered him. Nsika put the strap of his little bag around his neck and shoulders and walked back home. He passed by the church and, out of usual curiosity, peeped around to see what was going on. He had done so on several occasions, and sometimes the parishioners would come out and invite him to a prayer service or a doctrine class, which amused him very much. In fact, he had formed friends at the parish and was always helpful to Father Robert whenever he could. That was where he had met and made friends with the recently baptised Michael.

'Nsika, Nsika, over here!' Michael called out to him, and Nsika joined them for the prayer service.

After that, there was a doctrine class about the saviour walking over water and another prayer, and then they were allowed to go home. It didn't take long, just barely an hour. Nsika found the stories from the book he had now come to know was called 'the Holy Bible' very interesting.

As they both walked back home, Michael, as usual, explained the deeper meaning of the reading and the doctrine. 'You see, Nsika, if only we had faith, we could walk over the Akiki and the Chwa and the Moja Rivers without needing a bridge. This is the message of the Lord to us today. This makes me feel strong, Nsika. All I need to do is to trust, and all my problems will be solved.'

'Yes, I am sure with enough trust, even a chicken can walk over the Akiki, but, Ndikwa, how can you explain that the same people who enter into this church to sing praises to your new *god* can do the things they have done to us? I don't remember what happened, but I know these people did something terrible. And then I heard of the three men who were caught and what they did to them and the others who were disabled. There is something evil either about these people or about their *god*. That is why I don't believe that they are worshipping something good, Ndikwa. But let me ask you this. Do you believe? Do you really believe? This same *god* they speak of, of his peaceful nature, and that all you need to do is trust him and that you can do whatever you want? Ndikwa, do you really believe that this *god* they worship is the same as Si? Si tells us never to attack unless to defend, but these people, they come here on big boats, and they kill us, and they take whatever they want. What kind of *god* gives his people only the power to destroy? Ndikwa, think.'

They arrived at Ndikwa's home. Ndikwa's mother was preparing the fire for the evening meal. She saw them and invited Nsika to join them for dinner, but he declined politely, leaving her with a disturbed Michael.

At the end of the week, Ndikwa met Nsika at Kamuel's house and offered to help him with the work around. Nsika introduced his friend to Christy as Michael, hoping that would impress her. It had the opposite effect. Experience had taught her to trust the unconverted natives more. Nsika quickly read that and explained that his friend was, in fact, Ndikwa, and she calmed down. When she was gone, Nsika and Ndikwa made fun about the change in colour of her face each time – she had turned from pink to red and then blue and then back to pink – and laughed even more at the expressions and reaction to each name. Christy eventually got used to Ndikwa and welcomed him whenever he came. She called them her 'native sons'.

Over time, Michael remained Michael, but slowly, Nsika's questioning began to take effect. Michael started asking questions at doctrine class that could be answered neither by the doctrine teachers nor by Father Robert himself. The usual answer he was given was 'That is what the Holy Bible says' with a definitive tone, which was growingly unsatisfactory. He tried his best to relate the cobras' deeds with the preaching in the church, but the more he tried, the more disparity he observed, and the day came when he walked out of the church during service and never returned.

He couldn't explain to his Christian parents why he had left church, so he decided to go to help Nsika with the house chores just to kill time. When the family came back home, Christy opened her arms.

'Michael, you came to help.'

'No, Ndikwa came to help.'

* * *

Cornell and his greatest apostle (Cornelius) were unhappy not only because they had not been invited to the barbecue but also what pained them even more was the fact that the natives, especially the church workers, sang the praises of Kamuel as if he was the new commander. Cornelius was particularly bitter because he had spied on Kamuel the whole while he had worked on the bridge with the natives, hoping that

Kamuel might do or say something that he could use against him, but got nothing.

After a few hours of grumbling, Cornell and his apostle agreed that the best way to get information about Kamuel was to get a house help to do the espionage. However, that was tricky because Kamuel already had two. The only choice they had was to persuade Kamuel to take an assistant, which wasn't difficult because he needed one.

Fidelis was a little lazy but very meticulous in his work. He had helped Merritt out with some tasks from time to time, and that was how Cornell knew he was the man for this job. Cornelius outlined the job description, and Cornell motivated Fidelis by giving him some money and a pair of shoes.

Kamuel could feel that there was something odd about this situation but couldn't quite put a finger on it. Fidelis was successful in his first mission, reporting to Cornell about Kamuel's plans to return. Cornell quickly curbed that by tasking Kamuel with building the new school for the church.

Ndikwa met Fidelis by chance once when the latter came to the house to drop Kamuel's briefcase. They knew each other well, but ever since Ndikwa had stopped going to church, Fidelis hadn't seen him. Ndikwa explained why and told him about Nsika and how nice it was working here for Kamuel. Ndikwa later introduced Nsika to Fidelis, and Nsika opened up naively.

The three boys had a lot in common because they were all about the same age. Even though they talked to one another in the native Baluma language, they all understood the cobra's language, with the exception that Fidelis could write in the language. They had interesting debates about the cobra religion, and each seemed to enjoy the growing friendship. Fidelis resisted at first to the ideas against the religion and slowly pretended to give in, feeding all the information back to Cornelius almost on a daily basis.

Unfortunately, Fidelis blew his cover too soon. Once, when they were eating in the kitchen, Fidelis began to talk about his family and their conversion to the new religion and then used that opportunity to enquire about Nsika's family. Nsika told him about his parents and Mama Sawa and Uwa and later about Wandi playing the role of father for him. Fidelis asked him a lot about Wandi, and Nsika had no problem explaining the relationship and his admiration for Wandi, even going further to talk about how great a warrior he was and that he hoped to be like Wandi someday. Nsika noticed Fidelis's eyes flip in a peculiar manner every time he mentioned the name of Wandi, as if he had just received an award, so he stopped talking. He trusted Fidelis, but Fidelis's expression made him uneasy. After that incident, he gradually got cold towards Fidelis and never opened up, at least not in that manner again. They would talk about everything and nothing, but Nsika evaded any questions about Wandi.

'So this Wandinendi fellow is part of the resistance we hear of?' Cornell fingered his beard as they walked along. 'Then he must know where he lives or how we can get to him.'

Cornell's evil mind went to work as he thought it through. If he openly confronted Wandi, he would raise the alarm, and the others would go into hiding. He needed to go about this prudently. He didn't want an uprising. The next set of ammunition would take another month before it arrived.

'Maybe we should find them out one by one and then kill them quietly, bass.'

'Yes, but how?'

'Poison them quietly.'

'No, ask Fidelis to find out whatever he can about this Wandinendi and his entire family. A man like that would have several wives in this village. In the meantime, we do nothing. I will speak to Ottuwa and see if he knows anything.'

Kamuel moved farther into the shade and stopped his breath as Cornell and Cornelius walked by.

* * *

'Wandi, I don't know how this happened, but that evil cobra knows you are the leader of the rebellion. I wiggled my way out of it by telling him that it was your elder brother who defended us against the slave takers, and that explains why anybody would think you would do such a thing,' Ottuwa told Wandi as soon as they were in his secret chambers that evening.

'Nsika must have let something slip. I will find out, but knowing my name is not a problem. Catching me is. We have attacks planned but not enough ammunition, so we need to wait until the cobra's next supply. In the meantime, we prepare for our final attack.'

'They are also losing soldiers. Several of them took ill at the coast and died the last time they transported the rubber. I don't think they have asked for more soldiers yet. The evil cobra is still trying to find out what happened. I sent him a few members of the Ngui to "help" because I want to know what they know.'

There was a knock on the door, and Wandi changed the subject abruptly.

'How is the baby doing?'

'That baby is now an old man and growing fast. He will see his eighth harvest this month.'

The door was opened, and Aruma let Balumakazi in. Balumakazi – or simply Kazi, as he was called – had inherited his mother's beautiful large light brown eyes and long eyelashes to give him a feminine look and his father's short round blunt nose and big lips. He also had very big strong white teeth, which, as he grew older, seemed to be growing bigger than his mouth so that when he smiled, the first thing that caught the eye was his teeth. For a child who had started with a keen appetite, he had strangely lost interest for food ever since he started walking. Kazi could eat one meal of beans or pap in the morning and not be hungry until two days later. Aruma had to stand over him with a long stick to make sure he finished his meal. He loved accompanying the female servants to help them carry water at the stream and the males to split the wood but was not very helpful around the house besides that. Kazi never even knew when his clothes needed to be washed. Tall for his age (in fact, much taller than most fifteen-year-old boys), he was lean and hard but not physically very strong. He loved wrestling and running competitions. Because of his height, people always overestimated his real age. Only those who still remembered the time he was named (nine days after his birth) actually believed he was only eight.

Ottuwa had married two other wives after Aruma and had had six other children with them over the years. Aruma had not been able to conceive after Kazi because of illness, but Ottuwa never complained. Sometimes he wondered whether that was not the punishment for what he let the Ngui do to Lemi. He therefore developed a soft spot for the child and drew Kazi close to him. Kazi was charged with the special task of giving his father his bitter drink for the evening. Ottuwa liked that because it gave him a chance to be close to the boy. The boy spent most of his days with his mother or doing one or another craft with his peers and hardly ever spent enough time with him, so in the evenings when the boy came with the drink, they would talk until the boy got too tired and had to go to sleep. He made Kazi sit beside Wandi, and the two had a long conversation. Wandi was amazed at how much the boy knew about fighting and the current events about the cobras.

'So what do you think we should do to the cobras?' Wandi asked, amused at the brightness in Kazi's light brown eyes as they discussed the subject.

'We should send them back to their own kingdoms. What are they doing here? We need to fight them off.'

'And how do you suggest we go about that?'

'Well, during the period before the great return, we used to hide in the forest. Our warriors stayed here in Lumani and kept on fighting until they won, and we could come back. Why don't we all go into the forest again?'

'Hmmm, that is a good idea. I will ask Papa to think about it.'

'I have told him several times, but he won't listen.'

Kazi was perplexed when Ottuwa and Wandi burst out laughing.

From time to time, Kazi would follow Wandi into the forest with his father's permission to train with the warriors. Well, it was more that Wandi made him think he was really training to satisfy him. The warriors found his company amusing because his enthusiasm to fight didn't seem to match his understanding of the situation.

'Why do you think we have to fight?' they would ask.

'Because that is what Baluma warriors do. We fight, destroy our enemies, and bring our people back to the land,' he would answer.

Over time, Wandi taught Kazi how to use a dagger in a defensive manner. The boy enjoyed it and took his lessons very seriously. Wandi made sure to remind him never to use the dagger at home or on anybody during playtime. Just to be sure, he never let the boy return home with it. Instead, he kept the dagger with him and only brought it out during training time. He also taught the boy to use a gun when he felt he was ready.

Kazi learnt very fast and was extremely flexible and creative. He would use his teeth to get out of the grip of anybody holding him. That was a method of self-defence Wandi had not seen in all his years. Wandi didn't stop or discourage him from doing so because the technique amused him as much as the boy's zeal. Teaching Kazi reminded him so often about Vumanga. He was about Kazi's age when Vumanga had begun to train him, and the boy seemed to enjoy the training as much as he had so many years ago.

* * *

'So you wouldn't know a man called Whan-di-nun-di, would you?' Kamuel said, sipping his coffee.

Nsika knew the cobra accent well enough to know he was referring to Wandi. 'No, sir.'

'In that case, I couldn't send him a message through you. Pity.'

'Is he a friend of yours, sir?' Nsika queried in a calm voice, but as he fixed his eyes on the table and wiped with more caution than usual, he let off more emotion than he realized.

'Yes, he is a good friend of mine, but he is in a bit of trouble. Some people are looking for him and his whole family, so he needs to run as fast as he can.'

Nsika didn't say a word after that, but Kamuel knew he would relay the message. Kamuel left the house after that and didn't return the whole day.

Nsika tried as hard as possible to act normal. After he was done fetching water for the house, he thought of turning down Christy's meal to save time but realized that might draw the attention of Fidelis. He packed his bag slowly so as not to draw any suspicion as he talked with Ndikwa and Fidelis over the meal, and then he begged to leave on the pretext that Mama Sawa needed him to split wood that evening to dry in the morning. Leaving Kamuel's compound, he strode as he always did, but once he was around the corner, he took off in a mad run.

Bana ran to him when she saw him running home. He asked her if her father was at home. She answered that he wasn't but Uwa was. That was good enough for him. He transmitted the message and left.

Kamuel had followed Nsika a safe distance away. When he saw Bana, he recognised the little girl and made the connection: the notorious Whan-di-nun-di was, in fact, the man he had met at the stream. He almost fainted from the shock.

* * *

The construction of the school began with workers going about their tasks eagerly since they knew Kamuel was in charge. He gave them the usual breaks during working hours and stipends at the end of the week, with Christy playing her usual role of paymaster. The women tasked to fetch water always brought their youngest children along with them and let them play around the construction site.

Kamuel was sinking deeper and deeper into self-reflection until he got to a breaking point. He had to speak with the old man again, or he was sure to go mad. This time, he sent Nsika and Ndikwa, who were eager to bring Makafu to him. The conversation with Makafu was more relaxed this time, and Makafu tried to look less bored.

Kamuel came out of that meeting fulfilled and almost restored. They had shared a lot about their different beliefs and convictions, sometimes disagreeing to agree, but ultimately, both agreed on two main things: there was a supreme deity who was singular, and the cobra administration should not be in Lumani.

Makafu was taken aback by Kamuel's simplicity. Kamuel, on the other hand, was taken aback by Makafu's knowledge of the religion of Christianity and its deeper meanings beyond the Holy Bible. Kamuel had wanted to ask Makafu about Whan-di-nun-di but thought that would be inappropriate. Besides, he didn't know who else might be listening to this conversation. He stood up and thanked Makafu for the visit.

* * *

'Bass, bass, there is urgent news for you from the coast.' Cornelius ran in.

'Why? Is the ammunition here already?'

Cornelius handed the sealed telegram to Cornell and let him read in silence.

Cornell let out a torrent of curses as he read along, threw the telegram at the window, and yelled, '*Mary, mother of God!*' He grabbed one end of the table and threw it over, tore down the curtains, opened the cupboards, and threw all the glasses to the ground.

Cornelius watched him trembling, too afraid to ask what was wrong. Cornell's eyes and face were red with anger. He usually took hot liquor to calm himself down whenever he got agitated, but this time, liquor didn't seem to be what he needed.

Cornelius was about to run out when Kamuel walked in, making the pain more excruciating for Cornell.

'What do you want?' Cornell howled.

'I heard the yelling and thought I should find out,' Kamuel said calmly, perplexed.

'It is impossible to satisfy those fat cats no matter how much one tries. There is always something unsatisfactory to them. We supply more material, more frequently than Merritt ever did, but that is still not enough. Now they want ivory and timber as well and, even worse, think I am incompetent.'

Kamuel picked up the telegram from the floor. The information was worrying. The soldiers who had transported the material to the coast had all taken ill upon arrival, and most had died before the ship had arrived to take them home. The doctor at the coast had diagnosed food poisoning. Worse, their superiors had learnt of the sporadic attacks on Lumani and had noted that more soldiers had died over the time Cornell was in charge than throughout their history on that part of the continent. In addition, they had discovered that over a long time, the raw materials sent home were infected, which was why most of the cocoa and coffee was unusable by the time it arrived and the rubber was toxic. Therefore, the cocoa, coffee, and rubber, which were previously affordable, had to be sold at untenable prices, causing most consumers to turn to tea and other substitutes for rubber that were cheaper from other African regions. In the telegram, their superiors went on to suggest that Cornell explore other useful material from Lumani like ivory and timber and made note that they were sending in a *more competent* commander. Cornell would be relieved as soon as the commander arrived.

Kamuel replaced the telegram on the floor and took a chair as Cornell ordered for Ottuwa. This was the first time Kamuel would assist at a meeting between Ottuwa and Cornell. He had generally found a good excuse not to be around whenever such meetings were held because he didn't want to get involved in the politics of administration. This time, Kamuel wanted to assist to obtain information for himself. He and Christy had already been looking for an escape route, so he needed to gather all the information he could. Besides, if Cornell ever found out he had transmitted any message to Whan-di-nun-di, he would be hanged faster than any of the natives. He needed to make sure Cornell hadn't.

Ottuwa came into the room and sat down as if he hadn't noticed the disorder. After Cornell had finished ranting about the telegram, Ottuwa calmed his nerves as usual.

'It isn't possible that we picked up poisonous rubber and rotten cocoa and coffee. I gave out strict orders to deliver the finest to you. I will make sure this time myself. I apologise for the terrible situation. As a motion of good faith, I will begin to explore the possibility of timber and ivory for your exportation.' Ottuwa left.

There was something about Ottuwa's eyes that Kamuel didn't trust. He stared at him the whole while he spoke, and even when Ottuwa had left, Kamuel's eyes were still on the door that had been shut. Coming back to himself, he could feel Cornelius's gaze on him in return. Kamuel turned his attention to Cornell and pretended not to notice the gaze.

* * *

Cornelius whistled the whole way from his house to Cornell's residence, bouncing most of the way. He stopped sometimes to shake his waist to let off some of the joy. He had precious news for Cornell. Surely, after this piece of information, he would be given a promotion of some sort.

He stopped to fetch a ripe orange from a tree since the sun was burning hot, peeled it up, and was about to eat when he felt a sharp pain in his stomach. He clutched his stomach and looked down at it. His hands were streaming with blood. A second or two later, while his head was still bent downwards, he felt something hit the centre of his head. His feet gave way, and he fell. The only thing he could see ahead was the sky, and he felt his breath leave him.

Abimi signalled to the men behind him to pull the corpse into the bushes.

Ottuwa was sure the Ngui had been compromised but didn't know by whom or for how long. This, for two reasons. First, the information they had received from the spies was just too accurate to be a speculation by the cobras. The cobras already had knowledge that the rubber, cocoa, and coffee were being poisoned before delivery. They even knew the herbs that were used for the poisoning. Only someone in Ottuwa's close circle would have access to that type of information. Ottuwa began to reserve all sensitive information to himself and only speak with Wandi. For damage control, they had decided to eliminate Cornelius to begin with. Wandi had since found out from Nsika that Fidelis was the one who had filtered information on him to Cornelius, so they had Fidelis under close watch and knew he could not be in possession of that kind of information. It was as though the cobras were aware of everything discussed at the meetings of Ngui almost immediately after.

Second, the only sensitive information that the cobras had, seemed to be coming out of his discussion with the Ngui. Whatever information he had but hadn't shared with the Ngui, the cobras didn't seem to be aware of. For example, the cobras were aware that a final attack was in the making but not that Wandi was waiting for the next set of ammunition because Ottuwa had kept the last bit to himself for some reason unknown to him.

Cornell's informant in the Ngui handed over the same information he had given Cornelius. The orders had come from Ottuwa, and that was just one of the methods of retaliation. Besides that, there were the warriors who trained in Njuu in shifts and attacked sporadically, and then there were the spies set amongst the cobras, usually as helps around the house and assistants to feed information back. There was also the high priest Makafu who strengthened the warriors each time they were to attack and was responsible for the elimination of the native spies amongst the people. The natives also had spies in the church pretending to be converts but were actually there to watch Father Robert. The commander of the resistance, Wandinendi, was planning a final attack, but it was uncertain when it would happen.

Without any pretence or disguise, Cornell made Fidelis replace Cornelius as his native assistant and set him to the task Cornelius had not finished – to confirm the information about the poisoning of the raw materials and confirm from whom the orders were coming.

The screaming was deafening coming from outside. Ottuwa and Aruma stopped eating and stood up. She had just returned from a short vacation at her parents' place in the neighbouring clan and was telling him about it as they ate. The screaming was meddled with sounds of gunshots and cobra voices. Ottuwa took in a deep breath and walked through the door. Aruma followed.

'Do you know what you have cost me?' Cornell yelled.

'I am not sure I understand,' Ottuwa said composedly, pulling Aruma behind him.

By now, there was a large crowd around them at the palace because the natives, seeing so many cobras marching to the palace, had followed. The cobras were pushing the crowd back to let Cornell speak with Ottuwa. Kazi, in the crowd, ran to his father's side.

'You don't understand? Savage! I will bury you and your family alive!' Cornell said, slapping Ottuwa across the face.

It was as if the world stopped. Ottuwa's earring and crown fell across the ground. Two soldiers grabbed him to pull him to the ground, tearing Kazi away as they did. Aruma screamed and reached for Kazi just as he seized a gun off one of the soldiers and shot indiscriminately ahead of him at Cornell and the soldiers. One soldier hit Kazi on the back with the butt of his gun, and he fell.

His father stretched his arm out, drawing him to shield, and the other soldiers, in confusion, shot in Kazi's direction wildly, making the crowd berserk with such a rage that they attacked the soldiers. Panicked, the soldiers shot point-blank at the raging crowd. A pair of hands pulled an uncontrollable Kazi from the ground, still screaming, and carried him off.

When the soldiers had finally taken control of the crowd and the dust was cleared, they turned their attention back to the spot where it had all begun. Ottuwa and Aruma were still, Cornell was gasping for breath, and several soldiers were wounded fatally. It was unclear who had shot whom since there was so much confusion and shooting. The soldiers had Cornell taken back to his home for medical care and set on a destruction through the palace, desecrating even the most sacred places.

* * *

Nsika put some herbs to Kazi's nose to make him unconscious and ran the rest of the way. It was sundown by the time he got to Wandi's house. Wandi wasn't in, but Uwa was, so Nsika laid Kazi down to rest to let the herbs subside. He told Uwa what had happened at the palace and that he didn't know who had been killed or what had happened after he pulled Kazi from the ground. All he had seen was blood everywhere.

Luckily, Kazi hadn't been hurt. Kazi had been so compulsive, yelling and hitting all the way, that he had been obliged to put him to sleep to avoid them getting caught.

Wandi got home not long afterwards to hear what Nsika had to relate. Kazi woke up just as Wandi was giving Nsika instructions.

'Take this gourd of water and this dagger. They belong to Kazi. Run to Yaketu. When you get there, ask for the compound of Yem, son of Ngufo. He will take care of you both. *Go!*'

Nsika picked up the gourd and the dagger. Wandi threw Kazi over Nsika's shoulders, and Nsika disappeared into the night.

'Tomorrow before sunrise, you take your wives and children and go to my mother's place,' Wandi breathed heavily.

'Has it come to that?' Uwa looked back obstinately at Wandi.

'Yes! It has come to *that*!'

She needed a moment to get used to it because it was the first time Wandi had ever used an authoritative tone with her, but he didn't give her a chance to argue.

'If I find anyone here by sunrise, I'll cut my losses and kill them myself!' He stormed out.

* * *

They caught them on their way home, mutilated them, and wrapped the pieces up in a large cloth and dumped in front of Cornell's residence. Unfortunately, Cornelius was no longer there to keep a keen eye on unanticipated events at a time when Abimi's vengefulness was at its optimum. He knew where to hit in the places that hurt the most. Kamuel was in charge that evening and saw the bundle dumped. He counted eleven female heads. He knew most of the women and knew they must have been on their way back from church.

Kamuel sent for Father Robert and asked the soldiers to pack the corpses up properly in boxes. He wasn't sure on which side to be now. He was seeing savagery from both ends. When Father Robert arrived, he was equally horrified. The corpses were too bad to be kept, so they had to be buried the next day.

With Cornell injured, Kamuel had to take over the administration. The ammunition should arrive in a few days, and given what happened with the last batch, he needed to send a convoy to get the ammunition in safely. They would use that to restore order before the next commander arrived. But first, he had to deal with whoever had done this hideous act. His mind went straight to Whan-di-nun-di and his rebels. Kamuel spent the whole night strategising because they did not have enough ammunition to last longer than a day of fighting so needed to use what they had sparingly.

* * *

Wandi and Abimi looked over the weapons again. The bullets they had were not enough to last more than a few hours, but thanks to the warriors' creativity, they had more bullets of different kinds: corn bullets, cassava bullets, and yam bullets, all with the same effect. Once these 'home-made' bullets were discharged into a person's skin, they had the effect of absorbing as much fluid as they could. The effect was slower but just as effective because enough of such bullets would gradually stop the circulation of blood and cause a heart attack or suffocation, depending on where the bullet was lodged.

The next morning, on his way to Wandi's compound, Kamuel asked the driver to stop at Cornell's house so he could see how Cornell was doing. He came out distraught. Cornell was no friend of his, but he had never seen a more pitiful sight. Cornell was dying slowly and painfully. The painkillers didn't seem to be working, and the two bullets he had taken in were lodged in places that were too close to his heart and his spine. He was also getting paranoid, yelling out at people whom only he could see in the room. The doctor told Kamuel there wasn't any hope. Father Robert had been there that morning to administer the extreme unction, but Cornell had refused, accusing him of plotting his murder and covering it up with a sacrament.

When Kamuel got to Wandi's compound with a group of soldiers to get him arrested, there were just a few servants around, some chickens, and one or two goats. Kamuel ordered the first servant he saw to tell

Wandi to come out. The servant explained that Wandi had disappeared, and he was not sure where the family had gone to since he worked only on day shifts. He too had met the place as empty as it was now. Because the servant was a frail old man, Kamuel couldn't get himself to arrest him or threaten him in any way. He decided to look around the compound himself.

He went in the direction of Wandi's house. The closer he got, the stronger he felt that Wandi was somewhere around him. He could smell him. The soldiers combed the compound and reported that they hadn't found him, but Kamuel was convinced Wandi was around somewhere. He could feel Wandi's eyes on him. To give faith a chance, he asked the men to let go and leave, and they would return the next day. They went from house to house, arresting young people at random, leaving the same message each time that their relatives would be released as soon as Wandi and the rebels were delivered to them at the administrative building.

Wandi and his rebels delivered themselves in a manner much unexpected. The attack began at Cornell's home just as the sun set. The warriors took the guards completely unawares. Cornell had been dead for a few minutes before the warriors got to him. They cut his head off, placed it on a stick, and posted in front of his house. The plantations were burned down, followed by the schools not far away. A few faithful hiding in the church were praying with Father Robert when they heard the banging at the door. They hid Father Robert behind the altar stone where they knew the warriors wouldn't bother to check. They also knew it was a matter of time before the warriors got in. They offered no resistance, and soon, the place was a cemetery.

As the warriors rampaged from clan to clan, they came across resistance not only from the cobras but also from the native converts who knew them better and therefore put up better resistance.

* * *

Kamuel got out of his car and instructed the driver to wait for him. He hadn't stopped by Cornell's house on his way back home because he couldn't stand the pain. Walking towards the main door of the house, he thought about Cornell and all the hideous things he had done to the people, yet seeing him suffer that much still made his heart ache. Thinking about the mutilated women, he still couldn't understand why the natives would pick innocent women instead of the soldiers like Cornell who were guilty.

The smell of Wandi intensified as he got to the door. A cold chill went down his spine as he realized he hadn't heard Maria's chattering or Christy's voice. He went spontaneously for his short gun at his waist, but when he looked around, he couldn't see anybody in sight. He ran for the door, opened it, and called out to Christy and Maria and was answered with a dead silence. He searched round the house, calling their names louder and louder, with his heart rising to his mouth.

'Shhh, you'll wake Maria up. It has taken me two hours to put her back to sleep. The gunshots in the distance woke her. What's going on?'

'I heard the rebels were attacking, so I sent the men out but am not sure where they are attacking from. We just need to hold the fort this evening. The ammunition arrives tomorrow.'

'So we aren't going back after all?'

'Christy, we will have to wait for the next commander before I can take permission. For the moment, Cornell is down, which puts me in charge until further notice. I can't just leave now.'

Christy shook her head and went to bed, slamming the door of the room behind her.

Kamuel knew he had hurt Christy but didn't have time to explain. He needed to get back to work. He went back out, got into the car, and headed for the administrative building.

The administrative building was already under attack. Kamuel chose to take the bush track to the building to get in unnoticed and join the defence. The prisons behind the building had been emptied and set ablaze, and the men Kamuel had captured earlier, along with other prisoners, had been freed and joined the warriors with a vengeance. From the outside, Kamuel could hear the fierce fighting between the cobras, the native soldiers, and the warriors.

Wandi stood there, so much like a statue that Kamuel almost missed him as he hurried towards the administrative building through the bushes with thick grass and tall trees. He was not dressed in the loose clothes he had had on the first time they met at the stream. He was dressed in a loincloth woven of a different kind that was specially made to blend with the colour of his skin. He had chains around his neck that carried strange medallions. He had on armlets, bracelets, and anklets and a special headpiece that was a little differently decorated from what Kamuel had seen King Ottuwa wear. Wandi wasn't armed to the teeth as Kamuel expected him to be, just a long gun and a sharp machete. Kamuel noticed droplets of blood on the bare side of Wandi's chest and face and guessed rightly they were not his.

He stopped about five feet away from Wandi but could still smell him. Wandi didn't move or attempt to; he just stood there, watching him. Not knowing what to do or expect, Kamuel drew his short gun and pointed it at Wandi. He blinked and put his finger on the trigger.

Considering that a move of aggression, Wandi tilted his chin upwards, and two warriors emerged up from the bushes beside Wandi and fired at Kamuel. Wandi simultaneously flung his machete at Kamuel, hitting him straight in the heart. Kamuel fell, and the two warriors ran forwards to take Kamuel's gun from him and looked around for any other cobras.

Wandi came to Kamuel's side slowly with his gun in hand, pointing directly at Kamuel's throat.

'Do you think that in another world we could... let's say... get to... get to know each other?' Kamuel coughed between bloodied teeth.

Wandi understood the language well enough to understand him but wasn't sure how to answer in the language.

As Kamuel lay there with straight long hair, a pair of strange coloured eyes that turned blue and green and then black, a straight pointed nose, and a mouth that spoke a language he couldn't understand, Kamuel seemed to be the enemy, yet somewhere deep within, Wandi knew there was a semblance, a commonness between them that he couldn't explain. He closed his eyes for a split second, and when he opened his eyes, Kamuel was dead, with his eyes still open and looking straight at him.

One of the warriors came back when Wandi was withdrawing his machete from Kamuel's heart.

'This one was a good cobra. He didn't deserve to die,' Wandi said.

'Neither did my wife and my two children,' the warrior answered Wandi without an iota of remorse.

* * *

There was something different about this battle. Wandi could feel Vumanga around him all the time. He wasn't sure what it meant. During the fighting, he hallucinated about Vumanga's last battle where he had fought by his side. Sometimes he actually thought he heard Vumanga whisper in his ears about forgiveness, but he had no time to let those thoughts take control.

He met Abimi on his way back from the administrative building. Abimi was on his way to the last few cobra houses.

'Abimi, Kamuel crossed me.'

'Good!' Abimi said, understanding the implication.

Wandi couldn't find the courage to sound remotely sympathetic to cobras with Abimi in this frame of mind, so he diverted. 'Why are we fighting? What are we killing each other for? So much blood for what, Abimi? Why can't we just make friends? I am tired of fighting.'

'I don't know about you, but I haven't forgotten my lessons, Wandinendi, son of Morewa. We fight to preserve our land, we fight to defend our people, and we fight to the death!'

'So be it then. To the death, my rainbow.'

'To the death, my *afomi*!'

Both men knew instinctively that those would be the last words spoken between them. When Abimi had spoken those words so many years ago, he hadn't thought that Wandi would remember them (because of Wandi's brash nature, it was always difficult to tell whether or not he actually heard anything the other person said), especially since Wandi had never repeated it. So it was the first time after the cave incident that Wandi had said the word, and both men knew it would be the last.

As Wandi fought, he saw Vumanga fighting at the other end. Sometimes he would seem farther; other times, he would seem nearer.

He felt a sharp pain in his heart and side. He turned to his left and emptied his barrel into the man who had shot him. Vumanga was already by his side.

'Wandi, I am here.'

He let his brother drag him into the cave. Abimi was already waiting for them there with a piece of roasted porcupine.

BOOK II

Dear Young Lion

CHAPTER 4

Even a goat has a lesson to lend.

Maidem Kayem

H E COULDN'T RUN as fast as he normally would because Kazi was heavy for his age, but he didn't stop running and made sure to keep close to the trees as they had been taught growing up. When he couldn't run anymore, he stopped and laid Kazi, who was wide awake by now, against a tree trunk.

'Why are we running away?'

'Shhh. We have to get to Papa Yem at Yaketu. We still have quite some distance left. Don't talk unless you really need to and don't drink too much water.'

'I can run with you. That way, you don't have to carry me, and we can be faster.'

Nsika ran with him some of the way, carried him whenever he got tired, caught bush rats, and roasted for them to eat. From time to time, they bypassed hunters who helped Nsika trace the paths better so that they could take shortcuts or avoid areas where they were likely to meet wild animals. Nsika noticed that strangely, the gourd was always full whenever he thought it needed to be refilled.

Kazi was quiet and obedient, but by the third morning, he was missing his parents. 'Why can't we go back to Papa and Mama? Surely, the cobras would have left by now.'

'Remember, I said we need to get to Papa Yem first. Then he will bring us back. That is what Papa Wandi said.'

'Why didn't Papa Wandi come with us?'

'He had to stay and help Papa. Now *shhh*. Don't talk too much, or you will get tired too fast for the journey.'

'But when will we get to Yaketu?' Kazi was near tears.

'If we run some of the way, by sundown, we'll be there.' Nsika, seeing that Kazi was suppressing tears, held him by the shoulders and drew him close. 'We will soon be there, young warrior. It is almost over.' He checked their gourd for water, and it was full.

They swam out of the stream. The day was hot, so their clothes dried fast. Nsika had only been to Yaketu twice with his grandmother but still had a vivid memory of the surrounding clans, so he knew by the short trees and tall grass they were in the last clan separating them from Yaketu. As he remembered, the people there were not very friendly but had a natural hospitality common to most people around that region.

He stopped at the market and spotted a fat motherly looking woman frying something for sale and chose to go to her for the help he needed. She had greeted him absentmindedly as she stirred her pot and asked her daughter to bring more spice for the soup in the pot beside. He asked politely what path was shortest to get to Yaketu. The word *Yaketu* seemed to catch her attention because at the mention of the name, she raised her head to Nsika.

'I am from Yaketu myself. I was there three days ago to see my mother.'

Nsika smiled, knowing this would work. 'That is nice to know, Mama. My brother and I are going there to meet somebody but don't know which path is shortest.'

'Ah, you are not from this clan? Ah, I see.' She turned to her daughter. 'Go and call your brother to help these strangers.' Then she turned to Nsika. 'My son will lead you to the path. He knows the way.' She continued to satisfy her curiosity for later use in gossip. 'So whom do you say you are going to see in Yaketu?' She bent down to draw the already-cooked fries out of the hot oil, pretending not to be too interested, but Nsika was used to that kind of body language. He was still searching for a diversion not to answer her questions when she noticed Kazi's eyes as they followed her hands to the basket and back. 'Have you been travelling for long? Why is your brother so hungry?'

It was excellent timing. 'No, we just started off, Mama, but we did not eat before we set off.'

'Hmmm, some women should not be allowed to have children,' she hissed as she wrapped up a few fries in a leaf and gave them to Kazi just as her son arrived. The boy was a little younger than Nsika but was friendly and didn't ask too many questions, which Nsika found convenient. He led Nsika and Kazi to the path and told them what way to turn at each angle. There were not too many angles, so Nsika could memorise them all.

As soon as they were out of sight, Kazi unwrapped the leaf. Nsika made him sit down to eat but didn't eat any himself. The boy ate hungrily, while Nsika pretended to be trying to trace the road, not to let Kazi see the desolation on his face. He felt so sorry for Kazi because he knew that child had no idea what had happened to his parents. He had seen it all as he dragged Kazi away but hadn't told him and wasn't intending to. That information was reserved strictly for Papa Yem alone on Wandi's orders. The boy was too young to receive it just yet.

Kazi licked his lips, wiped his hands on his clothes, and tugged Nsika's loincloth to let him know he had finished eating, his face much brighter now after the meal. Nsika made them walk first to let the meal go down. Then later, they ran, and soon, they were nearing the last stream, and by sundown, they were almost at Yaketu. They stopped to rest in a bushy area.

Kazi was trying to catch his breath when his eyes popped out. 'Nsika, look.'

Right there, a few paces from them, were some cobras speaking with two natives whom they could see were hunters. Nsika pulled Kazi close to him and leaned against the trunk of the tree nearest to them. The men were still talking when Kazi tried to stick his head out to see, but Nsika held him back firmly. The cobras were giving instructions to the hunters, and from what Nsika could hear, they were talking about elephants. Nsika didn't understand the natives because they spoke a different language but could understand the cobras who spoke the same language as the ones in Lumani. They were asking for elephant tusks.

When they finished and started walking away, Nsika presumed wrongly that he could sneak away unheard. He took Kazi's hand and a step forward.

'Who's there?' a cobra's voice echoed around the bushes.

Nsika grabbed Kazi by the waist, pulled him over his shoulder, and ran in the opposite direction farther into the bush. He could hear the natives running after him, so when he got to some rocks, he hid behind one to let Kazi down and to breathe himself. The two natives who had followed them decided to split and chase them in different directions because it was not easy to know where Nsika could be hiding because of all the trees and bush animals around making noises.

Nsika could hear him breathe as one of them approached the rocks. He signalled Kazi to not make a sound, and he bent down and filled his hands with the red moist earth around. Then he held his breath and closed his eyes to monitor the man's footsteps.

As soon as the man got to the edge of the rocks shielding them, Nsika jumped out and flung the earth into the man's eyes. The man yelled and dropped his gun, trying to get the earth out of his eyes. Nsika picked up the gun quickly and gestured to Kazi, and they both ran for their lives, only stopping when they got to the bush meat market on the outskirts of Yaketu.

Nsika gave Kazi the gun and made him wait for him in the bushes. He walked into the market, not drawing any attention to himself. Luckily, it was getting dark by now so that it was difficult to distinguish who was who, and added to that, the traders were busy packing up since it was the end of the market day.

Nsika walked by and took advantage of a careless trader who had left three small antelopes outside his stall to haggle with a difficult buyer. He stealthily pulled one of the dead animals by the hoof and made his way back into the bushes. He slung the antelope across his shoulder and held the gun in the other hand to disguise himself as a hunter.

The boys walked through the clan to Yem's place undisturbed and almost unnoticed with only an occasional 'Welcome back from the hunt.'

Yem was a short and very dark bulky man with a bald head and a thick moustache and beard that helped hide his broken brown teeth. With six wives and thirty-four children, his compound was always busy and noisy. He was no noble but was revered as one because he had beaten the odds to become one of the most successful farmers and, later on, businessmen in Yaketu. Being the first child and first son of a farmer with many wives and several children, life had not presented him with many opportunities, so he had had to make the best of every opportunity life presented him.

From the little land he had borrowed from his father, he grew crops and sold them mainly to people coming from other kingdoms. Most people did the same thing, but Yem did it better. In secret, he would carry his crops to the main entrance of Yaketu, where he knew most traders came through, and sold at slightly cheaper prices than the other Yaketu traders so that he quickly gathered a good number of clients.

As the demand increased, Yem borrowed a choice piece of fertile land from his father and grew more crops for sale and later employed farm workers to help him. Before long, he had swallowed up a good chunk of the market share. He didn't stop there; he also found a network of traders selling metals at cheap prices in other clans. He got a good supply and employed somebody to make hunting material for hunters. At first, he sold the material but, realising the business wasn't too profitable, decided to hire hunters instead. Yem made them hunt and pay him a third of their catch, which he would then sell.

These were but a few of Yem's different trades. Gradually, Yem's network increased and spread to every corner of Yaketu. Each time he developed a new successful trade, the nobles rewarded him with laurels, and to show off his achievements, he would take a new wife.

Life had also thought Yem to take advantage of every situation, even the most desperate, so while everyone saw the invasion of the cobras as a bad thing, Yem had learnt to use even that to his advantage. Noting the cobras liked chicken and beef which were not commonly eaten in Yaketu, Yem travelled north to buy cows and east to buy fowls to set up a cattle ranch and a poultry. He also engaged other businesses like supplying foodstuffs and fruits to the cobras. He supplied the cobra administration at exorbitant prices, making more than 700 percent profit from sales so that while everybody had one or another complaint about the presence of the cobras, Yem had none to offer because his fortune had more than tripled ever since.

The boys arrived in the compound and, presuming they were hunters coming to supply an order, were led to Yem's house in the middle.

Yem came out and frowned. 'These are not my hunters.'

'No, Papa. We come on behalf of Papa Wandinendi,' Nsika said, almost expecting him not to recognise the name.

But at the mention of the name, Yem relaxed and invited the boys in. He took the antelope from Nsika and ordered for food and water to be brought to them.

Nsika was too anxious to eat. What he had to say needed to be said to get the load off his chest. 'I have an urgent message for you alone, Papa.'

Yem discerned the implication. 'What is your brother's name?'

'Balumakazi, but they call me Kazi,' Kazi said before Nsika could answer.

'OK, Kazi, eat your meal and wait for us here.'

Kazi turned to Nsika for approval. Nsika nodded, and Kazi turned back to Yem. 'Yes, Papa.'

Yem smiled, understanding, and took Nsika in.

By the time they had got back, Kazi had eaten and was fast asleep. Nsika rushed to wake him, but Yem stopped him.

'The child deserves a good rest, and so do you. Tomorrow I will tell you what I think of all this. Now take the child to bed.'

* * *

The next morning, Yem put the boys in the charge of Mandara, his third wife, a very lively, very charming young woman. As soon as the boys were brought to her, she opened her arms to welcome them. Kazi easily took to her. When Mandara had shown them where they would sleep, she set about preparing a meal for them. Kazi was eager to help her, and she let him and taught him quite a few things about kitchen business. She had three little girls whom Kazi easily made friends with. The eldest was about Kazi's age, and the youngest was just a toddler.

Later that same afternoon, Yem called the boys to inform them he was going to make arrangements for them to be enrolled into school.

'The schools are run by the cobras, but they are good. Children who go there become very intelligent. They can read and write the cobra's language.'

Nsika was excited at the idea of going to school but had mixed feelings about being taught by the cobras. He did not want to be indoctrinated by their religion and betray his people the way he had seen the church workers back at home do, and he told Yem as much. For that, Yem had a piece:

'Learn everything you are taught, but don't believe a word of it. I am sending you there so you can learn to read and write their language. As a businessman, I can see the advantage of that kind of knowledge when I do business with them. The cobras have taken over, and we are all embittered about it, but if we want to survive, we need to learn their culture and language so that later on, we can beat them at their own game. How do you fight an enemy whose language and culture you do not understand? You both will start school next season. I have already informed the head teacher.'

Nsika conceded. 'Yes, Papa.' Then remembering what Yem had said last evening about telling him what he thought about what they had discussed, he added, 'You said we will talk today.'

'Oh yes. Uh, Kazi, go and help your mother. I'm sure she must be making dinner.'

'Yes, Papa.' Kazi ran off excitedly.

When Kazi was out of earshot, Yem cautioned, 'Now listen carefully. If King Ottuwa and Queen Aruma are dead and Wandi sent you here with the boy, it can only mean two things – first, a bloody fight was to ensue, and second, in King Ottuwa's close circle, Wandi did not trust anybody enough to protect the boy. It therefore means that there was a traitor in the house whose face neither Wandi nor King Ottuwa could see. Now to be safe, you boys will stay here with me, while I send my eyes and ears out to find out what happened after you left.'

* * *

Arnold was aghast when he got there. He almost thought he had arrived in the wrong kingdom and really wished he had. Corpses were littered the whole way, from the outskirts to the centre of the main clan where the administrative building had been established.

'Why did we stop?' he asked the driver.

'That's a wounded one of ours, sir.'

'And how would you know that?' Arnold was almost shaking in his knees from the horror.

'The colour of his skin, sir,' the driver said.

The soldier was too badly wounded to give them any useful directions, so the driver had him carried into the third van that followed theirs.

As they got deeper and deeper into the kingdom, they began to recognise the place better from the descriptions they had been given and from the piece of paper they had on which directions had been marked. Finally, they got to what they thought was the administrative building. It didn't quite fit the description because this one was shredded with bullet holes.

Arnold kept the hope that they were totally mistaken about the kingdom to which they had been sent. He asked his men to skirt around for any 'life' (meaning any of theirs). Most came back with nothing, and he was just about to be glad that he was right when one of the soldiers ran out of some bushes with bad news for him. He had found the corpse of Kamuel in the bushes and the corpses of several soldiers and other natives somewhere in the back. Arnold and Kamuel had been friends as boys. Even though they had been separated for so many years, he still recognised him.

They moved to the house nearby to find a decaying human head posted on a stick in front of it. The soldiers almost passed by, thinking it was the house of some fetish priest, when Arnold pointed out that the building was differently built from the other traditional ones they had seen around and, even though almost completely demolished, seemed more like one of theirs. The soldiers tried not to look at the posted decaying human head and went on to search the house.

They found two corpses (of theirs), one somewhere in the living room with a bullet in the back and another headless on a bed. Arnold thought to have the bodies of the soldiers pulled out and wrapped in cloth to be taken back to the coast for processing and shipping back home, but because most were too bad to make the journey or with too many missing parts, he decided to wrap up only the ones that could make the journey. It turned out that there was only Kamuel's corpse and a few others they saw in the back of the administrative building that could make the journey.

Arnold couldn't stand the stench of the house, so he decided to step out. The door at the right side squeaked, and somebody coughed on the other side of it. He stopped and drew his gun. The soldier at his side stepped forward towards the door, while Arnold moved back and pointed his gun straight at the door.

The soldier moved to the side and struck the door handle with the butt of his long gun and then jammed the door open to a painful cry of 'Mercy, please! Mercy!'

Out stepped Father Robert, who explained to them that he had been hiding there since last night when the war broke out. Meeting Father Robert irritated Arnold; he was actually in the right kingdom but was relieved that he might at least have an idea of what had happened in this cursed place.

The soldiers had washed and wrapped up Kamuel's corpse and brought it in to the house. They laid it on the long dining table. Arnold moved forward to take one last look at it. Father Robert was being taken out when he decided to console Arnold and offer him blessings.

After the prayers, Father Robert asked Arnold, 'Did you know him?'

'Yes. Well, not really, but we were friends as boys, and we met briefly sometime before he was drafted for Africa.'

'He was a good Christian, a good man. I wonder what would become of his wife and child now.'

'Oh, he has a wife? Can you give me her address? I would need to get the corpse to her.'

'His family is here with him. At least, they were until last night before the killing spree started.'

Arnold would have loved to let Father Robert get a bath and some rest, but he couldn't hold himself back. 'Father, we need to get to his house now, to get his family out.'

'If they are still with us.' Father Robert sighed miserably, driving flies away from his face with his left hand.

On the way to Kamuel's house, Father Robert told them not so summarily about the horrors of the battle the previous night.

'I was closing up the church with the catechist when it all started. A few faithful natives came to seek refuge in the church from the pagans, so we reopened the church for them and closed the doors to pray for the angel of death to pass us over. When the banging on the door started, I thought it was just another desperate native, and knowing it was too dangerous to reopen the door, we decided to let God take care of him and continued praying, but as the banging got more menacing, we knew they were upon us. They hid me behind the altar stone, and I prayed that they would be spared, but God had a different plan for them. The doors were finally broken down, and I don't quite remember what happened after that.

'When I woke up, all I could smell was death in the sacred place. The next place I could think of was Cornell's, so I tried to venture out. I had not been walking for long when a stream of these pagans sprang up from the bushes to chase me right into Cornell's house. Luckily, there was this little room in the side where I usually did confessions for the soldiers and other native faithful, so I ran in and hid there because it is inconspicuous. I did hear them shooting but didn't know who. Convinced it would last for just a while before Kamuel restored order, I waited there, but it only grew worse. The killing didn't stop. I had to pray myself to sleep.

'I am still surprised I made it to the next morning, and that is where you found me. Honestly, it was as if a demon had taken over the natives. They were so ferocious. It was unbelievable. I saw as I ran to Cornell's place the same good boys I had seen around this place and even hoped to convert rushing out to fight and chase even me. I wasn't even sure why they were fighting us. How is it possible for people, from one day to another, to do such evil to innocent people? And Kamuel, poor man, one of the simplest I ever met.'

Arnold was getting weary of his whimpering when Father Robert pointed out, 'There it is. That's where he lived.'

They got to the main door and, realising it was locked, went round the back to find that it was just as well sealed. After banging and calling out, receiving no reply, Arnold decided to break in and prepared himself for the worst. Luckily, it was not difficult to find Christy and Maria hiding inside a wardrobe in one of the rooms in the little house. When Arnold introduced himself as the new commander who had known her husband, Christy didn't need to be told the rest. She burst out crying, and Maria, confused and frightened, clung to her mother.

Arnold had them packed and ready to go to the coast with one of the vans later that evening, in the same van that would be carrying Kamuel's corpse and the others. A few other families that had been spared for one reason or another were also put onto the van for the coast because they were all suffering from the trauma. Arnold couldn't deal with the situation and take care of the families at the same time. He would have loved to do more for Christy, but there was nothing he could do besides return her husband's corpse to her. At least once she got back home, she could give him a decent burial.

Father Robert, after giving Arnold all the information he possibly could, decided to go along with the families to the coast to later board the ship back home for 'a well-deserved break', as he put it. With that same van, Arnold sent word for more ammunition and reinforcement. He had no idea what he would have to deal with so preferred to have as many soldiers as he could on the ground. He also sent home the few surviving soldiers, most of whom were too traumatised to stay but managed to get some more information about the kingdom before they left.

Since all the cobras who could speak the native language were either dead or sent off by Arnold, the cobras went around cleaning up the administrative building themselves and digging mass graves for the corpses of the natives they found there.

After about a week, a few people started coming out of their hiding places. One or two people approached the administrative building to peep but ran off whenever they were beckoned. Remembering Father Robert mentioning a Fidelis and showing him the place around which he lived, Arnold decided to make this person his first point of contact.

'Fidelis!' Arnold shouted out when he got around the neighbourhood that was still littered with corpses. He could hear people in the houses stop moving and even feel them watching him, so he added, 'Father Robert told me you're a good friend of his. He said if I needed help, I could come to you.'

There was silence for a few minutes, and then a door cracked open, and a young man stepped out, holding his right elbow in his left hand behind his back with an expression of uncertainty.

Arnold tucked his gun back and moved slowly towards him. 'Fidelis?'

'Yes, bass.'

'Yes who?'

Fidelis stepped back, quickly his expression of uncertainty turning to fear, thinking he must have said the wrong thing.

Realising he had said the wrong thing, Arnold added, 'OK, OK, don't be afraid. Come forward. We need to talk, you and I.'

Fidelis fed Arnold the information as he ate hungrily. Arnold asked many questions, and Fidelis answered between mouthfuls and offered much more. Arnold had his cook pack a large pack for Fidelis to take home and asked him to be back the next morning.

'Well, Father Robert did prove to be of some use after all, telling us about this fellow,' he said when Fidelis left the house. 'After all that has happened, we couldn't have run this place without that kind of information, especially about Cornell, which brings me to think we will have to change strategy.'

* * *

In the week Arnold and his cobras were busy gathering up corpses of their own, Makafu and his priests had been doing the same thing. The corpses of King Ottuwa and Queen Aruma had already been brought to him by the priests. The bodies of important commanders, particularly the *afomi*, were never left to rot in the battlefield; they were always taken to the secret cave and preserved there. Makafu had seen Vumanga carry Abimi's and Wandi's bodies to the cave, so he sent his priest to collect them and bring Uwa along. He couldn't ask for Abimi's matriarch because the woman was a convert who, now convinced she should be the only wife, had set about causing mayhem in Abimi's household. He couldn't summon any of Abimi's children either because they were at war with one another about their father's property and over birthrights.

Three rituals needed to be performed, one for Ottuwa and Aruma, one for Wandi, and one for Abimi since, even though they were close, came from two separate lineages. The corpses were prepared and the burial sites drawn out around the shrine. The ritual for the two warriors would last seven days, but the one for Ottuwa would last nine days. This, because of their different ranks, according to Baluma spirituality. Makafu prepared to determine Ottuwa's successor on the ninth day, along with the burial.

He filled his calabash with fresh water, poured a powder into it, set it on the altar, drew out an enneagram around it, placed the ornaments in the required places, and held Ottuwa's staff above the calabash. The other priests joined him in a circle around everything, and the session began, with Uwa in the back.

The mantle fled on Kazi. Through the water in the calabash, he could see that the boy was still too young and with no knowledge of Baluma spirituality. He would need to find a priest to guard and groom the boy and an interim to run the kingdom in the meanwhile.

Makafu poured out the water in his calabash, refilled the calabash with muddy water, took the king's ring, and dropped into the water. After the prayers were said, Makafu put the tip of the staff into the water. The water cleared up and revealed a distant cousin of Ottuwa: Sigue, a noble from the Ngui, very wealthy and very influential who, despite not being an orator, always managed to get his points across concisely and understandably.

It was hard to find a successor amongst Wandi's living children. The one the ancestors had pointed to had died prematurely in the battle. The next one pointed out was a blossoming child with a radiant aura but still had a lot of growing to do. Makafu told Uwa she would have to be a patient matriarch and stay alive to coach the successor as Wandi would have done. He handed Wandi's ornaments to her for her keeping.

The next ritual was impossible to perform. There was too much commotion in Abimi's family and too many conflicting auras, with some wives using poisonous herbs and others performing different evil rituals against the others. Ever since they were introduced to the concept of an only wife, each wife wanted to be that *only* wife. Consequently, each group of children wanted to be the *only* successors to their father's property.

The water in the calabash just kept on swirling around and never settling. Makafu ordered one of his priests to assist Abimi's family until the storm passed, and at that point, he would re-perform the ritual to determine the successor, so he kept Abimi's ornaments with him for that reason and simply performed the burial rites.

In seven years, they would return to unearth the graves of Wandi and Abimi and extract the skulls to hand over to the successors and, two years after that, do the same for King Ottuwa.

* * *

The people were beginning to starve and desperately needed to get back to the farms and their normal livelihood, but the problem was that there were too many corpses around, too much fear and uncertainty, and no leadership. With the spread of the news that both Wandi and

Abimi had been killed, most of the warriors who hadn't died fighting, had either given up and returned home or run back into the forest.

Arnold needed the kingdom cleaned up of the corpses because the whole place stank of the rot of decaying bodies. He needed a native leader to get the people to do it and found one in Fidelis, who could communicate with both the people and his soldiers.

Most families had lost at least two or more members in the war. Crops had been burnt up as the warriors set fire to the plantations and other buildings. As destitute as the people were, they held certain spiritual beliefs that took precedence over their suffering and made the task of cleaning up excruciating for Arnold. Their spiritual beliefs did not allow them to touch bodies that were already in such a degraded state of deterioration. They needed to get people they called 'buriers' to get the bodies together and then bring the priests in to perform rituals of cleansing, which involved sacrifices of animals they did not have, to purify the land and appease their ancestors because the blood-soaked soil angered the ancestors. Neither Arnold nor any of his men could bear the stench any longer, so Arnold gave in to the people's demands and got the necessary animals for sacrifice and everything else necessary for the 'buriers' and priests to perform the rituals.

Two weeks later, the land was cleaned up, and as the people resumed their livelihoods, Arnold could finally begin to establish his administration. Fidelis easily recruited workers, and even though the church was not yet functional, the catechist held prayer sessions every day and made more and more converts by the day so that when Father Robert returned, a triumphant welcome was prepared for him. Life began to blossom again in Lumani, and Fidelis, as the newly appointed foreman, recruited large numbers of his friends from church and even beyond, like Ndikwa.

No one seemed to talk anymore about the warriors; it became a taboo subject. The few warriors who still had fire in their hearts abandoned their families and retreated to Njuu. The forced labour was resumed, this time with little resistance from the Baluma. More cobras came to settle over time, and the plantations and schools resumed as before. The people never forgot their culture and traditions but weren't beholden to them any longer as they were before. Makafu and his priest now lived permanently in the forest, so getting to them was tedious for the people. Because Sigue was only interim king, he did not have as much authority as a king would have had, neither in the Ngui nor amongst the people. Cultural festivals were no longer celebrated with as much merriment. Parents instead fought to send their children to school, where baptism was obligatory. The young people were growing up with less and less knowledge of their culture and more and more knowledge of whatever the cobra was teaching.

Arnold didn't have as tough a task as he had expected to run the kingdom. Sigue was totally cooperative (because in exchange, Arnold offered to let him continue his trade without paying any taxes to the cobra administration). Together with the help of a close informant in the Ngui, Arnold could keep an eye on everybody else who could be a threat. For example, he was informed that Ottuwa had a son who had disappeared after his father and mother had died. The other children had stayed in the palace with their mothers and were now in the care of Sigue. Arnold figured out that if none of Ottuwa's other children had been enthroned as king, it could only mean that Ottuwa's successor was the child who had disappeared. He therefore made Fidelis keep a keen eye on Sigue and everybody in the palace so that if the child ever returned, he would *know what to do*. Arnold was also aware of the fact that there were warriors who had survived the battle that had claimed the lives of almost all the soldiers and that some of the warriors had set up a camp in the forest to launch attacks.

Fidelis was instrumental in recruiting spies to identify the families of the warriors and where they lived so that when the warriors returned to their families, as they did occasionally, Arnold would arrange to have them arrested and killed quietly without causing any anxiety amongst the people. Arnold was also aware of Ottuwa's manner of poisoning the cocoa and coffee, so he had the work in the plantations strictly supervised to prevent Sigue from getting any ideas. Arnold was doing a good job for the cobras back home. They were impressed with his results and sent more ammunition and soldiers to support him.

Yem prepared to go north. He needed more cows to feed the increasing need in Yaketu and didn't trust his assistant Jonas to get the job done properly. He had spent a huge sum to send Jonas north the last time, but that dull fellow had returned with ill-bred cows, and on close inspection, most were sick. Had it not been for his cunning, he would never have been able to resell the cows. He was getting older and weaker and needed somebody to do the runaround jobs for him but couldn't find a suitable person. He had tried to train his sons, but each had proven useless. In Yem's opinion, they had to have inherited their mothers' genes; such laziness couldn't have come from him.

He wrapped up his luggage meticulously, ensuring they were tightly bound, and then took a bath and set about preparing himself for the journey, wrapping himself with several pieces of cloth and jewellery. In truth, Yem was a very vain man who wore more jewellery than all his wives put together. It was as if for every necklace or bracelet he bought for any of his wives, he bought two for himself. Yem always wore at least six rings on his short stumpy fingers. He was still fitting on his jewellery and admiring his outfit when one of his helps came with news from Lumani. Yem finished dressing up and sent for Nsika.

'I should be back by month end, just in time to take you both to school myself. We will monitor the situation in Lumani, and if things continue to be calm, you can go and see Uwa and your grandmother during the school break. In the meantime, you stay here with me.'

Nsika told Yem about the little 'job' he used to do for Wandi.

'We will talk about that when I return. I will teach you how to use it to make money.'

* * *

'What's your name?'

'Balumakazi, but they call me Kazi.'

'Surname?'

Kazi was confused. He didn't know what that meant. He looked up at Yem beside him, holding his hand.

'Yemumi,' Yem answered.

And so Kazi got registered as Balumakazi Yemumi. The middle-aged woman filled in the register, took out a school bag from the box beside, put in two books and a few other accessories like pens, pencils, a ruler, and an eraser, and handed it to Kazi. She waved them aside to receive the next on the queue.

Yem took Kazi to the next office, where the teacher gave Kazi a classroom and a seat number. The teacher led them towards the classrooms and then told Yem he couldn't go beyond a certain point. Kazi wouldn't move a step farther until Yem assured him it was all right and that he would be properly taken care of.

The class was noisy, and the first day was very confusing and difficult for Kazi. It was the first time he was meeting so many of his peers all at once and in the same room (as a little prince, particularly one who was his mother's heartbeat and his father's breath, he was secluded from the rest of the children). Kazi was glad when the day was over.

However, true to himself, by the end of the week, Kazi was the most famous pupil in class. Kazi was good at sports and arithmetic and talked so interestingly about school whenever he came home that Mandara was determined that Ndana (her first daughter who was a year younger than Kazi) would start the following year.

Nsika too began classes in the same school (with the name Nsika Yemumi), but his classroom was two blocks away from Kazi, which meant that they could only meet at break time. Nsika improved his understanding of the cobra's language and learnt to write it as well. He also loved drawing and painting.

At the end of the first trimester, they were given a break for the Christmas season. Both had done well in school, so Mandara killed a large chicken for them. Nsika seized the opportunity that break to see Yem about returning to Lumani to see Uwa and Mama Sawa.

Yem had just received news from Lumani that the situation was calm, and he told Nsika so but added, 'Experience has thought me that the water in which a crocodile swims is always very calm on the surface.'

Yem arranged for Nsika to go back to Lumani with a very good plan on his mind. 'If you go back to Lumani as you went, you will make yourself an easy target for the cobras because we natives don't just travel such distances for courtesy visits. You need a disguise. You will therefore go to Lumani as a trader. If this trip goes as planned, we can establish trade between Lumani and Yaketu and use that as a pipeline for information. We get information and make money at the same time.' His eyes glittered as he thought of the greater prospects within their reach.

Yem gave Nsika everything he needed to look like a trader: goods for sale, one or two servants, a donkey, a herd of cattle, and so on. Nsika had begun to develop a beard by now, so the part of a young trader suited him well. Mandara made him promise to return soon. Nsika and Kazi had become like the sons she didn't have.

Kazi was sad that he couldn't make the journey with Nsika and wasn't satisfied with the answer of 'It's too dangerous'. He was eager to see his parents again and his brothers and sisters. He wouldn't bid Nsika goodbye and kept to his room the whole day, only coming out to eat when Ndana persuaded him to.

When he got back from lunch, Kazi lay down on his bed and tried to sleep, but there was a hard bump on the side of the bed that made it uncomfortable to sleep. He decided to get whatever it was out of there, so he got out of bed and pulled up the mattress. It was the gourd of water that he and Nsika had used on their journey to Yaketu and a dagger that he immediately recognised, the dagger Wandi had used to train him. He took both items out and sat beside the bed, staring at them. For the first time, he noticed an inscription on the dagger: *The warrior who stands first.*

His young mind raced. Nsika had told him early that morning that he had something to give him, but he had told Nsika off for leaving for Lumani without him and slammed the door on his way out. Nsika had called after him, saying it was important, but he hadn't wanted to listen. He remembered Wandi muttering something about a dagger before Nsika picked him up that evening and fled but couldn't remember exactly what. In Baluma, ornaments like these were never passed down until death. Kazi shuddered at the thought that his Papa Wandi may have been killed. He stubbornly dismissed the idea and put the dagger and gourd down on the bed beside his pillow and slept.

Wandi stormed into the room. *'Put the dagger and gourd in a safe place and make sure nobody finds them, silly boy!'*

Kazi woke up and did as he had been told.

* * *

Christmas was a busy period in Yaketu and especially busy for Yem since that was the period when he made the greatest turnover as usual from swindling the cobras of their money. He had chickens, cows, and eggs and all sorts of other products for sale. Kazi usually helped Mandara around the house, but this time, noticing Kazi was doing well in arithmetic, Yem decided he could make use of the boy's skills and asked Mandara to let Kazi help him instead.

He took the boy to his different stalls in the market and introduced him to all his traders. The boy would go around counting the stock every morning and evening and bring him an account. That way, Yem had a good pair of eyes on his stock. When Yem thought Kazi had learnt enough, he taught him how to trade, about profit margins and break-even points. Kazi learnt eagerly. It seemed to him like a straightforward process. Yem also taught Kazi about supply and demand and the age-old trick of withholding goods to cause a scarcity and then supplying the goods at a later date at higher prices.

When the time came, Yem told Kazi about his next project: the sale of a few cows to some cobras. 'Kazi, you say nothing the whole while, but watch what I do and how I handle things. When we return, you can ask me all the questions you want.'

'Yes, Papa,' Kazi answered as enthusiastically as usual.

By the time Kazi had woken, Yem had been up for almost an hour before him. Kazi went straight to the barn where he knew he would find Yem, and he did. Yem was *working* on the cows and chickens. Kazi asked him why they needed to be up so early since they had arranged to meet the cobras at noon.

'Shhh, this is important for the trade. Now be quiet and watch me closely,' he answered as he poured out more grain and water for the chickens.

Yem inspected the cows and sprinkled some dried herbs into the water. Kazi couldn't understand but helped. A few hours later, Yem began to weigh the chickens and later inspected the cows. The chickens had almost tripled in weight, and the cows were bloated in the stomach, making them look twice fatter than they actually were. He then went around marking the chickens and the cows for sale and preparing the cages for the chickens. He let his servants continue that task with instructions to keep feeding the chickens and cows.

'But, Papa, why do we have to make them look that way? They are much bigger than they actually are,' Kazi asked innocently.

'*Shhh*. By the end of the trading day, you would have understood. I said be quiet and watch me closely.'

And Kazi obeyed religiously.

They got to the cobras' residences by exactly noon, accompanied by a few servants. The bargaining began with Yem escalating the prices and complaining about how expensive chicken and cow feed were. The cobras bargained as best they could but still settled for a price six times the price of a well-fed cow (and these ones were not). The bargain for the chickens went pretty much in the same manner. As if they were bewitched, the cobras asked for eggs and milk, which Yem readily had for sale.

When they had settled on a price for a particular number of eggs and amount of milk, Yem asked his servant to have the eggs and milk brought. The cobras didn't count the eggs before paying, and Yem knew they wouldn't; neither did they know the difference between freshly squeezed milk and stale diluted milk. When Yem signalled the servant, the servant knew exactly what to do – give them half the number of fresh eggs they had agreed on and make up the difference with the rest of the rotten eggs they knew they couldn't sell in the open market, take out all the stale milk they couldn't sell and dilute it with water, and stir in soya powder for flavour to make the sale. The animals were untied and taken to the cobras' barn, the eggs and milk delivered to the cobras' kitchens, and the money paid, and Yem and the cobras held a toast to a wonderful Christmas season. Kazi was scandalised at Yem's crookery.

On their way back, Kazi asked, 'Papa, is that how it should... um, I mean, that was not right. We cheated them. Is that, er, how things should happen in business?' he finally coughed out.

'Like I said, be quiet and watch me closely.' Yem walked ahead of him and onwards as if ignoring him.

Kazi was devastated by Yem's attitude and couldn't digest it anymore. 'Papa, I want to learn from you, but I don't feel right about this, so tell me, is that *really* how business works? Do we need to cheat the people we sell to?'

'It depends on who you are selling to. When it's the cobras, then it is OK. When it is our own people, we cheat less. Stay close, and you will learn how to do *this* business. This is our own way of making the cobras repay a small portion of what they are taking from us. *This* is the way to make money, my son.'

'But why do we need to make money? Why can't we just trade with them as we always do?'

'You need to learn very fast that the language of the cobra is currency. Without currency, you are nothing in the eyes of a cobra.'

'Yes, Papa,' Kazi said, not quite sure if he wanted to learn how to make money anymore, much less *this* manner of making it.

'You need to start drinking palm wine. It is time for you to become a man,' Yem said, fixing his loincloth tightly onto his shoulders.

When the festive season was over, Kazi returned to school, missing Nsika.

* * *

Even though Nsika was bearded and differently dressed, Mama Sawa still recognised him when he walked into the compound. Nsika ran and hugged his crying grandmother. She looked frail but well. Uwa, on the other hand, couldn't tell who it was until he got really close. Uwa looked twenty years older than she had the last time he saw her; the loss of Wandi and her mother later on had withered her. Mama Sawa had been of great support to her during that period.

They sat down and told Nsika all of it and what had happened in Lumani ever since: the fall of the resistance after Wandi and Abimi's deaths, the change of administration and the new cobras, and the new foreman, Fidelis, who had been very kind to them and always came around to see how they were faring and had even persuaded them to enrol the children into school.

At the mention of the name Fidelis, Nsika jerked. He told them about Fidelis and how he had served as a spy for Cornell and informed on Wandi. At first, Mama Sawa and Uwa would not believe it, but as he gave details on Kamuel, Cornell, and Cornelius, they began to connect the dots. Fidelis, whom they had never known before, had been so sympathetic to the family, and they had drawn him so close that they had even invited him to secret family discussions where they had talked about the warriors in the forest and the flight of Nsika in his presence.

Uwa had noticed Fidelis's keenness in listening but simply thought he was concerned for them. She had poured her heart out to Fidelis during her period of mourning and had talked about certain warriors and their families who later on disappeared or met with strange accidents, Mama Sawa had grumbled about the warriors in the Njuu not doing enough to protect the people from the cobras, and on and on it had gone. They then realized that the trend was that every time they had spoken to Fidelis, the situation had only got worse.

Mama Sawa wasn't sure how they should react because if, as she said, they showed any suspicion, the next time that Fidelis turned up, he could have them killed, but at the same time, she was so emotional, she wasn't sure she could conceal her anger and resentment. They needed to hatch a plan before Fidelis showed up at the house the next time (and that could be anytime).

Uwa and Nsika were thinking about a solution when a loud 'Is anybody home?' came from the doorway. Fidelis walked in, smiling brightly as he always did. 'Good afternoon, Mama. I noticed you had a guest, so I came to greet him.'

The spy in Nsika came alive. 'Fidelis! It's me, Nsika,' he said and threw his arms out.

Fidelis was taken completely aback. 'Nsika? The same one who worked with Master Kamuel?'

'Yes, the same one.'

Mama Sawa couldn't bear it.

'Let me take Mama Sawa to bed. She is not feeling very well. I will be back. We have a lot to catch up on,' Nsika said quickly before she could let anything out and took his grandmother out to her own house.

Uwa sat there quietly and gracefully, asking after Fidelis's family as usual and offered him something to eat. Being married to a warrior turned guerrilla for thirty-seven years had refined her nerves for this kind of scenario. She understood Nsika's game and played along, never giving off the slightest hint.

When Nsika got back, he joined Fidelis at table and spoke at length about how he had had to hide Mama Sawa on that fateful night and flee for his life. He told a story of how he had met and began working for a trader who had been very kind to him and who, after a few months, had lent him some money to begin his own business. He now lived permanently in the Fefe kingdom. The goods he had brought were partly for sale and partly for the family, and for old times' sake, he offered Fidelis a goat from the herd he had brought. Fidelis felt smaller and smaller as Nsika bragged about his growing business.

Not to be left behind, he told Nsika about his work with the cobras, how he was in charge of the whole kingdom, and how even the interim king called him 'sir'. He only missed that he would have loved for a *real* king to bow to him; that the interim bowed was not satisfactory enough. Fidelis also gave off that he couldn't wait for the real successor to be crowned because it was the first time in Baluma that they had an interim. 'They made us feel like their servants. Now we have the chance to make them kneel to us and beg for mercy as they made us.'

Nsika gave him a look of such admiration as he spoke that he continued on, talking about how feared he was. He could make people disappear or order for their deaths. He spoke of the fact that he had direct audience with the cobra in charge: the big bass, Master Arnold.

Nsika concluded that they had both done well since the war and that they should remain friends to help each other. Fidelis went off with his goat, promising to protect Nsika's family at any cost, and Nsika promised in turn to come for trade more often in Lumani in spite of his success abroad.

Nsika returned to Uwa after seeing Fidelis off. She held out a grey handkerchief that she had pulled from Fidelis's side pocket as he sat beside her.

'I will take this to Makafu tomorrow night,' she said with an embittered look on her face.

Nsika came to her side and held her as she cried. 'I'll go with you.'

'No. If you come, you'll draw too much attention. The guards wouldn't bother much with an old woman.'

Nsika couldn't sleep that night, ruminating over the conversation he had had with Fidelis. He knew Fidelis to be a traitor but not to this extent. With all this treachery, where did he expect his body to be buried? The Baluma had a very strict culture concerning traitors. When they died, they were burnt and the ashes scattered into the Akiki River. That was why the tides in the Akiki were never stable. The goddess of the river received the ashes of the traitors and punished their souls for eternity. Surely, Fidelis knew that.

* * *

Through the calabash, Makafu could see her coming and sent his young apprentice out to get her. The apprentice met her with a calabash of cold water at the last brook that separated the shrine from the forest as she struggled to get across. It was as if she was summoning all the strength she had in her bones to step on one stone after the other. In two hops, he was at her side and helped her over the brook, sat her down, and let her drink before holding her up and helping her to the shrine.

'Was it not enough that they took my husband? Now they have sent a snake into my house?'

'I know, and I will deal with him,' Makafu offered, trying to calm her.

Makafu and Uwa had only met for the first time when he had summoned her for the ritual of Wandi. He had been amazed at her aura. She was stronger than any priestess he had ever met, and yet she wasn't one of them. Her strength had calmed his heart upon meeting her. Uwa had never come to Makafu ever since Wandi's burial, and she had not surprisingly accepted his passing with such grace and strength that when he saw her through his calabash with a disturbed aura, he knew there was something terribly wrong.

'Kill him.' Uwa held out the handkerchief.

Makafu tilted his head pleadingly. 'But we can simply make him sick. The cobras will have no use for him then.'

'That is what my husband would have said. For all his mercy and goodness, they still left me a widow. Kill him, or I will do it myself.'

'The cobras will replace him with someone else in no time. Why don't we use him?'

'We will use the next one! Kill this one.'

Uwa was ordering at this point, and Makafu knew he had no choice. He took the handkerchief from her, tore it into three pieces, and set it on the altar to conduct the ritual.

Nsika stepped in just after the final prayers were said. He had dodged his way through Arnold's forest guards and wiggled through the priests on guard at the entrance to Makafu's shrine by telling them that Uwa had asked him to follow her but that he had got the news late.

'I asked you to stay back. You will draw attention to us.'

'Papa didn't ask me to obey you. He asked me to protect you. Besides, I didn't draw any attention. He taught me well.'

Uwa didn't have the time or energy to argue with Nsika. 'Is it done?' she asked Makafu.

'Yes.'

'Let me see.'

Makafu gave her some water to wash her eyes and let her look into his calabash (a favour he never did for anybody, but then Nsika was not the only one Wandi had asked to protect Uwa and his family). Uwa handed the calabash back to Makafu, satisfied with what she had seen, and let Nsika take her home when he was done talking with Makafu.

During the week, Nsika decided it would be best to stay with Mama Sawa and Uwa for longer than they had agreed under the pretext of selling off his goods to collect more information. Staying with Uwa and Mama Sawa, he learnt about the warriors in Njuu and gathered information from all angles and, as much as he dreaded it, even attended church sessions for this same reason. He didn't have his Papa Wandi to guide him anymore but had learnt enough in the few years being with him. In the months that followed, Nsika and Uwa were inseparable. She taught him a lot more about espionage than he had learnt through the few years of working in Kamuel's house.

He lured Fidelis close for information, but meeting Ndikwa again was tricky. He kept on dodging because he wasn't sure what face to put up. He had once showed Ndikwa who he really was, and they had made sincere friends, but times and things had changed. He had seen Ndikwa several times in a distance but always found a convenient excuse whenever Fidelis asked for them to meet. But he knew he couldn't keep up the pretence for too long because at some point, Fidelis would get suspicious.

'Why don't we have a drink together? All three of us, for old times' sake.'

'Who is the third person?' Fidelis asked.

'Ndikwa. I have been meaning to see him for so long but never had the time. Now that I have sold all I came to sell, I have enough time for us to catch up.'

'You mean Michael?'

'Oh yes, Michael, but then you know I never converted, so remembering the Christian name would be a challenge,' Nsika covered up, wondering what Fidelis meant by insisting on Ndikwa's Christian name.

When they met the next evening, Nsika could not believe his eyes. Ndikwa looked as if he bore the problems of everybody in Lumani on his two shoulders. He had also grown a beard and some muscles so that he looked physically healthy, but there was a sadness in his eyes that even a bright smile upon seeing Nsika again and loud laughter from cracking jokes could not conceal. Still, given the environment, Nsika was not sure on whose side Ndikwa was, so he decided to stay safe, calling him Michael and asking about his 'achievements' since the battle. Fidelis left them for about an hour to attend to an urgent call from his *bass*. Ndikwa, without any forewarning, began to talk in a hushed voice about life since the battle.

'When Fidelis asked me to work with him, I thought the work was simple and straightforward, to re-establish order and help the people with their daily lives, but the job got dirtier and dirtier. We snitch on people and report them to the master, and terrible things happen to them. At some point, when I couldn't take it any longer, I told Fidelis, and that was when it all started. Papa and Mama had died during the battle, so it fell on me to take care of my three younger sisters. Fidelis, whom I thought to be my brother, threatened to do bad things to my sisters if I didn't cooperate. I tried as much as I could, warning people in secret, helping them escape when things got really bad, and keeping as much information from Fidelis as I possibly could. Working every day with Fidelis for his master and against my own people is tearing me to bits, but I have no choice. He has made me do terrible things, Nsika. I cannot even begin to tell you. I will go to my grave a traitor. Our ancestors will not accept me, and my body will be burnt and my ashes scattered on the Akiki. I am willing to go through that if that will keep my sisters safe. Once they are married, I will flee Lumani forever to avoid the disgrace.'

Nsika stayed still and quiet all the while because he was considering two possibilities. One, Ndikwa was being Ndikwa, and the other, Michael was acting on behalf of Fidelis. Seeing the sincerity in Ndikwa's eyes, he was tempted to believe the former but, for prudence's sake, chose to act like the second.

He gulped his palm wine down and said, 'You are doing great work here.'

'But of course, he wouldn't be my assistant if he was not the best at his job.' Fidelis rejoined them.

An idea sparked in Nsika's mind. 'Michael, I will need a gun and maybe a bow and arrow or two. I need to go hunting tomorrow to take some Lumani meat back to sell in Fefe.'

'I will give you what you need tomorrow morning. What time do you intend to start off?'

'The afternoon seems like a good time, so we can meet in the morning.'

'Yes. Are you still staying at Mama Sawa's in the next clan?'

'Yes, yes.'

'See you in the morning then.' Ndikwa made his excuses and left.

Fidelis and Nsika shared another pint of palm wine before parting for the night.

* * *

'Let me show you the way into the best parts of the forest for hunting.'

'Don't be so worried about me. I'll know. I grew up here, you know.'

'I mean the place is surrounded by soldiers. If I am with you, they will let us by without any questions.'

'OK, let me get dressed.'

As they walked through to the forest, everything he came across was exactly as Uwa had said it would be. They came across several soldiers. There were two on guard almost every ten trees. Arnold had completely secured the periphery of the kingdom so that the warriors in Njuu had such a tough time breaking through the different lines of defence that they could not make any significant attacks on Lumani without being caught and summarily dealt with.

The interesting thing about Arnold's administration was that he did not carry out any public executions or punishing to give the people the impression of normality around the kingdom. However, there were so many disappearances that the people developed an incredulity towards one another that was fast becoming a life pattern. At gatherings, people talked in proverbs and told stories that were extremely ambiguous so that even those involved in the conversation were most often at a loss on whose side the speaker was on. It went without saying that some people took advantage of this situation of extreme wariness to either settle old scores or amass wealth for themselves by ratting on others or just plainly and simply making up false tales. Part of the reason Ndikwa could not forgive himself was the fact that Fidelis, in order to enrich himself, had made up stories about a few influential men and had made him testify as his witness.

'Forgive me, Nsika,' Ndikwa said, breaking the silence.

'But you have done nothing wrong, Michael.'

'You wouldn't be calling me Michael if you trusted me.'

'That's what I heard you're called, and I didn't want to offend you.'

'Cut it out, Nsika. I know you better than that. You didn't fool me, you know. I knew you were spying for Pa Wandi at Kamuel's place. I never mentioned it because I knew you would deny it, and I understood that but hoped that one day you would trust me enough to talk about it. Nsika, I am not asking you to confess anything to me or even to trust me. I am just asking you to help me if you can and in any way you can. I have three sisters whom I need to protect. I cannot run out of here and leave them behind because we both know that that hyena will feed on them. We all need to escape together, and if it comes to the push, I prefer for them to escape. That way, I can stay back and face the cobras. I will deserve whatever death they sanction me to. I am a traitor and deserve to die like one. Nsika, if you can help me, say so now or let me look for hope elsewhere.'

'What is your name?' It was a trap question from Nsika.

'Ndikwa,' Ndikwa said, understanding the coded language.

'Tell me something you know that I don't. Then I might think about what you have said.'

'I will tell you two things. First of all, there is a traitor in the Ngui, Pa Utatu. He has been feeding information to the cobras. What I am not sure of is for how long and on what he has been snitching, but I know for a fact that he informed them on the warriors in Njuu and their families. Second, that witty cobra has a kill order out on Balumakazi, the son of King Ottuwa. If you find him or anybody whom you think might know where he is, tell them not to let him return. Rumour amongst the cobras is that the boy is successor to King Ottuwa. They say we can identify him by a mark that would have been imprinted on his chest below his left breast if he is successor. From what Fidelis tells me, Pa Utatu also informed that this Balumakazi was taken to safety before the battle. The cobras have combed the whole kingdom but found nothing. This is why everybody in the cobras' circle is on alert for the boy or anybody who would have the mark. King Ottuwa's family is being closely watched by Fidelis and his crew, including me.'

'We missed an antelope,' Nsika said, attempting to divert the conversation.

'We will miss many others if you don't help me, Nsika.' Ndikwa was desperate.

'What do you want?'

'To get my sisters and myself out of this kingdom.'

After a longer pause and Ndikwa's glaring eyes, Nsika said, 'I can take your sisters with me, but only the ancestors know what will happen to you after that.'

'Take my sisters. I deserve whatever will come to me.'

'Show me to Njuu.'

'We can't go there, not today and not with me, but I can give you directions.'

They hunted the whole day and returned home with two antelopes and three bush pigs. When they had set the animals for smoking for the journey, Nsika took his chances.

'Let's say I take your sisters for a visit to Yaketu.'

It was neither a statement nor a question, but Ndikwa understood. 'Not Fefe?'

'No, that was meant for Fidelis.'

Ndikwa was so grateful for the vote of confidence that his eyes teared up. When they hugged, they both knew they had not changed from who they were when they shared those meals of roasted cassava and palm oil at Mama Sawa's.

* * *

When Nsika arrived with the three young ladies, Yem raised his eyebrows. 'I don't remember this part of the agreement.'

Nsika cut in. 'They are my sisters, Papa, not my wives, I brought them to see Yaketu, especially to meet you.'

He told Yem about the favour he was doing for Ndikwa, the search for Kazi, how things had changed in Lumani, and that he would go to Njuu to make contact with the warriors. His plan was to enter Njuu from the other side because as things were, nobody could get to Njuu from Lumani unnoticed, and Arnold had his eyes and ears everywhere. It would mean a longer and more dangerous journey.

Yem decided that Nsika's plan was good but needed refining. The girls were put up in one of Yem's many houses around the compound and registered in school a few weeks later.

Kazi was ecstatic seeing Nsika again. He had missed him so much that all was forgiven and forgotten. He told Nsika what had happened after he had left, from the ornaments under his mattress to Yem's crookery and everything happening in school day by day. He was disappointed that Nsika wouldn't be returning to school with him but was grateful he would be seeing Nsika more often. He asked after his parents, his stepmothers, and his brothers and sisters, but Nsika evaded the questions cleverly.

* * *

'Did you really think I wouldn't find out?' Fidelis said, cleaning his gun.

'Find out what?' Ndikwa tried to look puzzled.

'Your sisters left with Nsika.'

'They will be back before school resumes. They haven't left for good.'

'Are you lying to me, Michael?'

'Why would I want to do a thing that could cost me my life?'

'If they aren't back by the time school resumes, what do you think I should do?'

'Strangle me, for example.' He had seen Fidelis do that on numerous occasions.

Ndikwa wondered whether this was the moment he should turn on Fidelis. It had been three days since Nsika had left. They must have arrived at Yaketu by now, so he had nothing to fear anymore. The only thing that worried him was what would happen to Nsika the next time he returned to Lumani. Ndikwa decided that he needed to take Fidelis along with him to his grave.

The end of the week was a good time. Once he had finished his supervision of the plantations for the week and given Fidelis an account, he would sneak into Fidelis's house and wait for him to return home. Usually, Fidelis was drunk when he returned home on Friday evenings because he spent them drinking with his master. That would make Ndikwa's task easier. He could kill him quietly in his room, and everyone would blame the liquor.

Ndikwa finished up his work, reported to Fidelis and left, waited a few hours, and then sneaked into Fidelis's house and into his room as planned. The moon cast a ray of light into the room, but it was still dark enough. Ndikwa chose a good corner in the darkest area and waited. He ignored the stale blood smell around the room because Fidelis, being a murderer, usually had that same pungent stench around him after doing special 'tasks' for his master. Standing there in the small dirty space behind the cupboard, he asked his mother to forgive him for what he was about to do. He had become a different man from what she had taught him to be but not out of choice.

Fidelis was taking long to return, so he distracted himself with thoughts of meeting his father again in the land of the ancestors and marvelled at what the place may look like. As he was growing up, before his parents had converted to Christianity, they had always taught him that the land of the ancestors was a land of eternal peace and rest where only those whose lives on this earth the ancestors were pleased with were welcomed. That thought discomforted Ndikwa, so he tried to stop his thoughts at that.

The smell of blood was so pungent now that he couldn't breathe properly any longer. He moved slowly to the window beside him to let his nose out. The smell at the window, which was near the bed, was even more pungent, so he followed the smell, and it led him to the bed.

Lying there was Fidelis, motionless. Ndikwa put his hand to Fidelis's heart but couldn't get a beat. When he shook him violently and still got no response, he turned the lights on. The bed was soaked in blood.

Ndikwa turned Fidelis's body over to see three deep wounds cut in his back. Turning off the lights, he replaced the body, opened the door of the room quietly, and hurried out of the house, making sure to leave everything in its place as it had been when he arrived. He held his breath as he made his way back to his house, trying not to walk too fast to arouse suspicion, and only breathed again when he got home and had locked his door properly.

Ndikwa had gone to Fidelis to kill him, but somebody had gone ahead of him. He couldn't figure out who or for what reason. In Lumani, that kind of a death was only reserved for somebody who had betrayed his family profoundly. Ndikwa knew Fidelis had spent the last year betraying and killing everybody around him but couldn't think of anybody or family in particular whom Fidelis was that close to.

In his little house, it was difficult to feel alone, so he kept on checking. He finally lay down but couldn't find any sleep, so he woke and packed. When the soft cool breeze of the early morning began to whisper, he picked up his small pack and, walking down the lonely paths of dew-wet grass, made his way to Yaketu.

* * *

Nsika poured the fresh cool water over his head and shoulders and looked up to the sky. They had been riding on those bicycles for quite a few days, and his waist was hurting badly. Ndikwa had joined him in Yaketu a week later, and they had spent the next few weeks planning this trip and months preparing for it. They needed to get in contact with the warriors in Njuu, but as Nsika had told Yem, getting to Njuu from Lumani was impossible. They needed to get there from the back. The forest was dangerous and almost impossible to cross for a mere human, but with the help of Yem, they were making it through. Both Nsika and Ndikwa had been surprised at how much Yem knew of Njuu and how well he could locate it and even tell them what they would need for the journey but didn't have the courage to ask him, and Yem hadn't offered any information to assuage their curiosity. In any case, they had followed Yem's directions to the letter, sleeping where he had asked them to and riding through the paths he had indicated.

By the morning of the third day, they were in Njuu. Neither Nsika nor Ndikwa had been to Njuu before. They had only heard of it growing up as the place the Baluma used to hide in the days of the slave takers. Nevertheless, they were determined to make contact with the warriors and rebuild the resistance or contribute in whatever way they could to take out the cobra administration.

They saw the hedges that Yem had described, put their bicycles aside, and walked towards them, slowly watching where they placed their feet each time until a hushed 'Nsika' came from beside him just when he was about to call out to Ndikwa.

They both had knives held to their throats. It was as if it had all happened while they had blinked. The secret code that Yem had given them didn't help much. They were dragged farther inwards and made to tell the story of how they had discovered that place and what they were there for. As they answered question after question, it became clearer and clearer that there was no real leader amongst the warriors. The warriors did seem to have a notion of ranks and a unified front but not of a centralised leadership around any single warrior. Nsika took advantage of that crack in the wall.

'Baluma is so subdued now with traitors behind every tree. What traitor in Lumani do you know would risk his life to make the journey to come around from the back?'

Now that was a question none of them had asked themselves yet. A few warriors grouped together for a moment to discuss the thought-provoking question, therefore exposing themselves for Nsika to count them all, six in total, and he took note of all their faces and made out that they were the decision makers.

Nsika and Ndikwa were unchained but not free to go. The two were questioned for a long time by the decision makers, who kept on interrupting one another until they were convinced the boys were on their side. The warriors were impressed that Nsika had known Wandi and admired Ndikwa's courage despite working for Fidelis (whom they all knew well) to try to help as many people as he could and then finally escaping.

There were deeply dividing factors amongst the warriors. One caste felt that they should brave Arnold's guards and attack immediately and insisted that the more time they wasted, the more time they gave the cobras to poison the people. There was another caste that believed that the best strategy would be to go back to Lumani, infiltrate the cobra's administration, and cause an implosion. Yet another caste held that continuing with the struggle was futile and that they should try to reach an agreement with the cobras; the only problem was finding the leverage with which they could negotiate. To add to this mayhem, discontented church workers and other faithful who had deserted the church and, as a consequence, had been ostracised had somehow joined the warriors in Njuu, bringing along with them new Christian perspectives on how the cobra could be overcome. All the attacks on Lumani attempted so far had been so weak and ineffective that the warriors were losing faith.

It followed that throughout the week the young men stayed with the warriors, integrating was not so easy because of the different factions, and taking one side or another in an argument could be a dangerous thing. Sometimes tensions rose so high that the warriors raised arms against each other. Who was on whose side was decided by the slightest of things or presumed body language, and even an occasional nod at a single statement a warrior made was enough to condemn one to one side or another.

The evening before they were to return to Yaketu, Nsika and Ndikwa decided to brave it. They met the six commanders Nsika had identified and tricked each one to coming for the meeting by telling them that the five others had agreed to come. When they met, Nsika tried his best to sound wise, talking about the importance of an espionage force and telling them of the days when he worked with Wandi and how much that helped in designing the attacks, not just in terms of the number of warriors that would be needed but also on where to attack and most importantly how to attack. Nsika advised about the importance of working with the high priest for spiritual strength and the importance of never going to war without the blessings of a priest and surprised Ndikwa and even himself with the amount of detail he had on Baluma spirituality.

The whole time he spoke, the warriors paid abounding attention and, when he was done, asked him to let them sleep over his idea and would let him know what they thought when he returned the next month as he had promised he would.

Nsika and Ndikwa went to bed with renewed hope.

* * *

Kolela Wa Leni was a very sickly child. He had bouts of severe pain in his stomach and chest and frequent fevers. He coughed painfully, and sometimes his legs or hands would swell inexplicably, or he would faint for no reason. He usually complained that there was not enough air in the room, especially when there were more than two or three people, and would prefer to breathe through his mouth to take in more air. His father, Tima Ko Leni (a renowned herbalist and priest), had similar problems breathing and also experienced pain in his chest and stomach although not as severe. After trying all the herbs he could on the boy with few positive results, he decided to take him to Makafu.

Kolela's problems were not spiritual, actually, but Makafu took the boy in because he understood Tima's plight. Kolela's mother had died in childbirth, and taking care of the sickly child was becoming tedious for even a very patient Tima. When the child's father was killed at the palace that afternoon before the battle, he knew he would have to raise the boy himself.

Kolela was stubborn but very adorable. He wanted to know everything and asked questions about everything. At the time he received the child, Makafu's shrine was still close to the main kingdom, but with the cobra invasion, Makafu had moved his shrine deeper into the forest, about seventy miles to the east of Njuu, which meant that there were no children around the shrine, so Kolela had no friends, but that did not deter him. He made up games that he would play by himself as if there was another person playing with him. Like most children, Kolela loved to play under the rain. The trouble was that because he was prone to infections, he couldn't play in the rain without being in bed sick for the next week. Makafu had to lock him in his room each time the clouds gathered to prevent him from going out.

Kolela was so stubborn that whenever Makafu wanted him to sit down, he would tell him to stand up (knowing he would do the exact opposite). It became such a game between the two that whenever the child took ill, Makafu would come to his bedside and ask him to remain in bed. That would make Kolela laugh and forget his pain for a few moments. In spite of how much trouble he gave, Makafu missed Kolela whenever he fell ill and prayed that he would soon be well if only to give him trouble.

As the boy grew older, he got physically stronger and healthier, and the bouts of pain and fevers became less and less frequent. Because of his fondness for Makafu, Kolela decided to learn about Baluma spirituality and made Makafu teach him. He was a good student and learnt fast. Makafu watched the boy mature spiritually, never forgetting any lesson Makafu taught him.

By the time Kolela was fourteen, he was ready to be initiated into the priestly order. Makafu hesitated and delayed the initiation rite because he had never initiated a person so young. However, a few months later, he was obliged to perform the rite when he realized the boy had attained a higher spiritual rank than most of his priests. Kolela could see things through the calabash with his naked eyes that Makafu needed to wash his eyes to see.

At the end of the usual sunset prayers, the young priest put away the scroll and the chalk and spread the incense around. Makafu was getting very old now and couldn't hold himself up for very long without the help of his stick, so he sat down on the mat and drew the calabash towards him. After Kolela had filled in the water and herbs, Makafu put the tip of his stick into the water. Kolela watched as the water cleared up, and Kazi's image emerged.

'Balumakazi?'

'He is in your charge until he returns. Teach him to learn from the goats around him. Even a goat has a lesson to lend. Get your things packed. You go to Yaketu tomorrow. I already told Yem to expect you.'

Kolela looked back into the water and saw Kazi playing with somebody. 'That one as well?'

'No, Nsika is in my charge. He has made contact with the warriors at Njuu as I asked him to, and I am already monitoring him.'

CHAPTER 5

Dear young lion,

  No matter how tough the jungle or rough the path or tall the trees, the son of a lion is a lion.

  Your paws may be fragile, your stride short, your pounce a mere bump, and your roar barely audible.

  Be patient. Give yourself time to grow. Time flies, you know, and before you know it, the lion in you will emerge, fearless and unconquerable, even beyond the grave.

Maidem Kayem

I T WAS A well-reputed Christian boarding school run by the priests and nuns with both boys and girls. The dining halls, classrooms, and playing grounds were all shared, but the boys' dormitories were separated from the girls'. Almost all Yem's children (of secondary-school age) had schooled there, and he had been impressed with the grades they got (even though unimpressed with what they had become after that), so when the time came for Kazi to go off to secondary school, Yem sent him there, and Kazi loved it. He was enjoying school and getting good grades in his subjects, and Ndana, who had joined him a year later, made good company because they consoled each other when they were bullied and developed new tricks together on how to dodge one or another school activity like clearing grass or scrubbing floors. There were a few of Yem's children in the school when Kazi got there, but he wasn't as close to them as he was to Ndana because they lived together in the same house.

Kazi was especially good at literature and maths. He loved reading William Shakespeare and acting in the plays they staged in school except when they made him act *Macbeth* because he thought Macbeth was foolish for letting a woman convince him to do evil, plus Lady Macbeth reminded him of Yem's crooked business ways. He also loved calculating angles and vectors and the abstract thinking in physics. When the time came to choose between reading the sciences or the arts, he chose the sciences because in spite of his love for literature and his developing oratory skills, he wanted to go on to study architecture at university.

The idea was sparked by Mandara, who often made remarks that Kazi had a very inventive imagination. His new-found siblings (especially Ndana) teased him about being 'tall for nothing' because he was tall but wasn't physically very strong, so there was a lot around the house that a person of his height was expected to be strong enough to do that Kazi couldn't (of course, they were all forgetting that, in fact, Kazi was just too tall for his age).

Kazi found a way of getting about tasks that were too physically demanding for him by using his imagination. A good example was with splitting wood. One of the tasks Mandara had charged him with was helping the servants split the wood, and she liked the wood chopped up in narrow pieces because she said that they burnt better and gave off more flames. Though his axe was always well sharpened, Kazi found it extremely difficult to split wood because he didn't have the physical strength to hammer the axe down with enough force to get through. To get around that, he would spread the wood out in the sun at the beginning of the week to let it dry more, and then at the end of the week, he would split it much easier so that the servants choked on their own laughter when they realized he was splitting up more wood than them. Mandara always told him that he should be a builder when he grew up.

As he grew older, especially entering the senior years of secondary school, Kazi took on more physically demanding sports in his curriculum like boxing, wrestling, and weightlifting to build his muscles. Bodybuilding was hard, but Kazi made himself do it if only to avoid Ndana's teasing. An added reason that he never let anyone but Nsika know was that at school, he had once engaged in a quarrel that had led to a fight with a short stout boy. The end result was that the boy had beaten him up in spite of his height, and as if the beating was not enough, the story spread quickly throughout the school, and soon, all the girls who had found conversations with him interesting were suddenly more interested in what the short boy had to say. He set his mind to it and built up as much muscle as he could. By the time he was nineteen, he had enough muscles so that he didn't look so lanky in his shirts anymore.

In the senior years of high school, they were introduced to the subject of history. This was a compulsory subject for all students of the class. They were taught about heroes like Napoleon Bonaparte, Queen Elizabeth I, King James I of Aragon, Christopher Columbus, Kaiser Wilhelm, and the just-ended world war. Kazi loved the subject, especially the war bits. It reminded him of his 'training' with Wandi in the forest. They were also taught about the conquests of Africa, which was termed the Dark Continent. Kazi presumed that Africa was called the Dark Continent because everybody around was dark-skinned until a student asked the question and was given the reply that Africans lived in the Dark Ages before the coming of the white man and that the white man had come with the objective of 'civilising' the Africans and bringing them to light. The next question on Kazi mind was 'What is civilisation?' and he asked. The answer he received set his mind into commotion.

'Africans were savages before they were discovered by the white man, pretty much like the Native Americans, but thanks to the education they received and which you are now receiving, they have become better people. For example, before the white man set foot in Africa, Africans were cannibals who ate one another, but because of the education they received, they no longer eat one another or at least not as often.'

When Mandara came to see them at school the next Sunday, Kazi started with that. Mandara laughed until her ribs hurt. 'Your father sent you here to learn what the cobras teach you, not to believe what you are taught.'

As the history lessons went on and on about the greatness of European war heroes and the 'salvation' they had brought to Africa,

Kazi began to try to connect that heroism with the cobra invasion of Lumani and Yaketu, and with each lesson, his doubt increased. Discussions with his classmates demoralised him because contrary to him, most of them believed in the idea of the cobra's 'civilisation' and the 'bringing to light' of the Dark Continent. Nsika had told him to keep his mouth shut about where they came from or what he knew, so he couldn't talk about Wandi or his parents or other Baluma heroes or even about Queen Nzinga from the south, King Hassan from the north, or Dr Mojola Agbebi and Bai Bureh from the west, whom they had been told about growing up.

In frustration, he dodged as many history lessons as he could, and in the few he did attend, his discontentment was obvious. He would roll his eyes around and hiss during the class so much that very often, the teacher would dismiss him from class, which actually was his aim. After a while, the history teacher understood that he was doing that on purpose and put him in the spotlight in every class, asking him questions on the subject as if to make sure he had understood the lesson but really to watch him suffer as he recanted the glories of the white man in Africa. Kazi compounded his problems by throwing disdainful looks at the teacher and hissing each time his name was called.

As if the teacher had told the other teachers about him, Kazi found himself under the watch of every teacher. The prefects in school began to watch him too, and his life at school became painful and labourious. He was punished for every little offence. There were times when he would be out on punishment the whole day long while everybody was in class, which meant he would have to stay up until very late at night copying notes and studying to catch up. Luckily, his classmates felt sorry for him and tried to help as best they could. They would usually help him copy some of the notes or teach him what had been taught in class. Kazi became hateful of the cobras, and the constant punishment only served to fuel the growing hate.

The history lessons were one thing, but the religious classes got first prize when the teacher referred to African religions as pagan religions (a concept that most of his classmates seemed to agree with as well) and then associated African religions with evil rituals such as human sacrifices and crowned it all by inferring that the white man had brought salvation to Africa through the introduction of Christianity and the principle of one supreme god. If the reverends hoped to subdue him, they were only helping assemble and twine the delicate wires of their own time fuse.

* * *

Nsika was making a lot of money from the trips between Yaketu and Lumani and, in addition, collecting a lot of information both ways to help in Njuu. However, beyond Yaketu and Lumani, the world was changing. Lumani now belonged to a different 'country' from Yaketu, which meant that Nsika needed a pass every time he crossed and had to pay more tax. He didn't mind because he was making so much money that the added taxes had no effect on his income. Besides, there were ways of 'getting around' the taxes with Yem's mentorship and the 'friends' he had made himself at the borders, which had been cut just at the borders before Yaketu.

With time and dedication, he was able to shrub seedlings of unity amongst the warriors, now guerrillas, and, with the money he made, buy weapons and smuggle to Njuu. The resistance was taking shape and form, especially since the guerrillas had brought their families to live with them in Njuu so that the place was becoming like a small village. There were teachers, herbalists, and priests, including Makafu, who, with Kolela gone off to Yem, had temporarily moved to Njuu to join the resistance.

The guerrillas, with the information Nsika provided, succeeded in breaking some of the defence lines Arnold had placed and returned to organising sporadic attacks on Lumani whenever they found an opening. This not only took the cobras by surprise but also did a lot of damage to them because there were many more cobras in Lumani than before (thus providing more and easier targets). Plus, because Lumani was now part of a larger country, there were fewer soldiers based in Lumani. However, Nsika felt that the guerrillas needing better training because they were not as prudent as before, and sometimes their attacks also claimed the lives of natives whom they never intended to hurt.

Arnold had left, and Derrick had replaced him, but life in Lumani remained pretty much the same because Derrick had the same governing style, and Pa Utatu remained the eye and ear of the cobra administration. The only saddening thing for Nsika was that he had buried Mama Sawa two years back, so he still felt a little pain each time he returned to Lumani, but Uwa was always consoling, and her warmth made it bearable. Mama Sawa had lived a long life, and he was grateful for that, especially because she had died of old age and painlessly in her sleep. Even though he had cried a lot, he felt favoured to have been around (on one of his business trips) when she passed.

Bana was growing into a very attractive young lady, and Nsika found it difficult not to notice. He spent long hours talking with her for no obvious reason to even himself. Being Wandi's successor, she had been modelled into a graceful, soft-spoken, light-footed, and majestic lady, and though she was enrolled into evening classes at the Christian school nearby, she gave priority to her duties as matriarch of the family. She was well indoctrinated on the Baluma culture and spirituality, and Nsika found it increasingly difficult to bring conversations to an end whenever he came around.

She was the only daughter of her mother, Wandi's second wife. Learning to be ladylike was challenging for Bana with only brothers around her. From her mother, there were four ahead of her and one behind, but as soon as her schooling for succession began, she was made to stay with Uwa, so she sobered down soon enough. She had such a grandiose air around her that Nsika sometimes stumbled over his words, taking it all in as they talked. His only problem with her was Apochezi.

Now Apochezi was a young man, a little older than Nsika, son of Bamba, Abimi's fourth wife, who was a Christian. She had been baptised Veronica while her husband was alive but couldn't have any of her children baptised (that is, if she wanted to live to see the next sunrise), so the year after his death, as soon as she had finished the mourning rites, she had had all four of her children baptised. She had chosen the name David for Apochezi (her second child and second son) because she loved the biblical David who was a great king as they had been taught at doctrine class. Bamba had a beautiful voice, which she lent to the church choir, and, when she learnt to read the bible, taught doctrine on Saturday afternoons, a task which the catechist had assigned to her specially because she was good with children.

She was one of the many Christians who believed that Christianity did not conflict with Baluma spirituality and that both could be done at the same time. She and her children participated wholeheartedly at mass on Sunday morning and then, at crack of Monday dawn, went to see a Baluma priest for what they called 'reinforcement', thus fulfilling the scriptures by 'giving to Caesar what belonged to Caesar and to God what belonged to God' – with no harm done.

Bamba's father was a poor farmer who had worked all his life to feed his family and raised his children not to expect much of life, but when Abimi came along, Bamba began to rethink that philosophy. Although she was the youngest wife, she easily became the most influential in Abimi's compound because she was smart and hard-working but also very manipulative and could talk her way out of almost any situation. She controlled everyone in Abimi's compound and decided what each person should think, do, or say, all except the first wife (Uzise), who felt that it was her Christian right to be the only wife. Each of the other wives felt *they* should be the only wife, but at the end of the day, Bamba made everyone else believe that had Abimi converted to Christianity. It would have been she, Bamba, who would have been chosen for the very simple reason that she was the one he always put in charge of running the farms and barns when he was away. Well, because she was doing a better job than anyone else could and because Abimi wouldn't have anyone managing his wealth but her, they didn't have any arguments to object, so they resigned that she must be right (all except Uzise).

Two years after his death, Abimi's spirit hadn't objected when the ancestors pointed to Apochezi. The priest approached Uzise and asked her to call for a family gathering, but because she and her children were on one side and Bamba had the other side (meaning everyone else) in the palm of her hands, nobody attended the meeting except Uzise and her children. The priest had to postpone the meeting and ask Bamba when she came to see him for her weekly prayers and blessings to assemble the family. Bamba was beside herself with joy when Apochezi's name was pronounced as successor. The patriarch of the family was naturally the firstborn, Hani, who was also firstborn of Uzise and would have a lot of influence in the family, but Bamba didn't mind that. It was sufficing that she had harnessed the position of successor.

Apochezi struggled with understanding Baluma spirituality, which his mother had little knowledge of but, true to herself, found out ways of getting him to know what she couldn't teach him. She introduced him to Makafu and to Bana (whose mother she had deliberately made friends with for her own use). Apochezi and Bana had unearthed their father's skulls on the same day at the same place, so forming friends wasn't difficult once they were introduced, and because Bana was so well instructed on the Baluma culture, Apochezi often stopped by for advice.

However platonic their relationship was, Nsika didn't see it that way. His heart ached each time he saw Bana smiling at Apochezi. When he had met Apochezi, Bana had introduced them and told Nsika that everyone called him Chezi as a nickname since that was what his mother called him, but Nsika continued to call him by his full name, Apochezi. He wasn't interested in any closeness with this man who always hovered around Bana.

On one of his trips to Baluma, Nsika thought of asking for her hand in marriage but wasn't sure what she would respond. Familiar as they were with each other, she never gave off any hint of feeling anything special for him. Another problem was that in Baluma, a man went to the girl's father to ask for her hand, but with Wandi gone, the situation was tricky. He made up his mind, mustered his courage, and approached Uwa on the subject one evening when he thought she would be willing to receive the idea.

'I think it is time I got married, Mama.'

'Then when you're ready, bring Yem to Tchakunte, Wandi's younger brother,' she said with a knowing look.

Nsika laughed at himself. 'But, Mama, why didn't you tell me this before?'

'Well, I am not sure how it is these days, but in our days, a man was a person who was brave enough to ask.' She winked at him.

That was the bravest thing he had done in his life so far.

* * *

Kolela set up his shrine in the inner room and used the first room as his bedroom in the lovely little house Yem had assigned to him at a quiet place at the edge of the compound. Yem had a servant assigned specially to him, and everybody wondered who this special guest was, but since Yem was ever so secretive, none dared ask. He had introduced Kolela to Kazi as Makafu's son whom he had brought to serve as a mentor to Kazi since Nsika was always on the road now. Kazi, on the other hand, had heard of Makafu but never met him. Nevertheless, he was always happy to make a new friend, and that made things easy for Yem and Kolela. Kolela taught him a lot about the behaviour of billy goats, about the manner in which a billy goat would retreat before it launched an attack, to take time to strategise and observe enough to understand the enemy before assault. Kazi took the lesson and put it into practice at school to avoid trouble as much as he could and, when he needed to attack, to have a clear-cut strategy. It usually worked well.

Whenever Kazi came home from school after several weeks (since the school was boarding), Kolela would call Kazi to his house and start with a general topic and then gradually delve into Baluma culture and spirituality. With the difficulty Kazi was facing at school and the turmoil in his mind, conversations like these were relieving. He asked about the subject of forgiveness, a much-debated topic in religious classes that had made him several enemies at school. Kolela taught Kazi about the Baluma perspective.

'In Baluma, we believe that Si is the ultimate judge. When you feel that you have been wronged, you go to Si's court and lay your case, telling him honestly what you have done and what the other person has done. After that, you have three options. You can carry out vengeance yourself, but in that case, you must state clearly what you want to do before Si, and when you do carry out your vengeance, you must do exactly what you promised, nothing more. Or you can ask Si to disregard the offence and not hold it against the one who offended you. Or in the worst-case scenario, where you have been hurt so much that you are beyond vengeance, you ask Si to handle it for you.'

'But how will you know if Si will avenge you? He might do nothing.'

'Smart boy. Most often, you will never even be aware when he takes vengeance.'

Kazi frowned. 'Or if he will.'

'He always does but not in the way that we want,' Kolela said, smiling at the boy, remembering himself asking Makafu the same questions.

After a moment or two of deep contemplation, Kazi asked, 'We don't have the concept of forgiveness then?'

'The second option is pretty much the same, but remember two things. First, the one who speaks the most about forgiveness is always the one at the receiving end of it. Second, don't listen to the cobras telling you to forgive. They say that not to face the consequences of the evil they are doing to us. They know that one day we will rise up against them.'

'But most of my classmates believe them, even defend the religion and the history they teach. How are we going to rise up when we believe that they are better than us?'

'Ah ha! Most but not all your classmates, so there is still hope.' Kolela sighed. 'All human beings are spiritual creatures. Even the cobras know that the day of reckoning is fast approaching. It is a matter of time, Kazi, it is a matter of time. A people without leadership are conquerable and easily divisible, but once the leader takes his place, the reign of the cobra will come to an end.'

And on went their conversations almost every evening. Kolela taught Kazi so much, it was difficult for Kazi to consume all at once. He would have to go back to his own room at Mandara's to ruminate for one or two days before coming back for more. Kolela was like a fountain of wisdom. Kazi didn't know Kolela or where he came from but was intrigued by him, and in his youthful enthusiasm to express himself (being completely deprived of that at school), he never asked Kolela where he was coming from or anything about him for that matter. And as life went on, he really never got to know him. Kolela did.

Yem sometimes came around to join them and led Kolela to explain certain details more to help Kazi understand better, and Kazi could see that Yem was encouraging of these conversations and felt special because no one else in the compound was given that privilege. He could also see that even though he was younger, Kolela paid him the respect one would normally pay an elder one but presumed that that was done to console him because of the ill treatment he faced at school.

When they taught him about Osiris, the god of goodness and prosperity who was killed by his brother Seth, the god of evil, that these two gods are present in every human being, and that the one that emerges is the one that is nurtured, Kazi asked how it was possible to nurture the Osiris in him when the society around him kept calling out the Seth. To that, Kolela explained that that was where the proof of real strength lay.

The teaching on the totems animated Kazi. The Baluma had a culture of totems, which they used to protect the tribe. These totems were real animals in the forest kept and controlled by the Ngui, who were of high spiritual rank. Whenever the tribe was under attack, the Ngui would send their spirits into the animals and use the animals to fight the enemy. It puzzled Kazi that they didn't seem to be doing anything against the cobras and wondered if he could. Kolela found the question amusing because he had asked Makafu the same question years back.

'I'm not talking about physical warfare but spiritual warfare, and you need to attain a certain spiritual magnitude to have that kind of power.'

Kazi was disappointed. His idea of sending his spirit into an animal and killing one or two cobras in the night had been foiled.

With time, Kolela introduced Kazi to Baluma rituals that he performed in Kazi's presence in the inner room of his house. About the reason they used the number nine in performing rituals, he detailed. One was for Si, the supreme and only one. Two was a number considered singular because when one and one were put together, they tended to behave the same. Three was the first number that represented plurality, and three times three was nine and so the plural of plurals, therefore infinity. Kazi was surprised that Yem seemed to know about almost all the rituals and even helped Kolela explain the meanings. Kolela taught Kazi the 'language of the ancestors', which was used in praying to Si, and then how to recognise certain basic signs like when there was going to be a thunderstorm or when there was going to be an extremely hot day or hot season.

The coaching was so subtly done that Kazi did not realize he was being 'prepared' until the day came when he was considered ready to receive what he had been 'prepared' for.

'My father, Ngufo, besides being a farmer was also a herbalist,' Yem said when he met them at Kolela's house one usual evening. 'And like all herbalists, he had some knowledge of Yaketu spirituality and could perform certain rituals for healing. Sometimes he would come across a difficult case that the priests of our land could not resolve, such as my ear disease, and would go to Pa Ngunep, the Baluma high priest, for assistance. He didn't like going to our priests here in Yaketu because they were too corrupt. They could be paid to heal or to kill depending on who paid or paid more. So once Papa realized how astute Pa Ngunep was, he made a habit of taking difficult cases to him directly, bypassing the Yaketu priests.

'Although they did not belong to the same spirituality, Papa and Pa Ngunep had a lot of respect for each other. As a boy, besides going along to have my ear treated, I often accompanied Papa on his trips to Pa Ngunep to help him and learn a few things for myself. It was there that we met Makafu, the current high priest. He was just a young apprentice back then but helped me as Kolela is helping you now. Makafu and I developed a closeness as we grew older so that whenever I had a problem, instead of going to our own priests here in Yaketu for assistance, I went to Pa Ngunep, and when Makafu was ordained, I continued with him.

'Contrary to what everyone thinks, the early years of my business were not easy. I suffered a lot. I was doing well until the other traders realized I was making progress. They did a lot to try to ruin my businesses, including spiritual attacks. Once, I dreamt that two large crocodiles were fighting each other in a bush. A baby tortoise was passing by as they fought. Being a tortoise, he couldn't walk fast, so as frightened as he was, his legs could only take him so fast. One of the crocodiles defeated the other and turned on the little tortoise struggling to get away. The crocodile caught the little tortoise by his shell and was about to chew him when the little one squeezed himself out of his shell, leaving the crocodile with the tortoise shell in his mouth. The little tortoise managed to get to safety but not before the crocodile had pulled one of his arms out of its socket. The next morning, I woke up with a paralysed arm. This is just an example to give you an idea, but there were many such attacks.

'Luckily, Makafu was an exorcist and helped me a lot. To strengthen me, he would take me to Njuu for rituals of cleansing and protection. Even when I began to prosper, from time to time, I still went to Njuu to meditate and say my own prayers as Makafu had taught me. Here is why I understand the Baluma rituals and am better versed in Baluma spirituality than in my own. It was on one of my trips to meditate in Njuu that I met your Papa Wandi. He was preparing the place to resettle the warriors to train for the resistance when we met. We hadn't met before but formed a friendship based on our common fondness for Makafu. After that, I stopped going to meditate in Njuu and instead chose another site in the forest, but I helped Wandi in my own way by supplying his warriors with weaponry and food supplies from here. Later on, I met Wandi's right hand, Abimi, and married one of his sisters, your mother, Mandara, and so the bond got closer.'

Yem paused to let that bit sink in, and when it had, Kazi nodded. Something inside told him this was not the end of the evening and braced himself for what was to follow, but Kolela picked that up.

'Papa Yem, it is getting late, and I have to be up early tomorrow morning for my sunrise prayers, so why don't we meet again tomorrow evening?'

* * *

When Nsika told Yem about his intention to marry Bana, Yem thought that the pressure of having to tell Kazi the truth had reactivated his ear disease.

'Have our ancestors stricken you with madness? They will not let you marry their matriarch. You will need to be a noble' – and then he remembered his own experience with Mandara – 'or at least be revered as one.'

'That's why I came to you, Papa.'

'Even at that, you will need someone in her family to speak in your favour.'

'I have Mama Uwa. I can swear for her. She will defend me.'

Yem had never met Uwa, nor had he known of her, but Nsika was so persuasive that he conceded.

'OK, so the only problem now is to get you into the ranks, but you will need patience. It will take a few months to get the Yaketu council to accept you. Only then will they agree to give you the title of noble through me. I have wasted a lot of time trying to get my useless sons into the council, but whenever the time came, they turned it down and left me out to dry, saying they want to read more books, and left for a different country.'

Nsika assured him that he was determined to marry Bana so would do whatever he needed to, to be accepted by her family.

* * *

The final two years in school were extremely trying for Kazi. He was bottling up so much frustration, anger, and resentment that he lost his cheerful smile and fun-loving ways. He closed up and built such a high wall around himself that he didn't let anybody through. With hate burning in his eyes, his gaze was so frightful that even Ndana became afraid of him. Unlike his former self, he followed the school curriculum strictly and attended all classes. The teachers and prefects found it difficult to find any reason to punish him and had to make up excuses from time to time. Kazi never defended himself, even when it was obvious that he had done nothing wrong.

One early morning, he was still sleeping when everyone was out taking a bath. The head prefect woke him up by pouring a bucket of ice-cold water on him. The wound underneath his left breast was still sore, and in the cold Hamattan morning, the pain was unbearable. Kazi yelled in agony, drawing the attention of the housemaster passing by.

'What's going on in here?' Mr Opoka demanded.

'I was waking him up. He sleeps too much.'

'But that is understandable. He was up picking beans till late last night. You punished him, remember?' Mr Opoka rebuked the head prefect. 'Kazi, get up and go and take a bath and remember to set your mattress out to dry,' he ordered and left.

Once Mr Opoka was out of sight, the head prefect kicked Kazi in his chest, reopening the closing wound. Kazi stifled his scream and struggled to get up, holding his hand to his chest to stop the blood from spurting. The head prefect hit him on the head and promised to make him suffer for drawing the attention of Mr Opoka. Kazi gritted his teeth in anguish. He had never imagined that his vow of silence about who he was would be this hard to keep.

During the next meeting, Yem and Kolela had reopened his mind to that afternoon when his parents were killed, Wandi's instructions to Nsika, and their flight from Lumani. Kazi then remembered that Nsika had never really told him how his parents were doing whenever he got back from Lumani and had diverted the conversation each time he asked. He remembered his dream about Wandi and the dagger and gourd. Kolela informed him that the dagger and gourd were in fact the heritage of the king as the supreme leader of the tribe and supreme commander of the army of the tribe, but because, during the days of the slave takers, the Ngui decided that the king wouldn't lead the battles any longer, it had also been decided that the ornaments would be given to the *afomi*.

The dagger and gourd were over seven hundred years old and had been given to their king as a present by a king from the Kush kingdom in the north-east, whose son's life the Baluma king had saved. Whenever the owner of these was in the face of death, the dagger would save his life if he used it, and the gourd, once water was filled in it, would keep on refilling itself with water until the owner found more water to refill it. The gourd and dagger were a source of life for the owner. A curse had been locked on it so that it could not be stolen or used by anybody to whom it had not been given, and if anyone tried to steal the dagger and gourd or use them without the permission of their owner, the act of theft would evoke a generational curse on that person and his lineage.

Wandi had inherited the dagger and gourd from Vumanga, and ideally, it should have been passed down to the next *afomi*, but Wandi had given Nsika the knife to use to defend Kazi and the gourd to help them on the journey and had asked him to give Kazi to keep for the next *afomi*. The next reason Wandi did not want to have the dagger and gourd on him during that fight was that he feared that if, as he and King Ottuwa had discussed, there was a traitor in the Ngui, under the circumstances, the traitor might get hold of the dagger and unlock the curse and use them for an evil objective against the kingdom. He decided it was better for the dagger and gourd to be as far away from the kingdom as possible while the situation was the way it was.

Kazi's emotions were usually easily distinguishable from the expression on his face (which was the root of all the trouble he had at school), but as Yem told Kazi about his parents and his Papa Wandi, watching his facial expression carefully each time he spoke, he couldn't make out what was going on in Kazi's mind. When he came to the part of the unearthing of the skull, he let Kolela explain.

'Life happens in cycles, and when our ancestors feel that our mission in our physical state is done, they ask Si's permission and call us back to them, and so we are transformed from our physical forms to spirit forms to continue the next cycle. After that, we can be sent back at a later time into this world for a different reason. When our loved ones die, we keep their skulls to keep them close to us and not neglect them because even though their physical life is over, they are not dead but have simply continued on to another form of existence and might return whenever Si chooses to send them back. Being close to us, they continue to watch over us and guide us in our daily lives.'

Kolela paused and let Yem explain to Kazi that his parents had been shot in the chaos and how Nsika had pulled him out of it. Kazi did remember shooting wildly at the cobras but didn't remember seeing his parents drop dead because he had fallen to the ground when his father pulled him out of their range, and Nsika had pulled him away as soon as the cobras shot back. Kazi was still processing that when Kolela continued.

'Because the king is our supreme leader, we use the number nine to perform all rituals related to him. Nine years have gone by since your parents passed. It is time to unearth their skulls and put them in your keeping. After that, we will prepare you for kingship, but the enthroning will have to wait till you return to Lumani when you are done with your school.'

'But Nsika says I can't return. They will kill me if I do,' a confused Kazi said.

'No matter how tough the jungle or rough the path or tall the trees, the son of a lion is a lion. You will return when the time is right. Your paws may still be fragile, your stride short, your pounce a mere bump, and your roar barely audible. Be patient. Give yourself time to grow, time flies you know and before you know it, the lion in you will emerge, fearless and unconquerable, even beyond the grave.'

Kolela's eyes sparkled as he spoke in a language that Kazi couldn't understand, and for the first time since knowing Kolela, Kazi thought he was not right in the head.

Kolela continued with even more puzzling words, 'We will mark you so that the enemy will know that you are special to us and keep away from you.'

Kazi had had enough. He had borne the revelations with grit, but the insane language was the last straw. He got up and, without excusing himself, walked out. He needed time to digest.

Kolela led the way to Makafu's shrine. Makafu was already waiting for them at the gravesite. The ceremony began with libations. As the grave was uncovered, Kazi looked in, almost hoping to see his parents' faces again, his mother's chubby jaw and his father's long chin and beard, but all he saw were scattered bones. He stepped back in pain, and tears flowed down his cheeks. Yem's hands on his shoulders gave him strength.

Kolela went down and picked up the two skulls and climbed back up. The skulls were cleaned up and placed on the altar. Makafu made incantations and sprinkled palm wine, corn flour, and other spices on the skulls.

'Balumakazi, son of Ottuwa, come forward,' Makafu said when he had finished.

Kazi could not feel his feet. Yem shook him and pushed him forward gently, following him behind. Kazi was in a daze when the skulls were handed to him. Kolela led them into the inner part of Makafu's shrine where there were so many other skulls placed in an orderly manner. He was made to place his parents' skulls on a particular spot beside a skull that had a hole in it.

'The skulls of King Tozingana and your other ancestors are lying here because King Ottuwa had all the skulls transferred here for safekeeping. The traitor in the Ngui is of high spiritual potency. If he should get his hands onto the skulls, he could destroy the lineage irreversibly. When you return, you can have them transferred back if you want. In the meantime, Kolela will bring you here for adulation whenever you want.'

'Why does that skull have a hole in it?' Kazi asked when he found his voice.

'That is the skull of King Tozingana, your grandfather. They were captured after a battle with the cobras. He was shot in the head before his feet were chopped off.'

Kazi went cold.

'Now step back, and let us mark you in front of your ancestors.'

His scream drowned Makafu's voice as the hot metallic sickle was placed on his chest, and he felt life leaving him. As always, his teeth were the strongest thing he had. He clenched his teeth to the piece of wood that had been placed between them and bit through it, spitting out the pieces as he attempted to push the old man off him. Yem and Kolela held both his arms backwards and fitted another piece of wood between his teeth, knowing that he wouldn't be capable of mustering the same strength at that moment. Kazi only breathed again when it was over. Makafu filled the wound with herbs that numbed that part of his chest, and for days, he felt nothing, but later on, as the effect died out, he began to feel a little pain when he stretched his left hand too far or too suddenly.

Standing there, taking a cold shower, he was freezing, and that helped numb the pain of the freshly reopened wound. He dried and oiled himself and then rubbed in some of the herbs Kolela had given him to help the wound heal. The herbs had a disinfecting and drying effect on the wound and dispersed the pain. He got dressed and prepared himself for breakfast. He had missed the morning mass and, of course, would be punished for that, but that didn't bother him anymore.

He was more concerned with concealing his emotions and going through the school year, and that was, in fact, why he had adopted the reserved, introverted attitude, which was confusing everyone. Also, the hate he had felt before was only superficial and was principally generated by the audacious condescension on his culture and people whom he was very proud of. This time, the hate came from a deeper place. The manner in which his parents and grandfather had been killed and the wickedness on his people, which Yem and Kolela had told him about, with the cobra invasion – all those stories were confirmed by Nsika, with similar stories about Lumani and the fact that he could not return home because there was a kill order out on him, his crime being successor to his father. The cobras didn't want a king amongst the people because they had realized that while the people didn't have a king, they were less given to rebellion and more easily manipulated.

The hate inside him was ripping his heart apart, and he wished he could talk to someone, but because of his vow of silence, he could only bare it through his eyes and wait until Nsika (whenever he was around) and Mandara visited on Sundays. Even when she came alone, Mandara listened and lifted his spirits by telling him that his time in school was almost over. He could persevere for the little while left, and he had barely an academic year and a half to go.

'Mr Yemumi, can you clean my office today?'

'Yes, sir,' Kazi answered his principal.

Father Gabriel handed the keys to him with a smile, but Kazi didn't smile back.

'By the time I get back, I expect you to have found a reason to smile.'
Father Gabriel winked and went off.

Kazi cleaned his office properly as he always did and then went to
the cupboard to get air freshener to spray around the office. Unlike
usual, the cupboard was closed, so he looked around Father Gabriel's
table for the keys. They were lying beside a book entitled *The Grateful
Negro* by Maria Edgeworth.

Kazi forgot about the keys and picked up the book and started
flipping through it. He knew about the word *Negro* because Nsika
had told him about it (it was a word that was used in Europe and the
Americas to refer to Africans and people of African descent). He could
also read Elizabethan English since he was good at literature.

He was still engrossed in the book when Father Gabriel walked in.
Kazi didn't hear him come in, and Father Gabriel seemed to like that.
He stood there, watching Kazi and following the expressions on his face
as he read a few pages. When Kazi finally realized he was not alone,
he replaced the book on the table and picked the keys up, opened the
cupboard, and sprayed around as if his reading the book was a non-
event. On his way out, he didn't look in the direction of Father Gabriel.

'Come and sit down. We need to talk.'

Kazi barely answered or contributed to the conversation, forcing
Father Gabriel into a monologue. The priest went on and on about
all the good things that the white man brought to Africa and how
they sacrificed his life for the service of Africa, and his advice was for
Kazi to understand how much he had been given by the opportunity
of education and to express some gratitude. He concluded that Kazi
should be friendlier and try to be of greater service. At the end of the
conversation, he offered to lend Kazi the book.

'Make sure to take care of it. Don't rip it apart. It is a book that will
help you understand what I have been saying. Let's see you express more
gratitude, young man.'

If Kazi's curiosity wasn't killing him, he would have shot the book
back at Father Gabriel. He had to clench his teeth together to control
his anger.

Kazi couldn't put the book down once he started. He forewent his homework during the study period and took the book with him to the dormitory to read at night when everyone was sleeping. He even took notes on the book, and when Nsika came to visit the next Sunday with Mandara, they discussed the contents of the book based on the notes he had made while Mandara talked with Ndana. The discussions with Nsika crazed him further as Nsika talked about the theory of white supremacy and perpetuators of the ideology like Josiah Clark Nott and Arthur Schopenhauer, the contribution of Africans to the world war and the lack of recognition or reward they had been given in return, and the American Ku Klux Klan and other white supremacist groups in the Western world.

He finished reading the book and needed to return it but didn't want to face Father Gabriel, so he waited for the next time he would clean Father Gabriel's office and placed the book on his desk. By some stroke of ill luck, Father Gabriel walked in just then.

'You finished reading the book? That's a good boy. Why don't we talk about it?'

As usual, Kazi let Father Gabriel indulge in his monologue. Kazi had a million nerves in his body, but Father Gabriel managed to grate on every one of them.

'Unfortunately, I don't share your opinion,' Kazi scoffed and stood up. 'We were doing well in Africa before you people invited yourselves. We have nothing to be grateful for.'

With that, he turned around and left before Father Gabriel could say anything.

* * *

Yem didn't have any difficulty persuading the Yaketu council to accept Nsika as a noble. His popularity did most of the work. The difficulty was in getting Nsika accepted by Bana's family. In the Baluma culture, when a man wanted to marry a woman, his father took him and a few other males in the family to see the patriarch of the woman's family to ask for the woman on behalf of his son. The woman's family would let them make their case and then ask them to return in a month to give them time to carry out a background check on the man in question. After a month, when the family returned, they would give them the results of the background check and, if they were satisfied with what they had found, would give their approval and then ask the woman in question if she had any objections to marrying the man. Only after that would discussions on dowry begin. Unfortunately, in Nsika's case, they didn't get to the point of asking Bana her opinion because the family objected for strong reasons.

His paternal great-grandfather was an evil slave who had killed his master before the birth of his master's successor and run away. Because of that, his master's family had cast a spell on his great-grandfather's lineage for nine generations. Nsika's own father was born into poverty and the stigma of a slave grandfather but had worked hard and acquired wealth enough to buy a seat on the Wemtii. However, because the spell had not yet been broken, it led him to an early grave before his own son was born and killed his wife (Nsika's mother) once she had finished suckling Nsika a few months later. If their blood were to be mixed with his through a child as a result of a marriage between him and Bana, the spell would be brought into the family.

Such were the accusations against Nsika that even Uwa could not defend him against. Yem was devastated. Nsika was in denial, and Bana never said a word.

Back in Yaketu, one night Nsika dreamt that he was back in Kamuel's house, cleaning, when he heard voices in the living room and peeped through the keyhole of the kitchen door to see who it was. He saw Uwa arguing with Tchakunte about him, asking Tchakunte to see a priest to break the spell and free Nsika. Tchakunte was explaining that it was not their place to get involved in Nsika's family affairs. Through the keyhole, Nsika could see Wandi standing in the corner, saying nothing, with a neutral expression on his face and a cow horn in his hands (which traditionally was used in drinking palm wine). Nsika was disappointed that his Papa Wandi wouldn't say anything to defend him, so he got up, opened the door, and walked into the room. Mama Sawa sat in a corner with tears in her eyes. Uwa and Tchakunte ignored him and continued arguing as if he wasn't there. It was as if they weren't seeing him.

'Uwa, leave this marriage business for us men. You women know nothing about protecting a family,' Tchakunte was saying.

Nsika walked up to Wandi. 'Papa, wouldn't you defend me? Wouldn't you say something? I am innocent. I know nothing of this.'

Still, Wandi did not reply or even look in his direction. He tugged Wandi's loincloth for attention but didn't get any.

Yem came through the door and asked Nsika to follow him, to which Mama Sawa looked at him and nodded with tear-filled eyes. As he left the room with Yem, he heard Uwa scolding Wandi.

'If you have already drank palm wine for Bana, you better let us know.'

Nsika woke up in cold sweat to hear Ndana knocking on his room door, telling him that Yem wanted to see him urgently.

'We will go to Makafu. There is no spell that he cannot break. Go to the barn and get a spotless white fowl. We will leave by noon.'

Nsika did as he was told, and they set off for the journey.

Makafu took the fowl from its cage and tied its legs together. The enneagram had been prepared with the necessary tree barks, incense, oil, and spices. Nsika was made to lie flat on his stomach with his arms stretched full length in front of him as a sign of submission facing the enneagram. Makafu sprinkled the spices into the calabash and threw the three cowries onto the ground to begin the ceremony. He was assisted by six other priests who stood three to one side of him and three to the other. Yem stayed in the back, watching in silence.

Nsika closed his eyes and put his forehead on the ground and, in his mind, kept on replaying the whole scene and Tchakunte's words about the history of his family. He didn't know what to think of his dream and why Wandi did not defend him. This was too complicated for him. All he wanted was to marry the most beautiful goddess he had ever seen.

The fowl grabbed Nsika's hair as it was placed on his head, with Makafu in full ceremony, incanting, and the priests answering in chorus whenever he paused. He ripped the fowl's head off, and the fresh blood streamed onto Nsika's head. Makafu threw the fowl's body into the calabash and blew some incense at Nsika and then asked him to get up and sit on the ground. He placed the calabash into Nsika's hands and asked Nsika to answer 'Imani' whenever he paused. Nsika answered obediently when he was required to, and at each point, Makafu would put a piece of tree bark between his teeth, chew, and blow out on him. Nsika couldn't tell which was worse: his curse, the stench of the freshly killed fowl in the calabash he was holding, the fresh blood dripping from his head, or the crumbs of tree bark moistened by Makafu's spittle on his face. At the end of the ceremony, Makafu poured the oil unto Nsika's head and let out a few more words that ended in a chorus of 'Imani'.

'You must have a good palm wine tapper. I have never drank any palm wine this good in all my years in Lumani,' Makafu complemented when they had finished dinner and settled down to drink.

'Well, Yaketu people have always been better at palm wine tapping. I have never understood why that is always a debateable subject,' Yem boasted.

Nsika was quiet the whole while. He was still depressed about the history of his family and how it was affecting him.

'Nsika, four generations later, the blood is more diluted, and because your mother's side is clean, the curse will be easier to uplift. Besides, because you are innocent, your ancestors will never blame you for this. We will just need to be patient because those people used very strong medicine. But trust me, I will clean out all the bad blood from your veins. I don't like people who throw medicine around carelessly in anger without thinking about the consequences of their actions,' Makafu consoled him.

'How long will I need to do this?' Nsika asked, trying to feign relief.

'Only three years, my son. Next year, same time, we do this again, and then the next year, and it will be over forever!' Then as if remembering something important, Makafu turned to Yem. 'Did you ask Tchakunte whether Bana was betrothed?'

Nsika's heart stopped.

Yem's eyes showed all the surprise in the world. 'I didn't think to ask. I presumed they would have offered me such information if there was any.'

'Well, as I performed the ceremony, I decided to check Bana just to make sure she didn't have anything that could contribute to strengthening the effects of the curse, and I saw Wandi taking palm wine from Abimi. Perhaps you might want to go back and ask them if they have anything more to tell you.'

* * *

At twenty-one years, Kazi stood at almost six-foot-five and, with a lot of hard work, was filling out several muscles, his only trouble being that he needed to eat properly and do heavy bodybuilding to sustain them. He was one of the top students in his class and usually received several awards at the end of the school year for academic excellence. He was now in the final year of secondary school and head prefect, not that he was interested in the position, but he was relieved because that meant that he couldn't be punished as he had for the last three years. His days of torture were finally over. All he needed to do now was to persevere through the history and religion classes, write his final exams, and be off to wherever he wanted in life. He was no longer interested in continuing on to university to read architecture. He needed to go back and join the resistance.

Yem had a good plan for him, which was usual since Yem knew exactly what everybody should do in life for the better objective of making money. The plan was that after Kazi finished school, he would go back to Yem to learn how to 'make money' (this time, Kazi had no objections to Yem's *manner* of doing business), and in time, he would join Nsika trading and spying between Yaketu and Lumani. When he was ready, Nsika would introduce him to the guerrillas in Njuu, and he would start training with them. It was a good plan, but life had a paradox that Kazi still needed to learn. Of his entire seven-year stay, that year turned out to be the most trying.

Father Gabriel pronounced his name carefully as he read out the prefect list for the school year. And as he walked up to the stand so that everybody could see him and followed him with his eyes, after the ceremony, he was called to the principal's office for a 'talk'. Kazi wasn't surprised that Father Gabriel was asking him to play foreman. From the stories about Cornelius, Fidelis, and Pa Utatu, he understood Ndikwa's plight even better now but was determined to handle this differently. It was his last year and he had nothing to lose, or so he thought.

He worked well with the girl's head prefect (Daniella) and was slowly learning to let people through his wall of defence as he solved everyday problems amongst the students. It was a whole new discovery for him as he relearnt to communicate with people on personal terms. All was faring well until the day came when a girl two classes behind got pregnant.

Daniella had come to him with the problem, not sure how to handle it. She had met the girl crying in the dormitory and had persuaded her to tell her what the problem was. The girl was from a Christian family and knew her father would disown her, as he had done with two of her elder sisters, if he discovered she was pregnant out of wedlock. He was a stern man who was determined to keep his name clean of any scandals. The girl was hesitant to tell Daniella who was responsible for the pregnancy but, for some reason, told Kazi when he asked. Kazi decided that he would let Father Gabriel know so that together, they could force the teacher to marry the girl. Daniella tried to make Kazi understand that Father Gabriel would not see things the way he saw them and that it was better to help the girl pack up and run to a relative who could take care of her until she gave birth. Her father would disown her eventually, but at least she wouldn't have to go through the trauma of public disgrace and all the mockery it would provoke from the students on top of her woes. Kazi insisted on letting Father Gabriel know. He was convinced that in spite of what he was, Father Gabriel would agree with him, a mistake he would take a long time to forgive himself for.

They stood for a while in front of his office, waiting for audience, and, when their turn came, went in and made their case for the girl.

'So instead of studying, these girls go around seducing teachers? Unbelievable!' Father Gabriel bellowed.

'The teachers should not be taking advantage of the girls, sir,' Kazi shot back.

'Mr Yemumi, your job is to discipline the students, not to make excuses for their lack of discipline. Now who is the girl in question? I want her brought in here immediately.'

'And what about Mr Adui? Shouldn't he be brought here as well?'

'Don't you question my orders, Mr Yemumi. Go and fetch this Eveline of a girl.'

Kazi and Daniella walked out, fuming. On their way to the dormitory, they talked about it. No matter what Father Gabriel did, they would confront Mr Adui later that afternoon.

Eveline stood in front of Father Gabriel with her head down and tears rolling down her cheeks. Daniella and Kazi stood behind the door outside the office so they could hear what was being said inside. Father Gabriel gave a sermon on the sin of fornication and the seventh commandment. Not only would he have to dismiss her, but also, she couldn't be allowed to receive Holy Communion in church ever again; she was excommunicated.

The sermon on Eve tempting Adam was taking too long for Kazi's patience. He left Daniella standing at the door and marched to Mr Adui's house – a very bad idea.

'Who's there?' Mr Adui said irritably.

'Mr Yemumi, I want to see you, sir.'

Mr Adui opened the door. 'I am busy now. Come back later.'

Since Kazi was tall enough, he could look past Mr Adui to see another female student sitting on his porch. All the goats Kolela had taught him about couldn't hold Kazi back. He launched himself at Mr Adui, pulling him out by the throat, squeezing so hard that he almost suffocated the man. Mr Adui struggled to get out of Kazi's grip, holding his hand and hitting him across the face. The response was a resounding butt to the head and a blow that sent him to the ground, throwing two teeth out of their sockets. The female student screamed and ran out of the house.

Kazi pounded and pounded a yelling Mr Adui until the yelling drew the attention of Mr Opoka, who shared the conjoining house. He rushed out.

'Stop! Stop! Mr Yemumi, what do you think you are doing?'

He tried to pull him back but couldn't match the young bull's strength. With one careless wave of his hand, Kazi put Mr Opoka out of the way and picked up where he had dropped Mr Adui. Two other teachers who lived nearby heard the yelling and joined Mr Opoka. It was only then that they were able to hold Kazi back. Mr Adui was rushed to the surgery, and Kazi was led to the principal's office, still fuming.

Father Gabriel had gone off to get Eveline packed and ready to leave and made Daniella help her. Mr Opoka took the moment as they waited outside the office to ask Kazi what was going on, and though Kazi was still too enraged to get his words out coherently, Mr Opoka got the message. He wasn't surprised at all because he had known of the affair between Mr Adui and Eveline. Well, it wasn't really an affair but something of the sort. He and several other teachers had noted Mr Adui for deceiving students into situations like these by promising to give them more marks in his subject or giving them test questions before the day of the test. Eveline had fallen into that trap, as had so many others. She was just the unlucky one who hadn't been prudent.

Whatever Mr Opoka thought or said had no influence on Father Gabriel's stance that it was the girls to blame. Kazi and Eveline were packed by dusk, with the difference being that because Kazi was already registered to write his pre-university exams in the school, he would return in a month when exams commenced. Kazi wasn't sorry for himself or what he had done to Mr Adui and had told Father Gabriel as much. His only regret was that he wished he had followed Daniella's advice and avoided Eveline the disgrace. Mr Opoka engaged to teach Kazi at home after school every day to keep him abreast with the rest of his class. It was only a month before the exams, so there wasn't much left to teach.

A week later, Mr Adui returned to school and continued in his same old manner, getting more victims, with Father Gabriel turning a blind eye and blaming the girls each time.

Daniella was out of breath by the time she got to Yem's place. The results were out, and she and Kazi and three others had been given scholarships to study in the United Kingdom. The results came out during their long holiday period. She had got the news first through Mr Opoka and had run to school to see for herself. Father Gabriel was asking for all five of them to come to the school to sign some documents for their scholarship. Kazi told Nsika about it and left with Daniella. He had a piece of his mind to give Father Gabriel and wanted to do it in person.

They knocked on Father Gabriel's door and waited. When he was ready to receive them, Kazi let Daniella go in first and waited patiently outside. He let the three others go in after her not to jeopardise their chances because, knowing Father Gabriel, the man could well burn the rest of the scholarships after he heard what Kazi had to say. Daniella came out beaming, and Kazi promised to visit her at her parents' place later that week so they could talk in detail.

Father Gabriel still begrudged Kazi for causing him so much resentment amongst the students and teachers. The moment Kazi left the school, Father Gabriel's life became hell. Daniella told everyone who cared to listen about the fight between Kazi and Mr Adui and the incident with Eveline that had led to it so that instead of laughing at Eveline as they normally would, they instead felt sympathy, even the most reverend of students. Mr Opoka, on his end, confirmed the story and spread the word amongst the teachers about Mr Adui and the fact the Father Gabriel was deliberately turning a blind eye. The rumours spread like wildfire around campus, with each group drawing conclusions on the possible reasons why Father Gabriel would be 'encouraging' Mr Adui, as they put it. One rumour suggested that he was of the same behaviour himself. Another was the suspicion that he and Mr Adui, who held the treasury together, might have some fishy business between them and yet another that perhaps Mr Adui had a few 'secrets' about him (Father Gabriel) that he couldn't allow to come to light.

Whatever the case might have been, though none of the rumours were backed by facts but mere speculations because Father Gabriel did not ever address the matter, he lost all the credibility he had amongst the students and teachers. Every time he was seen talking with a female student, students passed by throwing glances of suspicion mixed with humour, which made him so uncomfortable, he cut off from the female students all forms of conversation, hoping it would help, but it didn't. He got the same reaction even when he was seen with male students. Before he knew it, he was obliged to relieve Mr Adui of his duties, but since the right things done at the wrong time didn't really have much relevance, the rumours and speculations continued with even more vigour. He decided to ask his bishop for a transfer and had just finished drafting the letter when the results of the pre-university exams came in with Kazi's name at the top of the list.

'Sit down!' he ordered.

'I didn't come here to sit down.'

Father Gabriel looked up, aghast. 'What did you say?'

'Exactly what you heard me say, or are your ears giving you trouble?'

'Do you know I could tear up your scholarship right away and your future will be over?'

'That's precisely where you're wrong. I didn't come here to accept your pittance of a scholarship. I came to let you know that I am turning it down. You asked me a long time ago to show appreciation for what you and your people are doing here. Here is what I know. You killed my parents! But first, you kidnapped our people. Then you stole our land, enslaved us on our own land, destroyed the fabric of our society, and then asked us to kneel to your *god*. And now you offer us 'gifts' and expect us to be grateful? I suggest that you take the scholarship and go back to your own land. You called us cannibals, remember? That history class we had? So the first person I will eat the next time we meet will be you.'

* * *

'I thank you for receiving me. I was here two and a half months ago with my son to ask for Bana. You asked us to come back a month later, and we did. In that last meeting, you told us about my son's history. We went back and found all you said to be true about the curse on Nsika, and we accept.'

'Thank you,' they chorused.

'We went on to engage Pa Makafu to break the curse, and it's going well so far.'

'That is good,' the choir answered.

'However, there is one thing that disturbs me in my sleep.'

'Whatever it is, we shall find a solution,' Tchakunte said.

'It seems that at some point, Wandi took palm wine from Abimi. If I am mistaken, forgive me.' Yem sat down.

Tchakunte was at a loss for words. He was not aware about any such pact. Wandi had never told him, and he didn't know what to do. The choir was waiting for him to say something, and he couldn't think up any tale to tell.

'It is Abimi who named Bana,' Bana's mother stepped forward to explain. Her voice broke the awkward silence.

As it was in the Baluma culture, when an important person in the family died at about the time a baby was expected, if the child was born of the same gender as the deceased person, it was considered that the child had come to replace the one they had lost. Wandi lost his mother at a time his second wife was expecting a baby, but when the child arrived it was a boy, and she kept on having boys. It was therefore considered that his mother had not been replaced in his life, so he looked forward to having a daughter who took long in coming.

When Bana was born four years later, Wandi's gratitude was beyond measure. Abimi had been a constant source of consolation all along, so Wandi gave him the honour of choosing a name for the baby. Abimi had named the baby Bana (after a peculiar precious stone in the forest) and, after her naming, had asked for her hand for Hani, his first son. Wandi had drank the palm wine offered, but no dowry was paid; that part was to wait until Bana came of age. Only Bana's mother, Wandi, Abimi, and Uzise knew of this pact.

'Why didn't you say anything before? Why would you embarrass us like this?' Tchakunte demanded to know.

'Well, since nobody asks for a woman's opinion in the affairs of marriage, you didn't ask me, and besides, Uzise has told me *things* that I would rather not say' was the cheek he got in reply.

The news smashed Nsika, and Yem didn't talk about it after that day.

* * *

It was difficult finding a responsible son, and by responsible, Yem meant one who would handle his businesses instead of going to school. All his sons were either doing studies abroad or had joined the cobra administration as teachers. He had disowned the one who chose to join the religion and become a priest and cut him off completely.

Ndana finished school the next year and added to his woes by accepting the offer of a scholarship to study medicine in the United Kingdom. He couldn't see how becoming a doctor could be more desirable than getting properly married and starting a good luxurious life with the son of one of his rich friends. So many had been asking, and he had fended them off by telling them to let her finish school, but now that she had finished school, she wanted more school. Such genes, he was convinced, had definitely come from Mandara, who was overjoyed with the idea of having a very well-educated daughter – overly well, in Yem's opinion, and completely useless for him.

By the time Ndana returned in six years, she would hardly make an attractive bride. He would be obliged to reduce the dowry on her. The only consolation he drew from Ndana's sad choice was that she was a girl, and he had no use for a girl; he needed a boy to handle his business.

Yem's only hope left was Changara, who was in the United States studying for a master's in business administration. The boy was to return in a year after graduating, and Yem was hoping to persuade him to stay and run his businesses. Kazi was filling the spot temporarily, helping him run things from time to time, and from the way things were going, he wished Kazi were really of his lineage, but he knew that Kazi would have to return to Lumani someday.

If Yem considered himself a rich man when he tripled his fortune from the rip-offs and crooked businesses, well, Kazi made him look poor. Kazi perfected Yem's crookery, lust for money, and vanity and learnt to dress like him. A lot of resistance movements were hatching in Africa at the time, and Kazi took advantage of the moment. He bought weapons and medicines from the ship workers who stole them off the ships to supply the resistance movements. Some of his supply also came from his organised gangs who broke into military barracks to steal weapons. To launder the money he made, he set up shop as a supplier of medicines, car parts, and plumbing materials, which he bought from the coast and transported to the interior, especially to the regions that were hardly accessible where the cobra administration had set up hospitals and schools. He joined Nsika in supplying the guerrillas in Njuu by smuggling weapons, food, and medicines. Later on, he bought a few herds of cattle, sheep, and goats from Yem and began rearing but did not sell in the same markets as Yem to avoid the competition. He went farther away and hired vehicles to cross countries with his animals.

He also noticed that the cobra soldiers had a hard time coping with their duty stations in Africa and often resorted to drugging themselves to ease the depression. He remembered that in Lumani, there was a certain leaf that warriors used to ease pain from wounds sustained in battle, and that leaf had a hypnotising effect, very much the same as the cocaine the soldiers used. On his next trip to Lumani, he got the leaf and brought it back to plant in Yaketu, and in a matter of months, Kazi was the best thing that happened to the soldiers.

* * *

When the curse was finally broken, Nsika felt as if a heavy weight had been lifted off his shoulders. He came back to life, and the travesty

with Bana's family was an old book in his shelf. He engaged fully with
the espionage unit of the rebellion, communicating with other countries
around the region and collecting evidence on genocides and massacres
carried out by the cobras on the natives and putting it together for
pressure groups in Europe whom they had made contact with.

The training in Njuu brought back painful memories for Kazi,
remembering Wandi teaching him with the little dagger. Even now,
he still took the dagger with him to Njuu and had it on him when he
trained. He had been introduced to the guerrillas as the heir apparent,
and it was understood why he could not return to Lumani to be
enthroned. However, Kazi did enter Lumani under the guise of a trader.
He just covered up his chest properly, and Nsika made sure not to reveal
who he was to anybody, not even to Uwa.

The guerrillas had, over time, managed to break through a few
lines of the cobra defence and recoup a large part of the forest so that
hunters from Lumani had to stop hunting and turn to other activities
for a living. The resistance took on more vigour once Kazi joined them.
He united the natives and the Christians, and soon, they were training
as one. With the presence of a king, their divisions seemed of little
importance, and the authority was centred on Kazi. He was naturally
good at wrestling, a sport he loved as a child, so training did not prove so
difficult, and since living with Ndana's mockery had taught him to find
easy ways of doing difficult tasks, it was not long before the guerrillas
began to admire his fighting skills. He was by no means the strongest
or fastest but was undoubtedly the best strategist.

He twined the oily ropes carefully together and tied them around
the tree. He pulled the end to the next tree and went round the tree
and kept on doing that until he ran out of rope. At his signal, the men
opened fire. The rope and trees went ablaze, and the bullets rained. The
soldiers were taken unawares by the attack. Kazi shot down the last one,
and the last line of defence was broken.

Lumani was finally open to them. They had made sure to kill all
the soldiers on guard so that no one could go back to tell the story.

They had reliable information from Nsika about the plan of the
kingdom, where the residences stood, the new administrative block,

schools, churches, hospitals, and where the natives lived. Their attack had to be indefectible; there was no room for errors because if it failed, the cobra administration would not give them a second chance.

The genocides and massacres in other parts of the continent were lessons to remember as the cobras crushed mercilessly any resistance from the natives. The uprisings all seemed to take the same trend and follow the same strategy, so Kazi and his guerrillas needed to find a strategy that the cobras had not known or heard of before, and the clock was ticking because it would be a matter of weeks before the cobras discovered that the last line of defence had been broken and that they had been bared.

CHAPTER 6

It is all about the conqueror.

The conqueror always considers themselves superior, whether defined by race, tribe, gender, or religion. It is all about the conqueror and their victory and their politics.

So there is no racism, no tribalism, no gender superiority, no religious hatred, just a conqueror and a conquered – until we all learn not to conquer or be conquered.

Maidem Kayem

UTATU ENJOYED THE position of patriarch until Ottuwa stopped listening.

The truth was that Pa Utatu's case was not so different from a wife betrayed by her husband after several years of marriage. As successor to Sambinunba, he had promised himself to die before his king did. To build the composure he needed, Utatu submerged himself in his spirituality. This meant that he had to change his pattern of living. First of all, he stopped marrying new wives and drinking to excess and set himself on a path of righteousness. He marked out particular moments during the day and the night when he had to pray and perform rituals of cleansing and protection. It was hard in the beginning and a difficult sacrifice to make, but he was paid off eventually because as time went by, he saw himself attain spiritual ranks he never thought he was capable of. Thus, although younger than Tozingana, Utatu was able to counsel the king with the wisdom expected of a person much older than his years.

He deeply regretted that he had encouraged Tozingana to fight with the warriors in the battle that took the king's life, but no matter how much his remorse, the council was not willing to forgive so easily. He lost the popularity he had enjoyed for the last six years of the king's life (which were the first six years of his patriarchy), and soon, matters were discussed in his absence that he only discovered during or after the execution of the decision.

Believing as everyone did that the death of the king was his fault, Utatu tried to make amends. He offered an apology openly to the Ngui and offered sacrifices of pardon and cleansing to complement. He didn't let Ottuwa find it out from somebody else. As soon as the ceremony of enthroning was over, he went to see Ottuwa and related the story as honestly as he could, holding nothing back. Ottuwa understood him and assured him that he held nothing against him. Supplementary to that, Ottuwa believed as the Baluma believed that a king's life could not be taken from him by any mortal until Si said yes. Si had agreed for the cobras to take Tozingana's life, so no matter how wrong the advice from the patriarch may have been, the final decision had been Si's, and he had said *yes*.

Assured of the king's confidence in his loyalty, Utatu rebounded, serving with zeal and wisdom for several years, and in recognition, Ottuwa always put Utatu's opinion first. Utatu contributed to the idea of poisoning the rubber and burning the cocoa that was delivered to the cobras by teaching Ottuwa exactly how the cocoa needed to be burnt so that it would seem well dried but at the same time too toxic for consumption when ground and how to rub the poison into the rubber undetectably. He also remodelled Ottuwa's speeches, helped him memorise them, and taught him how to speak to command authority and win the people's trust. In many ways, Utatu was Ottuwa's right hand. So what went wrong?

The entire Ngui had been against that attack, but Utatu had convinced Ottuwa that the battle would serve for good use against the cobras and their religion. It was therefore on Utatu's advice that Ottuwa had defied the Ngui and asked Wandi to send his warriors to attack the church on that fateful Good Friday when all got killed and the three captured were brutally executed shortly afterwards. Following that, Ottuwa became unsure of Utatu's advice and stopped listening. He always asked for a second opinion to whatever Utatu proposed and passed all decisions by Makafu before making his final decision.

This hurt Utatu profoundly, given that it was his first mistake after several years of selfless loyalty, and then to put the icing on his frustration and bitterness, at least five of the other eight members of the Ngui had one or another grudge against him (owing to their conviction that Utatu had led Tozingana to his death and other petty disagreements they had had with him in the past). Whatever he proposed was never good enough. They shoved his ideas aside and continued the discussion as if he were not present, the end result being that even though, by virtue of his position as patriarch, he had a greater measure of popularity amongst the people than the other members of the Ngui, in terms of authority, he had almost none. He could even hear them whispering that he was the worst patriarch Baluma had ever had, and that cut through his heart like a sharp knife. He then realized it was useless to ask them for pardon because the reaction would be total rejection.

Utatu resorted to performing his rituals of pardon in silence until the day when the thought propped up in his head that he could turn the tables around for himself, all by himself. From what Utatu could see through his calabash, the cobras would never leave; this meant that the situation of invasion was permanent. Utatu decided that he could use the situation to make his life in this world comfortable. His frustration for lack of authority amongst the people and the resentment he felt in the Ngui, coupled with his collapsing hunting businesses, set Utatu on what later became a downward spiral.

For every piece of land that the cobras wanted, Utatu, in conjunction with Cornelius, convinced them to pay large sums of money for Utatu to perform the rituals required for them to take over the land. Once the money was collected and shared between the parties involved, Utatu would kill a chicken or goat, sprinkle the blood around the area to be occupied, and then put signs around (signs that meant exactly nothing) to give the impression a ritual had been performed. Later on, he would have the bird or animal roasted for his own consumption. This, because the problem with selling the land was that in Lumani, the culture was to let out the land but not to sell it because the Baluma believed that their land belonged to posterity. There were therefore no rituals designed for the sale of land in Baluma spirituality. So whenever land was *sold*, it had to be done in such a way that the impression was given that the cobras had yet again seized another piece of land, and on the other hand, the cobras had to be convinced that because of Utatu's rituals, they would be spared of the horror of the nightmares and the haunting of the houses that they faced on the choice piece of land (the seized lands that Makafu had performed the ritual upon with the spotless white chicken).

He therefore made himself a large fortune by *selling* off bits and pieces of the land to the cobras and sharing a small portion of that fortune with Cornelius (and continued with Fidelis) and his thugs who provided protection for him in exchange for his silence about the torture of the people. To strengthen his ties with the cobras, Utatu fed information on an almost weekly basis, especially about what was discussed in the Ngui, so that the cobras intercepted every move they made (this was what triggered Ottuwa and Wandi's suspicion that there had to be a traitor in the Ngui). In addition, because of his high spiritual rank, he could perform rituals to shield his treachery so that though Makafu could tell the traitor was close when he performed the rituals, he couldn't tell who whenever Wandi insisted for him to try again.

It followed that while other nobles were subjected to humiliation and indignity by the soldiers of the cobra administration, Utatu continued to enjoy reverence, and that with the normal presumption being that it was owing to his position as patriarch.

It took Sigue a few years to discover what Utatu was doing. All along, Sigue believed that the invasion had made Ottuwa paranoid and that besides Fidelis and his hood of traitors, the rest of the common people were decided against the cobras. The Wemtii might have been corrupted but not the Ngui, the most sacred brotherhood in the kingdom, and insisted on that when Ottuwa had told him about his suspicions. So if the information had not come through Mpima (Sigue's first wife), he would never had believed it. She was visiting one of Utatu's wives (Mama Teri), whose son had taken ill, when the woman began to brood about the child's sickness being a curse from the ancestors for Utatu's betrayal of the land. Mpima didn't understand at first, but when the woman explained what Utatu had in common with Fidelis, Mpima took the information straight to Sigue, who made the apocalyptic mistake of confronting Utatu head on.

The conversation went exactly as Utatu wanted it to go. He rationalised his actions based on his foresight about the permanency of the cobra invasion and that there was nothing more to lose. If they didn't *sell* the land to the cobras, the cobras would take it anyway. It was therefore no harm benefitting from an unredeemable situation. With regards to the torture the people were subjected to, Utatu stated his position poignantly.

'In all the years the cobras have been here, how many people opposed to the torture have been able to do anything to prevent it? Wandinendi? Abimisema? Who?'

Sigue had no arguments.

Another twist to this story was that Fidelis had cut off the traditional royal tax paid to the palace so that all forms of taxes were now paid to the cobra administration alone, and with the introduction of the monetary currency in Baluma and no source of making any, Sigue could only manage to feed his family and Ottuwa's family from the traditional donations made to the palace. Their wives (his and Ottuwa's) were obliged to take on jobs with the cobra administration to send their children to school. Things were getting increasingly difficult, and he was badly in need of financial help but had been too proud to ask anyone. Utatu already knew that and offered to buy his silence.

* * *

'Chezi, we need to start by eliminating the traitors before they discover the defence lines have been broken,' Kazi said, drawing out the map of Lumani in the dust. 'Where exactly is Pa Utatu's compound located?'

'Over there. There is a large school here, and he lives just behind it, and here is about where the entrance to his compound is.' Chezi pointed with a stick.

'That old goat needs to be killed quietly. I figure poisoning would be the best way.'

'Yes, I think I know how to get that done,' Chezi answered and sat down beside Kazi.

Seven years before, the two had met at Bana's wedding to Hani and had bonded like two drops of water. Nsika could not attend for obvious reasons, and in addition to that, Uwa's death two months prior to the wedding was such a terrible blow that it would take a long time for him to return to Lumani. He had other routes of trade now that were much more lucrative, and Uwa had been, until her death, the only reason he returned to trade in Lumani after the infamous saga. Yem had sent Kazi to represent the family at Bana's wedding as a show of good faith to Wandi's family.

Apochezi was an older man and liked Kazi's reserved but friendly disposition. Kazi, on the other hand, knew all about Apochezi, that he was Abimi's successor and an undercover guerrilla as well. He recognised him almost immediately because on their last trip to Lumani together to bury Uwa, Nsika had pointed Chezi out to him. For prudence's sake, he made sure not to reveal his identity as Nsika had cautioned, simply introducing himself as Yem's son.

'I am Balumakazi, son of Yemumi, but you can call me Kazi.'

'And I am Apochezi, son of Abimisema, but you can call me Chezi.'

He smiled and set his arms out for the traditional greeting where an older one held out his arms half-stretched with his palms turned downwards to signify a superiority in wisdom. Kazi let out his arms in full length with palms turned downwards in submission.

'Baluma... Kazi, where are you from?' There was something about the younger one's large light brown eyes and long eyelashes that seemed familiar, and he felt as if he had seen him before, but it was difficult to say where.

'Yaketu,' Kazi answered, raising his eyebrows and bringing his eyes to more evidence.

'So why do you bear a Baluma name?' Chezi asked through narrowed eyes.

Kazi had a snappy answer for that. 'My mother, Mandara, is from here. She is the sister to your father, Abimisema.' He knew from Kolela's lectures that even though the man was dead, in the Baluma culture, death in the physical life did not signify the end of life, and therefore, those who had passed were never referred to as of late.

'God of my ancestors! Mama Dara married into Yaketu a long time ago, and we never saw her after that! So you are her son?'

'Firstborn.'

'That makes you my brother, but don't get confused. I am still a lot older. Come, take a seat beside me.'

They talked and had lots of fun at the wedding, watching the girls and making fun of those who seemed to be looking out to make a 'catch' and disappearing and reappearing with a little more make-up than before.

During that wedding, something happened that Kazi found funny and easily forgot but Chezi found peculiar and always remembered. A lady approached both men and asked Kazi for the next dance. Kazi was not a good dancer and was always shy, but because she was pretty, he agreed. As they danced, the woman seemed to be virtually dancing all over him and whispering in his ears. He tried to keep away to avoid the pairs of eyes about them. After the dance, the lady tried to persuade Kazi to follow her home and pulled his left arm so much that Kazi squeezed his eyes in pain (the effects of the wound in his chest had not completely faded away by then). Chezi came to Kazi's rescue and afterwards had a filled afternoon teasing him about being a pretty boy and found it funny and even curious that the boy should be in such pain because a woman had pulled his arm. What Chezi thought was even more curious, though, was that despite the cheerfulness and loud laughter, when he looked deeply into the boy's eyes, it seemed as if the boy had lost a part of his soul because the smile never seemed to reflect in his eyes. If Kazi wasn't his brother, he would have thought he was an assassin or a spy of some sort.

Two years after that, they met again when Kazi started training actively with the guerrillas, and this time, Kazi's identity became known to all, including Chezi. The news did not surprise Chezi as much as it did everyone else because as a young teen, he had known Aruma very well and recalled going to the palace on one or another errand to see Aruma on behalf of his mother. On one of such occasions, he had met Aruma's only child at the doorstep and had asked the child for his mother. He thought it was a girl at first because the child was so pretty. The child ran back to get his mother, and then Aruma came out with the child holding onto her loincloth and hopping along, an attitude that was typical of little girls, not little boys. The next time Chezi came around, the child wasn't with her, so he had asked Aruma after her daughter, and Aruma had laughed.

'My daughter is actually a son, and he has gone to serve his father his bitter drink for the evening.'

Chezi had never seen the child again after that but remembered those bright, pretty light brown eyes with long eyelashes.

Kazi's face had matured since, and he had grown a beard, but his eyes hadn't changed. They were still so pretty, and in adulthood, it looked as if he had three sets of teeth instead of one. Chezi recalled then that at Bana's wedding, when the lady pulled Kazi's left arm, Kazi jilted with pain as if the edges of a healing wound had been torn apart. It came to him that the sadness he had noticed in Kazi's eyes had to do with the manner in which the young lad's parents were killed and what he had had to go through following that.

Sitting there beside him that afternoon, he recalled all that.

'We will take back our land, young warrior. We will!'

* * *

Her maids had scrubbed the pots to what they thought was clean, but she pulled them back out and asked them to start scrubbing all over again.

In more ways than one, Diyateri was a very clean woman and extremely hard-working. Most described her as a perfectionist. She had learnt to read and write at the primary school, behind which she lived and learnt arithmetic to help her keep the accounts of the bush bar she was running against Utatu's wish. He found it demeaning that any of his wives should work and, more so, run a bar. In Lumani, it was unheard of that a woman of status be caught at a bar, much less run it as a business, but Utatu's efforts in dissuading her proved useless. Running her own business kept her busy and provided her more financial ease. She was way too dynamic to stay at home just cooking and cleaning like the other wives did.

She sold palm wine and palm oil in a strategic area between the farms and the houses, and this made her several clients. Men coming home from work on the plantations liked to stop at her bar to have a cool drink before heading home, and women coming back from the farms needed palm oil for cooking in the evening.

Because of this business, Pa Utatu had segregated her from the rest of his family. She still lived in his compound but had little or nothing to do with him. Every other wife had turns at cooking his meals but not her, at least until such a time as she would decide to close shop and apologise for her stubbornness. If Pa Utatu had had a choice, he would have sent her back to her parents, but because both were dead, he was obligated by culture to take care of her until her children grew old enough to take over. The rift between them was common knowledge in Lumani. She could feel the scorn even from her servants when they gave her respect with difficulty or pretended not to understand her instructions.

Farra approached her gently. 'Good afternoon, Mama Teri.' That was how everyone called her. 'What is going on?'

'Ah, my daughter, these people have been working with me a long time but still don't know how to scrub pots. How is your mother?'

'She is fine, Mama. I came by to see if Papa Utatu is home.'

'He went for a meeting with Ngui. Is anything urgent?'

'No, I just thought we should talk while he was away.' Farra sat down on the stool beside hers. 'Is he still angry with you?'

'Things have got worse. Yesterday, he cursed my children.' Mama Teri paused and then heaved. 'As if they are not his children as well.'

'He has to be a wicked man to do such a thing,' Farra said, pretending to be sad.

'If I had somewhere else to go to, I would have left already.'

Farra motioned for them to take a distance from the servants. 'It is possible to get even with him, you know.'

'How is that possible in this same Lumani where a woman's word is worth nothing? Even if I took my case to Sigue, Sigue would take his side. They are both men,' Mama Teri said sadly.

'I didn't mean Sigue or the Ngui or Wemtii or any council of men. I meant that just you on your own can get even.'

'How so?' She looked at Farra as one may a deliverer.

'He is doing business with the cobras. Do you know that?'

'Yes, but what can I do?' Mama Teri sighed. 'That is why I am glad he no longer gives me any money. I don't want that money to curse my children. In fact, that is what we were quarrelling about last night when he decided to curse them for me.'

'Why don't you put a portion of this medicine into his food?' Farra whispered and held out a bundle to Mama Teri.

'My daughter, your Papa Utatu has strong medicine. Getting to him will not be easy, and he may catch me and kill me. What happens to my children then?'

'You don't cook for him anymore, so how will he know it is you? Besides, Kolela has prepared this thing specially himself, and you know how strong he is. You will not be caught because he will shield you. Now let us work out a plan.'

Farra went on for about an hour to convince her that this medicine would solve all her problems. All she had to do was put one portion of it into his food, and it would make him invalid for long enough. They devised the strategy together, and Mama Teri, being a wit, proposed even brighter ideas. Farra never told her that a single portion of the poison could kill a stout stallion.

'My first wife, my sorrow is beyond measure,' Mama Teri said, standing in the doorway of the kitchen.

'That is normal. You have many problems. If you were not so stubborn, your life would be easier,' the first wife of Pa Utatu said without raising her head from the bowl of plantains that she was peeling for his evening meal of porridge plantains.

'My first wife, things have got worse. Pa Utatu cursed my children yesterday.'

'Aieeee!' The woman stopped to sympathise. 'That is so wicked. Are they not his children as well? Come in and sit down. Tell me what happened.'

Mama Teri had got the woman exactly where she needed her to be. She offered to help her cook while they talked. The woman was so consumed by the story that she didn't notice Mama Teri sprinkle something into the dish served for Pa Utatu (actually, for maximum effect, Mama Teri sprinkled three portions instead of one). She gave the dish to her daughter to take to Pa Utatu and continued with Mama Teri until late.

Mama Teri's convincing was so effective that the first wife informed the others, and from that evening on, every single wife of Utatu became weary of him and tried their best to avoid him. It was one thing to quarrel with one's wife but another to curse one's children because of it.

When Pa Utatu took ill the next afternoon, none of his wives were willing to come to his side. Each time he called, the wives pretended to be busy and sent their children instead. Not being a fool, Utatu noticed the growing chasm and called a priest to his aide. The priest tried to find the source of the illness, but the more he sought, the more confused he became until he gave up. Utatu suffered for six weeks before his eventual painful death. His wives and children could hear him moaning but, unsure what his dying words would be, kept to their houses. The priest stayed by his side, bearing the pain with him until he exhaled to empty his lungs for the last time.

In Utatu's compound, his wives suspected he might have been poisoned but could not tell which one of them had done it and how, and no one thought of asking Mama Teri because she didn't cook for Utatu anymore. Furthermore, the priest had been unable to say whether it was poisoning or real illness. Mama Teri did feel a little guilty about it but shrugged it off quickly because even though she realized that she may have killed him unintentionally, she felt that he deserved it. At least now her problems were over.

Infanini, the new high priest, performed the burial rites, it was not his place to judge, but he couldn't help himself when he came to the part where he had to address the ancestors.

'We have not burned his corpse to scatter over the Akiki because our patriarchs are chosen and ordained by Si. It is therefore on you to judge him. If you consider that he has lived a good life, then accompany him and defend him at Si's tribunal. But if you think as we do that he was wrong, then let him pay his debt in totality. With these spoken words, we send him off to you.'

* * *

Those six weeks Utatu took to die seemed such an eternity to the guerrillas that Kazi and Chezi began to question if Farra had actually done what they had agreed. She had always been a great emissary, but the thought that she might have inherited her father's treachery haunted their minds.

The nineteen-year-old had joined the resistance five years ago out of bitterness and a bid to clean her family's name or rather absolve them of their infamy. Daughter to Teresa, Farra was born out of wedlock to her mother two months after her father Cornelius had disappeared mysteriously. Most people presumed that he had run away out of guilt, but after his decaying body was found in the bushes, it became clear to everyone that he had been killed by the resistance. His body was burnt and the ashes scattered over the Akiki River, as was reserved for traitors.

Teresa's family tried to hide her pregnancy because everyone knew that Teresa had not been married to Cornelius nor had he ever intended to. She was one of the many girls around the clan whom Cornelius wooed for the fun of it. Her parents were planning on forcing Cornelius to make a decision when he disappeared suddenly. Unfortunately, since everybody knew everybody and watched everybody, the secret of her pregnancy was soon let out, and her family became a scum in the society, especially amongst the churchgoers. Her mother had to resign from her job of secretary in the Christian school, and her father, the assistant catechist, was made to leave his job and later died of depression. Teresa came to term and gave birth to a baby girl whom she called Farra (meaning 'to abandon') because she felt abandoned by Cornelius, the society, her fellow Christians, and even her closest friends.

Farra was a lively little girl who started walking before her first year and learnt to speak understandably before the end of her second year. She was too young to understand why their relatives hardly came around the house and shunned her whenever they did. They would pull their children away whenever they saw her playing with them and say something about bad blood that she never understood. Farra gradually got used to sitting in a corner and watching the other children play. She was only three when her grandmother saw her growing sadness and decided to send her to live with her own family in another clan to give her time to regain her cheerful nature. That seemed to work because the next time Teresa and her mother visited, Farra had become her cheerful self again. They decided that it would be better to keep things that way and let her stay with her grandmother's family, where the secret was not known.

Unfortunately, when her grandmother died, Teresa was obliged to bring Farra back to live in the main clan with her since she lived alone, and besides, Farra was about nine then, and it was time for her to start school. When she came to live with her mother, she was, of course, oblivious of the reason their relatives didn't visit much and insisted on paying them a visit sometime. Teresa tried to stop her, but she stubbornly insisted and returned with the broken heart that her mother had been trying to avoid. They had offered her a cold welcome and barely said a word. She could hear them whispering something about her but didn't know what. When she had tried to help with the cooking, her mother's cousin said something about not wanting the daughter of a prostitute and a traitor to touch her pots. Understanding why the statement was made was beyond Farra's years, but she did understand the meaning of the words and the disgust in the woman's eyes. Nobody noticed when she left the house with tears streaming down her face.

Farra regretted that she had ever asked when her mother told her the story. She wasn't old enough to fully understand the magnitude of her father's treachery, but she could feel a shame she couldn't bear, and her mother could feel what she felt. Teresa decided to return the child to her mother's family the next day and hopefully for good this time. She would be lonely living by herself, but a chance at her child's opportunity to live a life different from hers was worth any sacrifice she could humanly make. It was therefore very confusing for Teresa when Farra reappeared five years later and the reason for it. She had returned to join the resistance to spite everyone who called her the daughter of a traitor and to clean her family's name.

* * *

It was Chezi who had tasked her with the poisoning of Utatu, convinced that she could get the job done with the blink of an eye. When a week and another passed with nothing happening, Kazi was tempted to go there and drive a spear into the man's heart himself.

'The old wizard is dead at last,' Farra said shortly six weeks later.

'How can you be sure?' Kazi frowned.

'I told you, this matter is too serious to joke about – ' Chezi was reminding her when the traditional horns went off to announce the death of the patriarch.

Kazi and his guerrillas heaved a sigh of relief. They had been prepared several weeks before and were just waiting for Utatu to die. Also knowing how superstitious the Baluma were, they knew that as soon as word about the mystery surrounding his death got out through Farra, the confusion that would follow would serve them well.

* * *

In the seven weeks of mourning that followed, one could hear the sound of the most silent of winds blowing through Lumani. Confusion ravaged the kingdom as word about the suffering and mysterious death of the patriarch spread. It was the unsolved mystery surrounding his death that gave the panic legs and wings. Sigue was in a panic, the people were in panic, the Ngui was in panic, and the contagious agitation spread to the Wemtii and to the cobras after that.

The cobra commander Matthias had a slightly different governing style from his predecessor (Derrick). Matthias relied a lot on the secret service he had set up, which he made Utatu lead. With both the patriarch and the interim king on his payroll, he had a tight grip on Lumani. The trouble was that Utatu was so good at his job that Matthias had never thought of finding a replacement, and in his opinion, Sigue was too much of a coward to be suitable for the job. He needed a replacement who was as ruthless and egoistic as Utatu to continue his tenure peacefully. Therefore, with Utatu gone suddenly, he was destitute, especially with one soldier reported missing and the last disturbing piece of information Utatu had given him before he had taken ill. He hoped that the seven-week period of mourning would give him time to find one, but he was not so lucky.

* * *

'Surprise is our greatest ally. We have to attack by the end of the week, and we need to strike the enemy with a vengeance that sends terror to the rest of them in other parts of the country and the continent. I have experience trading weapons to resistance movements, and I can tell you that our victory will serve not just to restore our Baluma pride but also to encourage the other resistance movements around the continent. Our victory will sound the battle cry. The cobras are vindictive and greedy. We won't get a chance like this for another thirty years. Warriors of Baluma, I am Balumakazi, second son of Ottuwa, third son of Tozingana, eleventh son of Shesweh, and I will strike on the next market day because that is the kind of blood that runs in my veins. If anybody here disagrees, leave now, and I will hold you no grudge.'

Kazi struck his machete into the ground, and the guerrillas did the same to show oneness.

It was a tradition amongst Baluma warriors that before announcing a major battle, the commander would state his position, remind them of his ancestry, and then strike his machete into the ground. Whoever agreed would do the same to show that they accepted him as their commander, that they would fight by him, and that, for the duration of the battle, all discord and hatches they had with him or with one another would be buried and only unearthed after the battle was over.

Nsika stood behind him all the while, hardly believing that the little boy he had slung over his shoulders and fled Lumani with nineteen years ago had grown into such a strong man, commanding such authority and power and driving his machete into the ground with elegance and determination. He noticed that Kazi had the dagger and gourd strapped around his waist, and he asked in silent prayer for Wandi to protect the boy. No one except Kazi, Kolela, and Nsika understood what 'second son of Ottuwa' meant.

* * *

During that week, Kazi and Chezi laid out the final plan to the guerrillas, and Kolela performed the rituals for protection and victory. Infanini had not yet met the guerrillas because following Makafu's passing, he had gone through twelve weeks of fasting when he couldn't be in contact with anyone to prepare himself for ordination. Right after his ordination, the horns had gone off to announced the death of the patriarch. He had stayed in Lumani, trying to quell the panic and find a new patriarch (who turned out to be a matriarch), and sent word to Njuu, charging Kolela with the task of preparing the guerrillas and shielding their attack from the cobras and whoever Utatu's allies were.

They chose to attack at the darkest hour of the night when there was not a single star in the sky or shade of the moon. Farra supervised the little boys to tie the bundles on the branches of the trees that had been assigned to them. She went back and forth, making sure that all the trees in the strategic areas marked out had been loaded with the palm oil and kerosene bundles. It was the dry season, and the trees would catch easily.

Chezi got his troops to the hill overlooking the cobra residences, while Kazi targetted the administrative buildings and the prisons. The guerrillas were well prepared and well-armed, and the new ammunition that had been delivered two weeks back worked effectively, but they were extra prudent because this battle was crucial and because Nsika had informed them that there would be more soldiers than previously thought because Matthias had discovered that the guerrillas had broken the defence lines they had set up to shield Lumani from attacks. That was the last piece of information Utatu had given Matthias before he took ill. Matthias had followed up by reinforcing security with more troops in Lumani and was considering other ways of shielding the kingdom when Utatu had passed.

Farra was at the Matthias's doorstep with a basket of something. She knocked on the door and bent her head down to give the impression she was frightened and shy.

'Who is knocking at this hour of the night?' a cobra said, pulling his gun out. When he opened to a seemingly frightened young woman, he sighed and replaced his gun. 'OK, who is it that you want to see?' he said, knowing that in Lumani, young women seen with cobras were stigmatised, so to avoid that, some came stealthily at night to see their cobra friends.

Farra raised her head sharply as if she was having a hiccup, startling him. A second later, she threw the basket at him and ran off screaming. Out spilled its contents – the head of a soldier (the one soldier reported missing) who had been caught by the guerrillas and beheaded for the purpose as he wandered around the forest on a lonely evening.

Farra ran in a zigzag pattern to dodge the bullets the soldier shot at her as he chased her into the dark. The young boys heard Farra screaming and began to scream as well until she got to the first tree and lit it. They lit up their trees in answer, and Lumani came ablaze. That was the signal. The screaming and torching trees unscrewed the soldier completely. He stopped chasing and ran back to Matthias's house in fear.

Kazi's team attacked the administrative block and the prisons, with Chezi's team attacking the cobra residences and camps simultaneously. They went from one area to another, killing every cobra in sight and native soldiers who tried to fight back.

One could say that Ngemba was a very angry young native or, to be fairer, that his father pushed him to it. He had joined the guerrillas, trained with them, and was prepared to fight because he had grown up with the injustice of the invasion and had observed much more than what everyone thought he had. He helped with espionage and worked closely with Farra. Ngemba wasn't quick with his tongue or rough with his brush until pushed to the limits of his patience, but when it came to it, his physical strength and wit did all the talking. He was just sixteen but was strong and witty. He had challenged guerrillas much older and stronger than him during the trainings they had. Several of them admitted he was a nut to reckon with, and he grew only stronger with training. However, his slow speech and contemplative personality made him slow in reaction, and everyone, including his father, decided that he was unfit to be a guerrilla, at least not the kind they needed. Therefore, when the time came, his father asked him to stay home that night and keep watch over the family.

However bitter and angry Ngemba may have been that night; Chezi's problem was less about Ngemba's feelings and more about the safety of his family. He would not be able to explain to his wife or mother why he let Ngemba out that night to fight with him in a battle that he was doing for honour and, worse, a battle that he couldn't swear he would survive (and his own father hadn't). It was therefore to preserve Ngemba that Chezi decided to keep him home that night, even though the boy had proven himself in ways that had amazed even him. He had tried to explain to his first son what dangers lay ahead, but the crispy young man was too agitated for the fight, especially because, according to the plan, Farra would be at the head of it. His ego wouldn't let him sit at home while a girl fought. Chezi had to ask Bamba to intervene to persuade Ngemba not to follow him or do anything brash. Ngemba had promised Bamba by word of mouth, but because his heart wouldn't let him say it sincerely, Bamba kept him under close watch – but apparently not close enough.

* * *

He was told to watch over the family, and so he did, making rounds around the compound and keeping everybody from coming out, when they heard the screaming or the gunshots around them and anchoring the guerrillas his father had put on guard to put out what flames came through.

'Salana,' Ngemba whispered, 'take care of things here. Let me go and root these traitors out. I know more of them than anyone knows.'

'Who are you going with?' his younger brother asked.

'I will wake my friends up.'

'Ngem, Papa will not be happy if you step out of this compound.'

'I will not die. I am stronger than he or any of you thinks I am. Besides, I have some of the guns he left in his chambers.'

'You know where he keeps them? How did you discover that?'

'Well, contrary to popular opinion, I observe everything that goes on in this house and in Lumani.'

'Please be careful,' Salana said fearfully.

'Don't raise your voice. I will wake my friends up, and we will go out as a group. Keep things under control here while am gone. Can I trust you with that?'

'Yes, yes, you just be careful.'

Ngemba went out with the group and joined the guerrillas. They identified the homes, and their numbers fought for them, even though they were poorly armed (but for the few guns that Ngemba had distributed, all they had were machetes, kitchen knives, and a few pitchforks). They attacked their homes, burning down the houses and killing their families. When the native soldiers realized that they were being targetted, they began to desert the cobra army, taking off their uniforms and running back to their homes to pretend to be asleep with their families. Some were lucky, but most were not and were caught and killed on their way home or were killed right in their homes because one or another person recognised them. It was as if the Baluma had been waiting for this battle cry.

The group increased as they went on, and Ngemba had to admit that the battle was more horrifying than anything he had ever imagined. He prayed to Abimi to shield him from death.

The door of Matthias's office was broken down, and Kazi scanned through the office for notes and documents that they could use. He figured that typically, there should be a register where all the records of the soldiers in Lumani were kept (a thing he had learnt trading drugs to the cobra soldiers in Yaketu). That would give them a good indication of how many they were up against and where they were stationed. Drawing from his experience, he also expected to find a record of how much ammunition the cobras had and where it was stashed.

When Kazi found what he had been looking for, he skirted the office for anything else that might be of use. A sheet he picked up indicated the names of all the native soldiers. Another sheet had the names of all the nobles of the Wemtii and the Ngui. Some of the names had X signs marked beside them. He raised his head from the papers, and his eyes fell on a map. He had to squeeze his eyes twice and open them wide to believe what he was seeing. There, on the wall in front of him was a detailed map of Lumani, including the forest area beside it. An arrow pointed to the Njuu, and at the end of the arrow, scratchy writing read 'Base of the rebels'. There was a line drawn in red ink at the boundary between Lumani and the forest that had beside it 'Defence line broken, 7th October 1933.

The nine Baluma clans were well mapped out, with the names of each clan indicated, and there were dots on the places where the Wemtii and the Ngui lived, with their names and the number of people in their households noted beside the dots. The key of the map indicated the number of inhabitants of each clan and the number of nobles in the clan. With another squeeze of his eyes, he noticed there were X signs beside the same names as there were on the paper. This was too confusing to figure out with his heart racing. Kazi replaced the papers, collected the other documents that he needed, and locked the office. He put a few guerrillas to guard the building and continued with the troops to the next target, which was the prisons. Most of his troops were already on their way there by foot.

The driver ignited the engine of the van and started off. There was a gunshot, and the vehicle swirled in a zigzag pattern before hitting a tree. Kazi felt a thick substance on his shirt and rubbed it off before he realized it was the driver's brains. They got down and fired back in every direction into the night but weren't sure exactly from where the shots were coming. At Kazi's signal, the men took cover behind the trees and waited for the next round.

A few seconds later, the firing started again. This time, they spotted the direction of the attack. The cobras came out from the bushes and approached the vehicle slowly. A flame thrown their direction gave Kazi their exact number, and the firing continued. But when the guerrillas counted the bodies on the ground, there was one missing and a pair of legs on the other side of the vehicle. Kazi lay on his belly and aimed but missed, giving the cobra time to enter the van. Kazi needed to decide whether to blow up one of the four precious vans Yem had gifted them or preserve it along with the cobra's life. He took the grenade and threw it in anyway.

The explosion drew the attention of other guerrillas not far away and drew more cobras out of the bushes, reinforcing both sides. Kazi ran out of bullets and ducked behind a tree to reload. The pain in his left arm drew him to stop for a moment to realize he had been brushed by a bullet, and the wound was deep, but he had no time to pause. He stifled the pain and got out from behind the tree, firing as he ran towards the cobras. There was a last one beside the burning van, and he approached him and shot him dead as his men ran forwards in search of other cobras around. Kazi cut off a piece of the man's shirt and used it as a temporary bandage on his wound. When he stood up, he was almost shot by his own guerrillas who saw him from the back stooping beside the dead cobra and thought he was a cobra trying the help his comrade. Luckily, Kazi ducked in time and shouted out before their bullets could hit him.

They broke down the warehouse where the stockpiles of weapons were kept and helped themselves but had to walk to the prisons because the van was gone, along with the only guerrilla around who could drive it.

Kazi let the prisoners out, armed them, and grouped them. He told them the ultimate objective of the battle: to rid Lumani of the cobras. Most had been imprisoned there for months for committing offences like stealing a few hands of plantains or cassava or palm kernels from the plantations they worked on or other minor offences against the administration. Others were there because they had given support to the guerrillas in one way or another and had been caught. The prisoners had been planning their own escape, and some had been contemplating retaliation, so Kazi's attack came with perfect timing. Ridding Lumani of the cobras was all the prisoners needed to hear, and Kazi's army increased by the number of prisoners but for one or two who were too sick to fight. They headed to join Chezi at the residences and camps.

Terrifying screaming preceded the stampede that followed at the residences as the guerrilla bullets flew all over the place. The women tried to hide their children in every cupboard or closet possible, but the guerrillas' thirst for cobra blood was insatiable. They caught and killed everyone they found, from the master of the house to the littlest child.

Chezi was in no mood for a conscience check; he had loved his father, and nightmares about his father's last battle had haunted him his whole life. His hate for the cobras had grown steadily with every passing day, especially as they continued to tax the family even after his father's death, and Matthias had recently imposed special taxes on the families he considered 'rebellious families', which were actually the families of well-known warriors. Chezi had carried that hate his whole life, and this battle was the perfect platform to throw it all out. His guns shot perfectly, and he didn't miss a target. He was the best shot of the army, and on this night, he shot down especially the cries for mercy.

As they stormed from one house to another, they were received with more and more resistance because the cobras were waking up. The guerrillas hadn't anticipated that the cobras would have as many guns as they had in the residences. From the information they had received, most weapons were kept in the warehouse near the administrative building.

Chezi shot through the door before breaking it down. The house was quiet and almost seemed empty. The guerrillas went through, turning over everything, and Chezi went through the rooms again and again, cupboard by cupboard, until he opened up a cupboard that punched him in the face. His gun fell to the ground, and he had to wrestle the man. The guerrillas heard him struggling and shot the cobra in the head just as he planted a kitchen knife so deep into Chezi's lap that the edge of the knife almost came out at the other end. The cobra twisted the knife on his way down, and Chezi felt as if his leg was being cut off. Two women were found under the bed (one older, one much younger). Chezi ordered for them to be left alive. He and Kazi had decided earlier on that it would be necessary to keep a few alive to tell the story. They were bound and locked up in a little house usually used by the cobras as a doghouse.

A grenade was thrown through the kitchen window to wake them up. The family rushed out through the front door to meet their deaths. The guerrillas had surrounded the house, and Kazi was standing right in front of the door, waiting for the moment. As soon as the door was opened, he opened fire, eliminating the last family.

Chezi was getting weaker and dizzier from the wounds until it became apparent to his troops that the only strength he had left was the vengefulness in his heart. He was limping and slowing the group down but did not stop firing until Yango (one of his commanders) took command and asked for him to be made to rest in one of the residences until morning when they could fetch medicine and tend the wound. The camp where the soldiers lived had already been set ablaze by the guerrillas by the time Kazi and Yango got there and was a graveyard by the time they both left an hour later.

They had not yet decided whether to spare the priests and the nuns of Lumani. Kazi had nothing against this church but for what he considered false teachings. As long as they did not come between his independence and him, they could stay around, convincing anybody who was foolhardy enough to worship their white god. The churches were burnt down to make the point, and they marched on, leaving Nsika with the keys to Matthias's office (so he and Ndikwa could continue the study on cobra intelligence on Lumani) and Chezi in the company of a few soldiers.

The bloodiest battle in the history of Lumani (at least up until that point) lasted the whole night and some of the next day.

In the afternoon, the guerrillas took a rest and reported to have reconquered the entire clan, but they still had eight more to go. Kazi reminded them that the objective word was *surprise*. They needed to rest but also needed to get back to the battle as soon as possible because they couldn't let the cobras in the capital city have the time to attack before all Lumani had been reconquered. They agreed to continue at sundown when they were rested enough.

Chezi wanted to know what Kazi would do about Sigue as they studied the documents Kazi had taken from Matthias's office.

'We will leave that for the end. For now, I have asked Yango to dispatch a few men to guard the palace,' Kazi answered and then asked, 'Did you get Matthias?'

'No, but we know he is hiding in his house. We have circled the area and killed all the soldiers on guard. He is bound to rear his head at some point. I will come back for him when the battle is over.'

Chezi was not strong enough by sundown, even though he was determined to be. Kazi put him in the care of a herbalist who, by some miracle, persuaded him to heal a little before joining them again. They had the plan well laid out, so Chezi knew what the sequence of attacks would be on the different clans. He closed his eyes and tried to sleep.

'Papa, Papa, wake up.'

Chezi tried to open his eyes. The medicine the herbalist had given him made him sleep so deeply that he found it difficult to keep his eyes open for more than a few minutes. He tried to open them because the voice sounded so familiar, and then they shot out when he saw Ngemba sitting beside him.

'Ngemba! What are you doing here? Does your grandmother know where you are?'

'Papa, calm down. It is bad for you. The herbalist said you were stabbed with a poisoned knife, so I was worried.'

'What?' Chezi looked at the herbalist.

It all made sense that the venom of a snake would be the only thing that would have made him that weak and dizzy, especially when the knife had cut through a vein and the venom had had time to spread. But he wasn't forgiving Ngemba just yet.

'Go back home and stay there.' Then he noticed the guerrilla uniform and the bloodstains. 'What have you been doing, Ngem?'

'We are doing quite fine, Papa. We identified the houses of the spies and native soldiers and took them out.'

Chezi would have given him a beating if he wasn't so weak. 'I promise you, when the battle is over, we will let you join the army, but go home now and stay there until I return!'

'Yes, Papa,' Ngemba answered, but both knew he wouldn't.

Chezi closed his eyes and said a silent prayer for the boy.

* * *

At sundown, the troops regrouped for the next attack. The men cleaned their guns and machetes and sprayed incense on their bodies and around their noses to kill the smell of the blood.

Dozens of young men formed a group and marched behind the guerrillas (with Ngemba leading the pack), armed with spades, machetes, kitchen knives, and anything they could use as weapons. Throughout the war, the guerrillas never had to ask for help. The natives were extremely cooperative, feeding the guerrillas and tending their wounds, offering them shelter to rest before the battles. It was as if they had been waiting for this moment. This reaction warmed Kazi's heart as he realized Kolela had been right all along.

'A people without leadership are conquerable and easily divisible, but once the leader takes his place, the reign of the cobra will come to an end,' Kazi whispered the words to himself again.

Chezi rejoined them on the third day. His wound was still healing, but the poison was out, and the herbalist had tied the wound properly and numbed the area around it so that Chezi could run and fight without any problem.

The next clan had fewer cobras than indicated on the sheet of paper, so they wondered whether the cobras had got word about the attack and had fled. Nevertheless, it served their purpose well. The order was given, and they began to march on the next clan. As it was with the first battle, the young men, with Ngemba's engineering, joined the guerrillas each time so that by the time they got to the last clan, their victory was inevitable. In this last clan, they got the cobra soldiers at exactly the spots that were indicated on the paper and other information Nsika had discovered in the office.

A few hours later, the guerrillas sounded the victory horns, and they marched back to the main clan where it had all started. They counted sixty dead and a hundred and two wounded on their side. There was just one person missing: Matthias.

They broke down the door of Matthias's house and searched the house.

When they couldn't find him, Yango went out to see Chezi. 'He must have escaped through a window. The question is how.'

Chezi took his long gun and walked in. He sniffed the air like a trained dog and said, 'He is still in here. I can smell him.'

The guerrillas thought he was making one of his usual jokes when he went to check the living room and bedrooms and found them empty. They were awestruck when Chezi stepped into the kitchen and looked up.

'Come down here.'

Chezi shot at him to make him drop. Matthias had perched on a rafter of the kitchen ceiling all the while.

He was bound and taken to where the women were kept. The doghouse was not big enough to contain the three of them. Yango put Matthias's head and shoulders in first and then squeezed him in from behind, with the women screaming in pain all the while to the amusement of the guerrillas.

The whole war had taken four days and five nights to fight, but at the end of it, the guerrillas and natives were still not tired.

Kazi stepped onto a small platform that had been built for him to speak to the crowd. The platform was not built too high because he was already so tall. He looked like a pillar as he stood on it to announce that Lumani had been retaken. The crowd was berserk with excitement and emotion. Kazi couldn't believe it when he looked around and saw tears in the eyes of the most fearless of his commanders and thought it strange that Farra's eyes were still on fire after four intensive days of fighting. He took it all in for a while before he breathed.

'We have won the battle, but the war is not over. In the coming days, we will need to be more vigilant, better trained, and prepared for surprises. The cobras are greedy, and in spite of how much they have taken from us, they will return to take whatever is left. Never forget that! Our fight from now on is to defend what is ours, to preserve all what we have retaken from those who stole from us.'

After he stepped down from the platform, a woman walked out of the crowd and towards Kazi with a little baby in her arms, making him stop. She placed the baby in his arms with tears in her eyes. Kazi held the baby, not knowing what that meant.

'He is yours.'

Kazi was about to say, 'He can't be mine. I don't even know you,' when Chezi whispered in his ears to give the baby back and say, 'Take care of him for me.'

The woman added, 'You should have come earlier,' and went back into the crowd, leaving Kazi puzzled at that last statement.

The people did not know who he was or where he was from, but that was of little importance. He had brought them freedom, and their gratitude was all they had to give back to him. They hailed the man they called 'the tall commander' as he walked through the crowd to get back into the van.

In the van, Chezi explained to Kazi what the baby signified. In Baluma culture, the greatest gift a woman could offer a man was a child. But both wondered why the woman would offer her baby to Kazi, what she had to be grateful for besides the victory that had benefitted everyone, and what she meant by the last statement.

They later discovered that the woman was a widow whose husband had been helping the guerrillas with espionage by giving Nsika information about the number of troops in Lumani and the kind of artillery they had, information he had access to because he worked in the warehouse where the weapons were stashed. Someone had overheard him giving information to Nsika and told on him. They took him one night, and he never returned home. He was tortured to death because he wouldn't give up information on the Njuu and how many guerrillas there were. She also had three sons who were shot in front of her on the same night her husband was taken because they had tried to fight back. The cobras only spared the baby because he was too small, and then they defiled her and left. All this had happened barely two weeks before Kazi's attack.

* * *

When they had rested and decided on what next to do, they were approached by a goddess.

'Balumakazi, Nsika never mentioned how tall you are,' she said, half-smiling.

Kazi was flustered. The woman was so pretty, so composed, so magnificent, and as she spoke, she had such a grandiose air around her that humbled even a very proud Kazi.

He tried to sound charming, hoping to entice her. 'And how would a coquette know Nsika?' He lifted one eyebrow flirtingly.

'Kazi, I would like you to meet Bana, Pa Wandi's daughter, Hani's wife, my sister-in-law, and the new matriarch of Baluma,' Chezi said with an amused look in his eyes. It was the sort of fun that Chezi liked to make of Kazi, and if there was a hole in the ground, Kazi would have gladly jumped into it.

'Why don't you ask the ground to open up and swallow me, bush pig?' Kazi asked between gritted teeth.

* * *

Sigue peered through the half-closed window, trembling in his knees as he watched a man talking to Chezi in front of the palace entrance. He couldn't make out who he was but supposed that he must be a rebel because of the way he was dressed. He came away from the window and bit his thumb to think.

What could Chezi have in mind? And why did he need the stranger? Had he found the connection between him and Pa Utatu? With the cobras

all dead except a few who had been captured as he had been told, what did
Chezi intend to do now in Lumani?

Sigue racked his scarce brains but found nothing. He resigned that
if Chezi wanted the throne, he was free to have it as long as he let him
live. After all, the real successor was dead, so the throne was literarily
empty, and he wasn't eager to lead the people now that the cobras had
been defeated and the people were free again, and even if he was, he
wouldn't know how to.

When the knocking at the door started, Sigue didn't take any
chances. He crept under the bed and stayed there, even though the
knocking was done in the traditional manner where a person came to
the main door of the palace, knocked three times, waited, knocked
seven times, nine times, and then twelve times, and started over until
the door was opened. The palace guards stood there, numb, expecting
Chezi to break open and kill them all.

Mpima stepped forward and opened the door, drawing courage
from the fact that she had known Chezi as a boy and was on friendly
terms with his mother. Chezi had not forgotten his manners. He bowed
gently and asked to see Sigue.

Mpima looked at him with imploring eyes. 'You don't have to
kill him.'

'I do not intend to, Mama, but he needs to step aside.'

'How do you mean, step aside?'

Kazi stood behind him, looking around. The place had changed so
much. During the days, he used to sneak into Lumani under the guise
of a businessman. He sometimes stopped at a safe distance to look at
the palace nostalgically. It had seemed pretty much the same to him
then, but now on closer look, he could see that a lot had changed and
mostly for the worse. It was not as clean and well maintained as it had
been when his mother was alive.

Mpima saw him looking around. 'If you don't intend to kill him,
why is your guerrilla looking around like that, as if he wants to clean
out this place?'

'You will understand soon, Mama. Just let us see Pa Sigue.'

Kazi did not see why he had to haggle with Mpima. He stretched his long arms, pushed open the door, and strolled slowly into the house with the impunity of an owner. By now, Sigue had come out from under the bed and was sitting in a small stool in a corner, listening keenly with fright.

Without jostling the old man, Kazi pulled his jacket off and the T-shirt underneath it to reveal the mark underneath his left breast, causing Sigue to exhale and his eyes to multiply in size.

'*God of my ancestors!*'

'Get out of my chair!' The young lion set upon him.

Sigue nearly broke his back trying to get to his feet and then surrendered to the ground.

Chezi and Mpima were still standing in the doorway, watching them as it happened, Chezi with regalement but Mpima with fright.

* * *

The king's investiture was a long and time-taking process in Lumani, even for those who were involved. It first had to be proven that the one to be enthroned was indeed the one who had been chosen. Kazi couldn't see how that would be possible since the only evidence he had was the mark on his chest, and anybody could mark themselves. Neither did he understand the ritual performed where he was made to swear on his father's skull that he was indeed his son. When that was over, he noted nine other strange-looking stools around the one he was made to sit on in the middle of a room.

The Ngui came in and sat around him in silence. Infanini walked in and introduced him to these people as 'the boy we have been talking about'. To his knowledge, only the guerrillas and a few others like Nsika and Kolela were aware of his existence, but here he was in the middle of the old men, and Bana and two of them in particular looked at him with such a familiarity as if they had known him from the time he was a boy.

It was Kwahi who spoke first. 'Yes, that is indeed him. I can swear on my mother's grave for it.'

'So can I,' Tendo concurred.

'But given what happened in this council with Utatu, perhaps the others will need proof of it,' Infanini said.

'Of course. It is always better to make these things clear to everyone,' Kwahi agreed, and Tendo seconded.

The others wanted to know how such a thing could be kept secret for such a long time. They had kept it secret from the Ngui because of Utatu, Infanini explained. When it was time to mark Kazi, Infanini had informed Kwahi and Tendo and made them secretly assist to bear witness later on.

To satisfy the others and ensure no further doubt, Kazi was made to chew *the tree bark*. If he was not the one who had been chosen, he would develop sores on his feet and leprosy, and by the end of the third day, he would be dead.

After the three days were over, he was presented again to the Ngui, and this time, everyone cheered. Infanini and his priests took him away for nine days, during which he stayed at the shrine with no contact to anyone and eating once a day after sunset prayers, which didn't bother him except that doing business and making lots of money had also come with a habit of liquor in the evenings and a pipe of freshly ground herbs; the lack of these made the nine days very trying. He was not allowed to touch or speak to anyone around, not even the people who served him the meal. He wore a light cloth around his waist as his only form of clothing during the period. Every day, a priest came with a new cloth for him.

During the rituals, he was to keep silent and let the priests pray over him. All that was expected of him was that he had to do what the priests asked, raising his arms or bending his back in one direction or the other, and from time to time, 'wise men' would come to give him advice that he was not expected to respond to but simply to absorb.

All this was exasperating for Kazi. He didn't see why it had to be nine days instead of nine hours or nine minutes. He stalked around his room like a caged beast for the first days and then got calmer and calmer until he began to appreciate the sapience of silence.

Chezi was in charge of Lumani while Kazi was in 'preparation'. The nine days of prayers and fasting gave Kazi time to think about the kind of king he wanted to be. He promised his ancestors that if the cobras attacked while he was in preparation, he would forego his investiture to defend his people, but if they kept the kingdom calm and protected from attack until he finished, he would assume his throne as designed and, for the remainder of his life, fight every cobra who so much as dared to rear his head against Lumani.

Amongst the 'wise men' was Nsika. It was hard for him not to speak to Nsika when he came, but he succeeded because, knowing him, Nsika made it possible.

Kazi had his gaze on the setting sun when Nsika came into the room. The few days of prayers and meditation had increased Kazi's sensitivity, so he could feel Nsika around.

'Do not turn around, young lion.' He took a seat far off from Kazi in the opposite end of the room. 'People conquering people is not a new concept in the world, and the conqueror always considers themselves superior. I know that is what hurts you the most, and it hurts me too, but remember that this is not about some divinely ordained superiority but what the conqueror wants the conquered to believe. It is all about the conqueror and his victory. So don't blame Si. Don't turn your back on Si because of this. There is no racism, just a conqueror and his politics designed to make the conquered feel inferior. In the world, there will always be a conqueror and a conquered, at least until we all learn not to conquer or be conquered. Teach the world that!'

Kazi was so consumed with the words that he didn't know when Nsika left the room.

* * *

While Kazi was in seclusion, Chezi was up to mischief. He was in charge of getting the kingdom cleaned up and the systems running again. Kazi had told him to keep the three cobras alive until he got back, and Chezi loved that Kazi was not in a hurry to send them back. He loved the idea of having cobras in his prison the same way the cobras did with the natives, and he paid them back in their own coin.

He had them put into a cage made of cane and rope and left under the sun the whole day every day. This quite excited the natives, who would come around and jeer at them, throwing bananas at them like they used to do with the natives. In the evenings, Chezi had the cage lifted and taken to the riverbank so mosquitoes could gnaw at their skin. They were beaten every day and fed once every three days. They were made to eat from the ground with their hands tied behind their backs.

Everything Chezi could remember had been done to those imprisoned by the cobras was done to them, until Matthias begged for them to kill him. Chezi gladly promised to grant him his wish.

* * *

On the ninth day, the palace was prepared for the enthroning at sunset. The walls were decorated and the place cleaned up, and incense was burnt the whole day. Three priests gathered in a particular area of the palace and burned herbs to stop the rain. Some people came to the entrance of the palace and stayed there the whole day, watching the preparation, including Mpima, who was there to take detailed notes for her husband. Sigue's family had been moved out of the palace. The only people left in the compound were Ottuwa's two wives and their children, Kazi's stepbrothers and stepsisters, whom he had not yet met. The traditional horns were blown the whole day long with different sounds to send messages around the nine clans.

He sat in the inner chambers of the palace where his father had been prepared and looked around the room, whispering a prayer to his mother.

'Mama, hold my shoulder as I take my oath. I want to make you proud. I need to defend our land for posterity so that our children will not have to live on foreign lands as I did, in hiding and fearful of coming home. I will fight to the death, Mama, to make you proud. I will, I promise you, because I know that that is the kind of king you want me to be. I refuse to live in submission, I refuse to live in indignity, and I refuse to run. Give me strength, Mama.'

Kazi shut his bloodshot eyes to rest before Kolela and Infanini came in to begin the pre-enthronement ritual. He had not slept for the last two nights because on the seventh night, he had been introduced to astral travel and led to the forest to meet his totem.

Kolela and Infanini taught him how to spread the herbs around, burn the incense, trace the sacred signs, and place the ornaments to gird the environment so that when he went to sleep, he could dissociate his body from his spirit and travel to see his totem. They performed the rites necessary to connect him to his totem: a cow elephant. It was unusual because typically, in Baluma spirituality, a man would be connected to a male animal and a woman to a female animal. But for Kazi, the ancestors had chosen differently, connecting him to a female instead. Infanini explained what a cow elephant signified.

'She exemplifies wisdom, authority, power, loyalty, stamina, commitment, and physical strength. As matriarch of her school, she leads the way in an inclusive manner, understanding that family is not just about blood ties but also those who are loyal and committed to the school. A cow elephant has no limits to the kind of sacrifice she can make for one of her own. In a period of draught, she draws water from her own body to feed the young. She gives up her own water to quench the younger ones' thirst.'

The last two nights had therefore been very exhausting for Kazi because sometimes he got the signs wrong or put herbs in the wrong places and so afterwards couldn't dissociate his body from his spirit. Kolela would have to do it all over again and wordlessly at that, which meant that he would have to watch Kolela carefully and remember it all through tired eyes and on an empty stomach.

And that was not the only problem. When he got to meet her that first night, his totem was totally unfriendly and completely ignored him. He had to go back and bring Kolela with him, hopeful it would help. She communicated with Kolela as if they had known each other for years, but with him, she looked at him as if she had more to teach him than he had to teach her. The first night was so discouraging and exhausting for Kazi, he never thought he would be able to communicate with her.

Luckily, on the second night, his adamancy got the better of him. When they were leaving her to go back to their bodies, Kazi told her, 'You are my shadow, and I will call you Khala whether or not it pleases you.'

She was silent for a moment or two. Then to their surprise, she raised her trunk and blew into the air with melodious harmony and joy. The sound was so deafening and the spiritual energy so powerful that their physical bodies turned, and it took three hours of Infanini's intervention to get the bodies and spirits to reconnect.

From that night onwards, Kazi developed a close companionship with his totem that stayed until the end of his life.

* * *

Infanini stood in front of him with eight other priests, four to his left and four to his right, each standing behind the other, forming a triangle. Kolela stood at Infanini's immediate right, holding a small bowl that was burning incense. The priest to Infanini's immediate left carried the sacred crown that had a sign of a torch and an axe crossing each other. After the prayers, they dressed him up with a blue woven loincloth and rubbed a paste on the mark beneath his left breast so that it glittered as if it had been lined with gold. They sat him down in a stool in the court of the palace, just a few paces behind the door of the main entrance. Then turned around and, maintaining their positions behind Infanini, walked slowly out to the yearning crowd. The Ngui and the Wemtii were already there in traditional regalia.

There was a large pot burning incense. The high priest stood directly behind it and, when the crowd settled, raised his head to the sky and said a prayer for the breaking of a new dawn. Two priests moved out of position and came to Infanini's side, one carrying a large axe and the other a burning torch. Kolela held the dagger and the gourd which, it had been decided, would henceforth be returned to the king's keeping instead of the *afomi*.

Infanini turned so that he had his back to the large pot and crowd and the door of the main entrance of the palace straight in front. 'The one that the ancestors have chosen, come out and take your place!' he called out nine times, raising his voice each time he called so that by the ninth time, it sounded as if his voice had reached the sky, and the sky answered back with lightning and thunder in broad daylight.

The palace doors were flung open, and Balumakazi came through slowly. The crowd was flabbergasted as it came through that the 'tall commander' was the boy they had been told had died nineteen years ago.

He approached Infanini and said, 'I am here to take my place.'

'Sit down and stretch out your right arm.'

Infanini put the blade of the dagger on Kazi's palm, and Kolela held the opened gourd underneath it.

'Are you prepared to protect the people of Lumani, from everyone, even from your mother?'

The question was repeated nine times, and each time, Kazi answered, 'I am.'

'Then seal it with your blood!' the high priest ordered.

Kazi closed his palm to squeeze the blade of the dagger. Infanini pulled the blade out, and Kazi reopened his palm to let the blood surface and then closed it again to let the drops of blood fall into the gourd. When Kolela had counted nine drops, he pulled the gourd away and closed its mouth. A priest rubbed some powdery substance into Kazi's open hand, and the blood stopped suddenly.

The crown was strapped around his head, the axe placed in his right hand, and the burning torch in his left hand as a rainbow circled the sky to signify the approval of the anointing by the ancestors and by Si, the axe symbolic of the king's protective role and the torch symbolic of wisdom and vision.

Infanini ended the ritual. 'Stand up and take your place, my king.'

King Balumakazi rose to his feet. The priests formed a triangle, with the high priest first in front of him. They stooped, bowed their heads, and touched the ground with their right hands in Kazi's direction. The Ngui and Wemtii bowed in the same manner, and the people followed.

The royal chair was brought out. Kazi sat on the chair and placed his right foot on the stool in front of it. The veneration began with the Ngui presenting Kazi with a bunch of palm kernels, which he threw to the crowd. In Lumani, that signified that the king was no king without his people; they gave to him, and he gave back to them. He was introduced to his father's wives and their children, who would now be his responsibility, and then followed the Wemtii, who introduced themselves, and then there was eating and dancing all through the night.

* * *

The two women and Matthias were cleaned up and put in the vehicle. Ngemba took the wheel because he was one of the few who could drive. Yango sat beside him in the passenger's seat. They weren't sure why Kazi had asked them to bring the cobras to him, and when Matthias asked, they told him as much. Ngemba felt like telling Matthias that he knew this was not well intended, but Yango's eyes on him wouldn't let him dare. As much as Ngemba wanted the independence of Lumani, there was something in him that felt pity for Matthias and the two women. He would have led them to the coast and cut them loose for the next ship, but he knew he couldn't try that, at least not under Yango's watch.

Yango made Ngemba teach him how to drive the whole way and even tried the wheel from time to time. He was clumsy behind the wheel and pressed too much on the accelerator, causing the car to jerk forward like a rocket. At times, he would press the clutch and the accelerator at the same time and then take his foot too briskly off the clutch, causing the car to stall. As serious as their mission was, the two made the journey fun.

The other reason Kazi and Chezi had wanted the two women and Matthias kept alive was to send a message to the cobra administration in the capital city. At the border separating Lumani from Alingafana, Kazi and Chezi, together with a few guards, waited patiently until the vehicle arrived. Ngemba and Yango stepped out of the vehicle and pulled the three cobras out.

Kazi pulled out a sharp dagger and approached them. He stood in front of the first woman and looked her deeply in the eyes for about five minutes. The hate in his eyes was worse than death. The whole place was silent. The guards were at attention, and only Kazi knew what would happen next. Kazi caught her chin as the woman tried to look down at the ground to avoid his eyes. He lifted her chin upwards and slit her throat.

The other woman (the older one) screamed in horror and tried to get away but was caught by the guards and pulled back. Matthias too was moving backwards but was pushed towards Kazi, who planted the dagger in his heart as if he was trying to bury a bean seed, a move that horrified Ngemba, and he let out a sharp sound that Yango stopped with his eyes.

The second woman was fainting from fear and screaming for mercy as Kazi looked down at her with the bloody dagger in his hands in the same way he had looked at the first. She stopped trembling and resigned herself, saying a prayer, when he lifted her chin in the same way.

Kazi waited for her to open her eyes before saying slowly, 'Tell Xavier that the calf has grown into a bull, and he will take no prisoners.'

She was numb with horror when she was bound and gagged and hurtled back into the vehicle and placed in the middle of the two corpses.

Ngemba sat behind the wheel, swallowed deeply, and squeezed his eyes to shut out the horror he had just witnessed. When he ignited the engine, he noticed that the trousers beside him did not belong to Yango.

'Papa!' Ngemba was startled.

'Just because you killed a few frightened men doesn't make you a man yet.' He glared. 'Now move this vehicle carefully and get us there alive, or I will kill you myself,' Chezi said sternly.

Ngemba did not decipher the concealed worry in his father's voice and muttered something about people who didn't know how to drive. Needless to say, he got a resounding slap in reply to bring him back exactly to Lumani where he belonged.

When they arrived in Georgetown, they abandoned the vehicle in the front of the colonial governor's office and disappeared into the crowd before anybody noticed what was in the vehicle.

* * *

Getting the kingdom back on its feet was Kazi's first challenge —
ensuring that the hospitals and schools continued to function, securing
the peripheries of the kingdom, resettling the priests and nuns on the
outskirts of the kingdom, recruiting into the military, and restructuring
the military order. He set up the administration and gave responsibilities
to each member of the Wemtii and the Ngui. Some members of these
councils disappeared quite so mysteriously, including Sigue, and were
replaced so fast that Kazi was forced to question at some point, but the
answer he got in response was always that when he needed to know,
he would be made to know. This left Kazi with mixed feelings about
the Wemtii and Ngui, but he was too busy to meditate enough to ask
further questions, much less demand answers.

The next problem King Balumakazi had, which he had not
envisaged, was the Christians. He had great difficulty persuading them
that he had nothing against their religion unless they stepped in his
way, and by that, he meant the independence of Lumani and total,
complete, and absolute autonomy. Getting the message across after
relocating the parishes was so challenging that he lost patience and,
in a speech he made at the next festival of the pig, stated that if they
wanted to worship, they were free as long as they were prepared to
journey to the new areas assigned for the places of worship, which were
at the peripheries of the kingdom. He was so upset that he warned in
that same speech that should any of them be caught to be cooperating
with the cobras, they would be treated to a very sad fate. To his surprise,
in spite of how enraged the Christians were, the Ngui did not have a
telling-off for him after he burst out at the Christians in that speech.
In due course, Christians began to move their homes closer to the
churches so that over time Baluma returned more and more to their
original way of worship, and the Christians moved to the peripheries.
For some Christians, the distance was discouraging, and they chose to
give up attending service.

Knowing that the new manner of travel was by car and that their
major handicap during the independence war was drivers, the new king
knew he had to get driving lessons underway. It helped that Changara
and Ndana were back from the west, and Yem had just purchased a fleet

of cars and buses, and with Kazi knowing Yem to never be a man of short sight, that meant drivers who could train more drivers.

Kazi felt bad that had still not succeeded in persuading Nsika to return to Lumani permanently, and now that Bana was the new matriarch and the most important member of the Ngui, it would even be more difficult. Kazi planned on returning to Yaketu as soon as his hands were empty to perform the ceremony of the Ngan, which was required of him. In Yaketu, when a son left his father's house to live on his own, his father had to give his accord and bless him before he set out on his own. This was done in a ceremony they called Ngan.

It followed like a curse that as soon as he was enthroned, the pressure for him to marry began to mount. It was unheard of that a Baluma king shouldn't be married, and even the Christians thought it strange. The reason they had welcomed an unmarried king in the first place was that he had led them to a victory over the cobras they didn't think was humanly possible, and with him as king, they had never felt stronger as a people for as far back as any sane adult could remember. But in spite of the respect they had for him as a leader, their traditional values came first, especially if he was to be their leader, and the Ngui gave him an ultimatum of three years to get at least one wife, or they would get some for him.

When, at the end of the second year, Kazi had not shown any interest in all the women introduced to him at the various festivals, rumours took root and bloomed into stories that people believed without a shred of doubt about their legitimacy. First, they said he was afraid of women because he was impotent. Then they said he had a secret wife, and when that story was tired, they said that his totem was a jealous female snake and wanted to have him all to herself, and this last story became the 'secret truth' about Kazi that everyone believed. Kazi himself could not care less about the pressure to marry or the hurtful rumours because he was so consumed with re-establishing the kingdom, securing it and building networks with the other resistance movements around the country, that marriage was the last thing on his agenda.

His reputation of ruthlessness and terror preceded him. The recapturing of Lumani in four days, the victory, and the declaration of independence thereafter had inspired other rebel factions around the country and even beyond. He had been contacted by a few who wanted him to train their guerrillas, so he had extended invitations to those rebel leaders, and already, the rebels had come into Lumani for training. Yem and Nsika kept the supply of ammunition steady. Even though Yaketu was not yet free, because Lumani was now free, smuggling the weapons was easier, and Kazi had secured the borders of Lumani.

A prince from a northern kingdom had invited him to train his guerrillas, and Kazi had agreed to make the trip. It was happening too slowly for Kazi but fast enough for the Baluma. They hailed their king, and already, some people had decided that he was the son of Si.

* * *

Xavier was the colonial governor who administered the whole country that Lumani formed a part of. He was always particularly interested in Lumani because of how wealthy it was in terms of raw materials and minerals. Lumani alone produced almost half of what the whole nation produced, including food. The climate was the best in the country, and the soil was fertile and could grow almost anything. The minerals in Lumani were not far beneath the surface, so capital investment was low for abundant rewards. He had been in contact with Matthias concerning the rebels in Njuu, and they were working on an assault on the Njuu when their source of information had been cut off with the death of the native patriarch.

The appointment of a new administrator of Lumani had been made that morning before the vehicle was parked in front of his office. The woman who was left alive was too traumatised to tell the full story, and the radio messages and faxes he had made to Lumani since the attack had still been unanswered. He couldn't march on Lumani in the blind; he needed a source of information from within and couldn't think of how to get one.

The word of the Lumani victory had gone around the country, provoking the rebel factors in other kingdoms of the country to increase their sporadic attacks on his administration, and these attacks were getting more and more support from the civilians. The summary executions he retaliated with had only served to excite riots and workers' strikes around the country. Rumours about uprisings for independence began to circulate as the recent declaration of the independence of the Lumani territory by the Baluma king reminded the people of the famous Battle of Adwa, in which the Italians had been defeated by King Menelik's army.

Xavier had been told by Matthias and even Derrick about this Balumakazi fellow growing up in exile, but he had dismissed it as folklore spun by the rebels to keep the people hopeful that their king would return someday to rescue them, but now the boy was back and calling himself a bull and declaring independence as if he even knew what that meant. He found it funny that the silly native didn't understand how stupid a bull was (except that in this case, Kazi was talking about a bull elephant, and he [Xavier] was not aware that the nickname of the Baluma was Elephant).

The governor looked blankly at the clock on the wall. It was four o'clock in the afternoon on 30th January 1934, exactly one year after his hero had been elected chancellor of Germany. He saw that as a signpost for the way forward, but it was the words repeated by the woman that he found deeply disturbing.

'What does the native chief mean by "taking no prisoners"?'

BOOK III

Blood and Vengeance

CHAPTER 7

It is important to know how to fight, even more important to know when to fight, but most important to know whom to fight.

Maidem Kayem

AMINATA WAS A very stubborn, arrogant, adulterine, and despicable woman, at least in everybody's opinion in the Kush. She was incapable of doing the simplest thing a woman was born to do, which was obeying a man's instructions. They talked about her so often that it had come to her ears, but she took it all in her stride. Over the years, she had grown so used to being shunned and ostracised that working without talking to anybody (except the patients she tended to as a nurse) the whole day long or walking home alone meant nothing to her anymore. She had made her resolve to never remarry or ever be forced into a marriage again in spite of what the whole world around her thought about an unmarried woman.

She took one more look in the mirror to circle her head scarf around her head. She liked it tied firmly enough but not too tight so that it wouldn't give her a headache. Getting it right was a job on its own. Then she placed another scarf over the first one to fall on her shoulders and passed one end of the cloth around to the other shoulder. Her bag in hand, she walked down the aisle of the hospital offices, waved goodbye to the security guard, and headed home on foot. She liked to walk home most evenings instead of being chauffeur driven. It gave her time to think and pray for the strength she needed.

It all started when she was halfway through high school, and her father and family decided that she had reached the age to be married.

An influential man, her father set her up to be married to a *good* man, and in the Kush a *good* man, was considered one who could take care of a woman as well as her father did or better (with the woman's opinion neither requested nor required for the decision). Aminata was made to stop school that she loved for a marriage she didn't want and to a man she didn't know. Her mother convinced her that she would learn to love the man and that eventually, she would find happiness with him, and she naively believed that.

But once she was locked in, Fadil broke every promise he had made to her parents. He beat her up for every reason he could find, and there were many, given that she was just sixteen and a nerdy character. The excuses her mother gave her for Fadil's behaviour always ended up in the conclusion that it was she who had provoked the situation. And then the day came when he beat her almost to death, and she was taken to hospital with a broken jawbone and shattered ribcage by a kind neighbour who had been eavesdropping. Broken physically, psychologically, mentally, and emotionally, she was led back to Fadil, made to apologise for provoking him into that temper, and instructed to be a good wife.

Walking back home that evening, she still remembered the date and time she was discharged from hospital – 2:07 p.m., 21st November 1923, three days after her seventeenth birthday.

Fadil was kind to her for about a week after that, and then it began all over again. This time, she didn't bother to go back to her mother because she knew that it would be her fault as usual, and so she decided it was better to get back at him in her own way. She went through his wardrobe, pulling out every bit of clothing and ornament he considered precious, put them in a heap in front of the house, poured out kerosene, and set a fire, with the servants watching in dismay and making notes for their master.

When those were burnt to the ground, she was still not satisfied. She went round the house, pouring kerosene around, opening up all the electric cables and gas pipes she could find, and then lit everything up to diminish her rage. The servants didn't stay back to watch the house burn; they ran to their master to tell all. Aminata felt a sense of freedom as she walked out of the burning compound. A voice in her sang all the way to her uncle's place.

She was always at peace at his place because her Baba Yusuf had a happy family with three wives and eight children and a loving first son (Ishmael) who was always protective of her. Baba Yusuf was the younger brother to her father and a businessman as well.

For the first time, she wondered why through all the time Fadil had tortured her, she had never thought of telling Ishmael. She made up her mind to correct that mistake the moment she stepped into the compound. Ishmael was usually away for long periods to some place that was kept a secret to everybody, but luckily, on this day, he was home resting when Aminata got there.

He smashed a window when she told him what she had gone through over the last year and a half.

'Why didn't you ever tell me?'

'I thought it was my fault. Mama told me so. I was supposed to be a good wife. She says a good wife does not make her husband angry. But I can't take it anymore. I can't be married to him. It is like living with a wild animal.'

'This marriage is over, trust me.'

And Ishmael solved the problem like a joke in two days. Fadil was made to pay a fine to Aminata, and the marriage was dissolved.

She went back to school joyfully the next academic year, but her joy was short-lived because in the middle of the year, her father had yet another eligible suitor. She had to admit Hameed was a handsome man, but there was something about him that didn't seem quite in place. She couldn't put a finger on what it was, but she knew something wasn't right. He looked as if marriage to him was a formality that he needed to do to fulfil all righteousness. She ignored her instincts and promised her mother she would try to be a good wife this time. Her mother told her that marrying Hameed came with a bonus: he was a well-reputed lecturer in geography in the Islamic University of Kush.

Hameed was very encouraging of her thirst for an education. He got her registered into high school again and helped her with homework after school. She made a lot of progress and passed her year-end exams to progress to the next class. He was good to her, soft-spoken and respectful and a total contrast to Fadil. Although it seemed strange that he insisted they kept separate bedrooms, she brushed it aside because she needed a space to study late into the night, especially when her tests and exams were coming up.

What she didn't have time to process was that sometimes at night, alone in her room, she felt as if there was a presence around her, and each time she had that feeling, she would wake up the next morning completely exhausted. Hameed would wake up with bloodshot eyes, and she would wonder if he had had the same kind of night.

This went on for about a year until one night when she stayed up late studying for a test, and a strange thing happened. The lights began to flicker, and the room got suddenly very cold. She got a blanket from the cupboard, wrapped herself up, and then decided to go to the kitchen and make herself a warm drink. Aminata turned the knob of the door, and there stood Hameed, right in front of the door, as if he had been standing there a long time. She stepped back to ask him if he needed something.

'Go back into your room, and stay there until sunrise.' His voice sounded as if he was speaking through a microphone.

'I want to make a drink. I am cold.'

'Get back!' he said again, looking at her as if he was about to eat her up.

She shut the door and turned the key twice. The lights continued to flicker, and the room continued to get colder. She wrapped the blanket around her and prayed and tried not to be afraid.

She must have dozed off because when she woke, the lights had stopped flickering, but the room was still so cold. Aminata thought that whatever had been happening was now over, and she could step out of her room to get her hot drink.

She turned the key and the knob, and what she saw would never leave her memory. Lying on the couch in the living room was her husband with a huge dog in raw physical intimacy.

She couldn't explain how she found the calm to tiptoe back to her room and shut the door noiselessly. The next morning, as soon as

Hameed went off to work, she packed everything that belonged to her without taking anything he had ever bought for her and disappeared.

When she appeared at Ishmael's doorstep with the story, he laughed so much that she thought she had imagined the whole thing. He explained that he knew of a cult where such things were practised, and he knew a few people who belonged to it but that he hadn't ever suspected that Hameed belonged in any of them, especially because Hameed was a well-behaved man in society and respected for his moral standing and even preached in the mosque from time to time.

Ishmael asked her to stay at his house in his father's compound for a few days while he went to see her parents to explain, but Hameed beat him to it. When Ishmael got to her parents' house, they had a different version of what happened. Hameed had caught Aminata with another man in his living room on the same morning she had left the house. As an early riser, he had left home for work at the crack of dawn but had to return home because he had forgotten to take his lecture notes with him, and there, he met them. The story was so well told and so explicitly too that even Ishmael began to have doubts about Aminata's version. If he had not known Aminata to be honest and hadn't noticed Hameed's lack of interest at the wedding and some other things Hameed had done, which he could corroborate with Aminata's version, he would have believed Hameed.

The argument with Aminata's parents took a long time, not just because it was her word against Hameed's but also because of her reputation of *stubbornness* with Fadil. When Ishmael explained once more the scene at the door of her room when it got cold and the blinking lights, Aamira (Aminata's mother) stopped arguing and contemplated it, but her father continued arguing, and after several hours of Ishmael trying to convince him, he still refused to believe the story about a dog because it sounded ridiculous to him. He couldn't understand why Aminata would tell such a lie. He sighed and let it go.

Her father had the wedding annulled because he knew he could not confront Hameed with Aminata's version, and in addition, Hameed had expressed a strong desire to end the marriage. It was just easier to refund the dowry and forget about the whole story.

It forever remained a mystery to Aminata that Hameed had come up with his story on exactly the same morning that she had caught him. She wondered if he and his dog had seen her tiptoe back to her room that night. She also wondered why her mother, who was so keen on telling her how wrong she had always been with Fadil, had never brought up the discussion on Hameed and the dog incident. Could it be that her mother had understood?

Also a mystery was that her father, who was always so quick to blame her for everything that happened in her marriage to Fadil, had not questioned her even once about what happened with Hameed. She had returned home and was given a house in her father's compound. A servant was assigned to her, and that had been the end of that story. Nobody ever talked of a suitor or marriage to her again, and she was happy about that. She graduated from high school three years later and enrolled into a two-year nursing course at the Islamic University of Kush and graduated with good grades.

Aminata pushed open the gate of the main entrance to her father's compound and walked to her little house, now a recognised nurse and midwife and good at her job. She loved soothing people in pain, bringing babies forth, and giving advice on a healthy lifestyle. She had lots of books to read in her spare time, and when she got tired of reading, she wove cotton for cloth. She was the happiest woman in a world where she was expected to be the saddest.

* * *

He sat at his desk, looking at the letter he had just received from the young bull, and cursed.

'The savage! Who the hell does he think he is, taking parts of my territory and offering a trading agreement? I'll show him who's in charge here!'

Xavier couldn't continue to wait for an opening. He had to retake the rebel section of the country. He bit his lower lip.

'Is anything the matter, sir?' said Maxwell, perplexed at his boss talking to himself.

'What do you know about this native chief of Lumani?'

'Well, not much, sir, just that he seems to have cut the Lumani village off from the rest of the other villages and that trading happens at the markets outside the village. The native soldiers say they he has turned Lumani into a fortress. They can't get in, not even under disguise. The border controls are too stringent.'

'What about the chiefs of the voodoo cults whom we had supplying the information? Have they not contacted us yet?'

'We lost all contact in December '33 after the slaughter, sir.'

'We have to consider that they have been eliminated by the chief's butchers. We will have to go in blind.'

'That will be suicide, Commander, sir.'

'Do you have an alternative suggestion?' Xavier asked him, throwing him that look he always gave Maxwell to remind him that before he was drafted for Africa, he was a cobbler from a working-class family with a wife and four children and eating from hand to mouth. Maxwell felt stupid instantly.

Xavier continued, 'I estimate that this chief cannot have more than three hundred fighters in that village, so get five hundred troops together and start the training. We receive ammunition tomorrow evening at the port, so that should secure a smooth victory for us at a time we need to deter the rest of the natives with any ideas.'

'Yes, sir,' Maxwell answered and left the office, feeling humbled. He wouldn't live to know that he had been right.

The attempt at reconquering Lumani ended up in a bloodbath that sent shock waves around the country and the continent. Xavier's troops did not get past the first line of defence.

Kolela was Kazi's third eye and warned of the attack and the particular hill they would attack from days before it happened. Kazi directed Khala to watch the hills and to signal the approach on the day before. She strolled the area by day and by night until the day they finally came.

For some inane reason, Xavier had ordered for a daylight attack, which made his troops even more visible. Khala saw them moving in the grass and let them until they had moved past her towards the camps.

Then from a tree behind them, she sounded her trumpet, confusing and distracting them to turn around. They opened fire in her direction. Smoke filled the air, and when the air cleared, she was nowhere in sight. She had done the perfect job to give Kazi and his troops enough time they needed to get in place.

Maxwell turned his attention back to the principal target, the first rebel camps, which were just a hundred metres off from them. They crawled until they got to a good shooting spot. Maxwell rose to his feet to gesture for attack, only to have his neck blown out by Ngemba's bullets.

Kazi shot at the barrel of kerosene that Yango had placed in a tree. It was the dry season, and the fierce wind carried the flames through the battlefield. Kazi loved to fight in the midst of flames. It was as if the flames roused his mania for war and nourished his fearlessness for the duration of the battle while assuaging his rage and longing for cobra blood.

As the bullets rained and Kazi ducked and swirled, he could feel Khala by his side, giving him the strength of will that he needed in a battle that made him feel that he was achieving something beyond Lumani, beyond himself, and beyond his soul. It was his first battle fighting with Khala by his side and the beginning of a thirst that he would never quench. Like liquor, the more he killed, the more he wanted to kill – an insatiable thirst.

The soldiers tried to run back, but Yango and his troops were already waiting on the opposite end. The cobras were surrounded, and the butchery of that battle (and the ones that followed Kazi through life) earned him the name 'the Terror of the Nine Hills'.

Farra led a few soldiers across the river that separated Lumani from the Tebo kingdom. She knew something was amiss when she saw the deserted outskirts and the empty bush meat market.

'Treacherous Tebo people, you remind me of my father,' she cursed under her breath, her heart burning. 'I think we should continue inwards and face them head-on,' she said with fire in her eyes.

'No. If they are not here, then they are probably aware of the attack today. The cobras must be in there guarding them.'

'So let us take them by surprise. Attack by surprise as we did the last time. I can go in and create a distraction. They won't even know what happened.'

'We retreat now to fight another day. This is only the first in a long war, Farra. We don't have to win every day. If we don't plan properly before we attack, we will be attacking to lose. It's not worth it. Come, let's go back.'

At Chezi's signal, the troops began to cross back to join Yango's battalion.

* * *

When Xavier didn't get any feedback from the Maxwell-led legion, at the end of the same week, he sent in double the troops he had sent the first time, but lamentably, the young bull had anticipated that. Kazi tackled from the front head-on, Chezi took the riverside, and Yango took the hills.

Nobody returned. No bodies were returned, and there was not a word to say who had won or who had lost. Xavier finally began to understand what the native chief meant by 'taking no prisoners'. He decided that a peaceful treaty with Lumani would give him time to re-strategise.

He was drafting the letter to Kazi when that dreaded phone call came through. His superiors needed an update on the Lumani case at a time when he couldn't account for almost half of his troops. He stuttered through the phone call and hung up. Then he faxed them, blaming the phone lines and bad cabling and giving a false version of the reality. That would buy him time until the next phone call, hopefully after the treaty had been signed. He had the letter sent off and was surprised that its bearer came back alive and with a message.

The meeting with Xavier was arranged at Alingafana, the dividing town between Lumani and Georgetown (the capital city, where he was stationed). It intrigued Xavier that this chief, unlike Chief Sigue, did not want to come to the capital city or hold a meeting in any of his exotic residences in the capital city but chose the small town hall in

Alingafana, a town that neither he nor any of his predecessors had ever bothered to build a single road through because there was nothing to exploit. The land was fertile, but the people were so lazy, they couldn't be persuaded to work. They planted crops around their homes and harvested to feed. Waking up in the morning, petty farming, basking in the sun for the rest of the morning, cooking and eating and then drinking until dusk – such was the life of the people in Alingafana, as simple as that. The cobras had been unable to persuade any of the young men from this area to join the army for any reward in the world; they would rather be whipped to death. Consequently, no investment had ever been made in that part of the country. The cobras had roads between Georgetown and the borders of Alingafana and from the borders of Alingafana to Lumani but none inside Alingafana itself. There were dust tracks that had been cleared up by native soldiers to let vehicles through from Georgetown to Lumani.

The Ngui convened with Kazi and decided that they needed bus stops and more hospitals and schools. The problem was getting staff to man the hospitals and schools. They had the equipment and material ready to build from what they had smuggled, but Kazi and Bana had to find the manpower by the time the buildings were put up. Xavier's peace treaty therefore came in timely fashion because that would ease the importation of teachers, doctors, and nurses into Lumani from other parts of the country and from across the continent. The workers would need to be paid for their services, and the Baluma had lots of timber and material to sell to the cobras. Kazi wasn't sure how easy it would be to get the cobras to accept to buy from them after defeat, but Bana was positive that the cobras would still buy no matter what because she had seen how much they were willing to go through to get the raw materials during the period of the occupation.

* * *

Kazi didn't know what to expect of the man, and neither did Xavier. Kazi imagined Xavier with the same features as Father Gabriel. Xavier imagined him as an uncaged beast, preferably a greasy bear, and when he did meet Kazi, he reckoned he hadn't been too far from his truth.

It was Nsika's idea that the meeting be held there for a reason Kazi didn't know of. The place was a deserted area of Alingafana with tall grass and short trees, a small town with lots of animals, like antelopes, zebras, and other herbivores. There was a lot of land, but the population was scarce and concentrated in areas around rivers. Nsika chose the town hall area because he knew how scarce the population was and how far they lived from the abandoned area, so whatever happened there wouldn't cause any anxiety amongst the people.

The town hall was a four-walled ramshackle with a dilapidating roof in the middle of a large bush. Each party had to bring chairs to sit on because the hall had none. Kazi's team arrived first and added a small table. Yango stood on guard outside.

The atmosphere was tense enough to generate electricity for the whole of Lumani when Xavier arrived and walked in to stare up at the Tower of Babel. The tower stared back down at him with its large light brown eyes and long eyelashes sparkling a strange radiance of terror and darkness harbingering death. The lean, firm, smooth black-skinned body glittered as if it had been sprinkled with gold dust and towered over him with stern authority, clothed in what the cobra beneath had seen Sigue wear whenever he came to the capital city, the difference being that with this tower, the cloth seemed better woven and better fitted around its shoulders and waist and with colours so bright that his eyes hurt.

Xavier scanned the tower from head to foot, eyes closing up as he took in the braided hair beneath the strange headpiece, the long earring hanging down the left ear, several rings on the fingers (with a peculiar ring standing out on the long finger of his right hand), the bracelets, the chains on his neck so long that one could comfortably tie a cow to a tree three miles away, and anklets that led to weird-looking slippers he had never seen before.

Xavier's eyes came back to their starting point, and when he stared into its eyes, something sank within him. For the first time in his life dealing with these natives, he felt vulnerable. He was grateful when the tower sat down wordlessly.

The cars were parked outside. The only door of the hall and all the windows were left open for light and fresh air because the place was stuffy with stale air. Noting there was only one rebel-dressed native standing outside the building, Xavier found the courage to clear his throat. Whatever happened during the discussion, he was sure that his twenty soldiers could overpower the four natives in the room and the lone one outside.

Concluding that they had the upper hand, Xavier put his words forward with an air of superiority. 'What do you want?' He regretted the moment he let them out.

He closed his mouth quickly and was quiet until Kazi spoke in what seemed like two hours later but was actually just about thirty seconds.

'We need to come to an understanding. I have retaken Lumani, and your attempts at re-stealing it have been futile. It is not my immediate intention to wipe you out, but if the need arises, I will. Let us say I am giving us a chance to be civilised or, as you would rather say, gentlemen. Simply put, we need to establish trade between your protectorate and my kingdom.'

He hated the way Kazi said *protectorate* as if he was running some kind of poultry and Kazi was a buyer.

'What kind of trade?' he asked, hoping Kazi would talk about raw materials in exchange for basic food and clothing but was disappointed when the elder-looking man standing behind Kazi placed a document in front of him and one in front of Kazi.

Xavier looked down at it and began to read. They had spelt out every term of the contract: what the trade would consist of, where it would be done, and the conditions for continuance or rupture of contract. If the contract did not seem so defensive and, to a large extent, unknowledgeable about the cobra administrative politics in the country and continent, Xavier could have sworn this had been drafted by a cunning lawyer.

'Four logs of timber and six sacks of cocoa at this price?' Xavier blinked in disbelief.

'Yes. For your first supply, we have eight logs of timber and twelve sacks of cocoa, so that will be thirty thousand. Rubber is a little more expensive. Turn to page twenty-five. Yes, over there, we have a basket of rubber at seventy thousand. And on the last page, page thirty-two, you have our terms and conditions of the trade. Don't worry about builders for us. We have some engineers coming back home this June and some architects, so we should be fine,' Kazi said sarcastically and remembered Father Gabriel and the 'help' he said the cobras had come to offer. His mouth curled up into an evil grin.

The sarcasm felt like sand in Xavier's mouth, but he had to swallow. His assistant was dead, and he had not found a believable story for his superiors, so he had been unable to request for another one. He was sitting there alongside his foot soldiers, who couldn't assist because they understood nothing of how a treaty should be arranged.

A sweat drop rolled down his cheek as a feeling of terror swept through him. It was a horror, a vengefulness in the air that he could not describe even to himself. He couldn't hold back the feeling that there was a beast around, a huge beast standing beside Kazi, ready to pounce on him any moment. Maybe it was the lady's gentle but majestic manner, sitting there with a blank expression, not giving off any emotions but obviously listening very keenly and taking in his every move, or perhaps the wise-looking elder man to the left (the one who had placed the file on the table without a word), who didn't look like a soldier but had something of a dangerous spy about him, or perhaps the unswaying gaze of the strangely dressed young fellow behind who looked like some voodoo practitioner engrossed in some satanic trance.

'You know the rest of the natives around the country don't think like you. In fact, they don't like you because they are smarter than you. They know that we are here for their own good, and they offer us their unwavering support. Of course, but a few of much lower intelligence rioting and rebelling out of ignorance, the rest of them are clever enough. Hold on to your village tightly, *Bolumkaz*, because that's all you will ever have – a piece of land and a few serfs to rule.'

'If we have nothing to offer, you're free to leave. If you think we natives are, by nature, beneath you, then leave. It is that simple.'

The words were so composedly, quietly, and firmly spoken that Xavier felt as if he was in the presence of a psychopath. It wasn't just the words that were spoken but the way this young native looked at him, as if he were a meal.

No matter how intimidating this savage was, Xavier was determined to show him what the world meant by *the superior race*, but when he signed, sighed, and spat out the last grains of sand between his teeth, he knew at once that was the wrong thing to have done. The natives understood the meaning, and a chill went down his spine as those four pairs of eyes gawked him.

Ngemba picked up Yango's signal, and before the soldiers could move, huge long guns were pointed at every one of them. With the blink of an eye, the bushes had turned into seventy guerrillas.

Somebody outside put his hand on his grenade and was about to throw it at the cobras before Ngemba cried out, '*Don't!*' but it was too late.

One cobra soldier panicked and shot at the guerrilla, wounding him in the shoulder, and the other guerrillas shot him down spontaneously. A cold silent breeze blew past, and Yango knew there was nothing he could do about what would happen next. He moved backward into the hall with two of his, pointing guns at the cobras, with Yango's fixed on Xavier.

The shooting began outside as the guerrillas responded in spontaneous and unapprehensive retaliation. Xavier and his cobras wanted to move but knew they couldn't. The last time they had heard this kind of shooting was in the summary executions of rebellious natives at Georgetown. It was a harrowing, terrifying feeling to hear their own screaming in agony.

When the shooting stopped, the tower rose to his feet, grabbed Xavier by the neck, and, in one spin, threw him to the ground, stopping his neck steadily beneath his large foot as the rest of Xavier's body struggled to challenge the weight. The two other soldiers tried to move but were stopped instantly.

Kazi took out his dagger and said to Xavier with that same ice-cold tone and terrifying calm, 'I don't take any prisoners, but because I need you alive, I will make an exception.' Letting go of Xavier's neck, he stepped back and motioned Yango to do the same.

Xavier grappled to his feet and dusted himself up. One of his soldiers picked up the file from the table, trembling, and they left. Yango still had his gun pointed as the three got into the vehicle and drove off, leaving the other van they had come with. Kazi, Kolela, Bana, and Nsika left the room.

Before getting into the vehicle, Kazi asked for Ngemba.

'That aggression was uncalled for! You should have stopped them. How can you command men you cannot control?'

Ngemba hung his head.

* * *

Raheel Ibn Fadir was one of the four princes of the north-eastern Kush kingdom, determined to bring the cobra invasion in the Kush to an end and force an election for self-determination. A successful businessman, trading in gold and cloth and owning several herds of cattle, sheep, camels, and goats, Raheel and three other princes of different families had, several years ago, founded and funded a guerrilla warfare against the cobra invasion. His father, King Saadullah, had commended the movement and funded it as well. The guerrillas had ample funding and artillery, but what Raheel and his comrades knew was that they did not have the necessary training to match the cobra army in a head-on assault. It therefore came as a lantern of faith that on one of his trading trips down south, he got wind of Kazi's victory in Lumani and the effectiveness of the military that protected it. He was impressed with the stories he was told and even more so when he sent emissaries to Lumani to get details of what had happened.

With his father's seal of approval, he extended an invitation to Kazi for cooperation on intelligence and requested for Kazi to make a trip to Kush to better organise and train his guerrillas. Kazi had agreed, but it took three years for Kazi to make the trip because of the distance and the fragility of the new independent Lumani kingdom.

Raheel didn't mind waiting because Kazi sent Ndikwa north to help during the waiting period with unbelievable results. The exchanges of intelligence they had during that period helped his guerrillas improve their espionage task force and information flow, and already, the guerrillas were attacking the cobras in sensitive areas, forcing them to retreat from several clans. By the time the three years had elapsed and Kazi was ready to go up north, the cobras occupied only a few dozen clans and the capital city, albeit with a strong hold in each.

Both Raheel and Kazi were eager to see each other because they had had so many exchanges between them but hadn't yet met. Both kingdoms had had a long history of friendship in the past, and Raheel's father, who was alive at the time, had been friends with King Tozingana and had known of but never had the chance of meeting King Ottuwa.

* * *

The place wasn't much different from where he had left it six years ago when he had moved to Njuu permanently. Kazi came out of the car and looked around. Yem's compound was busy as usual – children playing around, women shouting across to each other, and servants splitting wood noisily. He savoured the flavour of the dusty ground sprinkled with the children's early morning water as he had done so often with Ndana and his other adopted siblings so many years ago.

The aroma of the women's cooking of fried cassava and wheat flour puffs and beans for the morning meal filled his nostrils as he strode through the entrance of the compound with the nostalgic feeling of coming home from school in his childhood, a feeling he had taken for granted in his youth and had quickly forgotten since leaving Yaketu. Nobody noticed him walking home, even though he had so much difficulty keeping his steps steady.

She had her back turned to him and was tying her head scarf to start her cooking. He came close and, not to startle her, said quietly, 'Mama Dara.'

She turned around, looking first straight ahead to his chest and then upwards. 'Kazi?' She then threw her weight on him and screamed, drawing the attention of the whole compound.

Eager for gossip, others came around to see who it was but were not disappointed to find out. They sent word to Yem, who was at the outskirts of Yaketu, trading cows.

Kazi held her tightly as she cried. Ndana had just come back from an overnight shift and was fast asleep, but the screaming woke her up. She ran out to see what was going on with her mother.

'*Kazi!*' she screamed, and she too fell into his arms. If Kazi had not been in training for a long time, he would have had difficulty holding both.

Yem was proud of Kazi and couldn't hold himself back. He threw a feast every evening for the four nights until the Ngan. Changara had never met Kazi but was delighted to because Ndana had told him of so many fun memories. Ndana had returned from the United Kingdom with a crisp English accent, and Kazi found it difficult to understand her, but when she spoke the Yaketu language, she was just as fluent as she had always been, so they chose to speak that instead.

Kazi admired Ndana's new person. She was educated and composed and spoke intelligently, and so did Changara. He then realized why Yem always said that when people went to the white man's school, they always came out 'very intelligent'. A part of him missed going to study architecture, which he loved, but the bull in him had never let him forego his duty to Lumani for an education, not even now. He asked Ndana about getting books on architecture to tutor himself and was happy when she offered to order some for him. It had been a long time since he had read a single book, but he was sure there was a natural architect in him that would be awakened once he saw the drawings and the vectors.

He let her know that he needed help running hospitals and clinics that were being put up in Lumani. She promised to make contact with medical personnel she knew in other parts of the continent. They both realized it was going to be an uphill task but understood that the success of Lumani was not just a Baluma affair.

When they talked about her experience in university abroad, she complained about racism and her resolve to return once she had finished her internship, even though her mentor persuaded her to work in a hospital there.

'It was too hard, Kazi. I couldn't bear it. Maybe if we were there together, I would have been stronger, but I was alone. The patients would line up waiting, but once I walked in and they realized I was the doctor, they would leave one by one. Some even told me that they couldn't let a Negro treat them no matter how sick they were. My only patients throughout my internship were West Indians and Jamaicans and a few Africans. If I even made a suggestion about how a case of a white patient should be treated, even the white nurses would scorn me. It was hell, Kazi. I would rather bear Papa's nagging about being unmarried and too educated than bear that kind of treatment.'

Kazi put his palm to her face. 'But you made it, Ndana, and kept your pretty face intact through it all.'

They both laughed.

Changara leaned into the conversation, and they talked about Yem's businesses. Kazi told him all he had to tell about the crookery and was even more delighted when Changara talked about the guerrilla movement in Yaketu that he and Ndana had joined. They talked about guerrilla strategy and breaking the myth in Yaketu as it had been in Lumani that cobras couldn't die, about the resistance in Yaketu and how Ndana was helping with medicines and treatment for the guerrillas in secret. She worked permanently at Saint Anthony's Hospital, administering cobra soldiers when they were attacked to pick up information that Changara could transmit to the guerrillas. They agreed to ease the supply for medicines to Lumani.

The pair loved the struggle but had the eternal problem of Yem breathing down their shoulders, telling them to be cautious and not get into any trouble, while he himself supplied medicines to the guerrillas that his agents stole from the cobras. All this was kept from Mandara because they could not bear Mandara's tantrums if she ever discovered what they were up to. Changara was optimistic that the rebellion was having effect because the cobras were leaving Yaketu slowly, and just as he had sent Ndikwa to help the northern prince of Kush with espionage, Kazi offered the same for Yaketu.

Kazi's discussion with Yem, when they found time, was centred on Utatu's and Sigue's deaths. While Kazi had been involved with Utatu's death, he hadn't known about Sigue's death or why he was killed, for that matter. It was a few months later that Bana had told him.

During the meeting with the Ngui, he had specifically asked them to work with his guerrillas to uproot the traitors in Lumani. He simply asked for all of them to be eliminated and hadn't cared who the traitors were. About three weeks after his investiture, he was told of Sigue's death. Now he had known Sigue to be a man of no action but not a traitor of any kind. He was not told that Sigue had been eliminated. Instead, the Ngui informed him that Sigue had regrettably passed away after a brief illness. It was later on when he pressed Chezi to find out that he had, in turn, squeezed the information out of Bana that in fact, Sigue had been poisoned by the Ngui, and the reason had been explained. Kazi wasn't sure what to feel about Sigue, but something in him felt sorry. He told Yem he was intending to find the right time to confront the Ngui and ask for clemency in the future, in cases such as those where the person was induced into treachery out of desperation. Yem cautioned Kazi against that. He advised to instead consider carefully the full consequences of the orders he handed out as king because whatever he ordered would be effected to the last word and not just literarily, a lesson Kazi would need to remember for the duration of his reign.

The ceremony of the Ngan was held in Yem's house as tradition required. Kazi had bought the two identical robes and the two identical horns for palm wine that Yem had asked of him. Yem put on the first robe and poured some palm wine into one of the horns. He made a small speech to the crowd to recant how Kazi became his adopted son. Then he drank to empty the horn and asked Kazi to step forward.

Kazi held back tears when Yem pulled the robe over his shoulders and made him sit in his chair. Yem put his hands over Kazi's head, and as he spoke out the blessings, Kazi's mind went back to that early evening when Yem came out of his house and frowned. Palm wine was poured into the two horns. Yem held out one to Kazi, and the two drank to empty their horns.

Then Yem finished with 'Now you have paid your ransom!'

Kazi got out of the chair and hugged him.

* * *

Raheel was so high-spirited from the moment Ndikwa informed him that Kazi was on his way that he almost got caught by the cobras. In a loud voice one evening, he talked so excitedly about weapons that a cobra spy walking past his house overheard him, and the next morning, Raheel was quite surprised when the cobras appeared at his doorstep. They made a thorough search of the house but luckily discovered nothing because Ndikwa always hid the weapons in a little underground space in a discrete part of the floor concealed by a cupboard in one of the kitchens. That served as a wakeup call to Raheel, who needed to keep calm until Kazi and his guerrillas arrived two weeks later.

They drew up a training plan with Ishmael and a channel for weapon smuggling. The training was divided into three phases.

The first phase was physical exercise, which each person could do on their own around their houses but not as a group so as not to draw attention from the cobras. When the sun came overhead, they would go underground into a dugout chamber where it was cool and receive lectures on the history of the Kush and how it was invaded, the atrocities committed by the cobras, and the different invasion tactics they had used over the years.

In phase two, they would gradually move to a place far off in a desert area that Raheel and his comrades had prepared a few years ago with Ndikwa's help. Once they had all arrived, the program was physical training in the morning, counter-attack lectures underground in the afternoon, and, in the late afternoon, the trainings on weapons and equipment until late into the night.

In phase three, they would map out areas they could attack with minimum loss on their side and other factors like diplomatic tactics to blackmail the cobra administration to concede to the independence of the Kush.

Kazi actually found this training more exciting than his real battles. He was even learning to speak some Kush and some Arabic from Ndikwa, who acted as a translator. The guerrillas were uneasy about Kazi and thought he was too demanding as a trainer, but once small victories began to come in, they got hungrier and asked for more. They began to like him very much. Kazi developed a close relationship with Ishmael and Raheel and learnt a lot about the Kush and its people.

His only problem was the fact that because they were predominantly Muslim, they didn't eat pork, which he was used to, coming from Lumani, where pork was a stable meal. In consequence, he had even more difficulty eating in Kush than he usually had, and he compensated the lack of culinary satisfaction with liquor, which they regularly had, even though it was against their religious principles. Hunger and liquor were a bad combination, and by the fifth month, his weight loss became so visible that Ishmael noticed.

'Are you not happy with us here?' Ishmael asked one evening.

'I am and very much so. Why?'

'Kazi, your jawbones are beginning to show. So if you don't miss Lumani or someone in Lumani, then what is it that we are not doing?'

'Pork.'

Ishmael burst out laughing. He couldn't believe Kazi's problem was that simple. He told Kazi how they could get that sorted out.

There were places where pork was sold to cobras, albeit clandestinely because the natives' adopted Islamic culture was binding and sternly enforced by the local clerics. Raheel would be cross, but Kazi couldn't care less. He needed his pork, and Ishmael could get it for him. They agreed to meet at Ishmael's place early the next evening.

They sat talking and drinking liquor that had been supplied earlier. A lady walked in and placed the bowl of roasted pork on the table and left without a word. Kazi barely got a glimpse of her face before she turned around. He could see she had large beautiful eyes, a little like his, but what caught his attention the most was the porgy jaw, her spotless milk-brown skin that he had never seen before, and the lovely scent of her perfume. He really wanted to ask Ishmael but was too shy to raise the subject. He had established his reputation as such a focused and undistracted rebel leader whom his soldiers admired and looked up to and didn't want that image tainted with a lousy attraction to any woman, no matter how beautiful. He kept his mind on his pork and liquor.

* * *

The new ammunition supplied was as exciting for Kazi as it was for the guerrillas – the grenades, the guns, and, this time, even a few machine guns. Phase two of the training began in the desert. They decided to fake an invasion of the administrative building, the commanding cobra's office, which was the prime target. It would be difficult to attack because it was well-guarded, but Kazi wanted that attack to happen because, as he explained to Ishmael, it was highly probable that the offices would contain invaluable information about the cobra investments in the Kush colony as they had found in Lumani.

The practise session began with Ishmael at the front and Kazi leading the rest of the troops around the back of the makeshift building. Some guerrillas acted as cobras guarding the building, heavily armed, as the cobras always were; others posed as native Kush soldiers armed with only swords and short guns. Ishmael sounded the alarm, and the fighting began.

They used different sounds to communicate with one another, an essential thing Kazi taught them from his experience in Lumani. Since the cobras had native soldiers fighting on their side who could understand the local language and translate for the cobras during the fighting, it was not prudent to speak in the native tongue. Instead, sounds were used that only the guerrillas understood so that messages could be transmitted amongst the guerrillas to signal who was hurt, who needed reinforcement, and who needed to change direction or go into what hideout.

Kazi ducked and took cover near a sand wall covered by a tin roof to recharge his weapon as the blank bullets flew around him.

Bang! Something sharp hit the wall behind him, and then *ping!* It hit the tin roof and came down, tearing his face open from the area between his two eyes above his nose, cutting through. He closed his eyes spontaneously, and it cut past his left eye and around his jawbone before it stopped. A split second later, something else hit the wall behind him and bounced off onto his back. Kazi fell forwards on his knees with his face covered in blood and sand. He felt dizzy for a moment and then passed out before he could tell what had hit him.

It was the shrapnel of a blank bullet that had gone astray and made its way to the sand wall behind him and onto the tin roof to come tearing down his face. The second piece of metal came from one of the guerrillas' rusted swords and hit the same sand wall, knocking off on his back, tearing it deep open, almost to the bone.

'We can't take him to the hospital. The cobras would easily figure out what happened.'

'OK, take him to your place. We can get a doctor there in no time.' Raheel kept his voice down.

'Good idea, Baba. Rahim, come over and help me. We have to take him to my place,' Ishmael called out to Raheel's youngest child.

When they got to Ishmael's place, he administered first aid on Kazi's wounds and sent word for Aminata to come straight to his place from work. From what his servants (or, rather, spies acting as servants) had told him, most of the doctors had been compromised by the cobra regime for better pay. Raheel arrived at Yusuf's place and went straight to Ishmael's house, meeting Aminata at the doorstep. Ishmael opened up to them, arguing about the reason she was there.

'It's OK, Baba, I asked her to come. She will know how to treat the wounds.'

'But she is a woman. She cannot be allowed to see him undressed.'

'In case you have forgotten, I abandoned your retarded Kush traditions a long time ago. Besides, from what Ishmael tells me, the wounds are in his chest and face, so I should not have to see him completely undressed. Since that bothers you more than his life.' Aminata glared at her father.

'I forbid you from looking at me in that manner.'

'And I forbid you from deciding what I do or don't. You have had your say in my life, and we all saw where it ended me. From now on, my life and my decisions are mine and mine alone.'

'Keep saying that, and –'

Kazi's painful groan brought the argument to an end, and Aminata rushed to his side. She took a close look at the wounds and decided she needed more medicine from the hospital to clean the wounds and some antibiotic, painkillers, and anaesthesia. On closer inspection, she realized there were a few pieces of metal stuck in. She made Kazi lie still on one side and rushed back to steal what she needed from the hospital.

When she had finished stitching and bandaging the wounds, she put him to sleep and stayed the night at Ishmael's place to observe him. In the morning, she made some spicy meat soup and fed him. Kazi was half-conscious the whole while. He only came around fully the next evening but was still too weak to speak or keep his eyes open for long. Aminata cleaned the wounds again and noted to Ishmael that the wounds had begun to heal quicker than she had expected. Raheel stopped by now and then to enquire about Kazi from Ishmael. He wouldn't address Aminata about it, even though she was the nurse.

By late afternoon on day three, Kazi was strong enough to get up on his feet. He could feel the energy sipping gradually out of his body, so he bathed quickly and changed. For the last two days, he hadn't liked the idea of male servants he didn't know giving him a bath but couldn't object. He knew there was a woman who had fed him with lovely hot spicy soup and made him take medicines that put him to sleep almost immediately, but between sleep, he couldn't make her out. All he knew was that her scent seemed appealingly familiar. Kazi sat down on the bed with his palms facing upwards and stared through the window at the sun to say a short prayer.

He was just finishing when a chubby woman walked in. He turned around to the smooth well-kept milk-brown skin and porgy jaws, which he remembered from the pork feast in Ishmael's living room some months back. For a Tower of Babel, she was average height, but in reality, she was about five-foot-nine, which, in Kush, was, by no means, average height for a woman. She wore a loose gown that flowed down to her wrists and ankles and two head scarves, one that was tied firmly around her head and knotted behind and the other loosely hung on top of the first and circled around her shoulders. The woman looked patronizingly at him, and her scent filled his nostrils as she leaned forward to place the bowl of hot spicy soup in his hands. He took a sip and then another and closed his eyes to let the hot spice run down his throat.

'Could you thank the nurse who cooked this for me?'

She gave him an amused look that made him realize he was looking right at 'the nurse'. Kazi spontaneously rolled his eyes and laughed at himself, and she laughed with him. Their eyes locked for a brief moment, but she pulled her eyes away in a somewhat dismissive manner and cut her laughter short.

'How does my brave warrior feel today?'

Kazi took another sip at the soup. 'His name is Balumakazi.'

'A beautiful name for a beautiful pair of eyes.' Her smile lit up the room and his face.

That statement took Kazi aback. In Kush, women were shy and reserved, almost irritably timid for Kazi's liking (he preferred the Baluma and Yaketu women he was used to, who were outspoken), but here was a Kush woman who, unlike the rest, was not just bold enough to look him in the eye while talking but also complimented him without even thinking about it.

'And a radiant smile for radiant skin,' he complimented in return.

'If you didn't fight so much, your skin would be smooth as well.' Her lips sealed her teeth and curled up mockingly to one side as if she didn't believe him, with her eyes still fixed on him flirtingly.

'You must be Aminata, the outlaw.'

'The outlaw? Is that what I am called? Well, I can't say I dislike that nickname.' She sat down on the chair beside the bed.

'Well, I overheard Raheel call you that yesterday. Is there a reason to it?' He finished his soup and gave the bowl back to Aminata.

'My father has every name for me in the book.'

Kazi's eyes widened. 'Your father?'

'Yes, my father,' she said dismissively. 'I am Raheel Ibn Fadir and Aamira's firstborn.'

Kazi was getting more and more intrigued by this odd Kush woman. 'Why would a man as loyal and traditional as Raheel have an outlaw for a first?'

'There is a long story to it, but you need to rest now.'

She got up and left the room before he could say anything else.

Days later, Kazi returned to training with the guerrillas, and they were happy to have him back. Ishmael and Raheel couldn't believe how popular Kazi had grown amongst their people. They gave him a welcome back befitting of a king. Everyone wanted to be in Kazi's legion. He taught them how to aim without missing and how to use the sand to their advantage to wield up a sandstorm to mask their approach.

In the last few weeks they concluded the attack strategy and Kazi left Ishmael to it, he had been informed to return to Lumani for pressing issues. On the evening before his departure, he again asked Ishmael for a pork and liquor feast, and Ishmael obliged, not knowing Kazi had another reason for asking. They sat in the living room, talking about everything and nothing. The lady came in as usual and placed the pork on the table. This time, Ishmael introduced them and noticed that she avoided Kazi's eyes, even though Kazi tried to make eye contact, which he found odd for Aminata, whom he had known as she aged to be a very bold and obstinate Kush woman.

* * *

Kazi returned to an unrested Lumani, one he had never seen before. Chezi's messages to him had overly downplayed the real situation. Kazi was furious. The cobras, since the last time Kazi was home fifteen months back, had attacked twice. The first time was an attack destroying the markets in Alingafana, which had been established to allow for trade between Lumani and the rest of the country. That attack resulted in the deaths of several traders and buyers and the burning of several stalls in the market, discounting material loss. The second attack had been at the clinic on the outskirts of Lumani bordering Alingafana that sick travellers frequented. The attack claimed the lives of several patients and medical staff. The cobras had carefully manoeuvred both attacks to create the impression that it was the work of Kazi's guerrillas. The rumours spread fast that the guerrillas had turned on the people and that Lumani was under a new kind of invasion. Anti-guerrilla sentiments took root, and in no time, they were resented by the same people who once idolised them.

The propaganda by Xavier's government in the rest of the country lent spur to the stories that the native peoples were not ready for self-determination, and Lumani was a good example of non-white rule. Before long, the inflow of skilled and unskilled workers who loved to immigrate to Lumani to find work and earn a living for their families back home began to diminish.

Chezi was having a hard time persuading even those who had already migrated to stay. Even the plumbers and construction workers began to leave. The newborn country's economy began to plummet. Xavier's strategy was working as planned, and he denied all of Chezi's accusations. It had taken him seven years, but he had finally found a crack in the native chief's wall. The people had been through a brutal history of betrayal and inhumanity; rebuilding the people's confidence in themselves, unity amongst themselves, and faith in their ability to govern themselves would be an uphill task. They would run at the slightest sign of danger because they were still so fragile in many ways. All it took was a few drops of self-doubt splattered every now and then. Xavier was drinking coffee and eating toast and savouring it as he read the fax from his informant.

The other issue Kazi had was in tackling negotiations with other rebel leaders around the continent. They all wanted the same thing but had different approaches to attaining the same objective. The communications kept on going back and forth and didn't seem to be making any progress. There was a caste that believed their part of the continent was not yet ready for autonomy and that the cobras should be allowed to stay for longer, albeit with more rights for the natives; another caste preferred to foster peaceful negotiations with the cobras to persuade them to leave eventually. Kazi belonged to the caste that felt that a complete expulsion of the cobras and immediate independence was the only route to a future void of indignity. The independence of Lumani had, as Kazi predicted, created a ripple effect across the continent, and the uprisings against the cobras were becoming more and more frequent. But notwithstanding, the road bumps against them were never-ending and were nothing he had foreseen. He had naively presumed that all the natives of the continent would rally around his idea of total, absolute, and complete independence now, but the more he travelled around the continent to meet with the different rebel leaders, the more he discovered that his ideas were not always so welcome. The cobra indoctrination of the natives had deeper roots than he could ever have imagined. The cobras' influence, Kazi realized, was the most poisonous venom they had.

It was therefore a tumultuous period for Kazi trying to regain the confidence of his people, on the one hand, in the midst of the cobras' continued manipulation of his people from the outside and, on the other, to rally the other rebel leaders to a single ideology. The only silver lining Kazi could see in the horizon was what the radio called the 'Second World War' that was sweeping across Europe. The Leader of Germany had made one too many enemies, and they had turned on him. The direct effect on Lumani and the nation was a drastic reduction in the number of cobras, hence fewer to attack Lumani because of the shifting focus.

Kazi had been informed that in the other parts of the nation, natives were being drafted to help the cobras fight the infamous leader of Germany. He couldn't understand why an African would leave his enslaved land to help the cobras who had enslaved them get freedom from their enslaver. Whatever the reason for it, war in Europe was a good thing for Lumani. It was diverting the cobras' attention from them, at least for a while. He prayed it stayed long enough to let him reunite his people before the cobras returned.

Kazi delayed his return to Kush to convene the Ngui. The first decision they took was to allot a governor to each of the clans and whip up counter-propaganda. They also needed to establish a pipeline of communication between the guerrillas and the people. If the people knew the guerrillas better, they would be less likely to be suspicious. So far, the guerrillas had been trained very much like the cultural Baluma warriors who kept a distance between themselves and the common people to maintain a certain kind of mystery around them. Kazi changed that. The guerrillas were moved from their camps to live amongst the people and only returned to camp for trainings. The strategy worked, and it wasn't long before the people began to warm up to the guerrillas because their human side was more and more visible. He also penned a letter to Xavier as a final warning.

The sky was starless that night as Kazi stared up at it, consumed by his problems. He tried to pray but couldn't muster the concentration. He had only been leader for a little above seven years and was already so tired and angry that he was beginning to wish it could all end. He didn't know when Chezi and Yango entered the room and called his name. They had to shake him to bring him back to Lumani.

'You're tired, Kazi.'

'No, I am angry, Chezi. Angry with the cobras, disappointed with the Africans, and confused about what lies ahead.'

'You can't go on like this. You need to rest if even only for a week.'

'I don't have a week!' Kazi slammed, raising his voice.

'You have a week, Kazi. I am here, and the Ngui will not stop working until we have reversed this situation. They have already sent out the totems to protect the boundary with Alingafana, and Infanini is watching himself. The cobras will be in for a surprise the next time they attack. The Wemtii and the governors have been very effective in reaching out, and the people are responding. You can take a short rest for yourself. Besides, Nsika is back for good now and will be of great help.'

Hearing that Nsika had returned for good seemed to act like a relaxing pill on Kazi.

'What the people need at this point is assurance from their king,' Yango chipped in. 'But you can't go to them like this. They will see that you are worn out, and they will panic. A few days of rest will make the difference.'

'Am I that obvious?' Kazi was worried.

'Well, today at the meeting, you asked me the question about the clinic four times,' Yango answered.

Chezi said, 'Listen, I have already arranged a meeting with the new governor, Trevor, and he has agreed to meet in a fortnight. We can't have a tired king meeting with him. He has to feel the terror to get the message.'

That night, Kazi dreamt about his mother for the first time. He was lying somewhere in the forest near Infanini's shrine, and as he lay there, he could hear the fast stream rushing cool water that splashed out on him. Somewhere in a distance, he could hear Kolela's voice inside the shrine talking to his mother.

He heard his mother say, 'Shhh, keep your voice down, Kolela. You will wake the baby up.'

Kolela lowered his voice to a whisper, and Kazi couldn't follow the conversation. On the other side, Kazi could feel Khala lying beside him. She took some water in her trunk and poured it gently on his forehead. Strength sipped in, and he slowly opened his eyes and got to his feet.

Then suddenly, the scene changed, and he was in a desert. The cold evening wind blew around him, raising sand and whistling loudly. He looked ahead of him and saw his mother and Khala in the distance. His mother was stirring something in a bowl and seemed to be saying in Aminata's voice.

'Yes, this will calm him down. He will be all right after this. He is stronger than he thinks, and he will be all right. Take it to him,' she said and placed the bowl on Khala's head.

When Khala brought the bowl to him, it was the hot spicy soup that Aminata used to make for him when he was injured. He inhaled the vapour from the bowl, and every nerve in his body relaxed.

Kazi opened his eyes to a bright sunny morning. Nsika was the first person who came to see Kazi when his week of rest elapsed. Kazi didn't ask Nsika why he had returned, but Nsika knew that his decision had gladdened Kazi. They talked about the different problems in Lumani and decided that it was time for Kazi to speak to his people to sound a message of unity before he saw the new governor the next week. They talked about the war in Europe and the weakening of the cobra presence in the continent. They had to take advantage of the chaos to push as far as they could for independence, but that would not be possible without the unity of the African peoples.

Nsika wrote the speech for him and ended with the following:

'It is important to know how to fight, even more important to know when to fight, but most important to know whom to fight, for a people who don't know how to fight are easily defeated, a people who don't know when to fight attack at the wrong time and get defeated, but a people who don't know whom to fight kill each other, and the enemy buries them without a fight.'

* * *

Kazi returned to Kush four months later to complete the third phase: the attacks. All he had to do was to lead them into the first battle to give Ishmael and the other commanders the confidence they needed. Once that was over, they would take it from there. The target, as agreed, was the administrative building, precisely the commanding cobra's office, to obtain the information they needed. Kazi used the same strategy he had used in Lumani: an overnight attack. The advantage the guerrillas had was that they were used to the cold desert evenings after extremely hot afternoons, whereas the cobras found it difficult to adapt and usually fell ill because of the drastic change in temperatures. The soldiers on guard at the administrative building would make a fire in the evening and gather around it to keep warm while taking turns around the block, two at a time. There was also a lot of complacency on the part of the cobras because for the last seven or eight months, there had been no attacks from the rebels, and their spies hadn't picked up any information on a preparation for rebellion or an attack of any form. This was because Kazi had deliberately asked Ishmael to stop all attacks and play dead so that the element of surprise would have its maximum effect. In addition, with Ndikwa's help, they had identified key informants and eliminated them.

The attack went therefore relatively smoothly for Kazi and Ishmael. They surrounded the administrative block at about midnight, Kazi from the back and Ishmael from the front. They watched the soldiers do their turns for about thirty minutes, counting the exact number and noting where they stopped and checked and when they returned to the fire to let another pair take over. Two of Kazi's jumped over the fence from the back and targetted the two who were doing the rounds, opening fire immediately, taking them completely by surprise. The shots drew the attention of the others around the fire, and they rushed to the back. Kazi and the rest of the troops jumped over the fence and opened fire. The cobras dropped like stones. Some had the time or ill luck to turn around and run back, only to end up straight in the arms of Ishmael's team. It was over in no time.

The doors were broken down, and Kazi and Ishmael took out as much paperwork as they could. They found pretty much the same information that Kazi had predicted: a well-tailored map of the Kush, the names of the prominent personalities in Kush (including Raheel and Yusuf), the names of the informants, and all the posts of the cobra soldiers and the number of them at each post. One thing Kazi pointed out was that the rebel base in the desert was not marked on the map as he had seen with the Njuu. That implied, he told Ishmael, that the cobras had not yet discovered their base or the route through which weapons were being smuggled and also that the informants were not linked to any top-ranking people amongst the Kush natives. It was a good sign.

He rounded up his mission in the Kush a week later by cautioning Raheel and Ishmael on the need for a strong secret service, keeping the information about the rebellion watertight, and to use surprise as a key element in attack strategy. He also warned for them to expect retaliation from the cobras once the attack had been traced to the people. If the cobras had not yet reacted, it was because they were still trying to figure out where the attack had come from, but sooner than later, they would discover and strike back at the natives. Ishmael therefore had to move fast on the next attack. Their attack had sparked disarray amongst the cobras, and most were fleeing back home, but eventually, the cobras would reassemble. Ishmael had to reconquer a good chunk of the Kush before then, a good chunk that they could establish as independent of the nation and use as leverage to negotiate independence.

Raheel was especially glad that Ndikwa had married into the Kush and was in no mood to return to Lumani or Yaketu just yet. It therefore meant that he would stay to support them. He had learnt Arabic and Kush, and with a good understanding of the cobras' language, he would play a key role. Raheel also felt an indebtedness towards Kazi that was seldom felt around the Kush for a person they had known for scarcely four years. He couldn't let his guest leave without a significant reward, a precious gift that would keep the Kush people in Kazi's heart forever and by which the Kush could always remember him: a wife, the perfect symbol of gratitude from one man to another.

Kazi tried to evade the 'gift' by reminding Raheel at that farewell feast that he still had the dagger and gourd, which a Kush king had given his people a long time ago, and that the Kush already had a special place in the heart of Baluma that he and his people would never forget. The truth was that Kazi had lost taste for the Kush. Two years ago, Aminata had left to complete a bachelor's in nursing at the Islamic University of Fitume in the capital city, and when she had finished her training, she sent word home that she had taken up a position in a hospital there and would not be returning home anytime soon. Since Kazi had never discussed Aminata with Ishmael, he couldn't muster the gall to ask about her directly when she left.

Raheel refused to concede. He wasn't letting Kazi go off without a piece of the Kush. 'You will take a wife, my king.'

A prince revering Kazi as *his* king didn't take effect because Kazi's mind was in Fitume. 'I will take Aminata.' Kazi summoned every iota of humility he had in his body to say the name.

The effect was as if the pedal of a guillotine had been lifted.

'What?' Raheel harrowed, and Ishmael's mouth gaped open before they said again, 'What?' each repeating himself as if they thought they had whispered the first time.

'Aminata.' Kazi looked at Ishmael. 'I know she is in Fitume, but tell her I am asking for her.'

While Raheel sat scratching his forehead, Ishmael, being a younger man and knowing Aminata better, knew that there was a piece of the puzzle he had to be missing. But it was Raheel who went on talking as if he was seeing an apparition.

'Please take her younger one, Rifaat. Rifaat is a good, calm, wise one. She will make an excellent wife. This is my gift to you because, trust me, I am their father. Aminata is nothing but trouble in a loincloth.'

Kazi wasn't listening. 'Not for me, no. I have made my choice, and that will be Aminata or no one else.'

'But, King Balumakazi, you are not even sure she will say yes.'

'Why would you be worried about that? You never asked her opinion before,' Kazi said with a cheeky smile.

Raheel gave up temporarily, letting Ishmael continue. 'Aminata told me a long time ago that she didn't want to have any more of this marriage business.'

'You have said yourself that it was a long time ago.'

'You don't know everything, Balumakazi. You need to know the full story before you make this mis –'

'I do know the full story. She told me herself.'

'And? You still want to marry such a woman?'

'Before she told me, yes!'

'And after she told you?' Ishmael and Raheel asked in parallel.

'Even more!'

They had to let Kazi win.

Later in his house, still within Yusuf's compound (because in Kush, a person couldn't move out of their father's house or compound, as the case may have been, until they were to marry), Kazi and Ishmael had a one-on-one.

Kazi had never talked to Ishmael about women, mostly because he had never allowed the opportunity. He was so inclined to maintain the unbreakableness in his image that he never discussed anything about what he considered a weakness, such as 'having an attraction for women'. It was beneath him, he believed, and so did everyone in the Kush and Lumani – except, of course, Chezi and Nsika, who had, after several years of knowing him, uncovered that soft side of him, that he never let anybody get to know about. For them, it was intriguing, but for Kazi, it was an exposure he wasn't willing to share with anybody, not even them. It was a weakness he felt that, like any other weakness, should be concealed. Even with *choosing* Aminata, he was determined to show every sign of resolve but none of weakness.

Ishmael knew that he was missing something and needed to fill in the blank spaces. He remembered catching the moment when she had placed the bowl of pork on the table and avoided Kazi's eyes as Ishmael introduced her as the nurse. Thinking about it now, he recalled that Kazi seemed to be going out of his way to make eye contact, and Aminata, unlike her usual self, was not welcoming of it. At the time, he thought that that was odd behaviour from Aminata, given that, after her ordeals in the last twelve years, she had grown a boldness for men, which was unheard of in Kush. She wouldn't just make eye contact with the men but would also glare at any who looked her way in a suggestive manner to fend them off before they had even processed their thoughts. In all of what he observed, he had never given a thought to the attention Kazi paid Aminata because Kazi was generally bold and brash with a taint of arrogance – and especially with *women*! Kazi generally ignored women but not Aminata. Ishmael's eyes flashed.

'How do you know she will not be trouble?'

'I just know. Her problem is the Kush and its cultures, not with the whole world.'

'Have you met Rifaat? You might want to meet her before you make a final decision,' Ishmael said, emphasising on the word *final*.

'Yes. I have once' Kazi rolled his eyes and that ended the conversation.

After that, there was just one more hitch Kazi had to cross. On his wife's advice, Raheel insisted Kazi had to be initiated into the religion of Islam (which greatly contradicted what they knew of Kazi's Baluma spirituality) to marry Aminata. This prerequisite, they would have required even if he had chosen Rifaat but, of course, told him was only required because he had chosen Aminata. The move to deter him fell flat. Kazi agreed to be initiated. It bemused Ishmael to hear of the compromise Kazi was willing to make to marry Aminata because he understood that all this (the acceptance to join the estranged religion, the acceptance to do everything the Islamic way) was just a means to an end.

Raheel and Aamira were still in disbelief when Kazi returned with Yem, Changara, and Nsika. The wedding wasn't grandiose because in the Kush, nobody got too excited about a woman's third time around. Kazi was initiated with the name Souman, which Aminata had chosen for him. He knew that the Ngui would object to his first wife being from outside Lumani (just like with his father), but he was determined to make them accept Aminata, and he knew he could rely on Bana and Kolela for support. Besides, Kwahi and Tendo had told him they were just grateful he had finally come to his senses and that they would try to persuade the others. He had learnt of the opposition of his father's marriage to Lemi and how she had had a baby boy who died a few months before his own birth. He didn't know the details but knew that he was not his father's first, as most people thought. Infanini had tried to explain to him the reason why they couldn't have let the child live, but he didn't agree because he didn't see the harm. That was why he always referred to himself as the 'second' son of Ottuwa in spite of the Ngui's disagreement.

They left the Kush and stopped by Yaketu for Ndana's wedding, which was much more grandiose, not just because it was Ndana's first marriage but also because her father was the man called Yem. Yem fed the whole of Yaketu during the three days of celebration. And on the day of the wedding, he brought out all the rings and chains in his wardrobe. He was merrier than the bride-groom and danced until his waist hurt.

Kazi had much more than two weddings to celebrate. The British had attacked in the north and the east of the continent and were fighting against the Germans and Italians, and he was eager to see how that would turn out. Better yet, the supply of ammunition to Lumani was better than he had ever seen because of the war between the different cobra clans. They had even had to build special underground warehouses to stock because of the abundance of ammunition. The British were attacking on two fronts, and the inflow of ammunition was steady. It was easier for Kazi's 'suppliers' to get their hands onto the ammunition and siphon some out to Lumani. In addition, Raheel had, as another gift to Kazi, given him gold and contracts for trade with strong connections in the Middle East. Kazi's wealth would increase at a time he needed it the most. He was beginning to see a rainbow at the end of the storm.

* * *

Back in Lumani, integrating wasn't so easy for Aminata. These were a different people with a different language, a different culture, and a different way of life. Bana was most welcoming to Aminata. She helped her settle in and feel at home. Everyone around watched Aminata as if she was some strange breed of human they had never seen before. It helped that she spoke the cobra language which she used to communicate with everybody including Kazi but didn't help that she didn't speak Baluma. Kazi got servants who were more than willing to teach Aminata. From time to time, she disguised herself and went to help at the clinic. Kazi knew but didn't mind that she did that, but some others did.

The moment it was noticed that she was expecting her first, she received more visits and gifts than Kazi had after his investiture. No one talked aloud about a queen's pregnancy. No one asked questions, but everyone was watching keenly. Some said she was too old to give birth safely or to a healthy child, and that made the curiosity about her even worse. Luckily, her experience in Kush had toughened her skin, and so the rumours didn't cause her any pain. She gradually won the love and admiration of the people and of Kazi's half-brothers and half-sisters in the palace.

So much was the attention concentrated on Aminata that no one noticed anything curious about Bana except Bamba. She knew that Hani had gone south with his second wife for trade. They had stayed there for over seven months and had only returned two weeks ago. So how come Bana's belly was protruding with an almost six-month pregnancy?

Now there was never any love lost between Bamba and Uzise, but they both had the habit of watching every move of their daughters-in-law, not because they would or could do anything about misbehaviour but because it made for good gossip and time off from their squabbles with each other. Besides, Bamba loved to watch Uzise's children and their wives to assure herself that her own house was in better order. And so Bamba told Uzise, who asked Hani, and Hani asked Chezi, who asked Bana, although he already knew the answer.

He had asked Nsika cunningly once why he was not interested in getting married, and Nsika had given him some clever excuse about the dangers of espionage, not knowing that Chezi (through his mother, of course) knew the story about Nsika asking for Bana's hand and the saga that followed. Chezi had also noticed the closeness between Nsika and Bana and guessed that they were having an affair but didn't think they would take it this far. Bana was the matriarch of Lumani, and Hani was patriarch of his family. This kind of behaviour was unacceptable in every language and from every perspective. According to Baluma custom, Hani was allowed to ask for Nsika to be exiled.

'I never asked for a marriage with Hani.'

'Did you object to the six children you have with him?'

'I haven't said I am unhappy with him. I just mean that my heart has always been with Nsika. Having children with Hani didn't change that.'

'Hani will be right to ask for him to be exiled. He cannot stay here.'

Actually, Hani was simply acting surprised when his mother asked him and was hoping that Chezi would not be able to get a confession out of Bana. He knew much more about what was happening than everyone else thought he did. He knew about his father's pact with Wandi because his father had told him when he had wanted to marry the woman who was now his second wife. His father had asked him to hold on because he could not marry any other woman before he had married Bana, and Bana was not yet of marrying age at the time. He knew about the fact that Yem and Nsika had come to ask for Bana's hand when he was away trading in the south and that the only thing that had stopped the marriage from happening was the betrothal, which could not be reversed now that both Wandi and his father were dead. He also knew from the way Bana behaved whenever Nsika came around that she must still have strong feelings for him. He knew what was going on but never asked. He knew that they were both sneaking away from time to time because of the guilt in her eyes, sometimes when she had been away for a few days without an explanation.

Hani wasn't hurt; neither was he upset with Bana or Nsika. He sort of understood her and Nsika's frustration. It was the same thing he felt when his father asked him to marry Bana first. The only reason he had married her was because his father had made him promise, but in reality, it was his second wife whom he loved. He understood Bana's frustration being married to him because he felt the same way. Bana was much prettier and younger than his second wife, but he couldn't get himself to feel anything special for her, and he knew she felt the same about Nsika and him. What he did to honour the promise he had made to his father was to treat Bana with respect and understanding and provide for her whatever she needed. But with his second wife, he had something special that he couldn't share with Bana. The advantage he had was that being a man, he could take two wives, but she couldn't take two husbands. It was a pain they all (Bana, Nsika, and him) would have to live with for the rest of their lives, a pain not caused by any of them but by circumstances none of them could control.

'I will take care of the child' was all he said when Chezi told him.

'And Nsika?' Chezi had always known how much Hani loved and protected the family and, as a result, had great respect for him as patriarch but didn't realize how much sacrifice Hani was prepared to make to keep the family unit together.

'Leave him alone.'

Hani closed the chapter.

CHAPTER 8

To hate is to love the one you loathe.

Maidem Kayem

MANDARA WAS INCONSOLABLE. Kazi didn't know what to say to make her feel better. Twenty-seven years had flown by since he had lost his own father, and somewhere along the way, Yem had made him forget that parents were not immortal. The pain he felt went even deeper when he looked at Yem's lifeless body on the table, covered in the traditional leaves and torches burning incense around it, no rings, no bangles, no chains or any of his expensive clothing, just Yem as he had come into the world, covered with a simple white cloth beneath the leaves. He hadn't aged by a day. As he lay there, he looked the same age as when Kazi saw him for the first time that early evening when he came out of his house and frowned. His thick moustache and beard still looked so fresh and his bald head shining with the coconut oil he always used to make it glow.

Regretfully, Nsika couldn't be there because he was following up on an important lead somewhere on the outskirts of Lumani. Kazi was glad when Ndikwa and his sisters arrived (amongst Yem's many adopted children). The herbalist said Yem had died of tiredness, but Kazi had difficulty reconciling that with the Yem he had always known – short, round, boisterous, with a never-exhausting flow of energy and ideas on how to make more money.

Changara was obviously in pain too and perhaps cried alone in his chambers because whenever he talked, it sounded as if he had just woken up from sleep. Kazi understood that being Yem's successor, Changara had to hold in whatever tears or weaknesses he felt lest he give their 'enemies' the impression of a weaker family. Ndana was in grief when she arrived with her husband and newborn. Her eyes were swollen and red, obviously from crying, but she had a mother to console, two younger sisters to look out for, and a baby that she had to suckle with a happy face. She buried her pain within and put up a strong front to support Changara.

The Yaketu priestly caste had threatened to curse the funeral and ruin the family because Yem, before his death, had called on Infanini to be by his side in his last moments and to carry out the funeral rites according to the Baluma spirituality when he passed. The priests could have made a good bounty from the death of a dignitary like Yem, but he had nipped that in the bud when he asked for Infanini to carry out the rites instead, and the Yaketu priests knew Infanini; the man never accepted payment for rituals. What made them even more disgruntled was that they could have taken advantage of some loopholes, usual in any family of that size to make some money for themselves, but Yem, being an organised man, had planned his succession so perfectly so that nobody was fighting over any property or succession when he passed.

Yem was well aware that his decision would annoy the priests, but he had made it because even though Pa Ngunep and Makafu were gone, the Baluma spirituality was the only kind that he had ever understood and that he ever had faith in. The Baluma god was the one who had helped him in the difficult moments of his life, and the rituals had always given him the strength and comfort to cope with the hardship he faced.

When the funeral rites were over, Changara was anointed successor and squelched the hostility of the Yaketu priests by giving them enough cattle to stop them from pronouncing curses on the family. Ndana's younger sisters went to stay with her at her new home with her husband. Mandara was too grieved to stay back in her home in Yem's compound after his death, and helping Aminata in her last weeks would take her mind off Yaketu for a while, so Kazi and Aminata took her along with them when they left.

On the way back to Lumani, Aminata couldn't reach out to Kazi, so she let him be. Kazi was disturbed by the dream he had on the night after Yem's funeral, another dream about his mother.

He was again lying by the stream nearby Infanini's shrine, feeling the fresh cool water splash on him as it flowed past.

Again, he heard his mother and Kolela talking, and again, she was saying, 'Shhh, keep your voice down, Kolela. You will wake the baby up.'

Kolela lowered his voice to a whisper, and Kazi couldn't follow the conversation. Again, Kazi could feel Khala lying beside him. She took some water in her trunk and poured some gently on his forehead. Strength sipped in. Slowly, he opened his eyes and got to his feet.

Then suddenly, again, the scene changed. He was back in his room in his father's palace, sleeping with careless abandon as he always did back then, when suddenly, his mother was by his side, shaking him violently.

'Kazi, wake up! Wake up, Kazi! They are killing us while you are asleep! They have torn open our wombs and ripped our children out!'

Kazi woke up in cold sweat to see Aminata sleeping peacefully beside him. He drank some water, opened the window, and prayed until dawn.

* * *

When Ngemba finished, the silence that filled the room was deafening.

Last Sunday morning, while Kazi was away in Yaketu, he was with Nsika in the thick bushes on the outskirts of Lumani, questioning the hunters they had caught. It was a usual Sunday morning, with the Christians attending Sunday service at the church a mile away where it had been relocated. The happy chanting of 'Alleluia, the Lord is risen, as he said' could be heard from miles away.

Nsika was standing beside the dead rhinoceros, talking to the two men on their knees. 'I wouldn't cause any harm to you if you just give me an honest answer.'

'Chief, it is not what you think. We are hunting this for our families. This is food for a month. We are just poor hunters struggling to feed,' the shorter of the hunters said.

'We both know your whole clan will be eating this animal for two months,' Nsika said.

Ngemba pointed his long gun straight at the hunter's head and put his hand on the trigger.

'Neither of you are from Lumani or Alingafana, nor are these guns and bullets the usual ones hunters use to hunt bush animals. Are you sure there is nothing else you have to tell me?'

The taller hunter decided that he was not prepared to die just yet.

Trevor had developed ways of earning his own money while he was governing. He hired poachers to get precious parts of hippopotamuses, elephants, and rhinoceros (teeth, tusks, and skins). These, he sent to the coast to be loaded on ships. The poachers also served as spies on Lumani. They noted everything happening on the borders and towns bordering Lumani and reported back weekly. On this particular Sunday morning, the hunters had come in through Alingafana and posed as buyers in the bush meat market between, and then they made their way to the thick bush area where the Christian mission had been relocated. The rhinoceros was not part of this plan, but they couldn't resist the urge to make a little extra money from their mission. They would sell the tusks to Trevor and the meat in the market at Georgetown.

Nsika and Ngemba safely assumed that Trevor already had information on how many defence lines they had, how many guards they had, and the shifts they took. The hunters didn't have the time to explain what their mission was on this particular day because it happened right in front of them as they stood there when the explosion and gunshots at the church area drew their attention.

There was smoke coming from one part of a small house beside the church that had been exploded. The cobras sprang out of a lorry and surrounded the church, causing frenzy. They were shouting out orders and hitting the faithful with the butts of their guns. They seemed to be asking them to walk out in a single file, but because of the screaming and the chaos going on, Nsika and Ngemba couldn't make out the words distinctly.

The cobras made the faithful line up outside and shot anyone who tried to resist. A young woman threw a piece of stone at one of the cobras, cutting him sharply above the eye. She took off running but was caught and pulled back to the entrance to the church. One cobra motioned for her hands to be tied up and stretched out; another one chopped off both with two strokes of an axe. Two little girls who protested were dealt the same.

The faithful got agitated and began to fight the soldiers as they struggled to break free. The commander gave an order, and the first four men in the line were cut loose and made to stand in a file. A single bullet was shot through the first one, and all four fell to the ground. The two at the rear were still moving when they fell. The cobras pulled them aside and mutilated them. That lesson sank in fast, and they stopped fighting. The rest of the faithful were bound and led into a lorry nearby. The old people were shot. Those left behind at the church were the dead, the wounded, and the maimed.

Ngemba turned to the two hunters. 'What just happened?' When silence followed, he struck one on the head with the butt of his gun. 'What was that about?'

'They are taking them to the coast. There is a ship that arrived in the early hours of the morning. The big chief asked us to watch here to make sure everything went as planned. We are to report back in the evening,' he said between bloodied teeth.

'Or else?'

'They will kill our families in Georgetown. They know where we live,' he said pathetically.

Ngemba was so torn between emotions; he didn't know what to do next. He turned to Nsika for help but was stone shocked to find Nsika rooted to the spot as if he had was going through an out-of-body experience. He tried to bring him back to earth, but Nsika was unresponsive. Ngemba and another carried Nsika to the van, tied the two hunters in as well, and drove straight to his father's house.

Chezi was on the veranda, consumed in some documents they had just received from the king of Fefe, when Ngemba's fingers dug into him by the shoulders.

'Papa, Papa, come quickly.'

Chezi turned around to an expression of fear and horror. He had never seen his Ngem this shaken. He held Ngemba's wrist tightly for a while, looking him straight in the eye in a way that sucked the trembling out of him.

When he stopped trembling, Chezi said slowly, 'What is it that I cannot solve?'

The young adult swallowed and calmed down.

Infanini was the first person whom Chezi called before he even made up his mind about the two hunters, and the results were no good news. The scene Nsika had experienced had prematurely reopened a book of horror that had been closed and kept safely away in a cupboard for over three decades. The healing had not completed when the cupboard had been broken open and the book reread by Nsika's yet unhealed mind. Infanini would have to take him to his shrine for a few weeks to fix him before he went mad or, even worse, psychopathic.

The spies had informed some time ago about Christians disappearing after Sunday service, sometimes a family or two or a small group of young men and women. They were more like arbitrary kidnappings, and from time to time, bodies were discovered in the bushes here and there, sometimes maimed, sometimes shot in the back as if they had been trying to run away. It was a mystery that Kazi and the Ngui were still trying to resolve. Infanini had talked about seeing ships at the coast, but nobody imagined this because the era of the slave takers was long over.

Chezi had got some intelligence about some massive kidnapping that was to happen sometime in the near future. Prudent and alert as he always was, he had sent Nsika and Ngemba to start the watch immediately but did not expect the feedback he was now receiving, at least not this soon and certainly not this horrific.

* * *

Patience was not one of Kazi's virtues, and Chezi knew that. Father Daniel was only making a bad situation worse by taking his sweet time coming out to the front of the church, where they were waiting. Kazi always had that deceptive calmness about him when he was going to do something horrific. It was a side of him that had developed slowly but surely over the years, and it was not in the interest of the cobras or anyone else to get him into that head space.

'What happened here?' Kazi asked in the cobra language, not answering Father Daniel's greetings and looking him straight in the eye without blinking.

'I do not know, Chief. I was in the back at the sacristy, changing, and when I came out, the faithful were gone, and the wounded were lying there alongside the corpses.'

'So you heard... nothing?' Kazi said the *nothing* almost in a whisper.

Father Daniel blinked. 'Well, it's not that I heard nothing. There was shooting, and I knew there was nothing I could do about it.'

'And... you have no idea where they were taken?'

'How should I know?' Father Daniel said, answering Kazi's question with a question.

Kazi walked past into the church.

'Wait, wait, Chief, you cannot get in there. That is the house of God. Only those who believe in him are allowed to enter his house,' Father Daniel protested, following Kazi.

The guerrillas forced open the double doors of the church, and Kazi walked in with the rest. Kazi looked at the sculptures and the altar, the tabernacle and the crucifix, the pulpit and then the pews. It reminded him of his days in secondary school with Father Gabriel. He moved along the aisle pew by pew. There was drying blood spattered on the ground between and on some of the pews. Some of the pews were broken as if there had been a stampede on the way out of church, which confirmed Ngemba's story. It looked as if somebody had tried to wipe the blood away in a hurry but couldn't get it off because the ground inside the church was made of rough concrete, so the blood had stuck to the concrete and couldn't easily be removed.

Kazi raised his head to find Chezi at the other end of the church. Chezi nodded. They both turned their eyes to the church worker standing beside Father Daniel who had been watching them keenly and moved towards him. The guerrillas understood the signal and caught him in spite of Father Daniel's protests. One of the guerrillas pulled out a blood-soaked cloth from the man's back pocket.

'You heard nothing?' Kazi said to him in Baluma, holding the cloth to his face.

The man pretended not to understand the language, so Kazi repeated the question in the cobra language.

'No, I was with Father Daniel in the sacristy.'

'And you saw nothing?'

'No, I didn't. I swear.'

'Then you never will,' Kazi said in Baluma.

'No, no, please don't!' the man said in Baluma as the guards pulled him to the side. The man's eyes were pulled out in front of a screaming Father Daniel.

When Kazi and Chezi left the church, the only thing they were certain of was that Father Daniel knew about what had happened there. But the rest remained a mystery. Why were the people kidnapped? Why were they taken to the coast? Infanini had seen ships, but the era of the slave takers was long over, so what was this all about? Nsika, who would have been able to resolve this, was in seclusion with Infanini for healing. Chezi's mind went straight to Farra.

Kazi penned a threatening letter to Bishop Ezra in Georgetown to ask for his people to be returned. The woman whose hands were mutilated couldn't tell the number of men and women and children, but she had counted eighty-four heads taken into the lorry. In his letter to the bishop, Kazi laid emphasis on the number of people taken and reversed the number to state a deadline for a response to his letter: forty-eight hours from the time the bishop received the letter that afternoon.

Bishop Ezra replied by the next morning in a condescending letter about the objective of the church in Africa.

I do not expect the likes of you to understand the service we render to you and your people and the sacrifice we undertake in coming here, the sacrifice that we made coming from our countries to this continent to save your souls. I only hope that in God's good time, you will understand and show some gratitude.

As for the faithful who were, as you claim, kidnapped from our church, I am convinced that they will fulfil whatever God has in store for them as in his plan, and we, as the church, will keep them in our prayers that they may fulfil God's will in their lives. I welcome the opportunity to speak with you and your people about what happened at the Saint Vincent's Parish on Sunday whenever my schedule permits me.

Kazi read the last two paragraphs aloud. His eyes were still fixed on the letter in disbelief. 'Who do these cobras think they are?'

'They obviously don't take us seriously,' Chezi was saying when Farra came in.

'Our sources say they took them to the coast and put them on the ship,' Farra said.

Kazi thought he was dreaming. 'But the era of the slave takers is long over...'

'Or so everyone thought,' Chezi completed the sentence.

'Apparently not. Our sources in the south say that in fact, it never really stopped. They just kidnapped people in fewer numbers and with less chaos. Every ship that comes to shore with ammunition, food, and clothing for the cobras goes back with a few natives, usually the church faithful, and usually after service or some gathering of the sort. They came this far this time because they know that the Christian churches in Lumani are on the outskirts and well beyond our defence lines. Nobody watches that area, so the people can easily be captured. From what the two hunters caught told us, this was their third trip here.'

Kazi and Chezi froze for a moment.

Then Chezi said slowly, 'Father Daniel has some explaining to do.'

'No, Father Daniel has some dying to do,' Kazi said. closing his eyes and breathing out audibly, a habit of his that always charmed Farra.

'If we kill him, we will never find out what the reason for the kidnapping is,' Chezi injected.

'And you think a cold-blooded reptile like Father Daniel will tell us what his brothers are doing?' Kazi asked, opening his eyes while Chezi considered it.

'We can perhaps press him. I noticed the cobras don't have a very high affinity for pain. They easily break down,' Farra said eagerly.

'It is against our culture to torture our enemies. Our spirituality forbids it,' Chezi slammed.

'Is it also against their culture to kill? Their spirituality forbids it, but they do it with impunity,' Farra shot back, raising her voice.

'I have a meeting with the king of Fefe in three weeks. He is asking for our help. We will ask him to get what information we need in exchange,' Kazi interrupted them both and went on to lay out a plan that he would pass by the Ngui later on in the day.

Farra listened in admiration as Kazi made out what to do next. His long eyelashes blinking, his one hundred spotless white teeth, his full lips, the mark across his face tracing from between his eyes and circling his jawbone, stopping before his left ear – she was not listening to him as much as she was concentrated on his handsome features. Even though Kazi never paid her any attention, she always secretly had deep admiration for him as a warrior, which had grown into an attraction as she grew older. She knew she was not the only young woman in Lumani (of both the married and unmarried) who felt a strong attraction for Kazi, but she knew that what she felt was something more special than just the physical attraction.

Kazi was her ideal warrior. His body looked as if it had been made of fine wood, smoothened and shining to perfection, like a carving. He was an ideal hero not just as a symbol of resilience and victory over the cobras but also of a pride she had been longing for her whole life. What made her even more beholden to him was how much he defended her in the army. She had, for a long while, been the only woman in the resistance who was engaged in physical combat and had worked hard to earn her place, but because she was a woman, the men had difficultly according her the same respect they did one another. There was also a lot of scepticism about her because her father's treachery had not been forgotten, and the fact that she was born out of wedlock made it even more difficult for her to command authority. Kazi had risen her to rank of commander and encouraged other women to join the guerrillas. Unlike the other men, Kazi didn't seem to think she had any less potential and encouraged her every step during training, even when she thought she should give up and leave the fighting to the men. He encouraged her and made her push herself to limits she never thought she could surpass.

Whenever they had to camp, Kazi treated her like a princess, assigning to her a special tent and making the men guard her the whole night. Later on, as the number of women increased, he expanded the amenities to accommodate the women and made the men accept them as equal guerrillas.

Farra only realized she was in love when Kazi came home with Aminata. She was disappointed and suffered a lot in silence, but she kept hope that she stood a tiny bit of a chance because a king was usually obligated by culture to take more than one wife. She was convinced that with some patience, her time would come, and unlike the other women who had the same objective, she worked closely with Kazi, so she could position herself perfectly when the time came.

When Kazi finished, she turned her head to see Chezi staring right back at her as he had been for the last twenty minutes. She pretended not to understand that he had understood and left the room without a word.

* * *

'There are too many converts amongst us. If we attack the churches, our own people will rebel against us. We don't want an insurrection,' Bana said.

'There will be no insurrection if we tell them what the churches are doing, and we make them see the woman and children whose hands were mutilated,' Kwahi said.

'We cannot wait to convince the people we need to strike first and then explain later,' said Kazi.

'Remember that the people are still fragile. Not long ago, it was so easy for Xavier to convince them that the guerrillas had turned on them. They are still trying to understand why the cobras would attack them and make it seem as if it were the guerrillas who did. The Baluma have many myths about the cobras, and these converts are the most difficult people to convince against the cobras. They will not believe that the cobras are still taking people from us. How will we justify burning down churches when they have been persuaded that our ways are pagan?' Bana insisted.

It took long hours and late into the night debating back and forth about whether to strike and when to strike. Kazi was resolved to strike, as were most of the Ngui, but Bana was hesitant about how the people would view an attack on the churches. Kazi turned down Tendo's suggestion that he delay the attack by three days and go to Georgetown to speak with Bishop Ezra first, give him another deadline on which to return the captives, and attack only after that. The deadline he had given Bishop Ezra was no longer relevant because the bishop had responded, albeit unsatisfactorily. They were all convinced that the Christian Church had come under the pretext of evangelisation but were, in practice, serving as an arm of the colonialists, and Kazi had a strong message to get across: the church belonged to the cobras, but Lumani belonged to him.

* * *

As they walked into the church to get the altar ready for the service, Farra hid behind the tabernacle and took aim. The deacon fell, the mass servant was propelled forwards, and Father Daniel ran out of the church screaming. His was the first throat slit by Yango that early evening and Saint Vincent's Parish the first of many destroyed.

Kazi's aim was to get eighty-four bodies, exactly the number that had been taken from Lumani to the coast, whether or not the clergy were involved. Kazi camped in the bushes while the fighting was going on. There were two teams, one led by Farra and Yango and the other led by Chezi. Both teams attacked Saint Vincent's first and then split to get to the other parishes.

The word got round, and in the last three parishes, the guerrillas met the place deserted. Kazi's thirst was not yet satisfied because he had only sixty-two corpses; he needed twenty-two more. Chezi asked for them to stop when they returned from the last parish. Even though his mother and Uzise were leading the anti-Christianity campaign that Kazi had sanctioned in parallel (on Bana's advice), he still had mixed feelings about killing clergy, especially the nuns.

'Let's stop here, Kazi. We have sixty-two corpses. That should send the message home clearly enough,' Chezi said, washing the blood off his hands.

'Not clearly enough for me. Are there any churches in Alingafana?'

'Kazi, please.'

'No! I need the exact number,' he said irritably. 'Yango!'

'There is just one parish in Alingafana, but it is no use going there because there are very few Christians there, and the place is usually empty.'

'What about beyond Alingafana, on the outskirts of Georgetown?'

'There are three parishes, but we are not sure about the number of clergy.'

'Can we get twenty-two heads from there?'

Seeing Chezi shake his head and look away, Yango hesitated. Kazi raised his eyebrows for an answer.

'Yes, my king,' Yango said reluctantly and looked down.

Getting to the outskirts of Georgetown was no longer a problem because they now had cars and a good number of guerrillas who had learnt to drive, including Farra, Kazi, and Chezi. There were priests, nuns, and even lay Christian missionaries. The guerrillas attacked, killing everyone who had come in the name of evangelisation. Well, the truth was that they killed every white person they saw in the parish, whether or not they were clergy. They stopped after the second parish and twenty-two more 'heads'. When the bodies had been chopped and wrapped up in cloth bags, they were loaded onto a lorry that had been stolen from a warehouse. Ngemba drove the lorry to the front of the cathedral in Georgetown and abandoned it there, a job he was getting good at.

Just after they crossed borders into Lumani, Chezi and his troops camped with Kazi in the bushes. That evening, he tried to take a bath but couldn't get rid of the smell of the blood in spite of the incense and perfume. He let Yango and Farra give Kazi an account of the mission and went to sleep, still feeling unsettled about what they had done. He didn't like this merciless side of Kazi that made him behave like a godless person.

Kazi laid his head down on his pillow, satisfied with the mission report and looking forward to returning to the palace in the morning. He missed Aminata. He was thinking about her when his head began to spin around. When he opened his eyes, he was in the forest beside Infanini's shrine. Khala was in labour, and Kolela was standing beside her, making incantations. For an elephant, she wasn't in labour for long before the calf came forth. Kolela cleaned the young one gently with water, and Kazi asked whether it was male or female. Kolela smiled but didn't answer.

Kazi was about to insist for an answer when he heard his mother laughing behind him. He turned around but couldn't see her. When he turned back towards Kolela and Khala, he saw his mother washing Khala up, saying, 'Can't you see? It's a male.'

Kolela set the young calf down to suckle. Kazi laughed at himself and was going to ask his mother what it felt like to have a baby when somebody with Chezi's hands began to shake him on his back.

Kazi turned around and was back in his tent, looking up at Chezi.

'Aminata has given birth.'

Kazi sat up. 'When?'

'Early yesterday morning, around this same time.'

It dawned on Kazi that if he had heeded Tendo's advice to delay the attack by three days, he would have been around during the birth of his son. The messenger from the palace told him that Aminata had not been in labour for long and that the baby slipped out so quickly that he almost fell to the ground. Mandara and a midwife had brought the baby forth.

The journey back took an eternity for Kazi. One could have thought Aminata had just returned from a vacation by the way she was going about the house.

'Aren't you tired, Nata?' Kazi said from the doorway.

'I gave birth to just one baby, King Balumakazi, not ten.'

They laughed. She led Kazi to where the baby was sleeping.

'I have decided to name him Yusuf-Ishmael,' Aminata said, taking the baby in her arms.

'Since when did women name children?' Kazi said without looking at her, knowing that she would object.

'Since we decided to make decisions for ourselves,' Aminata retorted, promptly making Kazi laugh.

It was that stubbornness she had that had made him fall in love and kept him there. She had a mind of her own, and one needed strong arguments to persuade her to think about changing it. The names weren't just arbitrary. They had been well thought out, and Kazi didn't have any arguments. He decided he would seek Kolela's advice first before settling on a Baluma name. Since Infanini was busy with Nsika, Kolela would be the one to name the boy on his ninth day.

Aminata gave the baby to him and showed him how to hold him. It was only the second time in his life that he had held a baby. The first was on the day of victory when the strange lady placed the baby in his arms and said, 'He is yours.'

Kazi refused to let his mind go back to that sad incident and focussed on his son. This time, the baby *was* his. The baby was huge and had large hands with long fingernails curled up in two tight fists. Kazi tried to undo the fists, but the baby objected, squeezing his fists in even tighter.

'He is as stubborn as his mother.' Kazi laughed.

'Then maybe he is beginning his life on the right fist.'

The baby opened his eyes and looked at Kazi skeptically, and then he closed them back and turned away. He started moving in Kazi's arms uncomfortably. Kazi tried to reposition himself, but no matter what position he took, the baby refused to settle down. Then the baby began to cry loudly. Kazi looked at Aminata, confused, and she took the baby from him, humming a little sound to make him stop. When he was calm again, she put him back in his father's arms, but this time, the crying was even louder, almost violent. Kazi gave the baby back to his mother, feeling hurt.

'Don't worry about it. He just needs time to get used to you.' Aminata smiled lovingly as she hummed the baby back to sleep.

When they thought the baby was fast asleep, they tried again, but the baby woke after only a few seconds and began to cry again, so Aminata had to take him back.

Kazi sat down, devastated. His first baby had rejected him.

* * *

In the days that followed, the news on radio was less about the Second World War going on in the east and the north of the continent and around the world and more about the 'Terror of the Nine Hills' who had slaughtered eighty-four innocent cobras for no reason. Condemnation flowed in from all directions. Words like *cannibal*, *butcher*, *ogre*, and *beast* were used against him, even by other African nationalist leaders. The anti-Christianity campaign in Lumani had helped keep the Baluma and other neighbouring kingdoms like Fefe and Yaketu steadfast in support of him, but the rest of the world beyond that had a totally different perception of him.

Bamba was aging but not enough to stop her from going around, campaigning as an ex-Christian about the ills of Christianity and the fact that the religion was just another arm of the colonial administration and its domination. Her charisma was unsurmountable, and she loved being in the spotlight, especially when she outshone Uzise. She got through to the most fervent of converts and even used biblical examples to illustrate to the people why Christianity was an evil religion that conflicted with Baluma spirituality. She exaggerated the kidnappings and created a culture of fear, suspicion, and resentment for anything Christian. Bamba cleverly didn't touch on the subject of Islam (since everyone knew that Aminata was Muslim and well loved by the people). She manoeuvred her way around that by encouraging the pig farmers and liquor traders and reminding every Baluma at every gathering about the importance of preserving culture and traditions like the festival of the pig. The effect in the long run was that no religion was welcome in Lumani altogether, a thing that would last for generations. Bamba had succeeded in making her name a household name as she always wanted. Whenever the subject of religion came up, the question 'But what does Mama Bamba think about that?' always came up.

Kazi wasn't bothered about his infamy in the slightest because he was preoccupied getting his firstborn to not cry when he carried him. So far, Aminata and Mandara had succeeded in getting him to carry the baby when he was fast asleep without any objection, and that was an improvement he was proud of. Whatever the world thought of him, he could sort out once his son had accepted him.

Kolela visited on the seventh morning with his calabash and many strange herbs. He laid the cloth down and drew the enneagram on it. Aminata had never seen this before, but because Kazi was comfortable with it, she didn't object. She held the baby and sat beside Kazi on the floor. Kolela plucked a strand from the baby's hair, cut it into three pieces, and placed them at different angles on the diagram. Into the calabash, he poured water and some sand. The water swirled around as his incantations got more and more intense, and then the water cleared up, and he looked into it.

'Weak outside but strong inside. Subtle and cautious but rebounding and indestructible. He will be patriarch and priest.'

The water stopped swirling and became still. Kolela rolled up his cloth and threw out the water from the calabash.

Kazi tried to think up a name suitable for a patriarch and priest, but by the ninth day, he had still not settled on a Baluma name. He resolved himself to keeping just the Islamic names that Aminata had told him about: Yusuf-Ishmael. After all, he thought, sitting there at the naming ceremony as Kolela and the priests carried on with the prayers, both Yusuf and Ishmael were good men, determined to fight for their people, and besides, Aminata had told him that Yusuf meant 'God gives' and that Ishmael meant 'one who obeys God', so he resigned himself to the names but didn't tell Aminata that lest she rejoiced too much.

Kolela called Kazi forward as was tradition at a naming ceremony, but Kazi, knowing that Aminata would not let him sleep if he went forward alone, held out his hand to her and brought her forward with him. Mandara, not to be left behind, followed Aminata. This was her first son and second grandson, and she had as much ownership of this baby as any other. So all three came forward to Kolela to assume ownership of the baby.

This was a first of its kind. When the priest carrying out the naming ceremony was ready to dedicate the baby, he called up the father or, better still, the *owner* of the baby because in the culture, mothers weren't considered to be owners. Here was the king and first advocate of tradition sharing his ownership with his wife and in such a public display of it, for that matter.

The murmuring through the crowd got louder and louder until one of the priests called for silence to remind them of the solemnness of the ceremony. Aminata was unmoved. She stuck her chin up towards Kolela as if she didn't hear the crowd behind her, and that made Kazi even more amused. It had always intrigued him that his people were so determined to uphold their culture and traditions about what women could or couldn't do but were not so determined towards the cobras and their completely estranged ways.

Kolela would usually have broken the small kola nut into two pieces, but with three 'owners' in front of him, he broke the little nut into four pieces, giving one to Kazi, one to Aminata, and one to Mandara and taking one himself. He said the prayers, and they ate. Then he took the baby in his arms and put some salt into the palm oil, making incantations the whole while, and then he asked Kazi, 'What destiny do you want for him?'

Kazi looked at the child for a while. Aminata looked at him, wondering whether he had forgotten the names she had chosen. The crowd was impatient, and the murmuring began again.

Then out of nowhere, Kazi said, 'Hlegiba Yusuf-Ishmael,' and the murmuring stopped.

The crowd was shocked by the choice of name, not the Muslim names but the Baluma name. The name had not been used for at least eight generations. Giving a child an ancient name had a strong meaning: that there was something in the past the people needed to be reminded of.

He dipped his thumb into the oil and rubbed it on the infant's head and lips. The baby clutched Kolela's thumb in his large hands and sucked the palm oil as if he understood the meaning of his name. Kolela dipped his hand again into the palm oil and put it to the baby's lips, and it happened again so that even the priests giggled.

'Hlegiba Yusuf-Ishmael, the people's lifeline. I place you today under the divine protection of Si to fulfil the destiny that has been set out for you. Your ancestors will guide you until your mission on this earth is completed. Whenever Baluma thinks that all hope is lost and the tribe is destroyed, you will emerge like a tiny root springing out of the ground with a green leaf to prove them wrong, to remind them that Si doesn't sleep. You will be the lifeline of your people.'

Kolela passed the baby to Kazi and, surprisingly, even though he was quite awake, didn't reject his father this time. He curled up and went to sleep for the rest of the ceremony, only waking when he needed to eat.

Later on, Aminata wanted to know why Kazi had chosen that name. Kazi told her the truth.

'I don't know, Nata. I really don't know.'

* * *

Infanini had the room prepared, and then he woke Nsika up himself and helped him up. His eyes were dazed, and he could hardly put one foot in front of the other. Over the last two weeks, the nightmares and the violent waking had gradually ceased. For the last three nights, at least Nsika had slept peacefully without waking. The high priest sat him down on a short stool in front of the cloth and calabash on the ground and made him rest his arms on his knees. Nsika shut his eyes and managed to hold his head up, even though the room was spinning around. Infanini crushed some herbs and put them to his nose, and the room stopped spinning.

The hot water was poured into the calabash and herbs sprinkled into it, producing a somewhat familiar scent, and the room got foggy. Nsika was back in Mama Sawa's house, talking to Natahi.

'Now let us start from the beginning.'

'They always bring them to the house for flogging. I am used to it. They flog them until they are bleeding, and then they let them go. The bridge has collapsed. It is nobody's fault. Even the younger basses say so. But Bass Cornell is not satisfied. I count one hundred men and boys. The boys are not much older than me. I know most of them. That's Ropo, and that's Mburi. I can see Ivumi in the back. He converted and now calls himself Paul. He has changed completely, but I can still recognise him. Over there, that's the mother of Mmani. She is crying for mercy. I can't see him, but if she is there, then one of her children must be there, maybe Mmani or his younger brother, Hile. She only has two of them.

'Bass Cornell is saying that there are not enough bullets to kill them. He is telling them to use machetes. They line them up and tie them by the hands and feet. As they are being led out of the compound, some of them have to hop because the ropes are tied too tight. I take a bucket as if I want to go and fetch water because I want to see what will happen. I lie down in a bush behind a small guava tree. They line them up by fives as if they are going to march. The families are crying and begging for mercy. Then they start five by five. They bring them to the front and make them kneel down and bow their heads.

'They raise the machetes and chop. The heads come off. Some bodies are moving, and the soldiers are holding the families back. Mburi is in the second set. He dodges, and the machete does not cut him completely. He tries to run, but they swing the machete again, and his body is running some steps without his head. They are laughing, and they bring forward the next five.

'I can see Mmani and Hile. They are holding hands. The machete comes down, and their mother collapses.

'When the soldiers are finished, they make the families dig a large hole and carry the bodies and put inside and cover the hole up again.'

'What about the church?'

'They are singing, the Christians, their usual songs. Then soldiers come out of the lorry and go to the entrance of the church. Somebody says something in church, and the people start running out. They line them up and tie them up. They start marching them to the lorry. Some of them have to hop because the ropes are tied too tight. This time, they take even the women and the children.

'One woman is fighting. She throws something at one of the soldiers. He falls to the ground. The commander says something, and she is caught and tied by the hands. She is pulled to the ground, and her hands are stretched out in front. They chop off her hands and leave her there on the ground, while the others continue tying people up. Two other little girls try to escape, but they are caught, and their hands are chopped off as well in the same manner.

'The crowd starts fighting the soldiers. The commander says something, and the first four men at the head of the line are put out and made to stand aside. One soldier shoots through the first man, and all the four men fall down. I can see the third and fourth men are still breathing. One of the soldiers sees them moving and chops off their legs and hands. The crowd stops fighting, and they are led to the lorry and laid down in the back, one over the other. Some of them are praying aloud, shouting about forgiveness, but I don't know what they did wrong.

'Some people are old and weak, like Mama Musaki and her friends. They shoot them. Somebody blows a whistle, and the lorry starts driving away.'

'What disturbs you the most about these two stories?'

Nsika was still for a while, and then he started rocking back and forth. 'The blood, the blood, the eyes pleading for mercy, the blood, the blood, the eyes, the eyes pleading for mercy, the blood...' He repeated himself several times, rocking back and forth each time.

Infanini put a hand on his shoulder to make him stop and put some herbs to his nose to bring him back from the clouds.

'Have you ever killed a man?'

The question seemed to take Nsika back to the clouds. He shook his head. 'No, no, no, never. Never had the courage. Never did it. The blood, the blood, the eyes, the eyes pleading for mercy, the blood, the blood, the eyes...' He rocked again.

'And what if your daughter were in danger?'

Nsika stopped rocking, his countenance changing.

'That is enough for today.' Infanini put herbs on his nostrils and led him back to his bed.

* * *

The meeting between the African nationalist leaders from eleven countries had been scheduled in Fitume. The Kush was still under colonial rule, but enough progress had been made with negotiations towards independence, so the African leaders were allowed to hold their conference there. They would take advantage of the Christmas and New Year season when most cobra commanders had gone overseas to hold as many meetings as they could and plan ways forward for each of their independence agendas. Each of the countries was in a totally different situation from the other, with different colonial invaders, different methods of oppression, and different strengths of the resistance movements. This was the root cause of the lack of understanding amongst them and the disagreements they had had in the past.

Kazi had succeeded in persuading the nationalist leaders of other countries that they all needed to come together to create a grey area and support each other. The meeting to be held was called 'Unity is not a choice'. In spite of his infamy, the leaders had an inexplicable liking for Kazi. His victory over the cobras had inspired them, and his continued maintenance of a small independent kingdom in the middle of a colonised country gave them the hope that self-determination was not just an illusion.

The year 1942 was coming to an end, and Kazi's notoriety as cannibal, butcher, ogre, and beast continued to spread. He flipped roughly through the letters on his desk that had been sent to him from Kush before opening up the newspaper included in the mail. In the front page was something about the commemoration of the death of Marcus Garvey two years earlier and his African nationalist ideologies, which were becoming wider spread amongst African nationalist leaders. Kazi saw something in small writing about the 'Terror of Africa' and a reference to page 6. He turned to page 6 and saw a whole page written about a certain King Buluka of Africa, described as a hideous cannibal. It took him reading the part about the slaughter of the clergy to realize they were actually referring to him.

Nsika had everything prepared for Kazi, including travel documents and speeches. Governor Trevor had taken ill and returned home for a while. From what Chezi said, upon his return, he seemed to be more inclined to hold talks about independence so much that he didn't object to Kazi travelling via the international airport in Menha. Kazi wondered why.

Eight months back, he had postponed the meeting with the king of Fefe because of the birth of his son. And since then, he hadn't had a chance to reschedule because getting used to the whole new world of fatherhood was a task more trying than killing cobras. An arrangement was therefore made for them to meet in Fitume three days before the scheduled meeting.

Another thing that made Kazi popular amongst the African leaders was that since the meeting was in Kush, Kazi took Aminata along to see her family. She had to take along their newborn because he was still suckling and because it was impossible to convince Mandara to stay in Lumani without the baby, a journey of one became a journey of four, including two servants, three maids-in-waiting, and four bodyguards. The maids took along their littlest children, about one or two each, and then the servants needed one or two helps, and then the bodyguards decided that they too needed to make one or two of their family visit this new kingdom outside of Lumani. And so while the other African leaders arrived with only one or two assistants, Kazi arrived in Kush with a herd.

The meeting with the king of Fefe was disheartening. The information about the continuous kidnapping of people from the continent to trade as slaves in the west left a bitter taste in Kazi's mouth. The kidnappings weren't just happening in Lumani but all over the nation and, as the other African leaders confirmed, even at the west and south coasts of the continent. So while the trade had been abolished on paper and was confirmed on radio and newspaper to have ended, it was still going on clandestinely on a smaller scale. This gave Kazi the chance to explain to the leaders why he had attacked the churches in Lumani months back and the result that no disappearances had happened ever since in spite of the churches' condemnation of him.

At the meeting, the first subject up for discussion was how to contact the Africanist movements in the west after Garvey's passing to get those freed slaves to come back to the continent. This was a subject that, after several days, was still unresolved because of the scepticism amongst the Africa leaders themselves. There was the conception that too much time had passed and that those taken would no longer fit into the African society. The Africans who had met those of African descent in Europe and the Americas couldn't seem to find common ground with them because of centuries of miseducation about their African origins and about the story of how they were taken. It had been engrained in these kidnapped Africans that the Africans on the African continent had willingly given them up and were unwilling to have them back. Kazi and a host of others believed in the principles of Garveyism, which had taken root in some parts of Britain, Jamaica, and the West Indies (but had very little effect on the Americans of African descent, where the greater population of slave descendants still lived), that all peoples of African descent be encouraged to return to the continent.

Kazi's speech centred on the grey areas that could be created amongst the African nations, about supporting each other by providing aid in terms of ammunition, food, medicines, and clothing to guerrilla movements in different countries. Together they set up a network across their countries and escape routes in the event that leaders had to escape to other countries to seek refuge for a while. He emphasised on the need for espionage, which could only be effective if there were no moles in the resistant movements.

A hot topic was the participation of African soldiers in the ongoing Second World War. Kazi was adamant that no African participate but rather let the colonisers kill each other off. He had rejected Trevor's call for African soldiers from Lumani and sent a strong message out to the rest of the nation, but his message had little effect because the people were enticed by the lofty promises of reward after the war. Most of the African leaders had fallen for it and encouraged their people to help the colonialists fight the war. Kazi questioned why he should help one enslaver fight the other. The stance taken was that they were choosing between the lesser of the two evils. Kazi disagreed.

By the end of the week-long conference, there were still several issues that remained unsolved, but Kazi was satisfied because the motion he came to put forward had been adopted. Grey areas had been created amongst the leaders. Henceforth, each guerrilla movement would not be acting as a single isolated unit but with sister units around its region, providing support to put up a stronger resistance, a first step in a journey of a thousand miles. Unity, they all agreed, was not a choice; it was the *only* choice.

* * *

It was a beautiful home on a hilltop that over looked the Moja River. In the mornings, the cool breeze filtered into the house to refresh it before the sun rose to warm it up, and in the evenings, when the sun went down, the breeze blew in to warm it up.

Nsika sat on his veranda, smoking a pipe. He knew he would never be allowed to give her a father's love, but just watching her playing by the river from a distance was satisfaction enough. He and Bana could no longer see, so they gradually grew apart. Hani's reaction had humbled them both. She had cut out this lovely piece of land for him on the hilltop of his choice as a parting gift. Uzise had named the baby after her, and no one would ever know the truth. Secrets like these were buried with those who knew.

Ever since the healing, he had had time to rethink his life and had resigned himself to die without a wife. The healing had given him the strength to face violence and blood, and he was determined to kill whatever he needed to kill to build a better Lumani for his Uzise. He was still head of the espionage force but had begun training and would be taking part in the next attack whenever it happened.

* * *

Kazi was encouraged by the progress that had been made so far. By mid-1943, the colonialists controlled very little territory within the Fefe kingdom. The Tebo uprising had pushed the cobras farther towards Georgetown. Other kingdoms began to rise one by one, and Trevor had lost control of almost two thirds of the nation. Because of the networks the natives had formed, there was a steady flow of ammunition to the resistance movements in all parts of the country, whereas the world war was crippling the cobra occupation in the country.

The only setback for the natives were the age-old grudges between the kingdoms. Some kingdoms still begrudged others for buckling to the pressure of the slave takers and attacking other kingdoms for slaves. Others accused some kings of making truces with the slave takers to protect their own kingdoms. These divisions weakened the native resistance and gave the cobras an upper hand in spite of how much territory the natives had recaptured.

The allies were winning the war. Germany was withdrawing from several territories. All the African leaders were excited except Kazi, who didn't see why he should be. The mail kept on flowing in from different countries about the victory of the allies in one or another nation. The next meeting of the African leaders was scheduled for August 1943. Kazi responded to accept the invitation. However, when the time came, he sent Nsika instead because Aminata was almost at term with their second child, and Kazi didn't want to repeat the mistake he had made with his first. And he was glad he didn't go because by the time the baby arrived, Nsika wasn't yet back from N'Gomda, where the meeting was taking place.

His second experience at fatherhood was very unlike the first. This second one was full of life and joy, completely trusting and welcoming to everyone who carried him. Kazi had no difficulty carrying him. Kolela described him as a warrior and likened him to other great warriors like Vumanga and Wandinendi with a zest for life and love; also that he was impatient and brash but extremely kind-hearted. Kolela's words about his second son reminded Kazi of himself before the world got in the way. He was resolute to keep the child's mind away from the evils of the world.

* * *

Bana had assigned a large chunk of land in a fertile area to her and several servants and farm workers, but there was nothing anybody could do to appease her. Mpima was a disgruntled old woman, and more was never enough. She hated Aminata for being the queen that she, Mpima, should have been. She hated Bana for being the matriarch that she, Mpima, could have been. She even hated Mandara for being the king mother that she, Mpima, would have been.

After a long time and lots of patience, she had finally got the noose she could hold around their necks to get whatever she wanted. A faithful servant of hers had brought her an invaluable piece of information from Chezi's compound some time ago during the preparations for the naming ceremony of Kazi's first son, but she decided to keep it to herself and use it at an appointed time. The appointed time for Mpima was once the three days of celebration were over and everyone had gone back to their daily lives. Unfortunately, Bamba had gone down with malaria before she had the chance to visit and had taken longer than expected to recover. Mpima waited patiently for Bamba to recover, reminding herself always of the fable of the patient dog. Once the time was right, she chose a warm afternoon to make the visit.

Now Bamba, on the other hand, had never liked Mpima. She thought her a usurper who didn't deserve all what she had been given.

Bamba merely tolerated Mpima to know what she knew and when she knew it and therefore keep her under control. That was how she had foiled Mpima's plans for more land and farm workers a year earlier. Besides, Bamba complained, Mpima's children were all sickly and weren't sure to live much longer. Four had died already, and there were only two left who were as sickly as the others who had died and, in her opinion, didn't have much more time left in this world, so who was she acquiring all this wealth for? Bamba may not have liked Bana for the simple reason that she was married to Hani, whose mother was her sworn enemy (she would have preferred for her to be married to Chezi; that way, she would have both successor and matriarch in her palm), but when it came to Mpima, Bamba and Bana were on the same side. The old woman was greedy.

Bamba was therefore not in a lively mood whenever Mpima came to see her and, on this particular afternoon, skeptical because of the spark she saw in her eyes when Mpima walked through the door.

'My sister, you have come to visit us.' Bamba grinned and hugged her in her usual charismatic manner, never giving off her heart.

'Yes, I thought I would come by and see how you are doing after the illness. It is always difficult at this age.'

Bamba was about to ask her what she meant by 'this age' and remind her that she was almost ten harvests younger, but she chose to stay focussed on the spark in Mpima's eyes. 'Yes, you're right, but I am much better now. Let us sit outside so I can get some strength from the breeze.' In reality, Bamba needed to sit outside because she wanted to see Mpima's facial expressions clearly.

The conversation went on for a long while about everything and nothing, and Bamba was almost thinking she was being paranoid when she heard Mpima say something about unfaithful women. She pretended not to understand what Mpima was insinuating and urged her on. Mpima fell for it and spilled all she had been told.

'Do you know that it is a well-kept secret that Bana's daughter, Uzise, is not really Hani's own?'

'Really? How so?'

'Well, they say that nobody knows the girl's real father but that Hani was away when Bana conceived.'

'Hmmm, one has to be careful with what one hears because I was here myself during that period, and Bana was obviously in about her second month before Hani travelled. In fact, that is why I visited so often after he left.'

Mpima blinked, her eyes expressing doubt now. She stopped for a moment to consider that perhaps her servant had got the wrong information. But to get what she wanted, she insisted on the story. 'Well, such rumours are never good for a family. It is important to keep them quiet. But that will take a lot of persuasion.'

'Who do we have to persuade? We need to act fast because this could cause significant damage to a family like ours. Mpima, you know our reputation.'

'I know, Bamba, and that is why I came straight to you once I heard it.'

Bamba put her hands over her head, pretending to be distraught. 'Whom did you hear this from?'

'Well, you know servants talk, and I listen, pretending not to understand. I am an old woman, so nobody thinks much of me,' she said, eyeing Bamba from the corner of her eye. 'But I promise you that I could stop this rumour once and for all. Bana just needs to understand what needs to be done.' Mpima looked forwards as if she was not talking to Bamba.

'I will let her know by this evening. Such things cannot wait, Mpima. They need to be resolved.'

And resolved it was, once and for all, as Mpima herself had said with her own lips. She took ill a few days later and was dead by weekend.

* * *

Trevor suffered a stroke and was taken out of the country for good. With the turmoil of the war, the headquarters could not spare a good commander to take charge of a single colony. Helmut, a lieutenant who had been discharged in the first few months of the war and had returned home to a life of misery, was more than eager to take on the task. Helmut was a man without honour and fought as such. He was promised stupendous benefits if he could regain the parts of the colony that had been seized by the natives and even more if he could recolonise the Terror's territory. He set his evil mind to work, and it therefore followed that while the world war was gradually coming to an end, the war in the colony was just beginning.

Helmut set out spies like fishing nets. There were several tribes and ethnic groups that had differences and grudges, but Kazi's doctrine of unity against the common enemy had sunk in so deep that Helmut was not able to penetrate enough to set one tribe against the other, at least not so soon. The one tribe Kazi had not convinced to fight in unity was the Menha tribe in the south. This was because of a long-standing grudge between the Baluma and the Menha, whom the Baluma had accused of making a truce with the slave takers to attack Lumani and other tribes in the interior and to kidnap them and trade as slaves in exchange for their own people being spared. Almost a century had gone by since the southern 'fish men' had stopped attacking Lumani and the Baluma had returned to their kingdom, but the grudge was still bleeding fresh.

All the tribes in the nation had made peace with Baluma in one form or another over the years. Even the Tebo king and his chiefs had made a public apology to King Tozingana, and the two tribes had reconciled, at least superficially, enough to support each other against the colonialists. But the grudge between the Menha and the Baluma remained fresh because while the Baluma were adamant about getting an apology from the Menha before considering the slightest possibility of reconciliation, the Menha were unwilling to apologise or show any form of remorse for the past. They accused the Baluma of burning down their clans and slaughtering their people in retaliation during the era and therefore considered that the score had been settled. In addition, the Menha maintained that they were forced to do what they did to save their kingdom, which was much smaller than the Lumani. Hence, though the Menha had just enthroned a new king who was willing to offer an apology and make peace with Lumani and Kazi was willing to bury the hatchet and move forwards, the wounds of their people were deeper than any of them could heal.

The new colonial administration could not take advantage of the rift just yet because the two tribes, though at swords drawn, were unwilling to betray each other. The Menha was in the territory that was still under colonial rule and had a rife guerrilla movement that acted independently of Kazi's forces, with the objective of liberating their people without support from Baluma. King Balumakazi was king of an independent territory who had a good supply of ammunition, connections, and hideouts all over the region and a guerrilla force that was more skilled than the cobra army. The Menha guerrillas, on the other hand, were poorly armed and ill-trained. Their attacks against the cobras were feeble and had little effect on the administration. Their guerrillas were dying in numbers, and the Menha knew they needed the Baluma support, but their pride was more important than victory and freedom.

Arbitrary arrests, public executions, and torture became symbolic of Helmut's administration. For every attack on his administration, Helmut retaliated by sending his soldiers out to shoot civilians indiscriminately on the streets. His spies picked out the families of the guerrillas, and a few months later, the guerrillas in the territories under his command began to desert, and the resistance weakened significantly, leaving him with Lumani as the only real threat.

Kazi's reaction was to create a safe haven in Lumani for the guerrillas and their families so that they could reside in Lumani, mobilise, and carry out attacks on the colony. This, therefore, created an exodus of natives from the colony to Lumani.

Helmut wasn't sitting on his laurels either. He systematically ambushed the moving families. His spies informed what route the people would take to get to Lumani, and then the soldiers would hide in the bushes and shoot them down as they passed by. Some eventually got to Lumani, but most were shot down and their bodies left to litter the roads to Lumani to serve as a warning for those who tried to escape. Helmut also had roadblocks for those who travelled by bus. The soldiers easily identified the families escaping to Lumani because they usually travelled with most of their belongings, and typically, there would be a family of women and children travelling without a father. That was the sign that the women were the wives of guerrillas. The soldiers at the roadblocks would get them off the buses and execute them on the spot.

Chezi mapped out a perimeter beyond the borders of Lumani that they could take control of. The territory didn't really belong to anyone; it merely separated one kingdom from another. Chezi got six teams of guerrillas to comb the area and secure it. That way, if the escaping population could make it into that perimeter, they would be sure to arrive at Lumani alive. Also, Nsika beefed up the espionage force with more women. The women always made more efficient spies, posing as farmers to watch the perimeters and sending the messages back.

* * *

Two chiefs slipped past the borders one night and were caught as they crossed the first defence line. They had risked their lives to escape to Lumani to ask Kazi for help on behalf of all the chiefs of Alingafana. Alingafana was under attack. The soldiers had occupied most of the town and patrolled the border with Lumani day and night. Helmut was preparing an assault on Lumani and had slaughtered hundreds of their people to deter anyone from helping the Baluma. Chezi had anticipated a move like that on Helmut's part and had the guerrillas prepared to attack Alingafana in less than a week. Nobody was more surprised than Kazi and Chezi when Nsika joined them in the van, dressed in full combat gear. Neither of them asked him why.

The objective was to eliminate all the soldiers in Alingafana and secure the territory by the border with Georgetown. Farra was already at the borders between Lumani and Alingafana, waiting for them with two teams. The chiefs were taken along to direct them once they had penetrated the front lines. Nsika knew the town well enough, so he joined Kazi and Yango's team, while the two chiefs joined Chezi and Farra.

Making out the cobra camps wasn't difficult because they all had a signature mark: they hoisted their flag wherever they camped as a symbol of authority and dominion. The first team of guerrillas had to crawl on their bellies to take them unawares, but the shooting woke the whole town. The sounds carried even faster because Alingafana was on plane land, with very few trees and strong winds. The guerrillas seized control of two war tanks but could not use the tanks because they had never seen that kind of ammunition except on the black-and-white televisions the cobras owned in Georgetown. All they knew was that it was a killer machine that had exploded them in numbers. The colonial soldiers received reinforcement the next day, and the battle dragged on for two weeks.

The corpses were humped together when the battle was over and burnt. Not all the town had been taken, but the essential parts had, and the border with Georgetown had been secured. Whatever soldiers were still in Alingafana by then would be taken out in the next few days. The guerrillas locked down the town and moved from house to house, searching. They found one or two soldiers hiding amongst the people, mainly native soldiers who had been fighting with the cobras. These were easy to eliminate. The problem was the ones who had run into the bushes that were too vast for Kazi's guerrillas to comb. It would require collaboration on the part of the natives to get them all out, and these were natives who were not particularly keen on engaging in physical combat in any form, not even to defend themselves. It exasperated Kazi that his guerrillas would have to do most of the defending themselves.

Besides a small shoulder injury, Nsika had been outstanding in the first battle of his life. He was almost as good a shot as Chezi, and that made most of the guerrillas wonder whether he had not just been pretending not to know how to fight all this while to avoid combat. He agreed to stay back to clean out Alingafana. Farra and her teams retreated to the border of Lumani, and Kazi returned to his family in Lumani.

* * *

The relationship between the boys was singular. The first one, Giba (shortened from Hlegiba), was extremely timid and reserved and wasn't comfortable with anyone except his mother and Mandara. He learnt to walk before he was ten months old but didn't talk until he was well over a year old. Giba was independent and comfortable in his own company. Once he had been fed, he could be by himself the whole day. He loved holding his mother's loincloth and following her around the house as she supervised the servants. Because he was ever so quiet and never complaining, only his mother knew when he was ill. Only she could tell when his emotions changed, happy or sad or sorry for something he had done. For everyone else, he was difficult to read, including his father. He loved running, playing hide-and-seek and indoor games, and was very neat. He would get upset if his loincloth had the slightest stain on it. He inherited his mother's chubby form and radiant smile, but unlike his mother, he gave out his smile sparingly. He had his father's long eyelashes, and when he narrowed his eyes, it looked as if he had closed them completely.

The second one, Mungu (who had been named Ibrahim Mazimungu), was outgoing and lively, always up to one form of trouble or another, and showing strong signs of his mother's stubbornness. Mungu could talk coherently before his first birthday but took his time in walking. He loved to be carried and made no effort to walk on his own until Mandara forced him when he was about eighteen months old. Still, whenever he had the chance, he let anyone around carry him. Mungu was a charmer, and whenever he came in, the room would light up. As he grew, he developed a love for wrestling and boxing and hated losing a match. He needed to show off how strong he was. Needless to say, neatness was not one of his strengths. He was developing several teeth like his father and had his father's light brown eyes and lean body and had hair all over.

The two boys were fifteen months apart, but as they grew older, it was difficult to tell who the elder was. At playtime, Mungu always took charge, and Giba let him. He would say what game they were to play and set the rules; Giba would do as he was told. At meal time, Giba took charge, and Mungu let him. Giba would set the plates down, Aminata would serve them, and Giba would make sure Mungu ate every morsel of food. Even when he didn't want to eat, Mungu obeyed. It was a strange understanding they had, a partitioning of responsibilities and total respect for each other's authority.

Being the father of these two totally different characters was disconcerting for Kazi. While Mungu loved his stories of war, Giba was terrified by them. It usually happened when he was trying to explain to the boys why he went away from home so often and why he needed to fight. He kept the details of the killing to himself but told them of the fighting and how it was going on, thinking it would excite them as stories of Wandi always excited him as a boy and nurtured the warrior within. Mungu would listen with admiration and undivided attention, whereas Giba would turn away and find any excuse to leave the room or the table or wherever they were. He noted particularly that whenever he came home from a battle, Mungu would run joyously to him, whereas Giba would not let him touch him until he had washed and the smell of blood about him had been dampened by the strong perfume he always used. Kazi tried to make an effort to talk to Giba as often as possible and ask him questions to get to know him better, but once he started talking about being a man and what a man ought to do, Giba would curl into his fortress again and raise the wall that he had built around him that Kazi couldn't get through.

He was talking to Giba on the veranda one afternoon when he was told that Farra and a group of female soldiers were in the court asking for him. When he asked the servant what it was about, the servant whispered something about spies they had caught, and Kazi got up to leave. He was about to tell Giba to go off and play with Mungu, but the horror in the boy's eyes made him stop. The boy was holding his breath as if he could feel that his father was about to do something gruesome. Kazi stooped to talk to him, but Giba ran off before he could say anything. Kazi was heartbroken, but it didn't stop him from doing what he was going to do.

He had the corpses chopped up and scattered along the road from Alingafana to Georgetown. Giba couldn't have known what happened, but he wouldn't let his father near him for weeks after that.

* * *

Alingafana was now under their control, and the neighbouring Fefe and Tebo kingdoms had pushed the cobras out a week earlier. Helmut had been lying low for quite a while now, and Chezi was on the alert. He knew it was a matter of time before Helmut reared his head, but no one would have guessed what his next target would be.

The primary school behind the seventh hill was newly built, and Bana had designed it herself and had it constructed to provide an education for the children of the farmers in that area. Ninety-six children between the ages of seven and sixteen attended, and twenty-seven teachers worked at the school, supervised by a headmistress. Typically, in Lumani, Kazi funded the construction around the kingdom with the money he made from the gold trade and his other trades, and the teachers were paid by the parents of the pupils. However, in this primary school, to persuade the farmers who were reluctant to send their children to school, Bana paid the teachers herself.

At break time, the children all came out to play, while the teachers sat in the shade of a tree, talking. The explosion in the football field drew everyone's attention. The children were screaming and running away from the field. A little boy was lying in the middle of it with blood on his chest. The teachers ran towards the screaming children to see what was going on and tried to stop them from running, but the panic was intractable. The headmistress rushed out of her office. Six cobras descended from the farms and started shooting at everyone. They threw grenades into the school classrooms and offices to blow them up. The small infirmary attached to the school was blown up with the nurse on call.

The cobras were hardly recognisable because they had covered their faces in mud. It was just their hands that were still white, and that was how the farmer who watched from his farm knew the attackers were not natives. They scanned the farms towards which they saw the children running and shot dead every single one of them. When they were certain that everyone was dead, they disappeared into the farms from which they had come.

Before Kazi and Bana got there, Yango's team was on the spot. The farmer told them in what direction the men had left, and they followed the trail. Kazi walked to the middle of the football field, where the first victim lay. He knelt down and looked at the little boy. The boy could have been about Giba's age, five going on six. He took the body in his arms and looked up to the sky. He didn't know when the tears flowed and when they stopped, but he was sure that if it was the last thing he did, he would kill Helmut himself.

The farmer's trail led Yango to a children's clinic not too far off. By the time they got there, the place was a river of blood. All the patients, doctors, and nurses had been killed. The blood and the smell of the gunpowder was still fresh, so Yango knew they couldn't be far away. He caught an eye peering out from behind a curtain in one of the wards and drew the curtains apart, and there was a nurse with a two-year-old baby. She told them of the attack but couldn't give them any useful information on where the men had gone or what direction they had taken.

Yango was wishing he had Chezi's nose and instinct when he heard Chezi's voice outside. Chezi had been to the primary school and had followed them here with his team.

'Did you find anything?' Chezi said as soon as Yango stepped out.

'No, just a nurse and a sick baby, and she can't tell us where the men went to.'

Chezi asked the men to skirt around for footprints, and then he turned back to Yango. 'These are not regular soldiers. They have to be mercenaries. They have likely gone towards Fefe. That is the nearest kingdom, and it is likely that that is where they came from. It doesn't surprise me. We have told those foolish people time without number to secure their borders to Georgetown, but that fat king does nothing but eat and marry women. He is counting on King Balumakazi to save him each time. If we get there fast enough, we should be able to catch them in Fefe. They are cobras, so they cannot walk about freely unnoticed. They will have to take the bush tracks, which we know better than them. Helmut is sending us a sign.'

'A sign?'

'Yes, a sign. This is just a sign of what they are preparing for us.'

'By the god of my ancestors! A sign? On children?'

'Helmut is a man without honour, not that any of the cobras ever was, but he is much worse. I have heard of what he does in the nation. His soldiers surround a whole neighbourhood and burn it to the ground. Anyone who tries to escape is shot dead – men, women, children, even goats and chickens. They say he is the son of evil.'

The guerrillas came back. They had traced the footprints in the direction of Fefe. Chezi sent Farra ahead to close the entrance into Fefe from Georgetown to lock the cobras in Fefe so that they would have to swim across the rivers to cross.

True to Chezi's words, when they arrived Fefe, the whole town was in jubilation, celebrating the king's wedding to his twenty-third wife. Chezi and Yango didn't even bother to stop by the palace to pay their respects. They simply set about their business, fetched the cobras, caught them hiding in some bushes around a riverbed, and left without anybody noticing.

Kazi was again with Giba when the mercenaries were brought to him, and Giba ran off. Again, Kazi was heartbroken by his son's reaction but didn't hesitate to do what he wanted to do. This time, he didn't kill the men. He simply had their stomachs opened, the livers and kidneys removed, and had them taken back and laid at the entrance to Georgetown right beside where he knew the soldiers usually patrolled, knowing that by the time they were found, the scavengers in the bushes would have fed on them. He followed it up by blowing up a hospital and two schools in Georgetown the next week and crowned it all by severing a child's head, putting it on a stick, and posting it in front of Helmut's office. Farra and her team did a perfect job of it. If Helmut was called the son of evil, Kazi was determined to show him that he was the father of evil.

The orders made even Chezi, who was as vindictive as his father, shudder. He didn't know what to say to make Kazi stop this manner of killing. He understood the need to retaliate and make a significant statement to a beast like Helmut, but this was savagery. He decided to speak to Aminata about it.

Aminata told him frankly what she thought. 'He needs a voice of reason around him, and unfortunately, I cannot be that voice because he has nightmares about the cobras attacking his family, so he wouldn't listen to me. Farra could have been that voice. She has a lot of influence on him. But as a person, she has a lot of bitterness to get off her chest, and the war is a good platform to vent it. You have to ask someone else, maybe Infanini.'

Chezi asked Aminata carefully, 'Do you think he loves her?'

'Yes, he does – but not the way he loves me. He loves her like a sister. She just hasn't understood that yet.' She smiled. 'When she finds a good man, she'll take her eyes off him.'

Kolela had also been watching Kazi and was worried about this side of Kazi that was beginning to be the norm. Previously, Kazi would either kill an enemy or let him go; torture was not in his nature. This side of Kazi had once shown itself when Xavier was in charge, but when Trevor had taken charge and stopped the violence, Kazi became himself again besides his attack on the churches, which was understandable after the kidnapping. This Helmut had brought back the insanity. Kazi was like wood ablaze, and every drop of violence towards Baluma was like oil that only helped nurture the fire. Kolela decided to speak to Infanini about it, even before Chezi spoke to him.

Kazi wasn't surprised to see Infanini in the court, waiting for him. 'I know why you are here, high priest.'

'Then why did you make me come here, son?'

'These cobras need to leave, and the only way is to pay them back in their own coin. They don't understand the language of honour. It is futile to speak to them in that language. If we are having any effect on them, it is because we are speaking their language. Even Nsika has finally understood that.'

'We have a culture, a spirituality that we uphold as a people, and you, as king, know better than to reduce your warriors to beasts.'

'They already call us that. So maybe we need to live up to our reputation.'

'Balumakazi! You descend of a long line of brave kings. This kind of savagery should be beneath you. Those were children, and there were women amongst those killed too.'

'They killed our women and children too!' Kazi yelled, standing up. 'These people have slaughtered us for almost a century, not counting the years of the slave takers. We stood by our culture, our spirituality, and our honour for all those years, and how far did that take us? Where is Wandinendi now? And all those great warriors who stood to fight with honour against a people without any — where are they now?' Kazi's voice echoed around the court.

'If you don't stop this thing, this thing will kill you, son,' Infanini said calmly, and then he got up and left.

It was the last time Kazi saw him, but Kazi never forgot his last words.

When the twelve days of mourning were over and Kolela was anointed high priest, Kazi declared nine days of celebration. It wasn't customary to have nine days of celebration after the anointing of a high priest, but it had been fourteen years since the people had had a festival declared arbitrarily by their king, and from the way the people rejoiced, Kazi knew Aminata was right to have suggested that he did. They needed to take their minds off the perpetual state of uncertainty in Lumani and the sporadic attacks by Helmut.

During the celebration, Nsika stayed safely away from Lumani because he knew Bana and her family would likely be all over, and he might betray himself if he met his daughter in front of everybody. He, however, found courage from somewhere to meet Hani before the celebrations began. He greeted him and went straight to the point.

'I am here because Kazi needs help. He is becoming a person he is not. I watched him grow, and this person who kills children without mercy is not the same boy I fled this kingdom with. Life changes all of us, and it has changed me too, but there is a part of us that we should never lose. Kazi is losing that part of himself, and no one around him can talk that side back into him.'

'What about Farra?'

'She is worse than him. She is still trying to prove to herself that she is not her father.'

'OK, I will see what I can do.'

'Thank you, Hani.' Nsika turned to leave, and then he turned back around. 'And thank you for everything. I never had a chance to say it but am saying it now.' He walked quickly away.

* * *

Hani chose a time during the celebrations when Kazi was home with the family to stop by. He brought along Bana and her children. The children went out to play with Kazi's boys. Only Uzise stayed, whom he couldn't persuade to go with the other children because they were all boys, and she hadn't yet learnt to play their games. Hani motioned to Kazi for them to step away from the women. Uzise tried to follow, but Bana made her sit down beside her.

'You know my father was a very fierce warrior. I worshipped him as Mungu worships you. I wanted to be him as Mungu wants to be you.'

'Yes, but Giba hates the sight of me. He thinks I am a monster.'

'It is natural to be a monster when you have been through what you have been through. I used to be a monster myself. I know what you feel.'

'You? Of all the men in Lumani?' Kazi laughed and sat down.

Hani sat down beside him.

'You wouldn't know because you weren't born yet, but there was a time a long time ago when my father went to Njuu to train with Papa Wandi, around the time that King Tozingana died. I don't know who betrayed him, but later on, we were told that it was the son of a certain Mbunti, a palm wine tapper. I remember the boy. They used to call him Nyomi before he converted to Christianity and changed his name. The boy betrayed that Papa was one of the warriors, so they came and took us one late morning. They took Tchaleta, Tameko and I. They tied our hands so tightly behind our backs that it felt as if our chests would tear open, and they dragged us to the fat cobra's house. Then they put us behind the house and tied us to some pillars. They asked us where our father had gone to, and because none of us would tell, they whipped us on our chests until we bled.

'What they didn't even understand was that of the three of us who were taken, I was the only one who understood a little of their language because I used to help Mama with her church affairs, so I learnt with her to speak some of it. Tchaleta and Tameko didn't even know why we had been caught or what they were asking. Tameko always had problems breathing, and he has never been very strong. I almost gave my father up when I saw him in pain. I only stopped when it dawned on me that if I should give Papa up, there would be nothing to stop them from killing all of us. At least, while they had only us, they could only kill us, and Papa, as I knew him to be, would go after them.

'When they were tired of whipping us, they hung us upside down. Tameko was almost suffocating, so I swung myself across and caught a rusty metal edge with my chin so that he could lean on the back of my head and catch some air to breathe. I stayed in that position until my body was numb. When the warriors came to rescue us that evening, they had to carry me because I couldn't feel my body.

'The cobras had unleashed the monster in me, Kazi. We returned during the time a certain Arnold was in charge here. I joined a secret group of young men who, like me, had had similar experiences. We used to go around this kingdom, abducting white women and children. We would torture them and kill them slowly in the forest and bury their bodies there. We didn't do it every night or every week, just once or twice a month. Sometimes there would be three women, sometimes just one, or sometimes just a group of about four children. Whatever we could catch, we caught. We didn't kill them straight away. We killed them slowly, piece by piece, cutting them up and making them bleed slowly to death. It assuaged the pain we felt inside to torture a white woman or child and then watch later on as the family mourned.

'I grew particularly good at abducting children. I knew how to watch them without being noticed and what victim to target. It was so easy to get them. In the first few months, I thought that after I had killed a few, my pain would have subsided, and I would go back to being me, but each time I killed, I only got thirstier. Then one day I caught a little girl for amusement. I didn't really feel like killing a cobra that day, but I decided to do it just for the fun of it. She strayed into the forest. I saw her on my way out from hunting. I let her see me, and then I frightened her to make her run into one of the traps I had set for antelopes. She fell in, and I closed the trap and went home. I returned later in the evening and pulled her out. Then I tied her up and slit her in the left armpit to let the blood out slowly and painfully. I lit a fire and sat back to watch her bleed to death, and then I put her back into the antelope trap to let her rot. A few days later, her body was discovered and taken to her parents. Her death was blamed on wild animals, as all other disappearances were.

'I watched as her mother held her body crying and remembered how my own mother had cried when the cobras took my brothers and me away that morning. I had become the cobra that I hated so much. I realized on that day that to hate is to love the one you loathe. When you hate a person too much, you become that person without even realising it. And that is the worst punishment a person can ever deal themselves. I know it is difficult to fight these cobras without becoming them somewhere along the way. But I also know if there is one person who can defeat them, that person is you, Balumakazi, because you are a true son of this soil.'

'It's so hard, Hani. They will never leave us alone.'

'I know it's hard. That's why I don't blame you, and I believe that our ancestors have made it that way so that we understand that the only way to tame the beast is to be the beast. No one can tame the beast within you except you. I know because I have been that beast myself.'

* * *

Francis couldn't tell who was more evil than the other: Helmut or his assistant Nathan. They were like evil twins. Helmut had one leg, and Nathan had one eye. They complemented each other perfectly. There were hardly any conversations between them, but when there were, it was always some plan about torture or killing. Helmut would begin an evil trend of thought, and Nathan, who was always quiet and focussed on the jar of beer in front of him, would throw in a few ideas to make the plan juicier, with his one eye coming alight as he did.

Francis worked as an errand boy for the colonial administration to support his large family in Menha. He did his tasks dutifully and was grateful with the scraps from Helmut's table, but he never forgot that it was this same administration that had executed his father three years ago, and even his mother was not allowed to weep lest she be labelled a sympathiser of the guerrillas and made to meet with the same fate.

'We killed King Tozingana, and King Ottuwa came up. We killed that one and thought it was over, but decades later, we have Balumakazi on our hands, who is much worse than his father or grandfather. These people spring up like radishes in spring. You don't see the end of them. Do we have to uproot the entire family?' Helmut was saying as Francis placed the mail on the table.

'Unlike most native chiefs, he has just one wife and only two sons. We should be able to take them out easily enough,' Nathan chipped in.

Francis left the room and loitered around to eavesdrop.

'I have never seen people as stubborn as the Baluma. The moment you think you have solved the problem, they create another. Where did this Balumakazi crawl out of?'

'Wherever he crawled out of, we will uproot the tree. His small family makes it easier for us.'

'"Strike the shepherd, and the flock will be scattered." Wouldn't that be in the book of Matthew?'

Francis heard them laughing as he slipped behind the cupboard.

CHAPTER 9

Radicalism is the firstborn of injustice.

Maidem Kayem

AMINATA THREW HER comb at him, pulled the bowl of oil from the stool, and flung it at him as well.

'What has got into you? How could you even consider such a thing? You would sacrifice my son to defeat the cobras? I will kill you first with my bare hands!'

For all his fearlessness, Kazi couldn't get himself out from behind the door where he had ducked.

'You are not the man I married. What happened to you, Kazi? I escaped the Kush to end up with exactly what I was running from!' And she let out a torrent of threats.

A silence later, Kazi peeped out to see if there was anything in her hands. 'I married you, not the other way around.'

The jar almost caught him in the chin. 'If I had known you were like the rest of them, I would never have come here.' She cursed and left the room.

This was proving to be more difficult than they had thought. He changed to disguise himself and went to see Chezi.

King Eyame of Menha had approached Kazi during the last meeting of the African leaders in Yaketu to discuss a solution to the rift between their two tribes. The grievance between Baluma and Menha was centuries old, often accepted and ignored but now was in the way of the independence that both kings wanted. Eyame had suggested betrothing his first daughter, Dika, to Giba to force reconciliation. It was an understanding common in that part of Africa that when a prince of one tribe married a princess from an enemy tribe, the two tribes were considered to be married and, by virtue of that, unable to fight each other (at least not physically). Therefore, whatever grievances they had between them, both tribes would find themselves obliged to peaceful solutions. Although the two children had a long time to grow before they actually got married, once they were betrothed, both peoples would be bound going forward. Kazi had told Eyame he would consider it and send him a response.

After a few months of deliberating all the angles, Kazi and Chezi decided to accept the proposal. That, they had done without asking the Ngui or Aminata first.

Chezi had told him she would object and prepared him for it, but neither of them imagined a woman could unleash this kind of anger. Chezi knew Bana would object as well but thought they could find a way around both women. It turned out that they were wrong on both counts. Nobody in the Ngui had a problem except Bana, but then she was matriarch, and therefore, if she objected, the decision could not be acted upon until she had at least given her non-objection. Kazi had hesitated because he had not forgotten Aminata's past and what she thought about forced marriages.

On this afternoon, making his way stealthily to Chezi's compound, he was desolate, knowing that even if Bana approved eventually, it would take an eternity to convince Aminata, an eternity during which he wouldn't sleep.

'Chezi, we will have to find another way out. If we go ahead with this betrothal, my days on this earth will be numbered.'

'Calm down and tell me. What exactly did she say?'

'It was just as I told you. She wouldn't hear of it. She threw everything at me. Imagine, I had to hide behind the door.'

'Yes, that is difficult to imagine.' Chezi chuckled, seeing it in his mind's eye. He cleared his throat for the more serious matter. 'But what exactly were her arguments?'

'She said if she had known I would sacrifice her son, she would never have married me.'

'OK, so besides just the fact that her son is not choosing for himself, she has no arguments?'

'I told you about her, what happened before I married her, Chezi! She will not let me sleep. Do I have to speak in the language of the ancestors for you to understand?'

'At some point, she will have to sleep herself, so you will eventually sleep,' Chezi said calmly.

Kazi sighed, feeling even more desolate.

Chezi continued, 'Now let us think about this carefully. Bana has a strong influence on her. If we convince Bana, she can do the convincing for us.'

Kazi looked at Chezi as if he were mad. 'Convince Bana? You make it sound so easy, Chezi. How did her betrothal to Hani end up? Uzise is a living answer to that question.'

'That brings me to the third person – my mother. If she can convince a mass servant against his priest, then she can most certainly convince Mama Uzise about this. Then Mama Uzise can convince Hani, and Hani can convince Bana.'

'And you know that because...' Kazi said, still finding difficulty believing Chezi's optimism.

'Because Hani is a person who understands why sacrifices need to be made. Bana may not love him, but she has a lot of respect for him because he has treated her well.'

'What will I be doing in the meanwhile?' Kazi rubbed his hands.

'You will pretend to avoid Nata and do your best to look miserable to draw pity from her.'

'That wouldn't exactly be pretense.' He blinked. 'She wants to dig my heart out.'

'You should have thought about that before you went across the world to find the most stubborn woman on earth. Nobody is afraid of their wife in this kingdom except you.' Chezi was laughing at him.

And so Chezi convinced Bamba, who convinced Uzise, who convinced Hani, who convinced Bana, who convinced Aminata. But to punish him, Aminata let Kazi explain this complicated story to a seven-year-old boy and didn't accompany him to Menha. Kazi took his punishment solemnly.

* * *

The two boys played together a lot, but Giba didn't like that whenever he was winning, Mungu changed the rules to suit himself. That would degenerate into a quarrel and then a fight, which Mungu, being the stronger, usually won. Giba was stouter and Mungu leaner but much stronger – or, at least, so they thought, until Giba got really angry and gave Mungu a sound beating. However, that only happened once every very long time. It was as if Giba deliberately let Mungu beat him up, but the truth was he needed anger and pain to fight, which, unfortunately for him, seldom came around. In addition, fighting meant dirtying his loincloth and rubbing himself in dust, which he hated. So while Mungu fought for the pleasure of it and wrestled for the admiration of the girls, Giba didn't see a fight as a pleasurable thing and found wrestling or any combative sport repulsive. Mungu was the charmer and Giba the one who aged before his years.

Mungu seemed to understand it better than Giba. But for the fact that he would now have a wife like his father and so many men had, Giba didn't really understand what it meant, much less the reason for it. Dika was Giba's age but, unlike him, wasn't shy or reserved. She was also playful and adventurous and seemed to take more to Mungu than Giba when they were introduced. Giba wasn't actually sure what he felt about Dika. Mungu said that Giba would be a man because he now had a wife, so that was the way Giba chose to understand it because that was the only way he could.

'But that wouldn't stop me from beating you up whenever I want. All I can promise is not to do it in front of your wife.' Mungu laughed. Giba didn't find it funny.

King Eyame didn't make a big show of the betrothal because it had provoked mixed feelings in his inner circle. There were a minority who thought it as a good way of burying a hatchet they were tired of shouldering, but most felt that it hurt the pride of the Menha to offer that kind of apology. Eyame had had to use his power of veto to defy the council's decision. He welcomed Kazi, told the Menha the reason for the visit, and offered a small feast to celebrate. The palm wine was poured into the horn. Kazi offered the horn to Eyame. Eyame drank, and the bond between the two tribes was sealed. The ceremony was over in three days, and Kazi returned to Lumani. The Menha and Baluma would have to bury the hatchet whether or not it pleased them to do so.

* * *

The 1950s were indelible years on the African continent, and the first few years of the decade set the tone of the struggle for independence for the next two decades. The leaders of the struggle were forming political parties all over the continent and engineering the masses towards self-determination. The African peoples were maturing in the politics of the Western world, and the word of independence was spoken more freely and with greater understanding of its implication.

King Balumakazi and King Eyame formed a political party called the Convention of African Natives (CAN) whose propaganda centred mainly on promoting African nationalism and African native ideals, the return to their kingdoms and cultures as they had before the invasions. At the outstart, the CAN mainly consisted of the Baluma, Alingafana, and Menha peoples and was departmentalised into four groups to represent all partisans: the main wing, which was the general assembly and was presided over by a council composed of principally Baluma and Menha nobles; the women's wing, in which matters such as the role of the women in the liberation movement and the gender-specific problems they faced during the struggle were deliberated (an influence from the feminist philosophy that had swept across the world); the armed wing, which Kazi was in charge of; and the youth wing, which was formed sometime later once the young people gained an interest in political education and activism. It went without saying that Ngemba was at the helm of the youth wing, with Bamba serving as secretary general of the women's league and special advisor to the youth wing. Eyame assumed the position of party chairman.

Because of its tribal composition, the CAN was initially received with skepticism, but as the CAN's anti-tribalism and pro-Africanist propaganda spread, the preconception that the CAN was a tribal party composed of 'Baluma and friends' was dispelled, and peoples of other tribes began to join. King Balumakazi and his guerrillas had not just defeated the cobras in their territory but had also equally succeeded in establishing a political party that was influencing natives from the most illiterate and menial works of life to the Western-educated and most highly revered people in the nation. This, they did through Kazi's stroke of genius.

'They speak differently, but they all speak the same language. What we need is a translator. So get a farmer to talk to the farmers, a builder to talk to the builders, and an intellectual to talk to the intellectuals,' he said at the launching of the party, and it worked like magic. The CAN could communicate to the entire nation and push the independence agenda.

All this while, Kazi was known for his terror on the cobras and fearlessness in physical combat and everything that that encompassed – but not as an intellectual. African leaders referenced him as a war strategist and a 'go-to' hero when the cobras attacked, but nobody ever thought he could contribute much in political debates because he had, with his own mouth, rejected a university education and the privilege of travelling to the West. Therefore, through African eyes, he remained a semi-illiterate at best. In this new era, lawyers, sociologists, and political scientists were the new nobles, and everyone else was restricted to the same confinement: illiteracy. The world around him was therefore not prepared to receive this other side of Kazi, a side even more effective than a guerrilla, an ingenious strategist who had become more popular than the CAN, who seemed to not only know how to defeat the cobras physically but also how to play the tune to which all Africans of every walk of life could dance in unison.

The effectiveness, therefore, of his strategy and the popularity of the CAN party drew, as a result, both admiration from once-enemy tribes like the Tebo and envy from once-friendly tribal groups. One such group was the Fefe. The Fefe was amongst the most literate tribes whose scholars had benefitted from several scholarships offered by the colonial administration. The Christian missionaries had built several schools in Fefe because of its temperate climate. Even though Kazi's anti-Christianity campaign had eroded the number of faithful who attended service, the numbers of scholars continued to rise because the Fefe believed in the colonial system of education. There were lawyers, teachers, nurses, and doctors who had returned home from abroad and were a reference in their community. When the lawyers addressed the people in the Fefe language, their accents were slightly tainted by the influence of years in Europe so that they sounded like the white pastors who tried to learn and speak the native language, giving them a flare of superiority. All Fefe parents wanted an education for their children because that was the shortest route to reverence, especially for poor families.

The Fefe king had, as his spokesperson, one of such lawyers named Tesan, the daughter of one of the palace servants whom he had sent to the mission school to repay the servant for several years of good service. Later on, she won a scholarship to study law abroad. When Tesan returned home a political activist and feminist lawyer, the king had not paid much attention until the CAN was launched. His kingdom had benefitted of King Balumakazi's protection, and he was grateful for that but not grateful enough to entertain the thought that a Baluma might be president of the nation when it finally gained independence. He needed a Fefe in office to be assured of his influence in the new independent country. It was, therefore, with that in mind that he and the council of Fefe princes funded a new political party they called the African Patriotic Front (APF) and put Tesan at the head of it. Indeed, the singular agenda of the APF was to oppose the CAN. Tesan quickly whipped up support for the APF at a period in Africa when the popularity of the women's rights movement in the Western world was being embraced by political movements all over the continent.

To soothe his hurt, Kazi withdrew his troops from the borders between Fefe and Georgetown and reposted them at the borders between Lumani and Fefe, leaving the Fefe open to attack by Helmut's troops, justifying himself that if the Fefe king didn't support the CAN, he could henceforth defend himself. Chezi thought that move was unnecessary and childlike, but Kazi was too hurt by the treachery to think strategically.

At around the same period, a group of educated elites from varying tribes launched the Democratic Movement (DM). The founders were mostly the children of embittered World War II veterans who had returned home without any reward from the colonialists for their contribution to the victory of the allies. These lawyers and teachers who founded the party aimed to gradually move the country towards independence in a piecemeal strategy that they forecasted to enact slowly over the next twenty-five years, a striking contradiction to the CAN that wanted independence as soon as possible. Because, unlike the CAN and APF, the DM could not be pegged to any particular tribe or tribes, they garnished national support rapidly and soon became a real political threat to the CAN. At the head of the DM was a business lawyer called Winston Churchill Agili, whose father had named him after a British prime minister by the same name. Agili was an eloquent and convincing leader and soon came to be called fun names like Mr President and the Orator.

What made the CAN remain the people's favourite in spite of the ground the two other parties gained in the first two years of the 1950s was mainly Kazi's reputation as 'the Terror of the Nine Hills', which assured the people of some form of protection that they badly needed with a governor like Helmut in charge. For every attack on the natives, Helmut could be sure of retribution from Kazi and his invincible guerrillas. They had stretched their influence beyond Lumani and had bases in almost every part of the nation, including Georgetown. In recent attacks, Kazi had changed strategy to hit the Helmut administration where it hurt the most: their homes. Several soldiers stayed after that, but they put their families on ships back home and closed down most of the schools they had built. Helmut was forced to build camps for the soldiers, but even he knew that no matter how well the camps were guarded, they were an easy target for the guerrillas. The entire country had become a war zone. The administration's main defence unit was composed of the native soldiers they had recruited, brainwashed and trained to serve.

The political parties held rallies and encouraged nationwide strikes that were crippling the nation's economy at a time when cocoa and rubber prices were on the rise. Of all the tribes, the Baluma benefitted the most from the inflation because they had lots to sell to the cobras. In a naive attempt at breaking the people's spirit, Helmut had the leaders of the CAN, the DM, and the APF arrested, along with several party officials. Kazi's guerrillas broke them out of the prisons, leaving a trail of corpses, further reducing Helmut's infantry.

Eventually, by the start of 1953, Helmut buckled to the pressure from the three political parties to hold talks on self-governance for the African natives and draft a constitution. He made it seem as if he had, of his own choice, made the decision to sit down, but the truth was that the headquarters was tired of his failure in reconquering the whole colony (as their agreement held) and was also under pressure from resistance movements in their other colonies to hold independence talks.

In addition, the game was changing. The Second World War had given birth to a Cold War between the capitalist nations in the West and the communist nations in the East. The communist nations were lobbying African independence zealots to provide funding and political support for their movements in exchange for implementing communist administrations in their countries and thereby expand communist influence in the world. The dominant capitalist governments therefore had to race against time to secure as many colonies in Africa to sustain their capitalist economies and force capitalism on world politics. Helmut's hurt pride was, by all means, inconsequential to that agenda.

The three political parties held meetings in preparation for the eventual meeting with the Helmut administration. The first was a heated meeting, with accusations flying around that ended in catastrophe, with every party shouting at the other. The CAN accused Tesan and the APF of treachery, of turning their backs on the Baluma after everything the Baluma had done to protect them. They equally accused the DM of receiving funding from the colonialists of other Western nations and, in Eyame's words, 'trading one slave owner for another'.

The DM rebuked the CAN for being short-sighted in believing that the African natives were prepared to govern themselves autonomously at that point in time and maintained that their plan for a gradual move towards self-determination over the next two or three decades was the only plausible plan. Their funding, they said, came from other 'friendly' Western nations, though colonialists themselves, who wanted to see this colony developing and eventually independent.

Tesan and the APF officials stormed out of the meeting when she couldn't get the other two parties to give her an audience, much less consider her proposal for a referendum on independence.

As the day of the meeting with Helmut approached, the three parties began to understand that if they could not put up a united front against Helmut, their division would be used against them, and so because of that, the final meeting was more productive and more civil. They elected a team of representatives from each party, but as much as they tried to diversify the team, the Baluma seemed to occupy most of the seats. The APF and DM didn't grumble immediately, but their discontentment was clear in the speeches they made to their partisans after the meeting. The CAN retaliated by stating that the Baluma was the largest tribe in the country, comprising almost 50 percent of the population, so it was to be expected that if fairly represented, they should occupy a considerable number of seats on the team. The team of representatives later elected a representative to serve as the face and voice of the new coalition. They elected the orator: Winston Churchill Agili.

During the talks with Helmut, Agili pretended to push the agenda that had been agreed upon by the representatives, but by the end of the week-long talks, much to the distaste of both the CAN and APF representatives, it was clear that he was, in fact, pushing the agenda of the DM. A constitution was drawn up, and agreements were later signed by Agili and Helmut to adopt the DM agenda, which didn't give the natives any more autonomy than they had at the moment and spread out a plan for a gradual move towards self-determination over the next three decades.

What pained the APF was the familiarity they observed between the DM representatives and Helmut's officials. It was almost as if they were long-lost friends. They too began to question the source of the DM's funding and suspected that the CAN may have been right after all. The DM was receiving funding from the same people they pretended to be fighting against. The CAN and APF broke out, and the coalition crumbled. The DM was soon dubbed the 'native–colonialist' party and lost popularity amongst the natives as rapidly as it had gained it.

The political climate in the country may have moved on from direct physical conflict between the cobras and the natives to diplomatic talks, but Helmut hadn't moved on, and the information from the headquarters of their decision to retire him only strengthened his resolve to exterminate the Baluma and everything King Balumakazi represented. He had neither forgotten nor forgiven King Balumakazi for what his army had done to ridicule his administration.

Helmut threw the dice and put his support behind the DM party, freeing all political prisoners and pledging to see the colony through to independence – in thirty years. Agili and his officials, from thence, enjoyed the support and protection of the colonial administration. Helmut had the money to pay for the power Agili wanted, and Agili was more than willing to trade his soul for a few pieces of silver. Of all he had ever done to hurt Kazi, this was the most effective, but Helmut never found out.

* * *

The rainy season of 1953 brought with it more than just rain and hailstones. Helmut had recruited even more mercenaries to do the jobs that his ordinary soldiers couldn't do. He chose Askoto for their next move to provoke King Balumakazi, and Nathan had the perfect evil plan for a satisfactory retirement.

Askoto was a little-known kingdom to the north-west of Lumani with a population of barely the size of two of Lumani's smallest clans. It had some grasslands in the middle of the kingdom, surrounded by a mangrove with lots of swamps and mosquitoes. It was a kingdom that the Baluma was always skeptical of because of its influence to the north by Islam and to the south by Christianity. The Askoto held on to their traditional religions but blended well with both new religions so that it was never clear on whose side they were. During the colonial invasion, they seemed to be untouched and kept such a low profile through the years so that even in 1953, the colonialists still didn't have Askoto on the map of the colony. This was mostly because the Askoto were a people who learnt faster than any other.

When the slave takers first came into the kingdom and massacred them, knowing they couldn't fight back because of their small numbers and inferior weaponry, they cleared out a large area in the middle of the kingdom where the sun usually cracked the ground when it was overhead. In this area, they built small bamboo houses that they used to dry crops and reptiles they caught for feeding and retreated to the surrounding mangrove area. Every time the slave takers arrived at the kingdom, they found nothing but drying crops, mud water fish, and crocodiles. The slave takers tried to go into the mangroves to find the Askoto, but too many of them died trying without finding anybody, so eventually, they gave up the chase, thinking the people had migrated and the area was unoccupied.

Later on, when the colonialists arrived to settle in Askoto, the king made them live in the cleared-out area, convincing them it was the choicest part of the land and that the mangroves where the people lived would be unconducive for their tender skin. The colonialists grew weary of the sun cracking their skin during the day and the mosquitoes feeding on their blood at night. They abandoned the kingdom and went out in search of other lands with more favourable weather. And so the Askoto lived in the mangroves for a long time.

King Balumakazi's victory over the cobras twenty years ago had called the Askoto out of the mangroves, and their king was the first of all to offer friendship and loyalty to Baluma for more reasons than one. Kazi accepted the offer of friendship and allegiance, and the Askoto became a protégée tribe of Baluma.

There were one hundred and fifty highly paid mercenaries. Nathan was in no mood for any mistakes or excuses. He reviewed the plan over and over again to make sure that there was nothing his evil eye had not noticed and then signed to sanction the operation.

The coordinates were marked. The mercenaries were at the entrance of Askoto by four o'clock the next morning, parked their trucks in the bushes, and grouped into fifteen groups of ten with gas masks and machine guns. The order was spelled by the helicopters pouring poisonous liquid and gas from above. The mercenaries moved in, and the mangroves burned like the Sahel in the Hamattan. Because of the relative peace over the last two decades, most of the Askoto had moved out of the mangroves to the mainland. Those who weren't burned in their sleep escaped to receive their death in the open fields. The flames of the burning mangroves could be seen from Lumani. The wind carried the sound of the gunshots and screaming to the periphery of a sleeping Lumani. By the time Baluma woke, Askoto and everything in it had been razed to the ground.

* * *

'This is no time to discuss who should lead the country after independence. We are not there yet. The problem we have to solve is this Agili fellow, who has signed a pact with the devil. They will not be the only ones to suffer the consequences if the cobras stay for another thirty years,' Kazi interrupted the king.

'Succession planning is important. We are going to get independence – that is for sure – but then after we have it, who runs the country?' The king of Fefe pulled at his pipe again.

'And you are sure that we will get this independence because...' Chezi asked, trying to decide which was more annoying for him, the man's bulldog-like drooping jaws or his selfishness. He had never met this king before, but sitting close, he thought the man was really ugly.

'We have guerrillas to defend us. We will get our independence,' the Fefe king said, exhaling.

'Correction. *I* have guerrillas. *You* don't.' Kazi glared. 'Now the issue at stake here is that we need to galvanise more support to put the DM's agenda to rest. Some people are already welcoming the idea of postponing independence. If we let the cobras stay, what is to stop them from doing to us what they have done in their own countries?

Relegating us to second-class citizenship as it is now already in some parts of the continent? There is no future for us in letting them stay. Agili has betrayed us all. We can't let him make mockery of twenty years of our blood and sweat.'

'I understand, and I agree with you. But you do realize Tesan needs to be president. She is the only one who can run this country successfully.'

Chezi was going to give him a piece of his beautiful mind when a servant walked in. and the king let him speak. The news about Askoto ended the meeting.

Yango took a team and went to search for his wife and children. They looked through the carnage in what he recognised as his father-in-law's compound. His wife had taken the three children to her family for a short vacation because she wanted to be with her mother at the time the fourth baby arrived. He had visited them last weekend and was supposed to be back this Saturday morning.

His heart was beating fast as he went through the wreckage and almost gave way when he saw his wife's corpse. Beside her were the two youngest children. They had been roasted in their sleep.

Ngemba went through the house and saw two other corpses, one he recognised as Yango's mother-in-law and a little one beside which was once his eldest child. He put his hand to his nose and turned around to get out of there. Yango was right behind him.

'No, no, Yango, you don't need to see this.' He pushed him.

'Let me see.' Yango pushed him aside.

His eyes were blank, totally void of emotion, as if he was looking through a wardrobe to choose a loincloth. He took his daughter in his arms, holding her carefully. He lifted her and placed her beside her mother and two younger brothers in the other room. The men placed the corpses carefully into the van, and Yango took them back to Lumani for a proper burial. Ngemba's experience with Nsika had taught him how to interpret the behaviour of his comrades. The blankness in Yango's eyes told him this was far from over.

While the Ngui were in session, trying to figure out what must have happened or why, Yango took his troops north to Helmut's military base without approval or alerting his command. Farra had a detailed description of the place, a small town in the middle of a Sahel area occupied by a small population of natives and a lively place with good weather. That was where they trained the native soldiers they recruited. There was not much ammunition there, and the soldiers were trained with wooden guns and knives. Real guns and blank bullets were only used in the final month of training; only the cobras had live bullets. This was done mainly to protect the cobras in case the trainees, for one reason or another, turned on the cobras. The soldiers could bring the families along to live in the community nearby so that they didn't need to go home during the course of training. In the community, the administration had built a school and a small surgery. The tribal leader received gifts of liquor and money for his cooperation.

Yango's team camped in the bushes for days to study the area, and when the time came, they attacked in mercenary style after dusk. Ngemba thought the idea was to eliminate just the cobras, but he soon realized he was partaking in a massacre when the guerrillas shot at even the farmers returning to their homes with crops. They threw grenades into the camp before going in to finish the rest of the soldiers. By the time the cobras were all dead and they had got to the houses, most of them had run out of ammunition. Ngemba thought it would end there. It didn't.

The look in his eyes hadn't changed. Yango whistled and brought out his bow and arrows, and his men did the same. When they ran out of arrows, they used whatever they could to kill those who couldn't run. Yango was soaked with everybody else's blood when he walked back into the bushes with the head of a cobra in his hands. Ngemba shut his eyes tight and tried to be grateful he had survived the massacre.

'Yango! What have you done?'

Yango starred at Kazi, his eyes still blank. 'I think you should know that there is a kill order out on you and your children.'

'I know that, but how do you know?' Kazi frowned.

'We have a mole in Helmut's house. He informed Farra. They might have got my family first, but it is a matter of time before they get to yours.'

'Yango!' Kazi looked into his eyes.

'Helmut is determined to kill you before he gives Agili his independence.'

'I will take care of that! You, on the other hand, are not mentally fit to command anybody. I will send you to Changara in Yaketu. Mama Dara is on her way back tomorrow. You will follow her.'

'You can send me to meet my family if you like, but the cobras are coming for us. You cannot escape it. If you think I am possessed, then perhaps you need to go to Askoto yourself and see what they did there,' Yango said, actually looking like a person possessed.

'Enough! Go and get prepared. You leave tomorrow.'

When Yango was gone, Kazi put his head in his hands and tried to hope that neither he nor Yango was mad. Eyame had told him about Francis, and he had put Francis in contact with Farra. He had deliberately kept the circle of people who knew about the threat on his family as small as he could because the Baluma (because of their history) were a people prone to panic and superstition, and he already had more than enough to deal with. Why would Farra have let Yango into it? *Bedroom affairs*, he thought exasperatedly.

Chezi got up and walked across to Kazi.

'Kazi, Ngemba was involved in the massacre.'

Kazi looked up 'What?'

'Yes, he told me himself. He thought they were going there to kill cobras to get revenge for Yango's family. He was surprised when they turned on even the natives. He really didn't know Yango's complete agenda from the beginning. Knowing him, I know he is telling me the truth.' He paused for a while before speaking as if weighing the consequence of what he was going to say. 'What frightens me now is that he came back visibly shaken yesterday, but when I spoke with him this morning, he said he didn't like the massacre, but he loved the smell of the blood.'

Kazi starred as if Chezi was speaking a language he couldn't understand.

'Yango was always so composed. He was always the voice of reason and temperance. If these cobras have been able to change even him, then I don't know what they will turn Ngemba into,' Chezi said.

Kazi sank back into his chair. 'Yes, I can understand your fear, Chezi, but I can understand Ngemba even better. We lived on this land peacefully until the cobras arrived. They left, and then they returned with colonialism and destroyed our livelihood. We are asking them to leave, but they won't, and they continue the bloodshed with impunity. Their venom poisons everyone they cross. It poisoned me, it poisoned Farra, it has poisoned Yango and Ngemba, and it will poison you too, Chezi. Several Yangos will be born because of this for generations to come, even long after we are both gone. Somebody once told me that this is all about the conqueror and the conquered, but perhaps he left something out. Radicalism is the firstborn of injustice.'

* * *

The massacre at the military base was the final blow to his ego. Helmut tried as much as he could to delay his departure, but he knew the time was coming. The headquarters had promised him a house and monthly stipend in his retirement, but since coming to Africa, he had learnt to live like a king and wasn't so eager to return to an average life. The headquarters was not willing to invest in another military base because it was gradually pulling its resources out of its colonies in view of independence. The hydroelectric dam between Georgetown and Menha, which was the main source of energy for the cobras in the colony, had collapsed or perhaps blown up of its own accord but, whatever the case, had ceased to exist, and they were back to the Dark Ages. Fuel was precious, so the few generators they had were used to power the offices and radio station.

Helmut lit the candle on the table and remained firm to the promise he had made to himself – to bury King Balumakazi and his family – but the question neither he nor his twin could answer was how. His mind drifted to the natives and the political groups in the colony. If only he could get through to one of them. King Eyame, for one, was out of the question. The betrothal of his daughter to King Balumakazi's son had sealed off the rift between the two tribes and served as a magnet to most other tribes in the colony. They took the queue, and tribal reconciliation was becoming a song word. The extermination of the Askoto had only served to further enrage the natives against the colonial administration. Even the massacre at the military base was blamed on his administration. Tesan would have been a good choice, but with the Fefe king behind her, she was like a double-edged sword, and besides becoming president, her agenda wasn't clear. His only hope of refuge was Agili, but the man had problems.

They only realized that Agili's popularity and following had plummeted when he organised a rally in Georgetown that only a handful of natives attended, heavily guarded by native soldiers and complaining about death threats. They also knew that it was all King Eyame's handiwork but couldn't figure out how he had galvanised so much antipathy against the DM in the few weeks Agili had been away in meetings in the colonial headquarters. In the meantime, the CAN had grown stronger and bigger, and with all thanks to King Balumakazi, Helmut's troops and native soldiers were surrendering by the day and returning from the provinces to Georgetown. In truth, by the end of 1954, Helmut controlled the colonial province of Georgetown.

* * *

In the last meeting between the CAN and APF, they had agreed to force Helmut out, declare independence, and establish a federation of states that would take the form of the different kingdoms in the colony. The political parties would be gradually abandoned, and the states would each elect a representative. The representatives would then elect a leader to serve as the country's premier. This would prevent the tribes from feeling left out of national decisions and dissolve the myth that the CAN was a pro-Baluma party pushing the 'Baluma and friends' agenda. Kazi was satisfied with the outcome of the meeting in Menha. The Fefe king had finally come to his senses, and they had been able to pave a path to independence without him mumbling about a president Tesan when they had more pressing issues.

While the Kush received funding mainly from the middle-east that Kazi benefitted from, the communist countries had Kazi on their radar. He had received several communications from the communists by mail, and even though he hadn't yet replied, he was seriously considering it. His hesitation was mainly because of his skepticism over their offer for help, which didn't seem to require anything in return. Long years of dealing with the cobras had taught him what the English called 'no such thing as a free meal'. They were offering military and political support and strong diplomatic ties but weren't quite clear about what they expected in return besides 'friendship'. Aminata's question kept ringing in his mind: *What kind of person leaves his house to help a total stranger for the sake of friendship?*

The Arab nations had helped the Kush make significant progress towards independence, and a date had already been settled for 1st October 1955, which was the next year. Ishmael was already leading the party, and his political opponents didn't stand a chance against him at the election. But even in the Kush, there was a price. The contracts on the oil reserves were far from fair for the Kush people on whose soil the resources were found. Kazi didn't want to pay any price; he wanted total, complete, and absolute independence for the natives. Any help they received to achieve it would bind them in the same chains they were trying to break away from. At the last meeting with the leaders of the other African resistance movements, Kazi had fallen out with those who held the view that with the ongoing Cold War, African countries would have to choose one side or the other, saying there was no other option for African nations. But Kazi was adamant about a third option: that it was possible for an African nation to get independence without having to choose between two evil lords.

He threw the letters into the dustbin and went out to train. The agreement with the APF was to launch the assault on Georgetown by February 1955, and his troops needed to be prepared. It would be their final and most important battle.

Giba checked that Mungu was asleep before curling himself up in his own bed as he always did before his mother came to check on both of them. He closed his eyes to think why his mother's belly had swollen in the recent weeks. She was always chubby, but her stomach never protruded this much. Perhaps it was something she had eaten, or perhaps it was the illness she had recently complained about that made her so tired that she didn't have the energy to chase him around anymore. She had told him to wait a few more months, that once his sister arrived, they would play together. She said she was carrying his sister in her belly, but she had to have been lying because babies were carried on the back, not on the belly, and when he had touched it, he couldn't feel the baby, just a round swollen belly. She told him stories about the baby being inside her belly and that she knew it was a girl, but he didn't believe her. Babies could not be inside the belly where no one could see, and how did she know it was a girl?

The idea of a baby sister pleased him because dealing with a younger brother was difficult. A sister would be friendlier, but still, he had questions. He was ready with his questions for when she came that evening, but it was his father who opened the room door and blew the questions out of his head. His father had never come to make sure they were asleep; it was always his mother who did that.

'Giba.'

'Yes, Papa?'

'Is your brother sleeping?'

'Yes, Papa.'

'Good. Are you sleeping?'

'Yes, Papa.'

'No, you are not.'

'I am waiting for Mama.'

'She is sleeping. She needs to rest.'

'Why is she always tired? There are questions I have to ask her.'

'Shut up and follow me.'

Giba pulled on a loincloth and followed his father. They rode for a while, and then Kazi stopped the vehicle, and they stepped out. They walked into thick bushes until the forest. Kazi led Giba towards a cold valley with creeping roots and tall trees. Kazi hopped on one stone to get to the other, and Giba did the same, not understanding where his father was taking him.

They reached a fresh waterfall. Giba had never seen a waterfall before in his life, and he stopped and stood there, watching in awe as the waters splashed over the cliff and bumped fearlessly onto the rocks below. In his twelve years, he had never known that part of the kingdom existed. He had his moment before the 'I asked you to follow me' command came.

They got to a dry area. Kazi sat down and lit a small fire. Giba warmed his hands up by the fire. As the story of the dagger and gourd was told to him, he could see it in his mind's eye.

'Once you fill water into it, the gourd never runs dry. It keeps on refilling itself. And the dagger will save your life whenever you're in danger.'

'But what if somebody steals it?'

'It is locked with a curse. Whoever steals it will unlock a curse on his lineage for nine generations.'

Giba remembered that a priest had told him something about generational curses during one of their many conversations. He took the gourd in his hands and tried to look into it. When he turned it upside down, a few drops of water leaked out.

'Go and fill it up at the stream and drink from it.'

Giba filled the gourd and drank. He brought the gourd back to his father. His father drank and gave him back the gourd, and he could feel the gourd full again.

The dagger was smooth and sharp as if it had never been used. Giba read the inscription on the dagger, and a strange urge to use it came over him.

Kazi showed him how to use it and then said, 'You will keep these in your possession until the next king is enthroned.'

'But how will I know?'

'They will tell you when the time comes.'

Giba sat down beside his father, and for the first time, his father held him by the shoulders in a warm embrace. He laid his head on his father's breast and closed his eyes to enjoy the feeling of the tough muscles underneath the rough skin. He could hear the heart beat, and it brought to him the realization that his father was indeed human. The thought of his father's lack of immortality disturbed him.

He opened his eyes to a strange mark that he had never really noticed underneath his father's left breast. He poked it to see what it was and looked up to his father. Kazi's eyes were closed as if he was deep in meditation. He didn't move or open his eyes, but he answered the question he knew the boy wanted to ask.

'The mark of the leader. When the time comes, they will take the leader to the shrine and mark him to protect him. The skulls are usually kept in a sacred room in the palace, but I asked for them to be kept in the shrine just in case there is something they cannot see.'

'Papa, do you think something will happen?'

'I can see that we will get independence, that we will become the masters and owners of our lands again. What I cannot see is if I will be there.'

'Papa.' Giba was frightened.

'Shhh.' He put the child's head back onto his breast and held him there for a while. Then he moved him away slowly and looked into his eyes.

'You think I am a monster, don't you?'

Giba blinked hard, not finding the courage to give an honest answer.

'It's OK if you think I am a monster. I am your father. My duty is to protect you even from yourself. But never forget this – the cobra is greedy, and running away from him won't stop him from chasing you. The only choice we ever had was to turn around and fight him. It is the only language he understands. You may be too young to fight right now, but when you grow up, you will have to fight. You will have to fight because you are a man. There is always a man to protect a woman, but a man has only himself to protect himself and his family. God is a woman, Giba. She is not generous to us men. If we don't fight, we will die.'

Giba retained every word but understood none.

* * *

'Don't wake the baby up, Kolela. How often do I need to tell you to keep your voice down and let him sleep?' Kazi could hear his mother saying.

'But he needs to wake up. The child has fallen on his face.'

He heard the calabash drop from Aruma's hands and break on the floor.

Kazi woke up to Aminata's screaming.

Mungu had been playing hero in one of his usual warrior games and fallen from a height straight onto his face. The stones had cut him between his eyes and formed a semi-circle around his left jawbone. He was bleeding profusely when Giba ran to his side and turned him over. The doctor disinfected the wound on his swollen face and stitched it up. Mungu could hardly open his eyes, and he ran a high fever for several nights after that. Aminata was in tears not because she didn't think he would recover but because she had never seen Mungu that weak and helpless.

Giba was always pensive, but this time, he was more pensive than usual, and this time, getting to know his son better, Kazi noticed and called him aside beyond Aminata's earshot.

'What happened?'

'He was playing King Yangisa against the Islamic invaders. I wasn't interested, so I turned to play my flute, but I could still see him from the corner of my eye. Then he fell.'

Kazi knew there was more, and there was.

'Then I don't know. Maybe somebody pushed him. I don't know. I think I saw somebody push him. It was like one of the servants or maybe just somebody else. I don't know. When I looked up at where he had fallen from, there was nobody. Maybe I was just imagining because he has jumped from there several times, and he knows how to jump. But this time, he didn't jump. He actually fell.' Giba blinked through teary eyes.

'What have I told you about men who cry?' Kazi shook him.

Giba stifled his tears and swallowed. 'Yes, Papa.'

'Your brother will be all right. It is just a small wound, and he is very strong.'

'Yes, Papa,' Giba said knowing the wound was far from small, but because his father had said so, it had to be so.

Kazi didn't really sleep after that. He and his family could be Helmut's targets, but what would it serve anyone to hurt an eleven-year-old boy playing hero in his father's yard? And what did the disappearance of Francis mean? Francis's body had been found in a bush by one of Farra's men on an evening he was to meet with Farra but didn't show up. They had concluded he must have been killed by Helmut's henchmen because the marks on his body were proof that he had been tortured.

After that, they had changed the plan and moved the date of the Georgetown attack to April 1955. If Francis had revealed under duress, Helmut would be waiting for it in February. They had been right because when the assault didn't happen, Helmut grew mad and went out rounding up politicians from the CAN and APF parties, causing Tesan to flee the country.

Kazi decided to move his family from the palace in Lumani. When he returned after the Georgetown attack, he would deal with whoever was working against him in his household. Aminata was the one who was familiar with the servants. He hardly had any contact with them, and it would kill her to even think that a servant may have done this to Mungu, so he didn't tell her what Giba had said.

Everything was set for the march on Georgetown the next week. All but a few of the guerrilla units were set for the attack. They kept one unit back in each of the provinces, including Lumani, as a precaution in case at any time, they needed to fall back. They would drive through Alingafana to the outskirts of Georgetown in the evening and camp there, and in the night, they would split into three groups. Once the day broke, they would launch the assault on the town from the three angles – Alingafana, Fefe, and Menha – destroy the colonial military camps, march on the administrative buildings in the centre, arrest Helmut and his cronies, and seize hold of the airport and national radio station.

Before he had disappeared, Francis had drawn out the plan of the houses and offices and even the camps and the number of guards around each place. The whole plan depended on this assault. It was the trigger. Once they had captured Georgetown, they would get Tesan back into the country and organise elections. It was a perfect plan, but Kazi couldn't shake off the feeling that he was missing something.

The next morning, he ran over the plans with Chezi for the umpteenth time. Chezi could feel his worry, especially after Mungu's accident, and kept reassuring him that the last assault was the best they ever had and that all would go as planned. Aminata was almost at term, but he was prepared to forego being present at the time of birth to secure the independence that gave his entire existence any meaning.

Kolela came around the same afternoon. Kazi was used to his unexpected visits, but this afternoon, his mind was too preoccupied with everything going on.

He only came back to himself when Kolela said, 'Somebody pushed the boy. I am here to find out. Take me to him.' Kolela always liked to use short phrases when he was in moods like this to avoid explaining himself.

As he applied pressure on the stitches moving his hands to trace the wound, Mungu moaned painfully.

'Can you be a little less brutal? The child is in pain,' Kazi told Kolela, who ignored him and continued moving his hands over the boy's face. Then he stopped where the wound ended just before his left ear.

'Winston Churchill Agili. But I cannot see the face of the hand.'

He took out some powder and blew into the air, took one closer look at the wound, and then left.

Kazi didn't have the time to figure out why Agili would want to hurt his family, but once they had captured Georgetown and Agili along with it, he would find out why. He told Nsika about it later, and just like him, Nsika thought it would be a good thing to send his family off to Menha while they attacked Georgetown. There was no time to try to investigate. With Mandara gone and a mole in the house, Aminata would be safer in Menha. They sent Aminata and Mungu to Eyame two days before the day. She wasn't comfortable with the decision but was too tired to object, and Kazi was grateful she was. He took Giba along with him. He wanted his first son by his side when he spoke through that microphone at the radio station.

* * *

They set off in the late afternoon. Kazi sat in the back of the vehicle with Giba. They were getting friendlier and had lots to say to each other. For each of them, it was like making a new friend with a wonderful person. Giba was beginning to worship his father like Mungu did; the human side of his father both disturbed and comforted him. That gentle, caring side wrapped inside the toughness that he had been introduced to over the last few months was as appealing as it was frightening that his father was human and therefore mortal.

Kazi was finally getting to know this totally different human being who, unlike him and Mungu (or any other man in Lumani, for that matter), preferred gentility. Princess, a nickname Mungu had given Giba, fitted him so well, and even though he hated it, his father and mother joked a lot about it and teased him as well so that over the years, he had grown used to it, and it didn't annoy him so much. Even more amusing was that his first son had the finesse of a girl. His nails were always well filed into shape, his loincloth always well pressed and spotless, and he rubbed oil into his skin to make it glow like a bride on her wedding day. In many ways, his little princess reminded him of Yem. Even the dagger and gourd, which he had kept as best he could since Nsika had given him, had been cleaned extra well so that the dagger shone and the leather of the gourd glittered, and they were put into a little bag his mother had made for him that he strapped elegantly to his waist. All the vainess he had learnt from Yem hadn't taught him to be that meticulous about himself.

They rode past Alingafana and were approaching the camping site. Giba sat in the vehicle, eating the roasted plantain carefully so as not to stain his clothes as he listened to his father's story about Papa Yem's dealings with the cobras and the science of 'business'.

The vehicle stopped suddenly, and the guerrillas jumped out in a stampede. Bullets began to fly about. Kazi pushed Giba on to the floor of the car and jumped out. They had been ambushed!

The soldiers were in the bushes, firing at the convoy. Kazi took a grenade, uncapped it, threw it into the bushes where the shots were coming from, and ducked for the explosion. He could see Chezi two vehicles away, shooting at the other side into the bush. His shotgun had only one bullet left. The soldiers seemed to multiply each time he blinked. The guerrillas were responding, but it seemed an equal duel, with none dominating the other. Kazi used his last bullet to shoot at the tank of a vehicle closest to the bushes. It caught fire and acted as a shield.

He called out, 'Chezi!'

Chezi responded, 'Kazi!' and flung a long gun to him.

Kazi stretched full length, caught it in mid-air, turned the gun around, and began to fire, moving closer and closer to the bushes. A cobra stood up from the bushes and shot at him, missing his shoulder as he fired back. In over two decades of fighting, he never saw a cobra with the nerve to fire back at him face to face. When the cobra fell to the ground, Kazi noticed the cobra had only one leg.

That split second of distraction was all the cobra's evil twin needed. He felt for the trigger, raised the mouth of the gun to his one eye, and pulled, firing Kazi from the back and crashing to the ground from Chezi's bullets a few seconds later.

The world swirled around. Kazi's finger was still on the trigger when he felt his knees on the ground. He could see Khala running towards him in a craze, blowing her trunk, Aruma stood up screaming, breaking her calabash.

Chezi's voice was even farther off, but Kazi could hear him saying, 'Take the king to the vehicle. He is wounded.'

Kazi didn't feel wounded or feel pain of any sort but for the sand scrubbing his face. Khala was pouring fresh water on his forehead, refreshing him, his mother was running towards him. He felt his body lifted, the birds chirping and running for cover, and the sky grumbling.

He gasped and grabbed Chezi's left hand. 'Our land!'

'My king.'

Chezi led him into the vehicle and went back to the fighting, knowing he had to win back *their land*.

By sunset, the guerrillas had overcome the cobras and even had time to inspect the corpses to notice some of Agili's so-called politicians in uniform, lying dead in the bushes. Chezi continued with the plan as strictly as it had been agreed: Farra to take the Menha angle and Nsika to take the Fefe angle. He sent the orders out, and the teams dispersed into focus for the attack at dawn.

* * *

It wasn't rainy season yet, but the sky darkened, lightning flashed through the sky, and thunder roared from one end of Lumani to the next. The downpour of rain that followed didn't seem as if it would ever stop.

The edge of his stick brought the swirling to a stop. Kolela looked into the calabash.

Chezi, Nsika and Farra were in place, and everybody was set. The plan as going as Kazi had said, but Kazi's eyes were closed, and he couldn't see Kazi reporting on the radio station. Aminata was stressed and couldn't fight any longer. She was giving up.

The water swirled again, and he saw Giba lying beside Mungu in the bushes near a tree. He chewed the tree bark and looked again. The dead men were carried into the vehicle by the other men, and the vehicle was driven off by a man laughing happily with his comrades.

He threw out the water, rolled up his mat, and stretched up from the ground. He walked out of his shrine into the rain to observe the trend of the wind and rain.

* * *

Giba hadn't stayed in the vehicle where his father had laid him. He crept out from the other side and watched the fighting. He saw his father fall and got up to run towards him but was prevented by

Ngemba's hands on his shoulder pulling him into the back of a van. The door shut out the light from the world, and the van drove off amidst the craze of gunshots and yelling. Giba couldn't decide whether he saw his father motionless on the ground or, if at some point, he had moved and grabbed Papa Chezi's hand. His mind went blank.

Aminata went into labour when Ngemba and the guerrillas arrived at Eyame's palace at nearly midnight. In the morning, Giba was woken up to the cry of a baby, but neither he nor his brother were allowed to go in to meet the baby. Eyame put Giba and Mungu into a vehicle, gave the drivers and bodyguards instructions, and sent them off. Mungu still had the stitches across his face, but he was half-conscious. Giba wasn't injured, but the only thing that made him seem conscious were his two eyes that were open. The light had still not come back.

They stopped briefly at Lumani. The guards loaded some bags into the vehicle, and they set off again. By late afternoon, they had reached the border. A heated argument preceded the fighting at the border. The border patrol wouldn't let them by without a permit. They could easily have bribed the men if they had understood the language, but they didn't. A guard arguing that Mungu had been referred to a doctor at a hospital was holding out some papers and urging them to look at them and let them by. When one of the patrol guards punched him in the face for talking arrogantly, the other patrol guards around swam to reinforce, provoking a ferocious fight between the bodyguards and border patrol that erupted into cassava gunshots and machete blows (the border patrol at the colony in which Yaketu belonged were not armed with real bullets, so cassava bullets were used to improvise).

The light came back. Giba slipped out of the vehicle with his half-conscious brother hanging on to his shoulders and hid behind the vehicle. Seeing the fighting spiral out of control, Giba leaned his brother on his chest and crept out to the bushes beside them. He could feel his brother's breath and heartbeat, but Mungu was completely unresponsive when he shook him. He lay beside him until there was silence. Prudence told him to wait another while longer.

At sunset, Giba pulled Mungu's hand over his shoulder and sat him upright against a tree trunk. He crept to the place where the car had been. There was no car, no guards, and no driver but a few blood patches on the grass around. In the distance, he could see a patrol guard stop to light a cigarette. He figured that although it wasn't dark yet, the shadows had begun to form, so he could hide by a tree to figure out an escape plan if only he could see ahead.

He waited until the guard turned his back and then got up and ran as fast as he could to the nearest tree. His foot hit against something, and he fell, letting out a low scream.

The guard turned back around. 'Who's there?'

Giba crawled up and stood stone stiff beside the tree. He could hear the guard looking around the bushes. Luckily, the guard was alone. Giba held his breath and tilted his head around the tree to see where the guard was. The guard was going in the direction of the tree where he had laid an unconscious Mungu. His mother had always told him that the best decisions were made with a cool head because a person's thinking faculties are apt when the person is calm, a thing he always believed because it had always worked for him, but this was not a time he could be calm.

He felt for the dagger that his father had told him would save his life if ever he was in danger. He took the dagger out of the bag and, pulling it gently by the hilt out of its wrapping, held it as his father had taught him: the tip towards him and the sharp edge looking outwards. The weather was chilly, but Giba was sweating and blinking hard, repeating his father's words in his mind: *You will have to fight. You will have to fight because you are a man. God is a woman.* His heart beat with the rhythm as he repeated it over again, and the drumming gave him the courage he needed to step out from behind the tree.

'*Aieeee! Aieeee!*' he called out.

The man turned in the direction of the sound and charged towards him. Giba slipped behind the tree and climbed it rapidly (a thing he had learnt trying to escape Mungu's fighting). As soon as the man was near enough, he pounced from the tree, dagger first and legs straight onto the man's shoulders. His weight and the suddenness of the well-calculated angle brought the man crashing. In mid-air, he lifted the man's chin and dug his dagger as deep in as he could. By the time they were both on the ground, the man was lifeless.

He wasn't thinking about the dirt and blood on his cloth and the man he had just killed. He took the man's gun, even though he had no idea how it worked. He covered the man with the drying grass around and ran to check that his brother still had a heartbeat.

Giba looked through the long grass into Yaketu. At the end of a small path, there was a stock of logs on fire with a few people around it roasting some animal. Behind them was what seemed to him like a bush meat market with a small dark path leading to it. He went back to his brother and lay beside him to wait until it was much darker.

Giba put his hand over Mungu's mouth to stop him from groaning for water and persuaded him to persevere. He was glad that Mungu was now conscious, but the pus on his hand told him there was something wrong with the wounds. He lifted the cotton covering and saw the pus come out of the edge of the wound.

Mungu opened his eyes briefly and said painfully, 'Princess, why are we here? What happened?'

To Giba's ears, Mungu's voice sounded like his father's. It made him remember the gourd, and he felt his waist for it. He took it out of the bag and tasted. The water was fresh, as if it had just been fetched from a flowing stream. When he fed him, Mungu emptied the gourd. He remembered then that his father had told him that the gourd refilled itself, but now the gourd was empty. He felt desolate. Remembering that his mother had once told him that people who were dying were usually cold and thirsty, he felt for his brother's heart in panic and calmed a bit when he felt the heartbeat. Until then, he had been lying to his brother's left. He changed sides and lay to Mungu's right, putting his right hand over his heart to feel the beat and stop the mosquitoes from gnawing on their skin. Mungu couldn't feel the bites because he was sleeping, and Giba was glad for that.

When he could only hear the owls hooting, Giba checked the area again. The bush fire had been put out, and the place was silent. He pulled his brother up and limped towards the place of the bush meat market and hid in a small stall he found. He lay Mungu on the ground and closed the entrance with a cloth he found around the stall. Mungu was running a high fever and asking for water again. Giba summoned all the faith he had in his father to feel for the gourd again, and it was full!

When Mungu had drank and closed his eyes, Giba sat beside him, exhausted, with tears running down his cheeks. He was sobbing hysterically, asking God for his mother. He had been as much of a man as he could be and had come to the end of his strength, and he needed his mother to sort this out.

Mungu put his hand on Giba's. 'Stop crying, princess. When I have rested enough, I will get us out of here. You know I like to fight, don't you? I'm just tired now.'

Giba was about to tell him what had actually happened when the cloth covering the entrance was pulled aside, and a man peered into the stall with a lamp in one hand and a stick in the other. The stall lit up as if it had ten lamps hung around.

'What did your father tell you about men who cry?' He was looking at Giba sternly. 'Stop crying, you old man. They will find you and kill you.'

Giba was sure he had never seen this man whenever his father had told him that. What appealed to him was that the man's loincloths were so sparkling white and strapped so neatly and elegantly around his waist. There was a peace about the man's presence and in his voice that, in spite of the sternness, calmed him. Mungu was looking at the man obstinately, but when his brother wiped the tears from his face, he followed the lead; it was their language.

The man turned to Mungu. 'You will have enough time to fight, young warrior. Don't be in too much of a hurry.'

He put his lamp down and took off the cotton covering from the stitches. He washed the wound with water from the gourd and put some herbs on the stitches. The herbs stuck together and formed the new covering.

The man gave Mungu some herbs to chew and swallow and then said to both, 'Come with me.'

Giba helped his brother up and followed the strange fellow. When they had come out of the market, the man led them onto a path.

'Follow the elephant. She will lead you.'

'But what elephant?' the brothers asked simultaneously.

They followed the man's pointed stick to a huge beast in the distance. The elephant blew her trunk to beckon them. Both boys turned to thank the man, but he had disappeared as suddenly as he had appeared.

Mungu needed less help to walk by now. The herbs seemed to have given him strength, so they ran towards the elephant. Throughout the way, they never caught up, but she was always just a short distance ahead. It was as if the elephant could have gone faster but slowed herself to let them keep up. Whether they walked or ran, the whole town seemed to be asleep – no guards, no soldiers, no drunk people in the streets, just Giba, Mungu, and the elephant.

By the time they were at the last lap, the effect of the herbs had begun to wear out, and Mungu was weakening again. Giba held him up by the shoulders. The elephant led them to a large compound with several houses. Seeing the armed guards around and remembering the border patrol, Giba froze. The elephant was no longer around them. She had vanished like the strange man. Mungu looked dead, and Giba felt dead.

He was about to turn them around and limp away when 'Stop right there, or you will meet your ancestors this night!' echoed through the quiet night.

The only person who seemed to be awake in Yaketu that night was armed to the teeth with strange charms around his neck. He looked at them for a while with his long gun pointed straight at Giba's chest and then called another man identically dressed. They said something to each other in low tones and called another.

This one came to them and asked Giba carefully, almost as if his and his brother's life depended on the answer he gave, 'What is your name?'

'Hlegiba,' Giba said, knowing that nobody called him that so the strangers wouldn't know who they were.

'What is your brother's name?'

Giba held his breath and didn't respond.

One of the men whispered something in the man's ears about the wounded boy. The man drew closer to take a better look at Mungu.

Giba stepped back, pulling his brother with him and seriously thinking about the gun on his shoulders and the dagger in his waist bag. 'Please, please, we are just lost. We don't mean any trouble, please,' he said, thinking this was the end but grateful that Mungu was almost unconscious so he wouldn't feel any pain. He felt for his dagger but couldn't see how a single dagger and a gun he could not use would help him against these three heavily armed huge men.

'Of course, you are lost, Hlegiba Yusuf-Ishmael. You should have arrived here by sunset,' he said, exasperatedly straddling his long gun to his shoulder, leaving Giba with no time to process his thoughts or the man's words.

The man lifted Mungu into his arms as if Mungu weighed a feather, and the other two helped Giba from his staggering feet. They took them to a house in the centre of the compound and knocked on the door with urgency. The man inside came out and ushered them in without questioning.

The next morning, Changara drove the boys to an airport and put them on a plane. When they asked to where the plane was headed, he simply told them, 'The place where your father asked me to send you.'

* * *

Farra and her team took the main airport near Menha without much of a fight. Some stayed to secure it, while she stormed the radio station with another team. It was at the radio station that they met the cobras prepared to die before giving the place up, but Farra had more of a reason to fight. She hadn't seen it, but she had been told that Kazi had been injured, and that was more than enough motivation for more reasons than one. They took the radio station with such a barbarity that the microphone didn't work at first because of the blood around it. She sent out the message to let Tesan know it was safe to return and that the country had been taken from the cobras but said nothing else about the state of the country.

Chezi got his team into Georgetown through Alingafana, and Nsika came in from Fefe with another team. The cobras put up a good fight, but nothing defeats a man with no reason to live. The guerrillas used the ammunition in the military camp to attack the administrative buildings. Helmut and Nathan had shared information with the soldiers on a need-to-know basis, so when the soldiers were overpowered, they saw no reason to die and surrendered to Chezi's troops. A ship at the port docked for a while and then set off sail again before Nsika's team could shoot at it. By noon, a fax was sent to the headquarters.

Possessed with anger and vengeance, Nsika led a team to Agili's residence. He was shocked to find the place clean and empty, as if nobody had ever lived there. Chezi arrived shortly after with the same objective.

'This Agili snake knew we would come for him,' Nsika said, holding his wounded arm.

'We need to declare a state of emergency to control this,' Chezi said tiredly.

'I will get the message to Farra at the radio station.'

'And I will assemble the troops. We need to comb the town.'

Nsika turned to leave and then turned back, remembering. 'Oh, by the way, not a word about Kazi.'

'No, not a word,' Chezi agreed as if they had discussed it before. He felt for the wound in his side. It was bleeding, and he could feel the bullet near the surface. He had prayed to survive, but now that he had, he regretted he had.

* * *

Yango didn't ask for permission or follow protocol (he never did), so nobody was surprised when he barged into the room where the Ngui were in session.

'The children didn't arrive,' he said, still dripping from the rain.

'You crossed them. They arrived at Changara's in the first hours of the morning,' Kolela said.

'We would have noticed the vehicle if we crossed it.'

'Yes, yes, that is because those rodents at the border robbed the vehicle. The patriarch barely escaped with his brother.'

Yango was still taking that in when Bana said, 'Our victory came with a price...'

'Where are they now?' Yango shut his eyes, not wanting to hear it.

'Georgetown,' came from Kwahi. 'When the rain stops, we will send out the totems to protect Lumani. That is the best we can do.'

Yango walked through the door and jumped into the back of the truck.

'If we let the news out now, it will cause panic. So how do we make certain no one lets it out?' It was Tendo talking after Yango left.

'We can send out the word that he has been injured but is recovering with Kolela and will be back soon. But we will have to tell them about Nata – well, not all but at least something of it,' Bana proposed.

'Something like what?' they asked in unison.

'She wasn't young. There are several complications when an aged woman gives birth. After we have told the people that, we can do the funeral.'

That led to an argument because in Lumani, if a woman's husband was alive at the time she died, the woman could not be buried without her husband present, especially a queen. Even if he was ill or bedridden, he would be taken out on a stretcher to assist. Therefore, if Queen Aminata were to be buried publicly without Kazi present, it would raise even more questions, and the panic would be uncontrollable. They agreed to discuss it the next day and were going to disperse, but Kolela had one last thing to say.

'I saw Salana push the boy.'

Everybody stopped in their tracks because they all knew Salana was the son of Chezi and played a key role in their espionage. Nsika had commended him several times.

Kolela clarified, 'I mean Salana, Mpima's surviving son.'

Now that did not surprise anyone, least of all Bana. The surprising part was the how, especially since he had been able to shield himself from Kolela for over a week. His connection with Agili did not surprise them either, but how Agili had got to him did. Salana would be eliminated – that was for sure – but the question was who else needed to be eliminated whom Kolela had not yet seen.

'Do you think Agili might have got to the Fefe king?' Bana asked Kolela after careful thought.

'Anything is possible. The Fefe king is an ungrateful man.'

The Ngui were silent for a long while, everybody thinking deeply about the implications but nobody with the courage to voice their thoughts. For the first time, they dispersed in silence, the atmosphere thick with their thoughts. Even Kwahi and Tendo, who always left together for Diyateri's bush bar, went their separate ways.

* * *

There weren't that many cobras in the colony at the time, so arresting them wasn't much of a problem for Yango. Chezi had ordered for the native soldiers to be left alone as long as they didn't fight back. Strangely enough, most of them had turned themselves in and asked to join the resistance army. They switched sides so fast, it took Chezi aback. Agili had still not surfaced, and Georgetown was too vast for the guerrillas to comb, even if he was hiding there. Tesan was already on her way back, as were several others who had fled for their lives.

The natives wanted the headquarters to send a representative to sign off papers that they could use to get their country recognised by the United Nations as self-governing and proceed to conduct a referendum for independence and presidential elections later on.

The communication with the colonial headquarters in the days that followed wasn't exactly smooth because neither trusted the other on their word. The cobras insisted on sending a representative with troops whom they said would be there just to ensure the safety of the cobras. The natives didn't trust the cobras to send troops for just that reason and stated that the only reason the captured cobras were still alive in the first place was that they had no reason to hurt the soldiers. They had simply disarmed them, but they were quite alive. All they needed was a representative to sign the papers, and that didn't have to be done by more than one person.

The headquarters only agreed to sign when they realized by the end of the second week that they could not retake the country without a long, tiresome, and very expensive war with the natives. Their economy was still recovering from the Second World War. Other colonies were asking for the same thing, and the last thing they needed was another war from a different angle. They sent a representative with a limited number of guards that Chezi and Nsika agreed to receive, and the natives had the captured soldiers ready with their belongings when the plane landed. The cobras were visibly surprised with what they thought was a show of good faith. This new Chezi surprised even Nsika. Kazi seemed to have taken a part of him with him.

A delegation from headquarters arrived a week later, and negotiations for a petition to the United Nations commenced.

* * *

The Ngui's silence fuelled rumours about King Balumakazi that spread through the country like wildfire in the Hamattan. Was he or was he not dead? If he was, then who had killed him? If he wasn't, then why was he hiding when his troops had won the battle and it was a matter of time before an independence declaration was made, the independence he had spent his life fighting for? What had happened to his family? Were they hiding with him, or had they been killed with him? What were the Baluma up to?

Such questions made even the most fanatical worshippers of King Balumakazi begin to doubt themselves, and the people pressured the Ngui for answers. The only person who didn't seem to be in a hurry to contribute to a solution was Kolela, insisting on not naming an interim and not explaining why. He was well known for his wise and visionary decisions, but this attitude in this very dire situation was nerve-racking. Tendo lost it.

'Have the evil spirits you exorcize got into you? We are here to find a solution, and all you can come up with is *Lumani will be governed neither by us nor by them.*' How does that help us?'

'For twenty-seven years!' Kolela finished his statement as if he had never been interrupted, stood up, and left the room.

A rainbow was crossing the sky to protect the tribe. Kolela went to his shrine to set up an altar to shield the boys from being recognised. With the kill order still active and the cobras determined to eliminate Kazi's family, it would not be impossible for the enemy to go as far as the Kush to find them. He also had to conclude the funeral rites. It was the ninth day since Kazi had exhaled, and he had brought Aminata and the baby home.

Bana stood up when the door closed.

'I am going to act as representative so that I do not have to take the oath. I will go to the people tomorrow and tell them exactly this – Kazi and Nata are both dead, and so are their boys. We will do the funeral and tell them that it is going to take a while for a successor to be named. In the meantime, I will assume the running of the kingdom, which is what the matriarch does in a time like this. I will tell them this for three reasons. First, it will bring the rumours to rest. The people will be very sad for a long time, but they will be at peace. Second, it will convince the traitors that it is safe to rear their heads and make it easier for us to uproot them. And finally, it will anger Baluma against the cobras and the traitors, and they will do the job themselves.'

'Their thirst for vengeance could spiral out of control. You are a woman. Can you control Baluma?'

'If you had a better suggestion, you would have said so.'

The Ngui had to submit.

Kwahi and Tendo walked to Diyateri's bush bar happy men. They drank until dawn, consoling themselves that since Hani was such a wise man, it should be all right, even if Bana was the figurehead.

Bana's announcement took not just the Baluma but the entire nation by surprise and caused havoc, especially amongst the guerrillas, so much so that Chezi had to come out of a hospital bed to speak to them. The one person who was relieved was Nsika because the announcement, just as Bana predicted, made the traitors more visible, with the only saddening thing being that he discovered there were quite a few in the same espionage force he had been running for over two decades.

There was an added bonus to Bana's announcement: Agili himself reared his head. One of his moles in Nsika's espionage force had passed on the information about the attack on Georgetown. Agili had then agreed with Helmut and Nathan to leave the country for the headquarters and come back in glory after the cobra victory. That plan was nipped in the bud with the death of Helmut and Nathan and the victory of the resistance army. He had been negotiating settling in the West with his colonial masters who had become totally uncooperative and lukewarm since the abortive attempt to reannex the country.

Luckily for Agili, as a cat who always fell on his feet, he had one more bargaining chip and used that to buy his asylum. King Balumakazi was a wealthy king with lots of gold, and according to his sources, several chests of gold had been delivered to the king not long before the attack on Georgetown. No matter how fast they were, those chests could not have been taken out of the country so soon; they had to be somewhere around. It was while the cobras were contracting mercenaries to make a way into Lumani – and, therefore, onto King Balumakazi's gold – that the information about the Lumani matriarch's announcement got to them. They had got rid of the Terror and Helmut in one go. They could now regain access to the colony's resources through Agili and get some gold to celebrate while at it. It was a win-win-win situation for them.

Agili spurred into action immediately, announcing his return to the colony. The DM's population may have plummeted, but with King Balumakazi's gold, he could pay his way back to popularity and have the backing of his colonial masters to crown it all. He announced his return on international media, stating that he had fled for his life for fear of the infamous Terror and that he felt safe to return home now. He concluded his press conference by thanking his colonial masters for being of great assistance to him in the moments when he needed them most. The DM officials began campaigning again and preparing their leader's return home – *in glory*. The small problem was that Nsika had anticipated that move, and if there was one person in the world Yango hated more than a cobra, that person was a cobra's servant, and for Farra, this Agili reminded her of the stories she had heard about her own father.

Meanwhile, Tesan returned to the country, and the referendum on independence went satisfactorily, with almost the entire colony casting a yes vote for independence. The APF put forward Tesan as their candidate, the DM put forward Agili, and the CAN put forward a relatively unknown Mpata Falina, but the CAN maintained its popularity because of Kazi's reputation and the recent happenings that had turned him into a martyr. The natives resolved to the CAN and everything Kazi had stood for.

Agili didn't make it to the election the next year. Indeed, ever since he had walked onto the political stage, he had spent his time making enemies of everybody whom he didn't need, so when his mutilated body was discovered in a bush near the Georgetown central market one morning, the question was not why or who was guilty but rather who had the most motivation to do it, a question that was difficult to answer or even speculate on because each group shared an equal piece of the pie.

There was Mpata of the CAN who had openly accused Agili of treason and then the officials of the APF who sulked about the funding Agili was getting from his powerful *friends* abroad and vowed to get equal funding for themselves to secure a win, and then there were the masses of people who felt that he was responsible for Kazi's demise. Even closer, in his own DM, there were several officials who were embittered that he had left them out to dry when the CAN guerrillas took over Georgetown and annexed the nation.

To crown it all, even before Agili was buried, his assistant Ebenezer Owaka connived with top DM officials and his powerful *friends* abroad to take on the baton as presidential candidate and acted as Agili's clone, his eagerness raising questions. The puzzle was too complicated to solve, so nobody wasted sleep over his demise. Needless to say that with Owaka in charge, the DM's chances of winning were reduced to very slim.

* * *

Two glasses clinked together at the dinner table. They had decided to work together for *their* greater good. Tesan was reluctant to accept the invitation at first, but Owaka's proposal was difficult to ignore.

He dragged the conversation on for as long as he could, talking about the gold King Balumakazi had, which could be of use to them both and the manner in which it could be taken, a tactic Agili had taught him and often used to bait a person they wanted to win over. When he was sure Tesan was running out of patience, he pulled out a card to whet her appetite, sampling Tesan's facial expressions carefully to mould his words.

'Neither of us can win. Even if we formed a single union, there still wouldn't be enough time or money – not even with King Balumakazi's gold – to bribe every chief or king in the country for their people's support, and the Baluma, who make almost a half of the voting population, would rather vote their king's ghost.'

Tesan's breasts fell at that point because with the Fefe king's support and promise to make whatever compromise Owaka asked of them, she was hoping that the meeting would serve to make her president since she was the more popular of the two. Reading her thoughts, Owaka moved in with the real reason for his invitation.

'We run to the end and lie low after the elections. Give him a year or two to give our *friends* time to set the stage. Then we move in.'

'What do you mean by that? If Falina wins, that will be *the* end.'

'*The* end for them but the beginning for us. This thing is working in other African nations perfectly. The people having been fighting a long time for this independence. They need time to lose faith. Running an independent former colony is not quite as simple as running a kingdom of homogenous people, and neither Falina nor anyone in the nation, for that matter, will find it an easy task. Our *friends* will take advantage of the tribal divisions, set the media and propaganda in rhythm, and help us capitalise on that for a coup.'

He looked at Tesan steadily as she thought for a moment about it.

'But the guerrillas...'

'Our *friends* will take care of that. Like I said, this strategy is working like magic in almost every part of the continent. Trust me. I am a meticulous man, and I have had enough time to do my homework.'

Tesan was getting nervous, realising she was getting nothing but promises out of this discussion. 'If I am going to lose the election, I will need something in return. There are a lot of people to whom I made promises.'

'Your king was a one-time friend of King Balumakazi. He should be able to help us get the gold. That is why I brought you in on this deal.'

She felt disappointed and upset by his condescending manner, but if she wanted to be president, she would have to follow Owaka's lead. This was not a time to talk about gender equality. However, she knew she had to be prudent with Owaka. If the information she had was anything to go by, then this fellow was worse than Agili. She set a trap.

'Assuming we get to the gold, I presume you would want a cut.'

'Let's cut it in half,' he suggested with feigned gratitude.

'The Baluma are well known for their powerful totems. We will need magicians to get anywhere near their palace. And then there are the guerrillas who have moved back.'

'You mean the gold is hidden in the palace?' Owaka tried to keep a disinterested look, but Tesan picked up the eagerness.

'Yes, that's where it is. We will get it when we take power.'

'We can use mercenaries. Our *friends* have lots of them,' Owaka said, unable to conceal himself.

'Baluma will not take that from us, and a civil war will upset our plan.'

Tesan knew that Owaka could not wait to get his hands on the gold because of the pressure from his *friends* and his own greed. She hoped that once she was introduced next month, she could start forming her own network amongst the *friends* and work her way to power. The nation had so much more she could trade than King Balumakazi's gold. The speed bump was that a good amount of the most valuable minerals of the nation were found in Lumani, and Baluma were a people with resolve. That was why she played Owaka, knowing that his greed would do the dirty work for her.

All Owaka, on the other hand, needed the meeting for was to confirm the location of the gold, a choice piece of information that Salana (who was the closest they could get to King Balumakazi) didn't have. After Agili's demise, the *friends* began to think they had been double-crossed. It created such a tense atmosphere that getting a loan from them was impossible without a clear path to the gold. Tesan's word and the Fefe king's confirmation were the clear path he needed to buy time and make a convincing case. That was Owaka's last shred of hope if he didn't want to be abandoned like Agili, and thanks to his wit and cunning, he had got what he wanted from Tesan. He would introduce her to some *friends* next month and put her on the spot. That way, if the information turned out to be incorrect, she would take the fall.

They shook hands and parted.

* * *

They found themselves more spiritually powerful as a people whenever they had a high priestess. A high priestess was always stronger than a high priest, they said. But ever since his anointing seven years ago, Kolela's reputation had preceded him, making him the most feared high priest in their history as a people. When he announced that King Balumakazi's palace had been sealed off, Kolela retreated to his shrine in Njuu and was never seen after that, at least not to bare eyes.

Nobody dared to come around the palace except a few fools who were seen sneaking in one night, never to return. What or whoever was in there, nobody, not even the Ngui, knew. The palace was a haunted place, with the smell of death, a mission unfinished, and a destiny interrupted. They said that there was a strange presence that circled the palace, and just before the cocks crowed in the morning, one could hear it whistling in a tune like the trumpet of an elephant.

The inauguration ceremony in the Federal Republic of Kush was superfluous at the very least. The people had fought their way to independence and voted the leader of their struggle into office. This was the day when it would all be officiated. They had borne the pain and deprivation that came with that kind of struggle, but it had paid off, and their joy was beyond saying.

The importance of this day in their history and lives and their expectation from their first president put immense pressure on Ishmael Ibn Yusuf. He felt more tired preparing for his inauguration than he had ever been chasing cobras around the desert. His only solace was Nsika, whom, with the help of Ndikwa, he had been able to contact to invite. He had also contacted Chezi, but Chezi had declined politely, sending Ngemba to represent him and stating other pressing matters that required his attention. Ishmael understood the unspoken words from his perspective. Both Nsika and Chezi could not afford to be out of the country at the same time, but the real truth he didn't know was that Chezi couldn't face the boys. He blamed himself for not protecting their father as Nsika had asked him to. Ishmael took care not to invite anyone else from Lumani to protect the boys.

Since the boys arrived over six months ago, he hadn't had much time with them besides stealing an hour or two to talk to them every now and then. But in spite of how little time he had spent with the boys, the difference was clear to him once Mungu had fully recovered. He missed his sister and her fiery husband intensely, but he couldn't let the boys see that. He set his emotions aside and tried to get to know them both. He had five children of his own, though a little younger than the boys, but still, he was a father and loved the boys as he loved his others.

It had been impossible to protect the boys from the information because it was all over the news, but Ishmael was determined to protect them from everything else. He had documentation processed to have them named Yusuf Ishmael Ibn Fadir and Ibrahim Ibn Fadir to conceal their identity. He covered all the tracks from Georgetown through Lumani and Yaketu to the Kush and kept the true identity of the boys a watertight secret, following up with stories so convincing that nobody ever thought to ask who the boys were despite the fact that neither of them spoke Kush yet.

When it was time, Ishmael got up for the stand and took Giba's hand, pulling him to his side and onto the podium. The crowd was merry and totally unconcerned with the boy beside him. The natural presumption was that that was his son, and indeed, in many ways, Giba *was* his son. There was a second reason Ishmael wanted Giba by him: it was the immense respect he had for the boy, not just a respect from one human to another but the kind one would have for a better person. Though just a boy, Giba reacted like an old man. He had met the boy as a baby when his father had come to the Kush for the 'Unity is not a choice' meeting and once after that on a visit to Lumani when the boy was just six years old. Perhaps that was why he had expected to meet two boys.

But when he got to know the boys, they both looked like boys, but one acted and spoke like a man. Mungu was a boy, but Giba was a man. At first, he was convinced it had to do with the trauma and had privately employed a psychologist to stay around the house to watch the boys closely. Mungu was reacting like every child would – emotionally with the crying, the screaming, and the erratic behaviour from time to time – but as with every child, he was coming to accept it and, after a while, healing visibly. Giba, on the contrary, handled himself like an old man with long years of experience and great wisdom.

The psychologist had said that Giba's mind was operating like the stomach of a goat, storing everything up to regurgitate later, that he was concealing all the pain and grief to do what needed to be done, and that his mind would process the emotions later, and he would begin to react to the pain. But there was something about Giba that made Ishmael's intuition tell him the psychologist was wrong. There was a tenacity and innate strength about Giba that was supernatural, and yet on the outside, he was just a boy like every other who needed protection.

He had known the boy's parents and larger family on both sides but could not pinpoint anyone whom the boy specifically took after but for his princess-like cleanliness, which his mother was known for, and his physical resemblance, equally divided between both parents. Giba was an enigma, a complex mixture of strength and weakness, of tenacity and fragility, an enigma Ishmael knew he would have to watch the boy grow to solve.

He read the speech Nsika had written for him in front of a sea of people, a speech that rippled and resonated through the resistance in every corner of the continent and ended with the following:

> *Of all the men in the world I ever met, of all the heroes I was honoured to meet, of all the kings I ever bowed before, there is one who always stands out. That man, that hero, that king, has taught me many things, but of all he has ever taught me, there are three things I will teach my children. He teaches me to fight! He teaches me to die! He teaches me to be native, as he is himself and always will be – pure, undiluted- native!*

FROM THE LION'S HISTORIAN

When Kazi fell, he was laid on a bamboo bed in the camp where Chezi left him in the care of Kolela to concentrate on the battle ahead. Kolela sat beside him in awe; the body was dead, but the spirit was alive and not giving up until the battle had been won. His heart was beating slowly, and he had lost a lot of blood from the nine bullet wounds in his back, but his eyes stayed open. His breathing was heavy and painful but steady, with his spirit accompanying his guerrillas. Sometimes it was as if he was telling them when to turn and what to look out for.

The next afternoon, Farra's voice came over the radio, and Kazi closed his eyes, smiling. Then his lips parted.

'Our land!'

Khala poured fresh cold water on his forehead to refresh him. Kolela was saying something, but Aruma stopped him as she stirred the hot spicy soup in the bowl for him. Kazi inhaled the delicious smell and exhaled as she put his head to her chest to feed him.

'Shhh, let the baby sleep,' he could hear her saying.

Chezi came in later to tell him that they had reconquered. He fell to his knees when Kolela repeated Kazi's words. Nsika stood at the door, remembering the day he fled with him. He could see Giba fleeing with Mungu in the same manner. The mercenaries were still in the country, and the kill order was still active.

Kolela picked up his stick and went to fetch Aminata and the baby. She had suffered a heart attack, and even though the baby girl was born alive, she had suffocated not long after.

Lumani survived the first and second civil wars that rocked the country's young democracy. The country went to war the first time after the DM and APF staged a coup that over threw Mpata Falina, and Tesan double-crossed the DM to take office. The Baluma were angered by it and staged another coup that overthrew Tesan and reinstated Falina. And after that, it was a cat-and-mouse game between the natives and the former colonialists. Finally, the Baluma got frustrated and pulled out of politics in Georgetown and returned to Lumani.

During the second civil war, the Baluma did not get involved; they let the other tribes fight one another. They were accused of selfishness by the Fefe and Quid tribes, who each wanted their support to defeat the other. Baluma remained the largest tribe in the country, and their vote or support could sway the war one way or another, but they chose not to get involved. And because they stayed out, the Alingafana and Menha stayed out, leaving the fighting between the Fefe and Quid tribes and other smaller tribes. Still, the second civil war destabilised the country enough.

There was a myth about King Balumakazi and Queen Aminata being alive that couldn't go away, that it was their ghosts protecting Lumani and that King Balumakazi would return to retake Georgetown. No matter how hard people tried to believe the contrary, something always brought the rumour back. Sometimes it was the flowers around the palace garden that always blossomed, even at odd periods of the year when all flowers were dried up, as if somebody was taking care of them. Sometimes it was the strange sounds that could be heard coming from inside the palace whenever there was a festival, the heavy rain with hailstones, the deafening thunder, and the lightning that sometimes killed people when it struck, especially around the same period of the year when the king had fallen. The myth was always fresh and refreshed with every new season.

Unlike in other provinces in the country where the kings or chiefs offered the administrative governor a house, in Lumani, nobody did because every house in the palace premises had something strange about it. The first governor sent to Lumani was cautioned by the Ngui before he moved in, but he was a man who didn't believe in the existence of supernatural forces. He packed his family in at the beginning of the week and packed them out at the end of the week. No governor was willing to administer in Lumani after that and so Lumani became like a country within a country, a kingdom within a country with its aristocracy and system of govenance.

* * *

A young man picked up the handset, thought for a while, and then placed the call. 'Joakim, the ammunition arrives at the port this evening. I am sending you the specifications of the container.' He replaced the phone and rubbed his eyes, exhaling audibly. The sunbeam came through the window and threw light on the scar on his face.

Ishmael drew his glasses from his face and placed them on the table. 'I still can't believe that after all these years, we are still falling for the same old tricks. The game has never changed. It is the rules that change, but every time they change the rules, it is as though our people need to be taught the same lesson all over again.'

'We have to prepare for the eventuality of another civil war.' He put his face in his palms.

'We can prevent it. I will speak to my friends.' The third one broke his silence.

'You mean your philosopher friends or your dreamer friends? Or perhaps you need me to read the note again.' He raised his voice. 'They have already armed the Quid and the Fefe. It is a matter of time before the fighting starts again. The OAU is powerless.'

Ishmael looked on as both men talked. If Aminata walked in here, she would not recognise her boys. They had both grown up so handsomely. Giba was always chubby and slightly shorter than Mungu, soft-spoken with a neatly kept mustache, still meticulous about cleanliness; his clothes were always well pressed and his perfume always strong. Giba was still the prudent old man, the wise one. Mungu was taller and leaner with his father's light brown eyes, a million white teeth, brash and impatient. There was so much hair on his chest and face that he had to shave inside his ears. His full beard, which he seldom shaved, almost covered his face. He was still the charmer. Mungu was a brilliant architect, and his work was all over the Kush. Giba was a cardiovascular surgeon in charge of the Queen Aminata Hospital of Fitume.

'You weren't listening to Baba. The game is the same. It is the rules that change. The battle to reconquer Africa will not be won with our fists but with our minds. People need to stop clamping their fingers together in a fist and clamp their minds together in focus. It is time for us to go home and teach our people that.'

* * *

The high priest sat on his veranda, burning incense and watching the rainbow in the sky at sunset. The rainy season was just coming to an end, and the clouds over Lumani were lifting. He inhaled the sweet scent of the incense and began to pray. Inside the shrine, the water in the calabash began to swirl. He liked his sunset prayers; he always felt as if the ancestors listened to him more at sunset than they did at sunrise. In the distance, he could hear the children screaming excitedly and running towards the shrine. He chewed a tree bark and blew the crumbs around to let them see him when they arrived.

'Mfile Nzuzu! Mfile Nzuzu! King Balumakazi is back, and he is in the palace! Come quickly!' the children cried out, running to him excitedly.

Mfile stood up slowly, stretching his usual old muscles, and followed the children. When they got to the palace, there he was – one leg on a crumbled wall and hands on his waist in typical King Balumakazi commanding style, looking around in bewilderment as if wondering what had happened to his house while he had been absent.

Hearing the noises behind him, he turned around to face Mfile – the light brown eyes, the one million white teeth, and the mark across his face striping between his eyes, embracing his left jawbone, and stopping before his left ear. He hadn't changed a wink in the twenty-seven years since he had been gone.

King Balumakazi narrowed his eyes as if he had seen Mfile before but couldn't remember exactly where. The children had followed the high priest into the compound and were all around them, chanting in excitement. King Balumakazi moved to avoid them as if he was allergic to children.

Mfile looked steadily at him with laughing eyes. 'Welcome home, King Mazimungu.'

Mungu frowned. 'What?'

'Where is the patriarch?'

'What patriarch?' Mungu's surprise was turning into confusion.

'I saw him come with you,' the other said, with his eyes laughing even more.

Mungu stepped back, scanning the man from head to toe.

The patriarch strolled out of the palace. 'Yes, I thought you would still be here when I returned, old crocodile.'

They laughed and hugged. Mungu, perplexed, was about to ask Giba how he knew this fetish-looking man.

'Meet Kolela Wa Leni, high priest of Baluma.'

A bull elephant blew his trunk to sound his presence. Giba introduced him to Kolela.

'I called him Kolela.'

Kolela sighed and gritted his teeth, not liking to be the namesake of a totem. He turned to Mungu.

'Would you like to see the skulls?'

ACKNOWLEDGMENTS

I could write a whole book on how I wrote this one, but I can't do that here so I will tell the world this: The greatest gift God ever gave humanity was the gift of family and that is why I believe he began our story with that concept.

Every chapter, every page and every word of this book, I dedicate to the greatest gift God gave me: My old bear, my grandson, koala, monkey and fluffy kitten. You will never know how much you did for me during those fifteen months of writing, but take this with you: when you get to God's tribunal, use this book as your bargaining chip.